Olive
A Novel

by
Dinah Maria Mulock Craik

Olive
A Novel
by Dinah Maria Mulock Craik

Copyright © 2024

All Rights reserved.

No part of this publication may be reproduced, stored in a retrieval system, or transmitted in any form or by any means, electronic, mechanical, photocopying or Otherwise, without the written permission of the publisher.
The author/editor asserts the moral right to be identified as the author/editor of this work.

ISBN: 978-93-63051-07-2

Published by

DOUBLE 9 BOOKS

2/13-B, Ansari Road
Daryaganj, New Delhi – 110002
info@double9books.com
www.double9books.com
Tel. 011-40042856

This book is under public domain

ABOUT THE AUTHOR

Dinah Maria Mulock was born on April 20, 1826, in Stoke-on-Trent, Staffordshire, England. She is frequently referred to as Miss Mulock or Mrs. Craik. Her best-known work is the novel John Halifax, Gentleman, which depicts the aspirations of English middle-class life in the middle of the nineteenth century. His uncertain circumstances had an impact on her upbringing and early years, but she received a decent education from a variety of sources and was inspired to pursue a career as a writer. She arrived in London in 1846, at the same time as her friends Charles Edward Mudie and Alexander Macmillan. She married George Lillie Craik in 1865, the nephew of George Lillie Craik, and a partner with Alexander Macmillan in the publishing house Macmillan & Company. In 1849, Mulock published her first books, and in 1853, she gathered them in Avillion and Other Tales. Nothing New, a compilation with a similar theme, was published in 1857. She released John Halifax, Gentleman in 1857, which outlined the ideals of English middle-class living. A Life for a Life (1859), Mulock's subsequent significant book, earned more money and was maybe more extensively read than John Halifax at the time. Later, Craik moved back to fantastical stories, and The Little Lame Prince was a hit (1874).

CONTENTS

CHAPTER I 7
CHAPTER II 13
CHAPTER III 20
CHAPTER IV 25
CHAPTER V 29
CHAPTER VI 38
CHAPTER VII 44
CHAPTER VIII 49
CHAPTER IX 56
CHAPTER X 60
CHAPTER XI 66
CHAPTER XII 72
CHAPTER XIII 81
CHAPTER XIV 91
CHAPTER XV 96
CHAPTER XVI 105
CHAPTER XVII 112
CHAPTER XVIII 120
CHAPTER XIX 126
CHAPTER XX 134
CHAPTER XXI 144
CHAPTER XXII 152
CHAPTER XXIII 159

CHAPTER XXIV	167
CHAPTER XXV	174
CHAPTER XXVI	182
CHAPTER XXVII	191
CHAPTER XXVIII	200
CHAPTER XXIX	209
CHAPTER XXX	215
CHAPTER XXXI	225
CHAPTER XXXII	231
CHAPTER XXXIII	239
CHAPTER XXXIV	246
CHAPTER XXXV	250
CHAPTER XXXVI	259
CHAPTER XXXVII	268
CHAPTER XXXVIII	275
CHAPTER XXXIX	283
CHAPTER XL	291
CHAPTER XLI	296
CHAPTER XLII	304
CHAPTER XLIII	310
CHAPTER XLIV	318
CHAPTER XLV	324
CHAPTER XLVI	333
CHAPTER XLVII	343
CHAPTER XLVIII	350
CHAPTER XLIX	358

CHAPTER I

"Puir wee lassie, ye hae a waesome welcome to a waesome warld!"

Such was the first greeting ever received by my heroine, Olive Rothesay. However, she would be then entitled neither a heroine nor even "Olive Rothesay," being a small nameless concretion of humanity, in colour and consistency strongly resembling the "red earth," whence was taken the father of all nations. No foreshadowing of the coming life brightened her purple, pinched-up, withered face, which, as in all new-born children, bore such a ridiculous likeness to extreme old age. No tone of the all-expressive human voice thrilled through the unconscious wail that was her first utterance, and in her wide-open meaningless eyes had never dawned the beautiful human soul. There she lay, as you and I, reader, with all our compeers, lay once-a helpless lump of breathing flesh, faintly stirred by animal life, and scarce at all by that inner life which we call spirit. And, if we thus look back, half in compassion, half in humiliation, at our infantile likeness-may it not be that in the world to come some who in this world bore an outward image poor, mean, and degraded, will cast a glance of equal pity on their well-remembered olden selves, now transfigured into beautiful immortality?

I seem to be wandering from my Olive Rothesay; but time will show the contrary. Poor little spirit! newly come to earth, who knows whether that "waesome welcome" may not be a prophecy? The old nurse seemed almost to dread this, even while she uttered it, for with superstition from which not an "auld wife" in Scotland is altogether free, she changed the dolorous croon into a "Gude guide us!" and, pressing the babe to her aged breast, bestowed a hearty blessing upon her nursling of the second generation—the child of him who was at once her master and her foster-son.

"An' wae's me that he's sae far awa', and canna do't himsel. My bonnie bairn! Ye're come into the world without a father's blessing."

Perhaps the good soul's clasp was the tenderer, and her warm heart throbbed the warmer to the new-born child, for a passing remembrance of her own two fatherless babes, who now slept—as close together, as when, "twin-laddies," they had nestled in one mother's bosom—slept beneath the wide Atlantic which marks the sea-boy's grave.

Nevertheless, the memory was now grown so dim with years, that it vanished the moment the infant waked, and began to cry. Rocking to and fro, the nurse tuned her cracked voice to a long-forgotten lullaby—something about a "boatie." It was stopped by a hand on her shoulder, followed by the approximation of a face which, in its bland gravity, bore "M.D." on every line.

"Well, my good — — excuse me, but I forget your name."

"Elspeth, or mair commonly, Elspie Murray. And no an ill name, doctor. The Murrays o' Perth were" — —

"No doubt—no doubt, Mrs. Elsappy."

"*Elspie*, sir. How daur ye ca' me out o' my name, wi' your unceevil English tongue!"

"Well, then, Elspie, or what the deuce you like," said the doctor, vexed out of his proprieties. But his rosy face became rosier when he met the horrified and sternly reproachful stare of Elspie's keen blue eyes as she turned round—a whole volume of sermons expressed in her "Eh, sir?" Then she added, quietly,

"I'll thank ye no to speak ill words in the ears o' this puir innocent new-born wean. It's no canny."

"Humph!—I suppose I must beg pardon again. I shall never get out what I wanted to say—which is, that you must be quiet, my good dame, and you must keep Mrs. Rothesay quiet. She is a delicate young creature, you know, and must have every possible comfort that she needs."

The doctor glanced round the room as though there was scarce enough comfort for his notions of worldly necessity. Yet though not luxurious, the antechamber and the room half-revealed beyond it seemed to furnish all that could be needed by an individual of moderate fortune and desires. And an eye more romantic and poetic than that of the worthy medico might have found ample atonement for the want of rich furniture within, in the magnificent view without. The windows looked down on a lovely champaign, through which the many-winding Forth span its silver network, until, vanishing in the distance, a white sparkle here and there only showed whither the river wandered. In the distance, the blue mountains rose like clouds, marking the horizon. The foreground of this landscape was formed by the hill, castle-crowned—than which there is none in the world more beautiful or more renowned.

In short, Olive Rothesay shared with many a king and hero the honour of her place of nativity. She was born at Stirling.

Perhaps this circumstance of birth has more influence over character than many matter-of-fact people would imagine. It is pleasant, in after life, to think that we first opened our eyes in a spot famous in the world's story, or remarkable for natural beauty. It is sweet to say, "Those are *my* mountains," or "This is *my* fair valley;" and there is a delight almost like that of a child who glories in his noble or beautiful parents, in the grand historical pride which links us to the place where we were born. So this little morsel of humanity, yet unnamed, whom by an allowable prescience we have called Olive, may perhaps be somewhat influenced in after life by the fact that her cradle was rocked under the shadow of the hill of Stirling, and that the first breezes which fanned her baby brow came from the Highland mountains.

But the excellent presiding genius at this interesting advent "cared for none of these things." Dr. Jacob Johnson stood at the window with his hands in his pockets—to him the wide beautiful world was merely a field for the exercise of the medical profession—a place where old women died, and children were born. He watched the shadows darkening over Ben-Ledi—calculating how much longer he ought in propriety to stay with his present patient, and whether he should have time to run home and take a cosy dinner and a bottle of port before he was again required.

"Our sweet young patient is doing well, I think, nurse," said he, at last, in his most benevolent tones.

"Ye may say that, doctor—ye suld ken."

"I might almost venture to leave her, except that she seems so lonely, without friend or nurse, save yourself."

"And wha's the best nurse for Captain Angus Rothesay's wife and bairn, but the woman that nursed himsel?" said Elspie, lifting up her tall gaunt frame, and for the second time frowning the little doctor into confused silence. "An' as for friends, ye suld just be unco glad o' the chance that garr'd the leddy bide here, and no amang her ain folk. Else there wadna hae been sic a sad welcome for her bonnie bairn. Maybe a waur, though," added the woman to herself, with a sigh, as she once more half-buried her little nursling in her capacious embrace.

"I have not the slightest doubt of Captain Rothesay's respectability," answered Dr. Johnson. *Respectability*! applied to the scions of a family which had had the honour of being nearly extirpated at Flodden-field, and again at Pinkie. Had the trusty follower of the Rothesays heard the term, she certainly would have been inclined to annihilate the presumptuous Englishman. But she was fortunately engaged in stilling the cries of the poor infant, who, in return for the pains she took in addressing it, began to give full evidence that the weakness of its lungs was not at all proportionate to the smallness of its size.

"Crying will do it good. A fine child—a very fine child," observed the doctor, as he made ready for his departure, while the nurse proceeded in her task, and the heap of white drapery was gradually removed, until from beneath it appeared a very—very tiny specimen of babyhood.

"Ye needna trouble yoursel to say what's no' true," was the answer; "it's just a bit bairnie—unco sma' An' that's nae wonder, considering the puir mither's trouble."

"And the father is gone abroad?"

"Just twa months sin' syne. But eh! doctor, look ye here," suddenly cried Elspie, as with her great, brown, but tender hand she was rubbing down the delicate spine of the now quieted babe.

"Well—what's the matter now?" said Dr. Johnson rather sulkily, as he laid down his hat and gloves, "The child is quite perfect, rather small perhaps, but as nice a little girl as ever was seen. It's all right."

"It's no a' richt," cried the nurse, in a tone trembling between anger and apprehension. "Doctor, see!"

She pointed with her finger to a slight curve at the upper part of the spine, between the shoulder and neck. The doctor's professional anxiety was aroused—he came near and examined the little creature, with a countenance that grew graver each instant.

"Aweel?" said Elspie, inquiringly.

"I wish I had noticed this before; but it would have been of no use," he answered, his bland tones made earnest by real feeling.

"Eh, what?" said the nurse.

"I am sorry to say that the child is *deformed*—slightly so—very slightly I hope—but most certainly deformed. Hump-backed."

At this terrible sentence Elspie sank back in her chair. Then she started up, clasping the child convulsively, and faced the doctor.

Olive.

"How daur ye speak so of ane o' the Rothesays?"

"Ye lee, ye ugly creeping Englisher! How daur ye speak so of ane o' the Rothesays,—frae the blude o' whilk cam the tallest men an' the bonniest leddies—ne'er a cripple amang them a — —. How daur ye say that my master's bairn will be a — — —. Wae's me! I canna speak the word."

"My poor woman!" mildly said the doctor, "I am really concerned."

"Haud your tongue, ye fule!" muttered Elspie, while she again laid the child on her lap, and examined it earnestly for herself. The result confirmed all. She wrung her hands, and rocked to and fro, moaning aloud.

"Ochone, the wearie day! O my dear master, my bairn, that I nursed on my knee! how will ye come back an' see your first-born, the last o' the Rothesays, a puir bit crippled lassie!"

A faint call from the inner room startled both doctor and nurse.

Olive: A Novel | 11

"Good heavens!" exclaimed the former. "We must think of the mother. Stay—I'll go. She does not, and she must not, know of this. What a blessing that I have already told her the child was a fine and perfect child. Poor thing, poor thing!" he added passionately, as he hurried to his patient leaving Elspie hushed into silence, still mournfully gazing on her charge.

It would have been curious to mark the changes in the nurse's face during that brief interval. At first it wore a look almost of repugnance as she regarded the unconscious child, and then that very unconsciousness seemed to awaken her womanly compassion. "Puir hapless wean, ye little ken what ye're coming to! Lack o' kinsman's love, and lack o' siller, and lack o' beauty. God forgie me—but why did He send ye into the waefu' warld at a'?"

It was a question, the nature of which has perplexed theologians, philosophers, and metaphysicians, in every age, and will perplex them all to the end of time. No wonder, therefore, that it could not be solved by the poor simple Scotswoman. But as she stood hushing the child to her breast, and looking vacantly out of the window at the far mountains which grew golden in the sunset, she was unconsciously soothed by the scene, and settled the matter in a way which wiser heads might often do with advantage.

"Aweel! He kens best. He made the warld and a' that's in't; and maybe He will gie unto this puir wee thing a meek spirit to bear ill-luck. Ane must wark, anither suffer. As the minister says, It'll a' come richt at last."

Still the babe slept on, the sun sank, and night fell upon the earth. And so the morning and evening made the first day of the new existence, which was about to be developed, through all the various phases which compose that strange and touching mystery—a woman's life.

CHAPTER II

There is not a more hackneyed subject for poetic enthusiasm than that sight—perhaps the loveliest in nature—a young mother with her first-born child. And perhaps because it is so lovely, and is ever renewed in its beauty, the world never tires of dwelling thereupon.

Any poet, painter, or sculptor, would certainly have raved about Mrs. Rothesay, had he seen her in the days of convalescence, sitting at the window with her baby on her knee. She furnished that rare sight—and one that is becoming rarer as the world grows older—an exquisitely beautiful woman. Would there were more of such!—that the idea of physical beauty might pass into the heart through the eyes, and bring with it the ideal of the soul's perfection, which our senses can only thus receive. So great is this influence—so unconsciously do we associate the type of spiritual with material beauty, that perhaps the world might have been purer and better if its onward progress in what it calls civilisation had not so nearly destroyed the fair mould of symmetry and loveliness which tradition celebrates.

It would have done any one's heart good only to look at Sybilla Rothesay. She was a creature to watch from a distance, and then to go away and dream of, wondering whether she were a woman or a spirit. As for describing her, it is almost impossible—but let us try.

She was very small in stature and proportions—quite a little fairy. Her cheek had the soft peachy hue of girlhood; nay, of very childhood. You would never have thought her a mother. She lay back, half-buried in the great armchair; and then, suddenly springing up from amidst the cloud of white muslins and laces that enveloped her, she showed her young, blithe face.

"I will not have that cap, Elspie; I am not an invalid now, and I don't choose to be an old matron yet," she said, in a pretty, wilful way, as she threw off the ugly ponderous production of her nurse's active fingers, and exhibited her beautiful head.

It was, indeed, a beautiful head! exquisite in shape, with masses of light-brown hair folded round it. The little rosy ear peeped out, forming the commencement of that rare and dainty curve of chin and throat, so pleasant to an artist's eye. A beauty to be lingered over among all other beauties.

Then the delicately outlined mouth, the lips folded over in a lovely gravity, that seemed ready each moment to melt away into smiles. Her nose—but who would destroy the romance of a beautiful woman by such an allusion? Of course, Mrs. Rothesay had a nose; but it was so entirely in harmony with the rest of her face, that you never thought whether it were Roman, Grecian, or aquiline. Her eyes—

"She has two eyes, so soft and brown—
She gives a side-glance and looks down."

But was there a soul in this exquisite form? You never asked—you hardly cared! You took the thing for granted; and whether it were so or not, you felt that the world, and yourself especially, ought to be thankful for having looked at so lovely an image, if only to prove that earth still possessed such a thing as ideal beauty; and you forgave all the men, in every age, that have run mad for the same. Sometimes, perchance, you would pause a moment, to ask if this magic were real, and remember the calm holy airs that breathed from the presence of some woman, beautiful only in her soul. But then you never would have looked upon Sybilla Rothesay as a woman at all—only a flesh-and-blood fairy—a Venus de Medici transmuted from the stone.

Perhaps this was the way in which Captain Angus Rothesay contrived to fall in love with Sybilla Hyde; until he woke from the dream to find his seraph of beauty—a baby-bride, pouting like a vexed child, because, in their sudden elopement, she had neither wedding-bonnet nor Brussels veil!

And now she was a baby-mother; playing with her infant as, not so very long since, she had played with her doll; twisting its tiny fingers, and making them close tightly round her own, which were quite as elfin-like, comparatively. For Mrs. Rothesay's surpassing beauty included beautiful hands and feet; a blessing which Nature—often niggardly in her gifts—does not always extend to pretty women, but bestows it on those who have infinitely more reason to be thankful for the boon.

"See, nurse Elspie," said Mrs. Rothesay, laughing in her childish way; "see how fast the little creature holds my finger! Really, I think a baby is a very pretty thing; and it will be so nice to play with until Angus comes home."

Elspie turned round from the corner where she sat sewing, and looked with a half-suppressed sigh at her master's wife, whose delicate English beauty, and quick, ringing English voice, formed such a strong contrast to herself, and were so opposed to her own peculiar prejudices. But she had learned to love the young creature, nevertheless; and for the thousandth time she smothered the half-unconscious thought that Captain Angus might have chosen better.

"Children are a blessing frae the Lord, as maybe ye'll see, ane o' these days, Mrs. Rothesay," said Elspie, gravely; "ye maun tak' them as they're sent, and mak' the best o' them."

Mrs. Rothesay laughed merrily. "Thank you, Elspie, for giving me such a solemn speech, just like one of my husband's. To put me in mind of him, I suppose. As if there were any need for that! Dear Angus! I wonder what he will say to his little daughter when he sees her; the new Miss Rothesay, who has come in opposition to the old Miss Rothesay,—ha! ha!"

"The auld Miss Rothesay! She's your husband's aunt," observed Elspie, feeling it necessary to stand up for the honour of the family. "Miss Flora was a comely leddy ance, as a' the Rothesays were."

"And this Miss Rothesay will be too, I hope, though she is such a little brown thing now. But people say that the brownest babies grow the fairest in time, eh, nurse?"

"They do say that," replied Elspie, with another and a heavier sigh; as she bent closer over her work.

Mrs. Rothesay went on in her blithe chatter. "I half wished for a boy, as Captain Rothesay thought it would please his uncle; but that's of no consequence. He will be quite satisfied with a girl, and so am I. Of course she will be a beauty, my dear little baby!" And with a deeper mother-love piercing through her childish pleasure, she bent over the infant; then took it up, awkwardly and comically enough, as though it were a toy she was afraid of breaking, and rocked it to and fro on her breast.

Elspie started up. "Tak' tent, tak' tent! ye'll hurt it, maybe, the puir wee——Oh, what was I gaun to say!"

"Don't trouble yourself," said the young mother, with a charming assumption of matronly dignity; "I shall hold the baby safe. I know all about it."

And she really did succeed in lulling the child to sleep; which was no sooner accomplished than she recommenced her pleasant musical chatter, partly addressed to her nurse, but chiefly the unconscious overflow of a simple nature, which could not conceal a single thought.

"I wonder what I shall call her—the darling! We must not wait until her papa comes home. She can't be 'baby' for three years. I shall have to decide on her name myself. Oh, what a pity! I, who never could decide anything. Poor dear Angus! he does all—he had even to fix the wedding-day!" And her musical laugh—another rare charm that she possessed—caused Elspie to look round with mingled pity and affection.

"Come, nurse, you can help me, I know. I am puzzling my poor head for a name to give this young lady here. It must be a very pretty one. I wonder what Angus would like? A family name, perhaps, after one of those old Rothesays that you and he make so much of."

"Oh, Mrs. Rothesay! And are ye no proud o' your husband's family?"

"Yes, very proud; especially as I have none of my own. He took me—an orphan, without a single tie in the wide world—he took me into his warm loving arms"—here herm voice faltered, and a sweet womanly tenderness softened her eyes. "God bless my noble husband! I *am* proud of him, and of his people, and of all his race. So come," she added, her childish manner reviving, "tell me of the remarkable women in the Rothesay family for the last five hundred years—you know all about them, Elspie. Surely we'll find one to be a namesake for my baby."

Elspie—pleased and important—began eagerly to relate long traditions about the Lady Christina Rothesay, who was a witch, and a great friend of "Maister Michael Scott," and how, with spells, she caused her seven stepsons to pine away and die; also the lady Isobel, who let her lover down from her bower-window with the long strings of her golden hair, and how her brother found and slew him;—whence she laid a curse on all the line who had golden hair, and such never prospered, but died unmarried and young.

"I hope the curse has passed away now," gaily said the young mother, "and that the latest scion will not be a golden-tressed damsel. Yet look here"—and she touched the soft down beneath her infant's cap, which might, by a considerable exercise of imagination, be called hair—"it is yellow, you see, Elspie! But I'll not believe your tradition. My child shall be both beautiful and beloved."

Smitten with a sudden pang, poor Elspie cried, "Oh, my leddy, dinna think o' the future. Dinna!"— — and she stopped, confused.

"Really, how strange you are. But go on. We'll have no more Christinas nor Isobels."

Hurriedly, Elspie continued to relate the histories: of noble Jean Rothesay, who died by an arrow aimed at her husband's heart; and Alison, her sister, the beauty of James the Fifth's reckless court, who was "no gude;" and Mistress Katharine Rothesay, who hid two of the "Prince's" soldiers after Culloden, and stood with a pair of pistols before their bolted door.

"Nay, I'll have none of these—they frighten me," said Sybilla, "I wonder I ever had courage to marry the descendant of such awful women. No! my sweet innocent! you shall not be christened after them," she continued, stroking the baby cheek with her soft finger. "You shall not be like them at all, except in their beauty. And they were all handsome—were they, Elspie?"

"Ne'er a ane o' the Rothesay line, man or woman, that wasna fair to see."

"Then so will my baby be!—like her father, I hope—or just a little like her mother, who is not so very ugly, either; at least, Angus says not." And Mrs. Rothesay drew up her tiny figure, patted one dainty hand—the wedded one—with its fairy fellow; then—touched perhaps with a passing melancholy that he who most prized her beauty, and for whose sake she most prized it herself, was far away—she leaned back and sighed.

However, in a few minutes, she cried out, her words showing how light and wandering was the reverie, "Elspie, I have a thought! The baby shall be christened Olive!"

"It's a strange, heathen name, Mrs. Rothesay."

"Not at all. Listen how I chanced to think of it. This very morning, just before you came to waken me, I had such a queer, delicious dream."

"Dream! Are ye sure it was i' the morning-tide?" cried Elspie, aroused into interest.

"Yes; and so it certainly means something, you will say, Elspie? Well, it was about my baby. She was then lying fast asleep in my bosom, and her warm, soft breathing soon sent me to sleep too. I dreamt that somehow I had gradually let her go from me, so that I felt her in my arms no more, and I was very sad, and cried out how cruel it was for any one to steal my child, until I found I had let her go of my own accord. Then I looked up, after awhile, and saw standing at the foot of the bed a little angel—a child-angel—with a green olive-branch in its hand. It told me to follow; so I rose up, and followed it over a wide desert country, and across rivers and among wild beasts; but at every peril the child held out the olive-branch, and we passed on safely. And when I felt weary, and my feet were bleeding with the rough journey, the little angel touched them with the olive, and I was strong again. At last we reached a beautiful valley, and the child, said, 'You are quite safe now.' I answered, 'And who is my beautiful comforting angel?' Then the white wings fell off, and I only saw a sweet child's face, which bore something of Angus's likeness and something of my own, and the little one stretched out her hands and said, 'Mother!'"

While Mrs. Rothesay spoke, her thoughtless manner had once more softened into deep feeling. Elspie watched her with wondering eagerness.

"It was nae dream; it was a vision. God send it true!" said the old woman, solemnly.

"I know not. Angus always laughed at my dreams, but I have a strange feeling whenever I think of this. Oh, Elspie, you can't tell how sweet it was! And so I should like to call my baby Olive, for the sake of the beautiful angel. It may be foolish—but 'tis a fancy of mine. Olive Rothesay! It sounds well, and Olive Rothesay she shall be."

"Amen; and may she be an angel to ye a' her days. And ye'll mind o' the blessed dream, and love her evermair. Oh, my sweet leddy, promise me that ye will!" cried the nurse, approaching her mistress's chair, while two great tears stole down her hard cheeks.

"Of course I shall love her dearly! What made you doubt it? Because I am so young? Nay, I have a mother's heart, though I am only eighteen. Come, Elspie, do let us be merry; send these drops away;" and she patted the old withered face with her little hand. "Was it not you who told me the saying, 'It's ill greeting ower a new-born wean'? There! don't I succeed charmingly in your northern tongue?"

What a winning little creature she was, this young wife of Angus Rothesay! A pity he had not seen her—the old Highland uncle, Miss Flora's brother, who had disinherited his nephew and promised heir for bringing him a *Sassenach* niece.

"A charming scene of maternal felicity! I am quite sorry to intrude upon it," said a bland voice at the door, as Dr. Johnson put in his shining bald head.

Mrs. Rothesay welcomed him in her graceful, cordial way. She was so ready to cling to every one who showed her kindness—and he had been very kind; so kind that, with her usual quick impulses, she had determined to stay and live at Stirling until her husband's return from Jamaica. She told Dr. Johnson so now; and, moreover, as an earnest of the friendship which she, accustomed to be loved by every one, expected from him, she requested him to stand godfather to her little babe.

"She shall be christened after our English fashion, doctor, and her name shall be Olive. What do you think of her now? Is she growing prettier?"

The doctor bowed a smiling assent, and walked to the window. Thither Elspie followed him.

"Ye maun tell her the truth—I daurna. Ye will!" and she clutched his arm with eager anxiety. "An' oh! for Gudesake, say it safyly, kindly."

He shook her off with an uneasy look. He had never felt in a more disagreeable position.

Mrs. Rothesay called him back again. "I think, doctor, her features are improving. She will certainly be a beauty. I should break my heart if she were not. And what would Angus say? Come—what are you and Elspie talking about so mysteriously?"

"My dear madam—hem!" began Dr. Johnson. "I do hope—indeed, I am sure—your child will be a good child, and a great comfort to both her parents;"— —

"Certainly—but how grave you are about it."

"I have a painful duty—a very painful duty," he replied. But Elspie pushed him aside.

"Ye're just a fule, man!—ye'll kill her. Say your say at ance!"

The young mother turned deadly pale. "Say *what* Elspie? What is he going to tell me? Angus"— —

"No, no, my darlin' leddy! your husband's safe;" and Elspie flung herself on her knees beside the chair. "But, the lassie—(dinna fear, for it's the will o' God, and a' for gude, nae doubt)—your sweet wee dochter is"— —

"Is, I grieve to say it, deformed," added Dr. Johnson.

The poor mother gazed incredulously on him, on the nurse, and lastly on the sleeping child. Then, without a word, she fell back, and fainted in Espie's arms.

CHAPTER III

It was many days before Mrs. Rothesay recovered from the shock occasioned by the tidings—to her almost more fearful than her child's death—that it was doomed for life to suffer the curse of hopeless deformity. For a curse, a bitter curse, this seemed to the young and beautiful creature, who had learned since her birth to consider beauty as the greatest good. She was, so to speak, in love with loveliness; not merely in herself, but in every human creature. This feeling sprang more from enthusiasm than from personal vanity, the borders of which meanness she had just touched, but never crossed. Perhaps, also, she was too conscious of her own loveliness, and admired herself too ardently to care for attracting the petty admiration of others. She took it quite as a matter of course; and was no more surprised at being worshipped than if she had been the Goddess of Beauty herself.

But if Sybilla Rothesay gloried in her own perfections, she no less gloried in those of all she loved, and chiefly in her noble-looking husband. And they were so young, so quickly wed, and so soon parted, that this emotion had no time to deepen into that soul-united affection which is independent of outward things, or, rather, becomes so divine, that instead of beauty creating love, love has power to create beauty.

No marvel, then, that not having attained to a higher experience, Sybilla considered beauty as all in all. And this child—her child and Angus's,—would be a deformity, a shame to its parents, a dishonour to its race. How should she ever bear to look upon it? Still more, how should she ever dare to show the poor cripple to its father, and say, "This is our child—our firstborn." Would he not turn away in disgust, and answer that it had better died?

Such exaggerated fancies as these haunted the miserable mother, when she passed from her long swoon into a sort of fever; which, though scarce endangering her life, was yet for days a source of great anxiety to the devoted Elspie. To the unhappy infant this madness—for it was temporary madness—almost caused death. Mrs. Rothesay positively refused to see or notice her child, scorning alike the tearful entreaties and the stern reproaches of the nurse. At last Elspie ceased to combat this passionate resolve, springing half from anger and half from delirium——

"God forgie ye, and save the innocent bairn—the dochter He gave, and that ye're gaun to murder—unthankfu' woman as ye are," muttered Elspie, under her breath, as she quitted the room and went to succour the almost dying babe. Over it her heart yearned as it had never yearned before.

"Your mither casts ye aff, ye puir wee thing. Maybe ye're no lang for this warld, but while ye're in it ye sall be my ain lassie, an' I'll be your ain mammie, evermair."

So, like Naomi of old, Elspie Murray "laid the child in her bosom and became nurse unto it." But for her, the life of our Olive Rothesay—with all its influences, good or evil, small or great, as yet unknown—would have expired like a faint-flickering taper.

Perhaps, in her madness, the unhappy mother might almost have desired such an ending. As it was, the disappointed hope, which had at first resembled positive dislike, subsided into the most complete indifference. She endured her child's presence, but she took no notice of it; she seemed to have forgotten its very existence. Her shattered health supplied sufficient excuse for the utter abandonment of all a mother's duties, and the poor feeble spark of life was left to Elspie's cherishing. By night and by day the child knew no other resting-place than the old nurse's arms, the mother's seeming to be for ever closed to its helpless innocence. True, Sybilla kissed it once a day, when Elspie brought the little creature to her, and exacted, as a duty, the recognition which Mrs. Rothesay, girlish and yielding as she was, dared not refuse. Her husband's faithful retainer had over her an influence which could never be gainsaid.

Elspie seemed to be the sole regent of the babe's destiny. It was she who took it to its baptism;—not the festal ceremony which had pleased Sybilla's childish fancy with visions of christening robes and cakes, but the beautiful and simple "naming" of Elspie's own church. She stood before the minister, holding the desolate babe in her protecting arms; and there her heart sealed the promise of her lips, to bring it up in the knowledge and fear of God. And with an earnest credulity, which contained the germ of purest faith, she, remembering the mother's dream, called her nursling by the name of Olive.

She carried the babe home and laid it on Mrs. Rothesay's lap. The young creature, who had so strangely renounced that dearest blessing of mother-love, would fain have put the child aside; but Elspie's stern eye controlled her.

"Ye maun kiss and bless your dochter. Nae tongue but her mither's suld ca' her by her new-christened name."

"What name?"

"The name ye gied her yer ain sel."

"No, no. Surely you have not called her so. Take her away; she is not my sweet angel-baby—the darling in my dream." And Sybilla hid her face; not in anger, or disgust, but in bitter weeping.

"She's yer ain dochter—Olive Rothesay," answered Elspie, less harshly. "She may be an angel to ye yet."

While she spoke, it so chanced that there flitted over the infant-face one of those smiles that we see sometimes in young children—strange, causeless smiles, which seem the reflection of some invisible influence.

And so, while the babe smiled, there came to its face such an angel-brightness, that it shone into the mother's careless heart. For the first time since that mournful day which had so changed her nature, Sybilla Rothesay sat down and kissed the child of her own accord. Elspie heard no maternal blessing—the name of "Olive" was never breathed; but the nurse was satisfied when she saw that the babe's second baptism was its mother's repentant tears.

There was in Sybilla no hardness nor cruelty, only the disappointment and vexation of a child deprived of an expected toy. She might have grown weary of her little daughter almost as soon, even if her pride and hope had not been crushed by the knowledge of Olive's deformity. Love to her seemed a treasure to be paid in requital, not a free gift bestowed without thought of return. That self-forgetting maternal devotion, lavished first on unconscious infancy, and then on unregarding youth, was a mystery to her utterly incomprehensible. At least it seemed so now, when, with the years and the character of a child, she was called to the highest duty of woman's life. This duty comes to some girlish mothers as an instinct, but it was not so with Mrs. Rothesay. An orphan, and heiress to a competence, if not to wealth, she had been brought up like a plant in a hot-bed, with all natural impulses either warped and suppressed, or forced into undue luxuriance. And yet it was a sweet plant withal; one that might have grown, ay, and might yet grow, into perfect strength and beauty.

Mrs. Rothesay's education—that education of heart, and mind, and temper, which is essential to a woman's happiness, had to begin when it ought to have been completed—at her marriage. Most unfortunate it was for her, that ere the first twelvemonth of their wedded life had passed, Captain Rothesay was forced to depart for Jamaica, whence was derived his wife's little fortune; their whole fortune now, for he had quitted the army on his marriage. Thus Sybilla was deprived of that wholesome influence which man has ever over a woman who loves him, and by which he may, if he so will, counteract many a fault and weakness in her disposition.

Time passed on, and Mrs. Rothesay, a wife and mother, was at twenty-one years old just the same as she had been at seventeen—as girlish, as thoughtless, eager for any amusement, and often treading on the very verge of folly. She still lived at Stirling, enforced thereunto by the entreaties, almost the commands, of Elspie Murray, against whom she bitterly murmured sometimes, for shutting her up in such a dull Scotch town. When Elspie urged her unprotected situation, the necessity of living in retirement, for the "honour of the family," while Captain Angus was away, Mrs. Rothesay sometimes frowned, but more often put the matter off with a merry jest. Meanwhile she consoled herself by going as much into society as the limited circle of Dr. and Mrs. Johnson allowed; and therein, as usual, the lovely, gay, winning young creature was spoiled to her heart's content.

So she still lived the life of a wayward, petted child, whose natural instinct for all things good and beautiful kept her from ever doing what was positively wrong, though she did a great deal that was foolish enough in its way. She was, as she jestingly said, "a widow bewitched;" but she rarely coquetted, and then only in that innocent way which comes natural to some women, from a universal desire to please. And she never ceased talking and thinking of her noble Angus.

When his letters came, she always made a point of kissing them half-a-dozen times, and putting them under her pillow at night, just like a child! And she wrote to him regularly once a month—pretty, playful, loving letters. But there was in them one peculiarity—they were utterly free from that delicious maternal egotism which chronicles all the little incidents of babyhood. She said, in answer to her husband's questions, that "Olive was well;" "Olive could just walk;" "Olive had learned to say 'Papa and Elspie.'" Nothing more.

The fatal secret she had not dared to tell him.

Her first letters—full of joy about "the loveliest baby that ever was seen"—had brought his in return echoing the rapture with truly paternal pride. They reached her in her misery, to which they added tenfold. Every sentence smote her with bitter regret, even with shame, as though it were her fault in having given to the world the wretched child. Captain Rothesay expressed his joy that his little daughter was not only healthy, but pretty; for, he said, "He should be quite unhappy if she did not grow up as beautiful as her mother." The words pierced Sybilla's heart; she could not—dared not tell him the truth; not yet, at least. And whenever Elspie's rough honesty urged her to do so, she fell into such agonies of grief and anger, that the nurse was obliged to desist.

Sometimes, when letter after letter came from the father, full of inquiries about his precious first-born,—Sybilla, whose fault was more in weakness than deceit, resolved that she would nerve herself for the terrible task. But it was vain—she had not strength to do it.

The three years extended into four, and still Captain Rothesay sent gift after gift, and message after message, to his daughter. Still he wrote to the conscience-stricken mother how many times he had kissed the "little lock of golden hue," severed from the baby-head; picturing the sweet face and lithe, active form which he had never seen. And all the while there was stealing about the old house at Stirling a pale, deformed child: small and attenuated in frame—quiet beyond its years, delicate, spiritless, with scarce one charm that would prove its lineage from the young beautiful mother, out of whose sight it instinctively crept.

Thus the years fled with Olive Rothesay and her parents; each month, each day, sowing seeds that would assuredly spring up, for good or for evil, in the destinies of all three.

CHAPTER IV

The fourth year of Captain Rothesay's absence passed,—not without anxiety, for it was war-time, and his letters were frequently interrupted. At first, whenever this happened, his wife fretted extremely—*fretted* is the right word, for it was more a fitful chafing than a positive grief. Sybilla knew not the sense of deep sorrow. Her nature resembled one of those sunny climes where even the rains are dews. So, after a few disappointments, she composed herself to the certainty that nothing would happen amiss to her Angus; and she determined never to expect a letter until she received it, and not to look for *him* at all until he wrote her word that he was coming. He was sure to do what was right, and to return to his dearly-loved wife as soon as ever he could. And, though scarce acknowledging the fact to herself, her husband's return involved such a humiliating explanation of truth concealed, if not of positive falsehood, that Sybilla dared not even think of it. Whenever the long-parted wife mused on the joy of meeting—of looking once more into the beloved face, and being lifted up like a child to cling round his neck with her fairy arms, for Angus was a very giant to her—then there seemed to rise between them the phantom of the pale, deformed child.

To drown these fancies, Sybilla rushed into every amusement which her secluded life afforded. At last, she resolved on an exploit at which Elspie looked aghast, and which made the quiet Mrs. Johnson shake her head—an evening party—nay, even a dance, at her own home.

"It will never do for the people here; they're '*unco gude*,'" said the doctor's English wife, who had imbibed a few Scottish prejudices by a residence of thirty years. "Nobody ever dances in Stirling."

"Then I'll teach them," cried the lively Mrs. Rothesay: "I long to show them a quadrille—even that new dance that all the world is shocked at Oh! I should dearly like a waltz."

Mrs. Jacob Johnson was scandalised at first, but there was something in Sybilla to which she could not say nay,—nobody ever could. The matter was decided by Mrs. Rothesay's having her own way, except with regard to the waltz, which her friend staunchly resisted. Elspie, too, interfered as long as she could; but her heart was just now full of anxiety about her nursling, who seemed to grow more delicate every year. Day after day the faithful nurse might have been seen trudging across the country, carrying little Olive in her arms, to strengthen the child with the healing springs of Bridge of Allan, and invigorate her weak frame with the fresh mountain air—the heather breath of beautiful Ben-Ledi. Among these influences did Olive's childhood dawn, so that in after-life they never faded from her.

Elspie scarcely thought again about the gay party, until when she came in one evening, and was undressing the sleepy little girl in the dusk, a vision appeared at the nursery door. It quite startled the old Scotswoman at first, it looked so like a fairy apparition, all in white, with a green coronet. She hardly could believe that it was her young mistress.

"Eh! Mrs. Rothesay, ye're no goin' to show yoursel in sic a dress," she cried, regarding with horror the gleaming bare arms, the lovely neck, and the tiny white-sandaled feet, which the short and airy robe exhibited in all their perfection.

"Indeed, but I am! and 'tis quite a treat to wear a ball-dress. I, that have been smothered up in all sorts of ugly costume for nearly five years. And see my jewels! Why, Elspie, this pearl-set has only beheld the light once since I was married—so beautiful as it is—and Angus's gift too."

"Dinna say that name," cried Elspie, driven to a burst of not very respectful reproach. "I marvel ye daur speak of Captain Angus—and ye wi' your havers and your jigs, while yer husband's far awa', and your bairn sick! It's for nae gude I tell ye, Mrs. Rothesay."

Sybilla had looked a little subdued at the allusion to her husband, but the moment Elspie mentioned the little Olive, her manner changed. "You are always blaming me about the child, and I will not bear it. She is quite well. Are you not, baby?"—the mother never would call her *Olive*.

A feeble, trembling voice answered from the little bed, "Yes, please, mamma!"

"There, you hear, Elspie! Now don't torment me any more about her. But I must go down stairs."

She danced across the room in a graceful waltzing step, held out her hand towards the child, and touched one so tiny, cold, and damp, that she felt half inclined to take and warm it in her own. But Elspie's hawk-eyes were watching her, and she was ashamed. So she only said, "Goodnight, baby!" and danced back again, out through the open door.

For hours Elspie sat in the dark room beside the bed of the little child, who lay murmuring, sometimes moaning, in her sleep. She never did moan but in her sleep, poor innocent! The sound of music and dancing rose up from below, and then Mrs. Rothesay's singing.

"Ye'd better be hushin' your puir wee bairnie here, ye heartless woman!" muttered Elspie, who grew daily more jealous over the forsaken child, now the very darling of her old age. She knew not that her love for Olive, and its open tokens shown by reproaches to Olive's mother, were sure to suppress any dawning tenderness that might be awakened in Mrs. Rothesay's bosom.

It had not done so yet, for many a time during the dance and song did the touch of that little cold hand haunt the young mother, rousing a feeling akin to remorse. But she threw it off again and again, and entered with the gaiety of her nature into all the evening's pleasure. Her enjoyment was at its height, when an old acquaintance, just discovered—an English officer, quartered at the castle—proposed a waltz. Before she had time to say "Yes" or "No," the music struck up one of those enchanting waltz-measures which to all true lovers of dancing, are as irresistible as Maurice Connor's "Wonderful Tune." Sybilla felt again the same blithe young creature of sixteen, who had led the revels at her first ball, dancing into the heart of one old colonel, six ensigns, a doctor, a lawyer, and of Angus Rothesay. There was no resisting the impulse: in a moment she was whirling away.

In the midst of the dizzy round the door opened, and, like some evil spectre, in stalked Elspie Murray.

Never was there such an uncouth apparition seen in a ball-room. Her grey petticoat exhibited her bare feet; her short upper gown, that graceful and picturesque attire of the Scottish peasantry, was thrown carelessly over her shoulders; her *mutch* was put on awry, and from under its immense border her face appeared, as white almost as the cap itself. She walked right into the centre of the floor, laid her heavy hand on Sybilla's shoulder, and said,

"Mrs. Rothesay, your husband's come!"

The young wife stood one moment transfixed; she turned pale, afterwards crimson, and then, uttering a cry of joy, sprang to the door—sprang into her husband's arms.

Dazzled with the light, the traveller resisted not, while Elspie half-led, half dragged him—still clasping his wife—into a little room close by, when she shut the door and left them. Then she burst in once more among the astonished guests.

"Ye may gang your gate, ye heathens! Awa wi' ye, for Captain Rothesay's come hame!"

Sybilla and her husband stood face to face in the little gloomy room, lighted only by a solitary candle. At first she clung about him so closely that he could not see her face, though he felt her tears falling, and her little heart beating against his own. He knew it was all for joy. But he was strangely bewildered by the scene which had flashed for a minute before his eyes, while standing at the door of the room.

After a while he drew his wife to the light, and held her out at arm's length to look at her. Then, for the first time, she remembered all. Trembling—blushing scarlet, over face and neck—she perceived her husband's eyes rest on her glittering dress. He regarded her fixedly, from head to foot. She felt his expression change from joy to uneasy wonder, from love to sternness, and then he wore a strange, cold look, such a one as she had never beheld in him before.

"So, the young lady I saw whirling madly in some man's arms—was you, Sybilla—was *my wife*."

As Captain Rothesay spoke, Sybilla distinguished in his voice a new tone, echoing the strange coldness in his eyes. She sprang to his neck, weeping now for grief and alarm, as she had before wept for joy; she prayed him to forgive her, told him, with a sincerity that none could doubt, how rejoiced she was at his coming, and how dearly she loved him—now and ever. He kissed her, at her passionate entreaty; said he had nothing to blame; suffered her caresses patiently; but the impression was given, the deed was done.

While he lived, Captain Rothesay never forgot that night. Nor did Sybilla; for then she had first seen that cold, stern look, and heard that altered tone. How many times was it to haunt her afterwards!

CHAPTER V

Next morning Captain Rothesay and his wife sat together by the fireside, where she had so often sat alone. Sybilla seemed in high spirits—her love was ever exuberant in expression—and the moment her husband seemed serious she sprang on his knee and looked playfully in his face.

"Just as much a child as ever, I see," said Angus Rothesay, with a rather wintry smile.

And then, looking in his face by daylight, Sybilla had opportunity to see how changed he was. He had become a grave, middle-aged man. She could not understand it. He had never told her of any cares, and he was little more than thirty. She felt almost vexed at him for growing so old; nay, she even said so, and began to pull out a few grey hairs that defaced the beauty of his black curls.

"You shall lecture me presently, my dear," said Captain Rothesay. "You forget that I had two welcomes to receive, and that I have not yet seen my little girl."

He had not indeed. His eager inquiries after Olive overnight had been answered by a pretty pout, and several trembling, anxious speeches about "a wife being dearer than a child." "Baby was asleep, and it was so very late—he might, surely, wait till morning." To which, though rather surprised, he assented. A few more caresses, a few more excuses, had still further delayed the terrible moment; until at last the father's impatience would no longer be restrained.

"Come, Sybilla, let us go and see our little Olive."

"O Angus!" and the mother turned deadly white.

Captain Rothesay seemed alarmed. "Don't trifle with me, Sybilla—there is nothing the matter? The child is not ill?"

"No; quite well."

"Then, why cannot Elspie bring her?" and he pulled the bell violently. The nurse appeared. "My good Elspie, you have kept me waiting quite long enough; do let me see my little girl."

Elspie gave one glance at the mother, who stood mute and motionless, clinging to the chair for support. In that glance was less compassion than a sort of triumphant exultation. When she quitted the room Sybilla flung herself at her husband's feet. "Angus, Angus, only say you forgive me before"— —

The door opened and Elspie led in a little girl. By her stature she might have been two years old, but her face was like that of a child of ten or twelve—so thoughtful, so grave. Her limbs were small and wasted, but exquisitely delicate. The same might be said of her features; which, though thin, and wearing a look of premature age, together with that quiet, earnest, melancholy cast peculiar to deformity, were yet regular, almost pretty. Her head was well-shaped, and from it fell a quantity of amber-coloured hair— pale "lint-white locks," which, with the almost colourless transparency of her complexion, gave a spectral air to her whole appearance. She looked less like a child than a woman dwarfed into childhood; the sort of being renowned in elfin legends, as springing up on a lonely moor, or appearing by a cradle-side; supernatural, yet fraught with a nameless beauty. She was dressed with the utmost care, in white, with blue ribands; and her lovely hair was arranged so as to hide, as much as possible, the defect, which, alas! was even then only too perceptible. It was not a hump-back, nor yet a twisted spine; it was an elevation of the shoulders, shortening the neck, and giving the appearance of a perpetual stoop. There was nothing disgusting or painful in it, but still it was an imperfection, causing an instinctive compassion—an involuntary "Poor little creature, what a pity!"

Such was the child—the last daughter of the ever-beautiful Rothesay line—which Elspie led to claim the paternal embrace. Olive looked up at her father with her wistful, pensive eyes, in which was no childish shyness— only wonder. He met them with a gaze of frenzied unbelief. Then his fingers clutched his wife's arm with the grasp of an iron vice.

"Tell me! Is that—that miserable creature—our daughter, Olive Rothesay?"

She answered, "Yes." He shook her off angrily, looked once more at the child, and then turned away, putting his hand before his eyes, as if to shut out the sight.

Olive saw the gesture. Young as she was, it went deep to her child's soul. Elspie saw it too, and without bestowing a second glance on her master or his wife, she snatched up the child and hurried from the room.

The father and mother were left alone—to meet that crisis most fatal to wedded happiness, the discovery of the first deceit Captain Rothesay sat silent, with averted face; Sybilla was weeping—not that repentant shower which rains softness into a man's heart, but those fretful tears which chafe him beyond endurance.

"Sybilla, come to me!" The words were a fond husband's words: the tone was that of a master who took on himself his prerogative. Never had Angus spoken so before, and the wilful spirit of his wife rebelled.

"I cannot come. I dare not even look at you. You are so angry."

His only answer was the reiterated command, "Sybilla, come!" She crept from the far end of the room, where she was sobbing in a fear-stricken, childish way, and stood before him. For the first time she recognised her husband, whom she must "obey." Now, with all the power of his roused nature, he was teaching her the meaning of the word. "Sybilla," he said, looking sternly in her face, "tell me why, all these years, you have put upon me this cheat—this lie!"

"Cheat!—lie! Oh, Angus! What cruel, wicked words!"

"I am sorry I used them, then. I will choose a lighter term—deceit. Why did you so *deceive* your husband?"

"I did not mean it," sobbed the young wife. "And this is very unkind of you, Angus! As if Heaven had not punished me enough in giving me that miserable child!"

"Silence! I am not speaking of the child, but of you; my wife, in whom I trusted; who for five long years has wilfully deceived me. Why did you so?"

"Because I was afraid—ashamed. But those feelings are past now," said Sybilla, resolutely. "If Heaven made me mother, it made you father to this unhappy child. You have no right to reproach me."

"God forbid! No, it is not the misfortune—it is the falsehood which stings me."

And his grave, mournful tone, rose into one of bitter anger. He paced the room, tossed by a passion such as his wife had never before seen.

"Sybilla!" he suddenly cried, pausing before her; "you do not know what you have done. You little think what my love has been, nor against how much it has struggled these five years. I have been true to you—ay, to the depth of my heart And you to me have been—not wholly true."

Here he was answered by a burst of violent hysterical weeping. He longed to call for feminine assistance to this truly feminine ebullition, which he did not understand. But his pride forbade. So he tried to soothe his wife a little with softer words, though even these seemed somewhat foreign to his lips, after so many long-parted years.

"I did not mean to pain you thus deeply, Sybilla. I do not say that you have ceased to love me!"

Would that Sybilla had done as her first impulse taught her; have clung about him, crying "Never! never!" murmuring penitent words, as a tender wife may well do, and in such humility be the more exalted! But she had still the wayward spirit of a petted child. Fancying she saw her husband once more at her feet, she determined to keep him there. She wept on, refusing to be pacified.

At last Angus rose from her side, dignified and cold, his new, not his old self; the lover no more, but the quiet, half-indifferent husband. "I see we had better not talk of these things until you are more composed—perhaps, indeed, not at all. What is past—is past, and cannot be recalled."

"Angus!" She looked up, frightened at his manner. She determined to conciliate him a little. "What do you want me to do? To say I am sorry? That I will—but," with an air of coquettish command, "you must say so too."

The jest was ill-timed; he was in too bitter a mood. "Excuse me—you exact too much, Mrs. Rothesay."

"*Mrs. Rothesay!* Oh, call me Sybilla, or my heart will break!" cried the young creature, throwing herself into his arms. He did not repulse her; he even looked down upon her with a melting, half-reproachful tendernes.

"How happy we might have been! How different had been this coming home if you had only trusted me, and told me all from the beginning."

"Have you told *me*? Is there nothing you have kept back from me these five years?"

He started a little, and then said resolutely, "Nothing, Sybilla! I declare to Heaven—nothing! save, perhaps, some trifles that I would at any time tell you; now, if you will."

"Oh no! some other time, I am too much exhausted now," murmured Sybilla, with an air of languor, half real, half feigned, lest perchance she should lose what she had gained. In the sweetness of this reconciled "lovers' quarrel," she had almost forgotten its hapless cause. But Angus, after a pause of deep and evidently conflicting thoughts, referred to the child.

"She is ours still. I must not forget that. Shall I send for her again?" he said, as if he wished to soothe the mother's wounded feelings.

Alas! in Sybilla's breast the fountain of mother's feeling was as yet all sealed. "Send for Olive!" she said, "oh no! Do not, I implore you. The very sight of her is a pain to me. Let us two be happy together, and let the child be left to Elspie."

Thus she said, thinking not only to save herself, but him, from what must be a constant pang. Little she knew him, or guessed the after-effect of her words.

Angus Rothesay looked at his wife, first with amazement, then with cold displeasure. "My dear, you scarcely speak like a mother. You forget likewise that you are speaking to a father. A father who, whatever affection may be wanting, will never forsake his duty. Come, let us go and see our child."

"I cannot—I cannot!" and Sybilla hung back, weeping anew.

Angus Rothesay looked at his wife—the pretty wayward idol of his bridegroom-memory—looked at her with the eyes of a world-tried, world-hardened man. She regarded him too, and noted the change which years had brought in her boyish lover of yore. His eye wore a fretful reproach—his brow, a proud sorrow.

He walked up to her and clasped her hand. "Sybilla, take care! All these years I have been dreaming of the wife and mother I should find here at home; let not the dream prove sweeter than the reality."

Sybilla was annoyed—she, the spoilt darling of every one, who knew not the meaning of a harsh word. She answered, "Don't let us talk so foolishly."

"You think it foolish? Well, then! we will not speak in this confidential way any more. I promise, and you know I always keep my promises."

"I am glad of it," answered Sybilla. But she lived to rue the day when her husband made this one promise.

At present, she only felt that the bitter secret was disclosed, and Angus' anger overpast. She gladly let him quit the room, only pausing to ask him to kiss her, in token that all was right between them. He did so, kindly, though with a certain pride and gravity—and departed. She dared not ask him whether it was to see again their hapless child.

What passed between the father and mother whilst they remained shut up together there, Elspie thought not—cared not. She spent the time in passionate caresses of her darling, in half-muttered ejaculations, some of pity some of wrath. All she desired was to obliterate the impression which she saw had gone deeply to the child's heart. Olive wept not—she rarely did; it seemed as though in her little spirit was a pensive repose, above either infant sorrow or infant fear. She sat on her nurse's knee, scarcely speaking, but continually falling into those reveries which we see in quiet children even at that early age, and never without a mysterious wonder, approaching to awe. Of what can these infant musings be?

"Nurse," said the child, suddenly fixing on Elspie's face her large eyes, "was that my papa I saw?"

"It was just himsel, my sweet wee pet," cried Elspie, trying to stop her with kisses; but Olive went on.

"He is not like mamma—he is great and tall, like you. But he did not take up and kiss me, as you said he would."

Elspie had no answer for these words—spoken in a tone of quiet pain—so unlike a child. It is only after many years that we learn to suffer and be silent.

Was it that nature, ever merciful, had implanted in this poor girl, as an instinct, that meek endurance which usually comes as the painful experience of after-life?

A similar thought passed through Elspie's mind, while she sat with little Olive at the window, where, a few years ago, she had stood rocking the new-born babe in her arms, and pondering drearily on its future. That future seemed still as dark in all outward circumstances—but there was one ray of hope, which centred in the little one herself. There was something in Olive which passed Elspie's comprehension. At times she looked almost with an uneasy awe on the gentle, silent child who rarely played, who wanted no amusing, but would sit for hours watching the sky from the window, or the grass and waving trees in the fields; who never was heard to laugh, but now and then smiled in her own peculiar way—a smile almost "uncanny," as Elspie expressed it. At times the old Scotswoman—who, coming from the debateable ground between Highlands and Lowlands, had united to the rigid piety of the latter much wild Gaelic superstition—was half inclined to believe that the little girl was possessed by some spirit. But she was certain it was a good spirit; such a darling as Olive was—so patient, and gentle, and good—more like an angel than a child.

If her misguided parents did but know this! Yet Elspie, in her secret heart, was almost glad they did not. Her passionate and selfish love could not have borne that any tie on earth, not even that of father or mother, should stand between her and the child of her adoption.

While she pondered, there came a light knock to the door, and Captain Rothesay's voice was heard without—his own voice, soothed down to its soft, gentleman-like tone; it was a rare emotion, indeed, could deprive it of that peculiarity.

"Nurse, I wish to see Miss Olive Rothesay."

It was the first time that formal appellation had ever been given to the little girl. Still it was a recognition. Elspie heard it with joy. She answered the summons, and Captain Rothesay walked in.

We have never described Olivet father—there could not be a better opportunity than now. His tall, active form—now subsiding into the muscular fulness of middle age—was that of a Hercules of the mountains. The face combined Scottish beauties and Scottish defects, which, perhaps, cease to be defects when they become national peculiarities. There was the eagle-eye: the large, but well-chiselled features— especially the mouth; and also there was the high cheek-bone, the rugged squareness of the chin, which, while taking away beauty, gave character.

When he came nearer, one could easily see that the features of the father were strangely reflected in those of the child. Altered the likeness was—from strength into feebleness—from manly beauty into almost puny delicacy; but it did exist, and, faint as it was, Elspie perceived it.

Olive was looking up at the clouds, her thin cheek resting against the embrasure of the window, gazing so intently that she never seemed to hear her father's voice or step. Elspie motioned him to walk softly, and they came behind the child.

"Do ye no see, Captain Angus," she whispered, "'tis your ain bonnie face—ay, and your Mither's. Ye mind her yet?"

Captain Rothesay did not answer, but looked earnestly at his little daughter. She, turning round, met his eyes. There was something in their expression which touched her, for a rosy colour suffused her face; she smiled, stretched out her little hands, and said "Papa!"

How Elspie then prided herself for the continual tutoring which had made the image of the absent father an image of love!

Captain Rothesay started from his reverie at the sound of the child's voice. The tone, and especially the word, broke the spell. He felt once more that he was the father, not of the blooming little angel that he had pictured, but of this poor deformed girl. However, he was a man in whom a stern sense of right stood in the place of many softer virtues. He had resolved on his duty—he had come to fulfil it—and fulfil it he would. So he took the two little cold hands, and said—

"Papa is glad to see you, my dear."

There was a silence, during which Elspie placed a chair for Captain Rothesay, and Olive, sliding quietly down from hers, came and stood beside him. He did not offer to take the two baby-hands again, but did not repulse them, when the little girl laid them on his knee, looking inquiringly, first at him, and then at Elspie.

"What does she mean?" said Captain Rothesay.

"Puir bairn! I tauld her, when her father was come hame, he wad tak' her in his arms and kiss her."

Rothesay looked angrily round, but recollected himself. "Your nurse was right, my dear." Then pausing for a moment, as though arming himself for a duty—repugnant, indeed, but necessary—he took his daughter on his knee, and kissed her cheek—once, and no more. But she, remembering Elspie's instructions, and prompted by her loving nature, clung about him, and requited the kiss with many another. They melted him visibly. There is nothing sweeter in this world than a child's unasked voluntary kiss!

He began to talk to her—uneasily and awkwardly—but still he did it. "There, that will do, little one! What is your name, my dear?" he said absently.

She answered, "Olive Rothesay." "Ay—I had forgotten! The name at least, she told me true." The next moment, he set down the child—softly but as though it were a relief.

"Is papa going?" said Olive, with a troubled look.

"Yes; but he will come back to-morrow. Once a day will do," he added to himself. Yet, when his little daughter lifted her mouth for another kiss, he could not help giving it.

"Be a good child, my dear, and say your prayers every night, and love nurse Elspie."

"And papa too, may I?"

He seemed to struggle violently against some inward feeling, and then answered with a strong effort, "Yes."

The door closed after him abruptly. Very soon Elspie saw him walking with hasty strides along the beautiful walk that winds round the foot of the castle rock. The nurse sat still for a long time thinking, and then ended her ponderings with her favourite phrase,

"God guide us! it's a' come richt at last."

Poor, honest, humble soul!

CHAPTER VI

The return of the husband and father produced a considerable change in the little family at Stirling. A household, long composed entirely of women, always feels to its very foundations the incursion of one of the "nobler sex." From the first morning when there resounded the multiplied ringing of bells, and the creaking of boots on the staircase, the glory of the feminine dynasty was departed. Its easy *laisser-aller*, its lax rule, and its indifference to regular forms were at an end. Mrs. Rothesay could no longer indulge her laziness—no breakfasting in bed, and coming down in curl-papers. The long gossiping visits of her thousand-and-one acquaintances subsided into frigid morning calls, at which the grim phantom of the husband frowned from a corner and suppressed all idle chatter. Sybilla's favourite system of killing time by half-hours in various idle ways, at home and abroad, was terminated at once. She had now to learn how to be a duteous wife, always ready at the beck and call of her husband, and attentive to his innumerable wants.

She was quite horrified by these at first. The captain actually expected to dine well and punctually, every day, without being troubled beforehand with "What he would like for dinner?" He listened once or twice, patiently too, to her histories of various small domestic grievances, and then requested politely that she would confine such details to the kitchen in future; at which poor Mrs. Rothesay retired in tears. He liked her to stay at home in the evening, make his tea, and then read to him, or listen while he read to her. This was the more arduous task of the two, for dearly as she loved to hear the sound of his voice.

Sybilla never could feel interested in the prosy books he read, and often fell half asleep; then he always stopped suddenly, sometimes looked cross, sometimes sad; and in a few minutes he invariably lighted her candle, with the gentle hint that it was time to retire. But often she woke, hours after, and heard him still walking up and down below, or stirring the fire perpetually, as a man does who is obliged to make the fire his sole companion.

And then Sybilla's foolish, but yet loving heart, would feel itself growing sad and heavy; her husband's image, once painted there in such glittering colours, began to fade. The real Angus was not the Angus of her fancy. Joyful as was his coming home, it had not been quite what she expected.

Else, why was it that at times, amidst all her gladness, she thought of their olden past with regret, and of their future with doubt, almost fear.

But it was something new for Sybilla to think at all. It did her good in spite of herself.

While these restless elements of future pain were smouldering in the parents, the little neglected, unsightly blossom, which had sprung up at their feet, lived the same unregarded, monotonous life as heretofore. Olive Rothesay had attained to five years, growing much like a primrose in the field, how, none knew or cared, save Heaven. And that Heaven did both know and care, was evident from the daily sweetness that was stealing into this poor wayside flower, so that it would surely one day be discovered through the invisible perfume which it shed.

Captain Rothesay kept to his firm resolve of seeing his little daughter in her nursery, once a day at least. After a while, the visit of a few minutes lengthened to an hour. He listened with interest to Elspie's delighted eulogiums on her beloved charge, which sometimes went so far as to point out the beauty of the child's wan face, with the assurance that Olive, in features at least, was a true Rothesay. But the father always stopped her with a dignified, cold look.

"We will quit that subject, if you please."

Nevertheless, guided by his rigid sense of a parent's duty, he showed all kindness to the child, and his omnipotent way over his wife exacted the same consideration from the hitherto indifferent Sybilla. It might be, also, that in her wayward nature, the chill which had unconsciously fallen on the heart of the wife, caused the mother's heart to awaken And then the mother would be almost startled to see the response which this new, though scarcely defined tenderness, created in her child.

For some months after Captain Rothesay's return, the little family lived in the retired old-fashioned dwelling on the hill of Stirling. Their quiet round of uniformity was only broken by the occasional brief absence of the head of the household, as he said, "on business." *Business* was a word conveying such distaste, if not horror, to Sybilla's ears, that she asked no questions, and her husband volunteered no information. In fact, he rarely was in the habit of doing so—whether interrogated or not.

At last, one day when he was sitting after dinner with his wife and child—he always punctiliously commanded that "Miss Rothesay" might be brought in with the dessert—Angus made the startling remark:

"My dear Sybilla, I wish to consult with you on a subject of some importance."

She looked up with a pretty, childish surprise.

"Consult with me! O Angus! pray don't tease me with any of your hard business matters; I never could understand them."

"And I never for a moment imagined you could. In fact, you told me so, and therefore I have never troubled you with them, my dear," was the reply, with just the slightest shade of satire. But its bitterness passed away the moment Sybilla jumped up and came to sit down on the hearth at his feet, in an attitude of comical attention. Thereupon he patted her on the head, gently and smilingly, for he was a fond husband still, and she was such a sweet plaything for an idle hour.

A plaything! Would that all women considered the full meaning of the term—a thing sighed for, snatched, caressed, wearied of, neglected, scorned! And would also, that every wife knew that her fate depends less on what her husband makes of her, than what she makes herself to him!

"Now, Angus, begin—I am all attention."

He looked one moment doubtfully at Olive, who sat in her little chair at the farther end of the room, quiet, silent, and demure. She had beside her some purple plums, which she did not attempt to eat, but was playing with them, arranging them with green leaves in a thousand graceful ways, and smiling to herself when the afternoon sunlight, creeping through the dim window, rested upon them and made their rich colour richer still.

"Shall we send Olive away?" said the mother.

"No, let her stay—she is of no importance."

The parents both looked at the child's pale, spiritual face, felt the reproach it gave, and sighed. Perhaps both father and mother would have loved her, but for a sense of shame in the latter, and the painful memory of deceit in the former.

"Sybilla," suddenly resumed Captain Rothesay, "what I have to say is merely, how soon you can arrange to leave Stirling?"

"Leave Stirling?"

"Yes; I have taken a house."

"Indeed! and you never told me anything about it," said Sybilla, with a vexed look.

"Now, my little wife, do not be foolish; you never wish to hear about business, and I have taken you at your word; you cannot object to that?"

But she could, and she had a thousand half-pouting, half-jesting complaints to urge. She put them forth rather incoherently; in fact, she talked for five minutes without giving her husband opportunity for a single word. Yet she loved him dearly, and had in her heart no objection to being saved the trouble of thinking beforehand; only she thought it right to stand up a little for her conjugal prerogative.

He listened in perfect silence. When she had done, he merely said, "Very well, Sybilla; and we will leave Stirling this day month. I have decided to live in England. Oldchurch is a very convenient town, and I have no doubt you will find Merivale Hall an agreeable residence."

"Merivale Hall. Are we really going to live in a Hall?" cried Sybilla, clapping her hands with childish glee. But immediately her face changed. "You must be jesting with me, Angus. I don't know much about money, but I know we are not rich enough to keep up a Hall."

"We *were* not, but we are now, I am happy to say," answered Captain Rothesay, with some triumph.

"Rich! very rich! and you never told me?" Sybilla's hands fell on her knee, and it was doubtful which expression was dominant in her countenance—womanly pain, or womanly indignation.

Angus looked annoyed. "My dear Sybilla, listen to me quietly—yes, quietly," he added, seeing how her colour came and went, and her lips seemed ready to burst out into petulant reproach. "When I left England, I was taunted with having run away with an heiress. That I did not do, since you were far poorer than the world thought—and I loved little Sybilla Hyde for herself and not for her fortune. But the taunt stung me, and, when I left you, I resolved never to return until I could return a rich man on my own account. I am such now. Are you not glad, Sybilla?"

"Glad—glad to have been kept in the dark like a baby—a fool! It was not proper treatment towards your wife, Angus," was the petulant answer, as Sybilla drew herself from his arm, which came as a mute peacemaker to encircle her waist.

"Now you are a child indeed. I did it from love—believe me or not, it was so—that you might not be pained with the knowledge of my struggles, toils, and cares. And was not the reward, the wealth, all for you?"

"No; it wasn't."

"Pray, hear reason, Sybilla!" her husband continued, in those quiet, unconcerned tones, which, to a woman of quick feelings and equally quick resentments, were sure to add fuel to fire.

"I will not hear reason. When you have these four years been rolling in wealth, and your wife and child were—O Angus!" and she began to weep.

Captain Rothesay tried at first, by explanations and by soothings, to stop the small torrent of fretful tears and half-broken accusations. All his words were misconstrued or misapplied. Sybilla would not believe but that he had slighted, ill-used, *deceived* her.

At the term the husband rose up sternly.

"Mrs. Rothesay, who was it that deceived me?"

He pointed to the child, and the glance of both rested on little Olive.

She sat, her graceful playthings fallen from her hands, her large soft eyes dilated with such a terrified wonder, that both father and mother shrank before them. That fixed gaze of the unconscious child seemed like the reproachful look of some angel of innocence sent from a purer world.

There was a dead silence. In the midst of it the little one crept from her corner, and stood between her parents, her little hands stretched out, and her eyes full of tears.

"Olive has done nothing wrong? Papa and mamma, you are not angry with poor little Olive?"

For the first time, as she looked into the poor child's face, there flashed across the mother's memory the likeness of the angel in her dream. She pressed the thought back, almost angrily, but it came again. Then Sybilla stooped down, and, for the only time since her babyhood, Olive found herself lifted to her mother's embrace.

"The child had better go away to bed," said Captain Rothesay.

Olive was carried out nestling closely in her mother's arms.

When Sybilla came back the angry pout had passed away, though a grave troubled shadow still remained. She made tea for her husband, tried to talk on common topics once or twice, but he gave little encouragement. Before retiring to rest, she said to him, timidly,

"There is no quarrel between us, Angus?"

"Not in the least, my dear," he answered, with that composed deprecation of any offence, given or received, which is the most painful check to an impulsive nature; "only, we will not discuss matters of business together again. Women never can talk things over quietly. Good-night, Sybilla."

He lifted his head a little, a very little, for her accustomed kiss. She gave it, but with it there came a sigh. He scarcely noticed either one or the other, being apparently deep in a large folio "Commentary on the Proverbs," for it was Sunday evening. He lingered for a whole hour over the last chapter, and chiefly the passages,—

> *"Who can find a virtuous woman;*
>
> *for her price is far above rubies.*
>
> *The heart of her husband doth safely trust in her:*
>
> *so that he shall have no need of spoil....*
>
> *She openeth her mouth with wisdom:*
>
> *and in her tongue is the law of kindness."*

At this, Captain Rothesay closed the book, laid his arms upon it; and sighed—O how heavily! He did not go to bed that night until his young wife had lain awake for hours, regretting and resolving; nor until, after many determinations of future penitence and love, she had at last wept herself to sleep for very sorrow.

CHAPTER VII

Looking back on a calm and uneventful childhood—and by childhood we mean the seven years between the babyhood of five and the dignity of "teens,"—it always seems like a cloudy landscape, with a few points of view here and there, which stand out clearly from the rest. Therein the fields are larger and the sky brighter than any we now behold. Persons, places, and events assume a mystery and importance. We never think of them, or hear them named afterwards, but there clings to them something of the strange glamour of the time when "we saw men as trees walking."

Olive's childhood was passed in the place mentioned by her father. Merivale! Oldchurch! In her future life the words, whenever heard, always sounded like an echo of that dreamy time, whose sole epochs are birthdays, Christmas-days, the first snowdrop found in the garden, the first daisy in the field. Such formed the only chronicle of Olive's childhood.

Its earliest period was marked by events which she was too young to notice, troubles which she was too young to feel. They passed over her like storm-clouds over a safely sheltered flower—only perceived by the momentary shadow which they cast. Once—it was in the first summer at Merivale—the child noticed how pleased every one seemed, and how papa and mamma, now always together, used to speak more tenderly than usual to her. Elspie said it was because they were so happy, and that Olive ought to be happy too, because God would soon send her "a wee wee brother." She would find him some day in the pretty cradle, which Elspie showed her. So the little girl went to look there every morning, but in vain. At last her nurse said she need not look there any more, for God had taken away the baby-brother as soon as it came. Olive was very much disappointed, and when she went down to her father that day she told him of her trouble. But he angrily sent her away to her nurse. She looked ever after with grief and childish awe on the empty cradle.

Olive.
"Olive, little noticed, sat on the hearthrug, fondling the sleepy cat, or gazing with vague childish reverie into the fire."

At last it was empty no longer. She, a thoughtful child of seven, could never forget the impression made, when one morning she was roused by the loud pealing of the Old-church bells, and the maids told her, laughing, that it was in honour of her little brother, come at last. She was allowed to kiss him once, and then spent half her time, watching, with great joy and wonderment, the tiny face and touching the tiny hands. After some days she missed him; and after some more Elspie showed her a little heap in the nearest churchyard, saying, that was her baby-brother's cradle now. Poor little Olive!—her only knowledge of the tie of brotherhood was these few days of silent watching and the little green mound left behind in the churchyard.

From that time there came a gradual change over the household, and over Olive's life. No more long, quiet hours after dinner, her father reading, her mother occupied in some light work, or resting on the sofa in delicious idleness, while Olive herself, little noticed, but yet treated with uniform kindness by both, sat on the hearthrug, fondling the sleepy cat, or gazing with vague childish reverie into the fire. No more of the proud pleasure with which, on Sunday afternoons, exalted to her grave papa's knee, she created an intense delight out of what was to him a somewhat formal duty, and said her letters from the large family Bible. These childish joys vanished gradually, she scarce knew how. Her papa she now rarely saw, he was so much from home, and the quiet house, wherein she loved to ramble, became a house always full of visitors, her beautiful mamma being the centre of its gaiety. Olive retreated to her nursery and to Elspie, and the rest of her childhood was one long, solitary, pensive dream.

In that dream was the clear transcript of all the scenes amidst which it passed. The old hall, seated on a rising ground, and commanding views which were really beautiful in their way, considering that Merivale was on the verge of a manufacturing district, bounded by pastoral and moorland country. Those strange furnace-fires, which rose up at dusk from the earth and gleamed all around the horizon, like red fiery eyes open all night long, how mysteriously did they haunt the imaginative child! Then the town, Oldchurch, how in her after-life it grew distinct from all other towns, like a place seen in a dream, so real and yet so unreal! There was its castle-hill, a little island within a large pool, which had once been a real fortress and moat. Old Elspie contemned alike tradition and reality, until Olive read in her little "History of England" the name of the place, and how John of Gaunt had built a castle there. And then Elspie vowed it was unworthy to be named the same day with beautiful Stirling. Continually did she impress on the child the glories of her birthplace, so that Olive in after-life, while remembering her childhood's scenes as a pleasant land of earth, came to regard her native Scotland as a sort of dream-paradise. The shadow of the mountains where she was born fell softly, solemnly, over her whole life; influencing her pursuits, her character, perhaps even her destiny.

Yet there was a curious fascination about Oldchurch. She never forgot it. The two great wide streets, High-street and Butcher-row, intersecting one another in the form of a cross: the two churches—the Old Church, gloomy and Norman, with its ghostly graveyard; and the New Church, shining white amidst a pleasant garden cemetery, beneath one of whose flower-beds her baby-brother lay: the two shops, the only ones she ever visited, the confectioner's, where she stood to watch the yearly fair, and the bookseller's whither she dragged her nurse on any excuse, that she might pore over its incalculable treasures.

Above all, there was fixed in her memory the strange aspect the town wore on one day—a Coronation-day, the grandest gala of her childhood. One king had died and been buried.—Olive saw the black-hung pulpit and heard the funeral sermon, awfully thundered forth at night Another king had been proclaimed, and Olive had gloried in the sight of the bonfires and the roasted sheep. Now the people talked of a Coronation-day. Simple child! She knew nothing of the world's events or the world's destinies, save that she rose early to the sound of carolling bells, was dressed in a new white frock, and taken to see the town—the beautiful town, smiling with triumphal flower-arches and winding processions. How she basked in the merry sunshine, and heard the shouts, and the band playing "God save the King," and felt very loyal, until her enthusiasm vented itself in tears.

Such was one of the few links between Olive's early life and the world outside. Otherwise she dwelt, for those seven years of childhood, in a little Eden of her own, whose boundary was rarely crossed by the footsteps of either joy or pain. She was neither neglected nor ill-used, but she never knew that fulness of love on which one looks back in after-life, saying deprecatingly, and yet sighing the while, "Ah, I was indeed a spoiled child!" Her little heart was not positively checked in its overflowings; but it had a world of secret tenderness, which, being never claimed, expended itself in all sorts of wild fancies. She loved every flower of the field and every bird in the air. She also—having a passionate fondness for study and reading—loved her pet authors and their characters, with a curious individuality. Mrs. Holland stood in the place of some good aunt, and Sandford and Merton were regarded just like real brothers.

She had no one to speak to about poetry; she did not know there was such a thing in the world. Yet she was conscious of strange and delicious sensations, when in the early days of spring she had at length conquered Elspie's fears about wet feet and muddy fields, and had gone with her nurse to take the first meadow ramble; she could not help bounding to pluck every daisy she saw; and when the violets came, and the primroses, she was out of her wits with joy. She had never even heard of Wordsworth; yet, as she listened to the first cuckoo note, she thought it no bird, but truly "a wandering voice." Of Shelley's glorious lyric ode she knew nothing; and yet she never heard the skylark's song without thinking it a spirit of the air, or one of the angels hymning at Heaven's gate. And many a time she looked up in the clouds at early morning, half expecting to see that gate open, and wondering whereabouts it was in the beautiful sky.

She had never heard of Art, yet there was something in the gorgeous sunset that made her bosom thrill; and out of the cloud-ranges she tried to form mountains such as there were in Scotland, and palaces of crystal like those she read of in her fairy tales. No human being had ever told her of the mysterious links that reach from the finite to the infinite, out of which, from the buried ashes of dead Superstition, great souls can evoke those mighty spirits, Faith and Knowledge; yet she went to sleep every night believing that she felt, nay, could almost see, an angel standing at the foot of her little bed, watching her with holy eyes, guarding her with outspread wings.

O Childhood! beautiful dream of unconscious poetry; of purity so pure that it knew neither the existence of sin nor of its own innocence; of happiness so complete, that the thought, "I am now happy," came not to drive away the wayward sprite which never *is*, but always is to come! Blessed Childhood! spent in peace and loneliness and dreams; hidden therein lay the germs of a whole life.

CHAPTER VIII

Olive Rothesay was twelve years old, and she had never learnt the meaning of that word whose very sound seems a wail—sorrow. And that other word, which is the dirge of the whole earth—death—was still to her only a name. She knew there was such a thing; she read of it in her books; its shadow had passed her by when she missed her little brother from the cradle; but still it had never stood by her side and said, "Lo, I am here!" Her circle of love was so small that it seemed as though the dread spectre could not enter. She saw it afar off; she thought upon it sometimes in her poetical dreams, which clad the imaginary shape of grief with a strange beauty. It was sweet to be sad, sweet to weep. She even tried to make a few delicious sorrows for herself; and when a young girl—whose beautiful face she had watched in church—died, she felt pensive and mournful, and even took a pleasure in thinking that there was now one grave in the new churchyard which she would almost claim to weep over.

Such were the tendencies of this child's mind—ever toward the melancholy and the beautiful united. Quietly pensive as her disposition was, she had no young companions to rouse her into mirth. But there was a serenity even in her sadness; and no one could have looked in her face without feeling that her nature was formed to suit her apparent fate, and that if less fitted to enjoy, she was the more fitted for the solemnity of that destiny, to endure.

She had lived twelve years without knowing sorrow, and it was time that the first lesson, bitter, yet afterwards sweet, should be learned by the child. The shaft came to her through Elspie's faithful bosom, where she had rested all her life, and did rest now, with the unconscious security of youth, which believes all it loves to be immortal. That Elspie should grow old seemed a thing of doubtful future; that she should be ill or die was a thing that never crossed her imagination.

And when at last, one year in the fall of the leaf, the hearty and vigorous old woman sickened, and for two or three days did not quit her room, still Olive, though grieving for the moment, never dreamed of any serious affliction. She tended her nurse lovingly and cheerfully, made herself quite a little woman for her sake, and really half enjoyed the stillness of the sickroom. It was a gay time—the house was full of visitors—and Elspie and her charge, always much left to one another's society, were now alone in their nursery, night and day. No one thought the nurse was ailing, except with the natural infirmity of old age, and Elspie herself uttered no word of complaint. Once or twice, while Olive was doing her utmost to enliven the sick-chamber, she saw her nurse watch her with eager love, and then sink into a grave reverie, from which it took more than one embrace to rouse her.

One night, or rather morning, Olive was roused by the sight of a white figure standing at her bedside. She would have been startled, but that Elspie, sleeping in the same room, had many a time come to look on her darling, even in the middle of the night. She had apparently done so now.

"Go to your bed again, dear nurse," anxiously cried Olive. "You should not walk about. Nay, you are not worse?"

"Ay, ay, maybe; but dinna fear, dearie, we'll bide till the morn," said Elspie, faintly, as she tried to move away, supporting herself by the bed. Soon she sank back dizzily. "I canna walk. My sweet lassie, will ye help your puir auld nurse?"

Olive sprang up, and guided her back to her bed. When she reached it, Elspie said, thoughtfully, "It's strange, unco strange. My strength is a' gane."

"Never mind, Elspie dear, you are weak with being ill; but you will get better soon. Oh, yes, very soon!"

"It's no that;" and Elspie took her child's hands and looked wistfully in her face. "Olive, gin ye were to tine your puir auld nurse? Gin I were to gang awa?"

"Where?"

"Unto God," said Elspie, solemnly.—"Dearie, I wadna grieve ye, but I'm aye sure this sickness is unto death."

It was strange that Olive did not begin to weep, as many a child would have done; but though a cold trembling crept through her frame at these words, she remained quite calm. For Elspie must be kept calm likewise, and how could she be so if her child were not. Olive remembered this, and showed no sign of grief or alarm. Besides, she could not—would not believe a thing so fearful as Elspie's death. It was impossible.

"You must not think thus—you must think of nothing but getting well. Lie down and go to sleep," she said, in a tone of almost womanly firmness, which Elspie obeyed mechanically. Then she would have roused the household, but the nurse forbade. By her desire Olive again lay down.

It had always been her custom to creep to Elspie's bed as soon as she awoke, but now she did so long before daylight, in answer to a faint summons.

"I want ye, my bairn. Ye'll come to your auld nurse's arms—maybe they'll no haud ye lang," murmured Elspie. She clasped the child once, with an almost passionate tenderness, and then, turning away, dropped heavily asleep.

But Olive did not sleep. She lay until broad daylight, counting hour by hour, and thinking thoughts deep and strange in a child of her years—thoughts of death and eternity. She did not believe Elspie's words; but if they should be true—if her nurse should die—if this should be the last time she would ever creep to her living bosom!

And then there came across the child's mind awful thoughts of death and of the grave. She struggled with them, but they clung with fearful tenacity to her fancy. All she had heard or read of mortality, of the coffin and the mould, came back with a vivid horror. She thought,—what if in a few weeks, a few days, the hand she held should be cold, lifeless; the form, whose faint breathings she listened to, should breathe no more, but be carried from her sight, and shut up in a grave—under a stone? And then where would be Elspie—the tender, the faithful—who seemed to live but in loving her? Olive had been told that when people died, it was their bodies only that lay in the grave, and their souls went up to heaven to be with God. But all her childish reasoning could not dissever the two.

It was a marvel, that, loving Elspie as she did, such thoughts should come at all—that her mind was not utterly numbed with grief and terror. But Olive was a strange child. There were in her little spirit depths of which no one dreamed.

Hour after hour she lay thinking these thoughts, horrible, yet fraught with a strange fascination, starting with a shudder every time they were broken by the striking of the clock below. How awful a clock sounds in the night-time, and to such a watcher—a mere child too! Olive longed for morning, and yet when the dusk of daybreak came, the very curtains took ghastly shapes, and her own white dress, hanging behind the door, looked like a shroud, within which— —. She shuddered—and yet, all the while, she could not help eagerly conjecturing what the visible form of Death would be.

Utterly unable to endure her own thoughts, she tried to rouse her nurse. And then Elspie started up in bed, seized her with burning hands, and asked her who she was and what she had done with little Olive.

"I am little Olive—indeed I am," cried the terrified child.

"Are ye sure? Aweel then, dearie, dinna greet," murmured poor Elspie, striving vainly against the delirium that she felt fast coming on. "My bairn, is it near morn? Oh, for a drink o' milk or tea."

"Shall I go and call the maids? But that dark dark passage—I dare not."

"It's no matter, bide ye till the daylight," said Elspie, as she sank again into heavy sleep.

But the child could not rest. Was it not cruel to let her poor nurse lie suffering burning thirst, rather than encounter a few vague terrors? and if Elspie should have a long illness, should die—what then would the remorseful remembrance be? Without another thought the child crept out of bed and groped her way to the door.

It is easy to laugh at children's fancies about "ghosts" and "bogie," but Dante's terrors in the haunted wood were not greater or more real than poor little Olive's, when she stood at the entrance of the long gallery, dimly peopled with the fantastic shadows of dawn. None but those who remember the fearful imaginings of their childhood, can comprehend the self-martyrdom, the heroic daring, which dwelt in that little trembling bosom, as Olive groped across the gloom.

Half-way through, she touched the cold handle of a door, and could scarce repress a scream. Her fears took no positive shape, but she felt surrounding her Things before and Things behind. No human courage could give her strength to resist such terrors. She paused, closed her eyes, and said the Lord's Prayer all through. But "*Deliver us from evil*" she repeated many times, feeling each time stronger and bolder. Then first there entered into her heart that mighty faith "which can remove mountains;" that fervent boldness of prayer with the very utterance of which an answer comes. And who dare say that the Angel of that child "always beholding the face of the Father in Heaven," did not stand beside her then, and teach her in faint shadow-ings the mystery of a life to come?

Olive's awe-struck fancy became a truth—she never crept to her nurse's bosom more. By noon that day, Elspie lay in the torpor which marks the last stage of rapid inflammation. She did not even notice the child, who crept in and out of the thronged room, speaking to no one, neither weeping nor trembling, but struck with a strange awe, that made her countenance and "mien almost unearthly in their quietness.

"Take her away to her parents," whispered the physician. But her mother had left home the day before, and Captain Rothesay had been absent a week. There were only servants in the house; they looked at her often, said "Poor child!" and left her to go where she would. Olive followed the physician downstairs.

"Will she die?"

He started at the touch of the soft hand—soft but cold, always cold. He looked at the little creature, whose face wore such an unchildlike expression. He never thought to pat her head, or treat her like a girl of twelve years old, but said gravely, as though he were speaking to a grown woman:

"I have done my best, but it is too late. In three hours, or perhaps four, all will be over." He quitted the room, and Olive heard the rattle of his carriage wheels. They died away down the gravel road, and all was silent Silent, except the twitter of a few birds, heard through the stillness of a July evening. Olive stood at the window and mechanically looked out. It was so beautiful, so calm. At the west, the clouds were stretched out in pale folds of rose colour and grey. On the lawn slept the long shadows of the trees, for behind them was rising the round, red moon. And yet, within the house was—death.

She tried to realise the truth. She said to herself, time after time, "Elspie will die!" But even yet she could not believe it. How could the little birds sing and the sunset shine when Elspie was dying! At last the light faded, and then she believed it all. Night and death seemed to come upon the world together.

Suddenly she remembered the physician's words. "Three hours—four hours." Was that all? And Elspie had not spoken to her since the moment when she cried and was afraid to rise in the dark. Elspie was going away, for ever, without one kiss, one good-bye.

Weeping passionately, Olive flew back to the chamber, where several women stood round the bed. There lay the poor aged form in a torpor which, save for the purple face and the loud, heavy breathing, had all the unconsciousness of death. Was that Elspie? The child saw, and her tears were frozen. The maids would have drawn her away.

"No—no," Olive said in a frightened whisper; "let me look at her—let me touch her hand."

It lay outside the bedclothes, helpless and rigid, the fingers dropping together, as they always do in the hour of parting life. Olive touched them. They were cold—so cold! Then she knew what was death. The maids carried her fainting from the room.

Mrs. Rothesay had returned, and, frightened and grieved, now wept with all a woman's softness over the death-bed of the faithful old nurse. She took her little daughter to her own sitting-room, laid her on the sofa, and watched by her very tenderly. Olive, exhausted and half insensible, heard, as in a dream, her mother whispering to the maid:

"Come and tell me when there is *any change.*"

Any change! What change? That from life to death—from earth to heaven! And would it take place at once? Could they tell the instant when Elspie's soul departed "to be beyond the sun"?

Such and so strange were the thoughts that floated through the mind of this child of twelve years old. And from these precocious yearnings after the infinite, Olive's fancy turned to earthly, childish things. She pictured with curious minuteness how she would feel when she awoke next morning, and found that Elspie was dead;—how there would be a funeral; how strange the house would seem afterward; even what would be done with the black bonnet and shawl which, two days since, Elspie had hung up against the nursery-door never to put on again.

And then a long silent agony of weeping came. Her mother, thinking she slept, sat quietly by; but in any case Olive would never have thought of going to her for consolation. Young as she was, Olive knew that her sorrow must be borne alone, for none could understand it. Until we feel that we are alone on earth, how rarely do we feel that we are *not* alone in heaven! For the second time this day the child thought of God. Not merely as of Him to whom she offered her daily prayers, and those repeated after the clergyman in church on Sunday, but as One to whom, saying "Our Father," she could ask for anything she desired.

And she did so, lying on the sofa, not even turning to kneel down, using her own simple words. She prayed that God would comfort her when Elspie died, and teach her not to grieve, but to be a good, patient child, so that she might one day go to her dear nurse in heaven, and never be parted from her any more.

She heard the maid come in and whisper to her mamma. Then she knew that all was over—that Elspie was dead. But so deep was the peace which had fallen on her heart that the news gave no pang—caused no tears.

"Olive, dearest," said Mrs. Rothesay, herself subdued into weeping.

"I know, mamma," was the answer. "Now I have no one to love me but you."

The feeling was strange, perhaps even wrong; but as Mrs. Rothesay clasped her child, it was not without a thrill of pleasure that Olive was all her own now.

"Where shall Miss Rothesay sleep to-night?" was the whispered question of the maid. Olive burst into tears.

"She shall sleep with me. Darling, do not cry for your poor nurse, will not mamma do instead?"

And looking up, Olive saw, as though she had never seen it before, the face which, now shining with maternal love, seemed beautiful as an angel's. It became to her like an angel's evermore.

How often, in our human fate, does the very Hand that taketh, give!

CHAPTER IX

Mrs. Rothesay, touched by an impulse of regretful tenderness, showed all due respect to the memory of the faithful woman who had nursed with such devotion her husband and her child. For a whole long week Olive wandered about the shut-up house, the formal solemnities of death, now known for the first time, falling heavily on her young heart. Alas! that there was no one to lift it beyond the terrors of the grave to the sublime mysteries of immortality.

But the child knew none of these, and therefore she crept, awe-struck, about the silent house, and when night fell, dared not even to pass near the chamber—once her own and Elspie's—now Death's. She saw the other members of the household enter there with solemn faces, and pass out, carefully locking the door. What must there be within? Something on which she dared not think, and which nothing could induce her to behold. At times she forgot her sorrow; and, still keeping close to her mother's side, amused herself with her usual childish games, piecing disjointed maps, or drawing on a slate; but all was done with a quietness sadder than even tears.

The evening before the funeral, Mrs. Rothesay went to look for the last time on the remains of her faithful old servant. She tried to persuade little Olive to go with her; the child accompanied her to the door, and then, weeping violently, fled back and hid herself in another chamber. From thence she heard her mother come away—also weeping, for the feeble nature of Sybilla Rothesay had lost none of its tender-hearted softness. Olive listened to the footsteps gliding downstairs, and there was silence. Then the passionate affection which she had felt for her old nurse rose up, driving away all childish fear, and strengthening her into a resolution which until then she had not dared to form. To-morrow they would take away Elspie—*for ever*. On earth she would never again see the face which had been so beloved. Could she let Elspie go without one look, only one? She determined to enter the awful room now, and alone.

It was about seven in the evening, still daylight, though in the darkened house dimmer than without. Olive drew the blind aside, took one long gaze into the cheerful sunset landscape to strengthen and calm her mind, and then walked with a firm step to the chamber-door. It was not locked this time, but closed ajar. The child looked in a little way only. There stood the well-remembered furniture, the room seemed the same, only pervaded with an atmosphere of silent, solemn repose. There would surely be no terror there.

Olive stole in, hearing in the stillness every beating of her heart. She stood by the bed. It was covered, not with its usual counterpane of patchwork stars, the work of Elspie's diligent hand through many a long year, and on which her own baby-fingers had been first taught to sew—but with a large white sheet. She stood, scarce knowing whether to fly or not, until she heard a footstep on the stairs. One minute, and it would be too late. With a resolute hand she lifted the sheet, and saw the white fixed countenance, not of sleep, but death.

Uttering a shriek so wild and piercing that it rang through the house, Olive sprang to the door, fled through the passage, at the end of which she sank in convulsions.

That night the child was taken ill, and never recovered until some weeks after, when the grass was already springing on poor Elspie's grave.

It is nature's blessed ordinance, that in the mind of childhood the remembrance of fear or sorrow fades so fast. Therefore, when Olive regained strength, and saw the house now smiling within and without amidst the beauty of early autumn,—the horrors of death passed from her mind, or were softened into a tender memory. Perhaps, in the end, it was well for her that she had looked on that poor dead face, to be certain that it was not Elspie. She never thought of Elspie in that awful chamber any more. She thought of her as in life, standing knitting by the nursery-window, walking slowly and sedately along the green lanes, carrying the basket of flowers and roots, collected in their rambles, or sitting in calm Sunday afternoons with her Bible on her knee.

And then, passing from the memory of Elspie once on earth, Olive thought of Elspie now in heaven. Her glowing imagination idealised all sorrow into poesy. She never watched the sunset, she never looked up into the starry sky at night, without picturing Elspie as there. All the foibles and peculiarities of her poor old Scottish nurse became transmuted into the image of a guardian invisible, incorporeal; which seemed to draw her own spirit nearer to heaven, with the thought that there was one she loved, and who loved her, in the glorious mansions there.

From the time of her nurse's death, the whole current of Olive's life changed. It cast no shadow over the memory of the deep affection lost, to say that the full tide of living love now flowed towards Mrs. Rothesay as it had never done before, perhaps never would have done but for Elspie's death. And truly the mother's heart now thirsted for that flood.

For seven years the little cloud which appeared when Captain Rothesay returned, had risen up between husband and wife, increasing slowly but surely, and casting a shadow over their married home. Like many another pair who wed in the heat of passion, or the wilful caprice of youth, their characters, never very similar, had grown less so day by day, until their two lives had severed wider and wider. There was no open dissension that the wicked world could take hold of, to glut its eager eyes with the spectacle of an unhappy marriage; but the chasm was there, a gulf of coldness, indifference, and distrust, which no foot of love would ever cross.

Angus Rothesay was a disappointed man. At five-and-twenty he had taken a beautiful, playful, half-educated child,

"His bride and his darling to be,"

forgetting that at thirty-five he should need a sensible woman to be his trustworthy sympathising wife, the careful and thoughtful mistress of his household. When hard experience had made him old and wise, even a little before his time, he came home expecting to find her old and wise too. The hope failed. He found Sybilla as he had left her—a very child. Ductile and loving as she was, he might even then have guided her mind, have formed her character, in fact, have made her anything he liked. But he would not do it; he was too proud. He brooded over his disappointed hope in silence and reserve; and though he reproached her not, and never ceased to love her in his own cold way, yet all respect and sympathy were gone. Her ways were not his ways, and was it the place of a man and a husband to bend? After a few years of struggling, less with her than with himself, he decided that he would take his own separate course, and let her take hers.

He did so. At first she tried to win him back, not with a woman's sweet and placid dignity of love, never failing, never tiring, yet invisible as a rivulet that runs through deep green bushes, scarcely heard and never seen. Sybilla's arts—the only arts she knew—were the whole armoury of girlish coquetry, or childish wile, passionate tenderness and angry or sullen reproach, alternating each other. Her husband was equally unmoved by all. He seemed a very rock, indifferent to either sunshine or storm. And yet it was not so. He had in his nature deep, earnest, abiding tenderness; but he was one of those people who must be loved only in their own quiet, silent way. A hard lesson for one whose every feeling was less a principle than an impulse. Sybilla could not learn it. And thus the happiness of two lives was blighted, not from evil, or even lack of worth in either, but because they did not understand one another. Their current of existence flowed on coldly and evenly, in two parallel lines, which would never, never meet!

The world beheld Captain Rothesay in two phases—one as the grave, somewhat haughty but respected master of Merivale Hall; the other as the rash and daring speculator, who was continually doubling and trebling his fortune by all the thousand ways of legal gambling in which men of capital can indulge. There was in this kind of life an interest and excitement Captain Rothesay rushed to it as many another man would have rushed to far less sinless means of atoning for the dreary blank of home.

In Mrs. Rothesay the world only saw one of its fairest adornments—one of those "charming women" who make society so agreeable; beautiful, kind-hearted—at least as much so as her thoughtless life allowed; lively, fond of amusement—perhaps a little too much, for it caused people to note the contrast between the master and the mistress of the Hall, and to say what no wife should ever give the world reason to say, "Poor thing! I wonder if she is happy with her husband?"

But between those two stood the yet scarce recognised tie which bound them together—the little deformed child.

CHAPTER X

"Captain Rothesay?"

"My dear?"

Reader, did you ever notice the intense frigidity that can be expressed in a "my dear!" The coldest, cruellest husband we ever knew once impressed this fact on our childish fancy, by our always hearing him call his wife thus. Poor, pale, broken-hearted creature! He "my deared" her into her grave.

Captain Rothesay also used the epithet with a formality which was chilling enough in its way. He said it without lifting his eyes from the book, "Smith's Wealth of Nations," which had become his usual evening's study now, whenever he was at home. That circumstance, rare enough to have been welcome, and yet it was not welcome, now subdued his wife and daughter into silence and quietness. Alas! that ever a presence which ought to be the sunshine of a household should enter only to cast a perpetual shade.

The firelight shone on the same trio which had formed the little after-dinner circle years ago at Stirling. But there was a change in all. The father and mother sat—not side by side, in that propinquity which is so sweet, when every breath, every touch of the beloved's garment gives pleasure; they sat one at each corner of the table, engrossed in their several occupations; reading with an uncommunicative eagerness, and sewing in unbroken silence. Each was entrenched within a chilling circle of thoughts and interests in which the other never entered. And now the only point of meeting between them was the once-banished child.

Little Olive was growing almost a woman now, but she was called "little Olive" still. She retained her diminutive stature, together with her girlish dress, but her face wore, as ever, its look of premature age. And as she sat between her father and mother, now helping the one in her delicate fancy-work, now arranging the lamp for the other's reading, continually in request by both, or when left quiet for a minute, watching both with anxious earnestness, there was quite enough in Olive's manner to show that she had entered on a woman's life of care, and had not learned a woman's wisdom one day too soon.

The captain's last "my dear" found his wife in the intricacies of a Berlin-wool pattern, so that she did not speak Again for several minutes, when she again appealed to "Captain Rothesay." She rarely called him anything else now. Alas! the time of "Angus" and "Sybilla" was gone.

"Well, my dear, what have you to say?"

"I wish you would not be always reading, it makes the evening so dull."

"Does it?" and he turned over another leaf of Adam Smith, and leisurely settled himself for its perusal.

"Papa is tired, and may like to be quiet. Suppose we talk to one another, mamma?" whispered Olive, as she put aside her own work—idle, but graceful designings with pencil and paper—and drawing near to her mother, began to converse in a low tone. She discussed all questions as to whether the rose should be red or white, and what coloured wool would form the striped tulip, just as though they had been the most interesting topics in the world. Only once her eyes wandered wistfully to the deserted "Sabrina," which, half sketched, lay within the leaves of her "Comus." Mrs. Rothesay observed this, and said, kindly—

"Let me look at what you are doing, love. Ah!—very pretty! What is Sabrina? Tell me all about her." And she listened, with a pleased, maternal smile, while her gratified little daughter dilated on the beloved "Comus," and read a passage or two in illustration. "Very pretty, my love," again repeated Mrs. Rothesay, stroking Olive's hair. "Ah! you are a clever child. But now come and tell me what sort of winter dresses you think we should have."

If any observer could have seen a shade of disappointment on Olive's face, he would also have seen it instantly suppressed. The young girl closed "Comus" with the drawing inside, and came to sit down again, looking up into the eyes of her "beautiful mamma." And even the commonplace question of dress soon became interesting to her, for her artistic predilection followed her even there, and no lover ever gloried in his mistress's charms, no painter ever delighted to deck his model, more than Olive loved to adorn and to admire the still exquisite beauty of her mother. It stood to her in the place of all attractions in herself—in fact, she rarely thought about herself at all. The consciousness of her personal defect had worn off through habit, and her almost total seclusion from strangers prevented its being painfully forced on her mind.

"I wish we could leave off this mourning," said Mrs. Rothesay. "It is quite time, seeing Sir Andrew Rothesay has been dead six months. And, living or dying, he did not show kindness enough to make one remember him longer."

"Yet he was kind to papa, when a child; and so was Auntie Flora," softly said Olive, to whose enthusiastic memory there ever clung Elspie's tales about the Perthshire relatives—bachelor brother and maiden sister, living together in their lonely, gloomy home. But she rarely talked about them; and now, seeing her mamma looked troubled, as she always did at any reference to Scotland and the old times, the little maiden ceased at once. Mrs. Rothesay was soon again safely and contentedly plunged into the mysteries of winter costume.

"Your dresses must be handsomer and more womanly now, Olive; for I intend to take you out with me now and then. You are quite old enough; and I am tired of visiting alone. I intended to speak to your papa about it to-night; but he seems not in a good humour."

"Only tired with his journey," put in the sweet little awdiator. "Is it not so papa?"

Captain Rothesay started from a dull, anxious reverie, into which his reading had merged, and lifted his face, knitted and darkened with some inward care, heavy enough to make his tone sharp and angry, as he said,

"Well, child, what do you want?"

"Do not scold Olive; it was I who wished to speak to you." And then, without pausing to consider how evidently ill-timed the conversation was, Mrs. Rothesay began to talk eagerly about Olive's "coming out," and whether it should be at home or abroad; finally arguing that a ball at Merivale would be best, and entering at large on the question of ball-costume. There was nothing wrong in anything she said, but she said it at the wrong time. Her husband listened first with indifference, then fidgeted restlessly in his chair, and at last subsided into an angry silence.

"Why don't you speak, Captain Rothesay?" He took up the poker and hammered the fire to small cinders. "Of course, you will be reasonable. Say, shall it be as I have arranged?"

"No!" The word came thundering out—as Captain Rothesay rarely thundered; for he was calm and dignified even in his wrath. Immediately afterwards he rose up and left the room.

Sybilla grew pale, sorrowful, and then melted into tears. She tried not to let Olive see them. She was still too faithful a wife to seek in any way to turn the child against her father. But yet she wept: and drawing her young daughter closer to her arms, she felt the sweetness of having a child—and such a child—left to love her. In proportion as the wife's heart closed, the mother's opened.

Ere long, Captain Rothesay sent for little Olive, to read the evening newspaper to him in his study.

"Go, love," said Mrs. Rothesay; and she went—without fear, too; for her father never said a harsh word to *her*. And as, each year of her life, the sterling truth and stern uprightness of his character dawned upon her, she could not fail to respect him, even while she worshipped her sweet-tempered gentle mother.

Captain Rothesay made no remark, save upon the subject she was reading, and came in with Olive to tea, just as usual. But when he had finished, and was fast sinking back into that painful reverie which seemed to oppress him, his weak ill-judging wife recommenced her attack. She talked gently when speaking of Olive, even affectionately—poor soul! She persuaded herself, all the time, that she was doing right, and that he was a hardhearted father not to listen to her. He did listen, apparently; and she took his silence for consent, for she ended with—

"Well, then, it is quite settled; the ball shall be at Merivale, on the 20th of next month."

Angus turned round, his blue eyes glittering, yet cold as steel—"Mrs. Rothesay, if you will worm the truth out of me, you shall. By next month you may not have a roof over your head."

He rose up and again quitted the room. Mrs. Rothesay trembled—grew terrified—but tried to reassure herself. "He only says this in anger, or else to frighten me. I will not believe it." Then conscience whispered, that never in her whole life had she known Angus Rothesay to tell a falsehood; and she trembled more and more. Finally, she passed into a violent fit of nervous weeping—a circumstance by no means rare. Her health was weakened by the exciting gaieties of her outward life, and the inward sorrow which preyed upon her heart.

This night—and not for the first time either—the little maiden of fifteen might have been seen, acting with the energy and self-possession of a woman—soothing her mother's hysterical sufferings—smoothing her pillow, and finally watching by her until she fell asleep. Then Olive crept downstairs, and knocked at her father's study-door. He said, "Come in," in a dull, subdued tone. She entered, and saw him sitting, his head on his hand, jaded and exhausted, leaning over the last embers of the fire, which had gone out without his noticing it. If there had been any anger in the child's heart, it must have vanished at once, when she looked upon her father thus.

"Oh! is that you, Olive?" was all he said, beginning to turn over his papers, as if to make a show of occupation.

But he soon relapsed into that unknown thought which oppressed him so much. It was some minutes before he completely aroused himself, and saw the little elfin-like figure standing beside him, silent and immovable, with the taper in her hand.

"Shall I bring your candle, dear papa? It is eleven o'clock and more."

"Where is your mother, Olive?"

"She is gone to bed;" and Olive paused, uncertain whether she should tell him that her mamma was ill. Again there was a silence—during which, do what he would, Captain Rothesay could not keep his eyes from the earnest, wistful, entreating gaze of his "little Olive." At last, he lifted her on his knee, and took her face between his two hands, saying, in a smothered tone,

"You are not like your mother; you are like *mine*—ay, and seem more so as you grow to be a woman."

"I wish I were a woman, that papa might talk to me and tell me anything which he has on his mind," whispered Olive, scarcely daring to breathe that which she had nerved herself to say, during many minutes of silent pondering at the study-door.

Captain Rothesay relapsed hastily into his cold manner. "Child, how do you know?"

"I know nothing, and want to know nothing, that papa does not wish to tell me," answered Olive, gently.

The father turned round again, and looked into his daughter's eyes. Perhaps he read there a spirit equal to, and not unlike, his own—a nature calm, resolute, clear-sighted; the strong will and decision of a man, united to the tenderness of a woman. From that hour father and daughter understood one another.

"Olive, how old are you?—I forget."

"Fifteen, dear papa."

"Ah! and you are a thoughtful girl. I can talk to you as to a woman—pah! I mean, a sensible woman. Put out your candle; you can sit up a while longer."

She obeyed, and sat with him for two whole hours in his study, while he explained to her how sudden reverses had so damaged his fortune that it was necessary to have a far smaller establishment than Merivale Hall.

"Not that we need fear poverty, my dear child; but the future must be considered and provided for. Your mother's jointure, should I die—nay, do not look sad, we will not talk of that—and then, too, your own portion, when you marry."

Olive blushed, as any girl of fifteen will do when talked to on such a topic, even in the most business-like way. "I shall not marry, papa," said she, expressing the thought which had come to her, as it does to most young girls who love their parents very dearly, too dearly to imagine a parting.

Captain Rothesay started, as if suddenly recollecting himself. Then he regarded her earnestly, mournfully; and in the look was something which struck on Olive's memory as though she had seen it before.

"I had forgotten," muttered Captain Rothesay to himself. "Of course, she will never marry. Poor child!—poor child!"

He kissed her very tenderly, then lighted his candle, and went upstairs to bed, holding her hand all the way, until they parted at her room door, when he kissed her a second time. As he did so, she contrived to whisper—

"Mamma is sure to wake; she always does when you come in. Kiss mamma, too."

Olive went to bed, happier than she could have believed possible, had any one told her in the morning that ere night she would hear the ill news of having to leave beautiful Merivale. But it was so sweet to feel herself a comfort to both parents—they who, alas! would receive no comfort from each other.

Only, just when she was falling asleep, the thought floated across Olive's mind—

"I wonder why papa said that, of course, I should never marry!"

CHAPTER XI

"Dear mamma, is not this a pretty house, even though it is in a town?—so pretty, one need hardly pine after Merri-vale."

Thus said Olive when they had been established some time in their new abode, and sat together, one winter evening, listening to the sweet bells of Oldchurch—one of the few English parishes where lingers "the curfew's solemn sound."

"A pretty house, if any one came to see us in it, my dear; but nobody does. And then we miss the close carriage so much. To think that I have been obliged to refuse the Stantons' ball and the dinner-party at Everingham. How dull these long winter evenings will be, Olive!"

Olive answered neither *yes* nor *no*, but tried quietly, by her actions, to disprove the fact She was but a child—scarcely would have been called a clever child; was neither talkative nor musical; and yet she had a thousand winning ways of killing time, so sweetly that each minute died, dolphin-like, shedding glorious hues.

A very romantic simile this—one that would never have crossed Olive's innocent brain. She only knew that she loved her mother; and therefore tried to amuse and make her happy, so that she might not feel the change of circumstances—a change so unimportant to Olive, so vital to Mrs. Rothesay.

Olive, this night, was peculiarly successful in her little *ruse* of love. Her mother listened while she explained a whole sketch-book of designs, illustrative of half-a-dozen modern poets. Mrs. Rothesay even asked her to read some of the said poets aloud; and though not of an imaginative temperament, was fain to shed a few womanly tears over Tennyson's "Queen of the May" and the "Miller's Daughter." Finally, she was coaxed into sitting to her daughter for her portrait, which Olive thought would make a design exactly suited to the heroine of the latter poem, and chiefly at the verse—

"Look through mine eyes with thine. True wife, Round my true heart thine arms entwine; My other dearer life in life, Look through my very soul with thine."

And, reading the verses over and over again, to bring the proper expression to her mother's face, the young girl marvelled that they brought likewise a look so sad that she would fain have made some excuse, and terminated the sitting.

"No, no, my dear; it amuses me, and I can talk with you the while."

But Mrs. Rothesay did not talk much; she was continually falling into a reverie. Once she broke it with the words—

"Olive, my child, I think, now we lead a quieter life, your papa will stay at home more. He seems to like this house, too—he never liked Merivale."

"Dear old Merivale!" said Olive, with a sigh. It seemed ages since she had left the familiar place.

"Do not call it *dear*. It was a dreary home. I did not think so at first, but I did afterwards."

"Why, mamma?" asked Olive. She was glad to lure her mother on to talk a little, if only to dispel the shadow which so ill became Mrs. Rothesay's still fair face.

"You were too young to know anything then—indeed, you are now, almost. But, somehow, I have learned to talk with you as if you were quite a little woman, Olive, my dear."

"Thank you, mamma. And what made you dislike sweet Merivale?"

"It was when your papa first began to take his long journeys—on business you know. He was obliged to do it, I suppose; but, nevertheless, it was very dull for me. I never had such a dreary summer as that one. You could not remember it, though—you were only ten years old."

Olive did remember it faintly, nevertheless—a time when her father's face was sterner, and her mother's more fretful, than now; when the shadow of many domestic storms passed over the child. But she never spoke of these things; and, lest her mother should ponder painfully on them now, she began to talk of lighter matters. Yet though the sweet companionship of her only daughter was balm to Mrs. Rothesay's heart, still there was a pain there which even Olive could not remove. Was it that the mother's love had sprung from the ruins of the wife's happiness; and that while smiling gaily with her child, Sybilla Rothesay's thoughts were with the husband who, year by year, was growing more estranged, and whom, as she found out too late, by a little more wisdom, patience, and womanly sympathy, she might perhaps have kept for ever at her side?

But none of these mysteries came to the knowledge of little Olive. She lived the dream-life of early girlhood—dwelling in an atmosphere still and pure as a grey spring morning ere the sun has risen. All she learnt was from books; for though she had occasional teachers, she had never been sent to school. Sometimes she regretted this, thinking how pleasant it would be to have companions, or at least one friend, of her own age, to whom she might talk on the various subjects of which she had of late begun to dream. These never passed the still sanctuary of her own thoughts; for some instinct told her that her mother would not sympathise with her fancies. So she thought of them always by herself, when she was strolling about the small but pleasant garden that sloped down from the back of the house to the river; or when, extending her peregrinations, she went to sit in the summer-house of the garden adjoining, which belonged to a large mansion close by, long uninhabited. It was quite a punishment to Olive when a family came to live there, and she lost the use of the beautiful deserted garden.

Still, it was something new to have neighbours. She felt quite a curiosity respecting them, which was not diminished when, looking out one day from the staircase window (a favourite seat, from which every night she watched the sun set), Olive caught sight of the new occupants of her former haunts.

They were two little boys of about nine or ten, playing noisily enough—as boys will. Olive did not notice them much, except the youngest, who appeared much the quieter and gentler of the two; but her gaze rested a long time on a girl, who seemed to be their elder sister. She was walking by herself up and down an alley, with a shawl thrown over her head, and her thick, black hair blown about by the March winds. Olive thought she looked very picturesque—in fact, just like some of her own fantastic designs of "Norna on the Fitful head," "Medora watching for Conrad," etc. etc. And when the young stranger drew nearer, her admiration was still further excited, by perceiving under the shawl a face that needed but a little romantic imagination to make it positively beautiful. Olive thought so, and accordingly sat the whole evening drawing it from memory, and putting it into various characters, from Scott, Byron, Moore, and Coleridge.

For several days after, she took a deep interest in watching the family party, and chiefly this young girl—partly because she was so pretty, and partly because she seemed nearly about her own age, or perhaps a year or two older. Olive often contrived to walk in her garden when her neighbours were in theirs—so that she could hear the boys' cheerful voices over the high hedge. By this means she learnt their Christian names, Robert and Lyle—the latter of which she admired very much, and thought it exactly suited the pretty, delicate younger brother. She wished much to find out the name of their sister—but could not; for the elder girl took little notice of them, or they of her. So Olive, after thinking and talking of her for some time, as "my beauty next door," to Mrs. Rothesay's great amusement, at last christened her by the imaginary name of Maddalena.

After a few weeks it seemed as though the interest between the young neighbours became mutual—for Olive, in her walks, sometimes fancied she saw faces watching *her*, too from the staircase window. And once, peering over the wall, she perceived the mischievous eyes and pointed finger of the elder boy, and heard the younger one say, reproachfully—

"Don't—pray! You are very cruel, Bob."

And Olive, deeply blushing—though at what she scarcely knew—fled into the house, and did not take her usual garden walks for some days.

At last, when, one lovely spring evening, she stood leaning over the low wall at the garden's end, idly watching the river flow by beneath, she turned round, and saw fixed on her, with a curiosity not unmingled with interest, the dark eyes of "Maddalena." Somehow or other, the two girls smiled—and then the elder spoke.

"The evening was very fine," she said; "and it was rather dull, walking in the garden all alone."

Olive had never found it so; but she was used to it. Her young neighbour was not; she had always lived in a large town, etc. etc.

A few more simple nothings spun out the conversation for ten minutes. The next day it was resumed, and extended to twenty; during which Olive learnt that her young beauty's name, so far from being anything so fine as Maddalena, was plain Sarah—or *Sara*, as its owner took care to explain. Olive was rather disappointed—but she thought of Coleridge's ladye love; consoled herself, and tried to console the young lady, with repeating,

My pensive Sarah! thy soft cheek reclined, etc.

At which Miss Sara Derwent laughed, and asked who wrote that very pretty poetry?

Olive was a little confounded. She fancied everybody read Coleridge, and her companion sank just one degree in her estimation. But as soon as she looked again on the charming face, with its large, languishing Asiatic eyes, and delicate mouth—just like that of the lotus-leaved "Clytie," which she loved so much,—Olive felt all her interest revive.

Never was there any girl over whom every form of beauty exercised more fascination. By the week's end she was positively enchanted with her neighbour, and before a month had passed, the two young girls had struck up that romantic friendship peculiar to sixteen.

There is a deep beauty—more so than the world will acknowledge—in this impassioned first friendship, most resembling first love, the foreshadowing of which it truly is. Who does not, even while smiling at its apparent folly, remember the sweetness of such a dream? Many a mother with her children at her knee, may now and then call to mind some old playmate, for whom, when they were girls together, she felt such an intense love. How they used to pine for the daily greeting—the long walk, fraught with all sorts of innocent secrets. Or, in absence, the almost interminable letters—positive love-letters, full of "dearest" and "beloveds," and sealing-wax kisses. Then the delicious meetings—sad partings, also quite lover-like in the multiplicity of tears and embraces—embraces sweeter than those of all the world beside—and tears—But our own are gathering while we write—Ah!

We also have been in Arcadia.

Gracious reader! grave, staid mother of a family!—you are not quite right if you jest at the days of old, and at such feelings as these. They were real at the time—and most pure, true, and beautiful. What matter, if years sweeping on have swept them all away or merged them into higher duties and closer ties? Perhaps, if you met your beautiful idol of fifteen, you would see a starched old maid of fifty, or a grandame presiding over the third generation; or perchance, in seeking thus, you would find only a green hillock, or a stone inscribed with the well-known name. But what of that? To you the girlish image is still the same—it never can grow old, or change, or die. Think of it thus; and then you will think not mockingly, but with an interest almost mournful, on the rapturous dream of first friendship which now came to visit Olive Rothesay.

Sara Derwent was the sort of girl of whom we meet some hundreds in a lifetime—the class from whence are taken the lauded "mothers, wives, and daughters of England." She was sincere, good-tempered, and affectionate; not over-clever, being more gifted with heart than brains; rather vain, which fault her extreme prettiness half excused; always anxious to do right, yet, from a want of decision of character, often contriving to do wrong.

But she completely charmed the simple Olive with her beauty, her sparkling, winning cheerfulness, and her ready sympathy. So they became the most devoted friends. Not a day passed without their spending some portion of it together—Olive teaching the young Londoner the pleasures of the country; and Sara, in her turn, inducting the wondering Olive into all the delightful mysteries of life, as learnt in a large home circle, and a still larger circle of society. Olive, not taking aught from the passionate love with which she looked up to her mother, yet opened her warm heart to the sweetness of this affection—so fresh, so sudden, so full of sympathetic contact. It was like a new revelation in her girlhood—the satisfying of a thirst, just beginning to be felt. She thought of Sara continually; delighted in being with her; in admiring her beauty, and making interests out of every interest of hers. And to think that her friend loved her in return brought a sensation of deep happiness, not unmixed with gratitude.

Sara's own feelings may be explained by one sentence of a letter which she wrote to an old schoolfellow. Therein she told how she had found "such a dear, loving, gentle thing; a girl, not pretty—even slightly deformed; but who was an amusing companion, and to whom she could confide everything. Such a blessing in that dull place, Oldchurch!"

Poor little Olive!

CHAPTER XII

As the summer advanced, Olive Rothesay and her new friend, sanctioned by the elders of both families, took long walks together, read, and practised. Not that Olive practised, for she had no voice, and little knowledge of music; but she listened to Sara's performances for hours, with patience, if not with delight. And when they talked—oh, what talks those were!

Now, reader, be not alarmed lest we should indulge you with the same. Go back into your own *repertoire* of early friendships, and that will suit us quite as well Still, we may just say that these young friends flitted like bees over every subject under heaven, and at last alighted on the subject most interesting at their age—love.

It is curious to note how the heart first puts out its tendrils and stretches them forth toward the yet unknown good which is to be in after-life its happiness and its strength. What folly of parents to repress these blind seekings after such knowledge—this yearning which nature teaches, and which in itself involves nothing wrong. Girls *will* think of love, whether or no! How much better, then, that they should be taught to think of it rightly, as the one deep feeling of life. Not, on the one hand, to be repressed by ridicule; nor, on the other, to be forced by romance into a precocious growth; but to be entered upon, when fate brings the time, rationally, earnestly, and sacredly.

Olive Rothesay found, with considerable pain, that Miss Derwent and she did not at all agree in their notions of love. Olive had always felt half-frightened at the subject, and never approached it save with great awe and timidity; but Sara did not seem to mind it in the least. She talked of a score of "flirtations" at quadrille parties—showed her friend half-a-dozen complimentary billets-doux which she had received, and all with the greatest unconcern. By degrees this indifference vanished under the influence of Olive's more earnest nature; and at last, when they were sitting together one night, listening to the fierce howling of the wind, a little secret came out.

"I don't like that equinoctial gale," said Sara, shyly. "I used to hear so much of its horrors from a friend I have—at sea."

"Indeed. Who was that?"

"Only Charles Geddes. Did I never speak of him? Very likely not—because I was so vexed at his leaving college and running off to sea. It was a foolish thing. But don't mention him to papa or the boys." And Sara blushed—a real, good, honest blush.

Olive did the same—perhaps from sympathy. She continued very thoughtful for a long time; longer even than Sara. They were not many days in making out between them the charming secret for which in their hearts they had been longing. Both were thirsting to taste—or at least to see each other taste—of that enchanting love-stream, the stream of life or of death, at whose verge they had now arrived.

And so, it somehow chanced that, however the conversation began, it usually glided into the subject of Charles Geddes. Sara acknowledged that he and she had always liked one another very much, though she allowed that he was fonder of her than she was of him; that, when they parted, he had seemed much agitated—and she had cried—but they were mere boy and girl then. It was nothing—nothing at all.

Olive did not think so; and, contrasting all this with similar circumstances in her pet poems and novels, she wove a very nice romance round Charles Geddes and her beloved Sara, whom she now began to look upon with greater interest and reverence than ever. This did not prevent her reading Sara a great many lectures on constancy, and giving her own opinions on what true love ought to be—opinions which were a little too ethereal for Miss Derwent's comprehension, but which she liked very much, nevertheless.

Olive took quite an affectionate interest in her friend's lover—for lover she had decided that he must be. Not a day passed that she did not eagerly consult the *Times*" "shipping intelligence;" and when at last she saw the name of Charles Geddes' vessel, as "arrived," her heart beat, and tears sprang to her eyes. When she showed it to Sara, Olive could hardly speak for joy. Little simpleton! she counted her friend's happiness as if it were her own. She kept the secret even from her mother; that is, in the only manner Olive would conceal aught from any one so beloved, by saying, "Please, mamma, do not ask me anything." And Mrs. Rothesay, who, always guided by some one, was now in a fair way to be entirely guided by her daughter, made no inquiries, but depended entirely upon Olive's wisdom and tenderness.

Charles Geddes came to Oldchurch. It was quite a new life for Olive—a changed life, too; for now the daily rambles with her friend were less frequent. Instead of which, she used to sit at her window, and watch Sara and Charles taking long strolls in the garden, arm-in-arm, looking so happy, that it was beautiful to see them.

Who can describe the' strange, half-defined thoughts which often brought tears to the young girl's eyes as she watched them thus! It was no jealousy of Sara's deserting her for Charles, still less was it envy; but it was a vague longing—a desiring of love for love's own sake. Not as regarded any individual object, for Olive had never seen any one in whom she felt or fancied the slightest interest. Yet, as she looked on these two young creatures, apparently so bound up in each other, she thought how sweet such a tie must be, and how dearly she herself could love some one. And her yearning was always *to love* rather than *to be loved*.

One morning, when Olive had not seen Sara for a day or two, she was hastily summoned to their usual trysting-place, a spot by the river-side, where the two gardens met, and where an over-arching thorn-tree made a complete bower. Therein Sara stood, looking so pale and serious, that Olive remarked it.

"Has anything happened?"

"Nothing—that is, nothing amiss. But oh, Olive, what do you think? Charles put this letter into my hand last night. I have scarcely slept—I feel so agitated—so frightened."

And in truth she looked so. Was there ever a very young girl who did not, on receiving her first love-letter?

It was an era in Olive's life, too. She even trembled, as by her friend's earnest desire she read the missive. It was boyish, indeed, and full of the ultra-romantic devotion of boyish love; but it was sincere, and it touched Olive deeply. She finished it, and leaned against the thorn-tree, pale and agitated as Sara herself.

"Well, Olive?" said the latter.

Olive threw her arms round her friend's neck and kissed her, feeling almost ready to cry.

"And now, dear, tell me what I must do," said Sara, earnestly; for of late she had really begun to look up to Olive, so great was the influence of the more thoughtful and higher nature.

"Do! Why, if you love him, you must tell him so, and give him your whole life-long faith and affection."

"Really, Olive, how grave you are! I had no idea of making it such a serious matter. But, poor Charles!—to think that he should love me so very much!"

"Oh, Sara, Sara!" murmured Olive, "how happy you ought to be!"

The time that followed was a strange period in Olive's life. It was one of considerable excitement, too; she might as well have been in love herself, so deeply did she sympathise with Sara and with Charles. With the latter, even more than with her friend; for there was something in the sincere, reserved, and yet passionate nature of the young sailor, that answered to her own. If he had been her brother, she could not have felt more warmly interested in Charles Geddes and his wooing. And he liked her very much, for Sara's sake first, and then for her own, regarding her also with that gentle compassion which the strong and bold delight to show to the weak. He often called her "his faithful little friend;" and truly she stood his friend in every conceivable way, by soothing Sara's only parent—a most irascible papa—to consent to the engagement, and also by lecturing the gay and coquettish Sara herself into as much good behaviour as could be expected from an affianced damsel of seventeen.

Charles Geddes went to sea again. Poor little Olive, in her warm sympathies, suffered almost as much as the young man's own betrothed, who, after looking doleful for a week, consoled herself by entering, heart and soul, into the gaieties of the gayest Christmas that ever was spent by the society of Oldchurch. Everywhere Miss Derwent was the belle, and continually did her friend need to remind her of the promise which Olive herself regarded as such a sacred, solemn thing.

The love-adventure in which she had borne a part had stirred strange depths in the nature of the young girl. She was awakening slowly to the great mystery of woman's life. And when, by degrees, Sara's amusements somewhat alienated their continual intercourse, Olive was thrown back upon her own thoughts more and more. She felt a vague sadness—a something wanting in her heart, which not even her mother's love could supply.

Mrs. Rothesay saw how dull and pensive she was at times, and with a tender unselfishness contrived that, by Sara Derwent's intervention, Olive should see a little more society; in a very quiet way, though; for her own now delicate health and Captain Rothesay's will, prevented any regular introduction of their daughter into the world. And sometimes Mrs. Rothesay, pondering on Olive's future, felt-glad of this.

"Poor child! she is not made for the world, or the world for her. Better that she should lead her own quiet life, where she will suffer no pain, and be wounded by no neglect."

Yet, nevertheless, it was with a vague pleasure that Mrs. Rothesay dressed Olive for her first ball—a birthday treat—coaxed by Sara Derwent out of her formidable papa, and looked forward to by both girls for many weeks.

No one would have believed that the young creature, on whom Mrs. Rothesay gazed with a tenderness, not unmingled with admiration, had been the poor infant from which she once turned with a sensation of pain, almost amounting to disgust. But, learning to love, one learns also to admire. Besides, Olive's defect was less apparent as she grew up, and the extreme sweetness of her countenance almost atoned for her bad figure. Yet, as the mother fastened her white dress, and arranged the golden curls so as to fall in a shower on her neck and bosom, she sighed heavily.

Olive did not notice it; she was too much occupied in tying up a rare bouquet—a birthday gift for Sara.

"Well, are you quite satisfied with my dress, dearest mamma?"

"Not quite;" and Mrs. Rothesay fetched a small mantle of white fur, which she laid round Olive's shoulders. "Wear this, dear; you will look better then—see." She led her to the mirror, and Olive saw the reflection of her own figure, so effectually disguised, that the head, with its delicate and spiritual beauty, seemed lifting itself out of a white cloud.

"'Tis a pretty little mantle, but why must I wear it, mamma?—the night is not cold." So little did she think of herself, and so slight had been her intercourse with the world, that the defect in her shape rarely crossed her mind. But the mother, so beautiful herself, and to whom beauty was still of such importance, was struck with bitter pain. She would not even console herself by the reflection, with which many a one had lately comforted her, that Olive's slight deformity was becoming less perceptible, and that she might, in a great measure, outgrow it in time. Still it was there. As Mrs. Rothesay looked at the swan-like curves of her own figure, and then at her daughter's, she would almost have resigned her own once-cherished, but now disregarded, beauty, could she have bestowed that gift upon her beloved child.

Without speaking, lest Olive should guess her thoughts, she laid the mantle aside, only she whispered in bidding adieu, "Dear, if you see other girls prettier, or more admired, more noticed than yourself, never mind! Olive is mamma's own pet—always."

Oh, blessed adversity! oh, sweetness, taught by suffering! How marvellous was the change wrought in Sybilla's heart.

Olive had never in her life before been at a "private ball," with chalked floors, rout seats, and a regular band. She was quite dazzled by the transformation thus effected in the Derwents' large, rarely-used, dining-room, where she had had many a merry game with little Robert and Lyle. It was perfect fairyland. The young damsels of Oldchurch—haughty boarding-school belles, whom she had always rather feared, when Sara's hospitality brought her in contact with them—were now grown into perfect court beauties. She was quite alarmed by their dignity, and they scarcely noticed poor little Olive at all. Sara, sweeping across the room, appeared to the eyes of her little friend a perfect queen of beauty. But the vision came and vanished. Never was there a belle so much in request as the lively Sara.

Only once, Olive looked at her, and remembered the sailor-boy, who was, perhaps, tossing in some awful night-storm, or lying on the lonely deck, in the midst of the wide Atlantic. And she thought, that when her time came to love and be loved, she would not take everything quite so easily as Sara.

"How pleasant quadrilles must be!" said Olive, as she sat with her favourite Lyle, watching the dancers. Lyle had crept to her, sliding his hand in hers, and looking up to her with a most adoring gaze, as indeed he often did. He had even communicated his intention of marrying her when he grew a man—a determination which greatly excited the ridicule of his elder brother.

"I like far better to sit here quietly with you," murmured the faithful little cavalier.

"Thank you, Lyle; still, they all look so merry, I almost wish some one had asked me to dance."

"You dance, Miss Rothesay! What fun! Why nobody would ever dance with you," cried rude Bob.

Lyle looked imploringly at his brother: "Hush! you naughty boy! Please, Miss Rothesay, I will dance with you at any time, that is, if you think I am tall enough."

"Oh, quite; I am so small myself," answered Olive, laughing; for she took quite a pride in patronising him, as girls of sixteen often affectionately patronise boys some five or six years their junior. "You know, you are to grow up to be my little husband."

"Your husband!" repeated Bob, mischievously. "Don't be too sure of getting one at all. What do you think I overheard those girls there say? That you looked just like an old maid; and, indeed, no one would ever care to marry you, because you were"—

Here Lyle, blushing crimson, stopped his brother's mouth with his little hand; whereat Bob flew into such a passion, that he quite forgot Olive, and all he was about to say, in the excitement of a pugilistic combat with his unlucky *cadet* In the midst of which the two belligerents—poor, untaught, motherless lads—were hurried off to bed.

Their companionship lost, Olive was left very much to her own devices for amusement. Some few young people that she knew came and talked to her for a little while, but they all went back to their singing, dancing, or flirting; and Olive, who seemed to have no gift nor share in either, was left alone. She did not feel this much at first, being occupied in her thoughts and observations on the rest. She took great interest in noticing all around. Her warm heart throbbed in sympathy with many an idle, passing flirtation, which she in her simplicity mistook for a real "attachment." It seemed as if every one loved, or was loved, except herself. She thought this, blushing as if it were unmaidenliness, when it was only nature speaking in her heart.

Poor Olive! perhaps it was ill for her that Sara's "love affair" had aroused prematurely these blind gropings after life's great mystery, so often

Too early seen unknown, and known too late.

"What! tired of dancing already?" cried Sara, flitting to the corner where Olive sat.

"I have not danced once yet," Olive answered, rather piteously.

"Come—shall I get you a partner?" said Sara, carelessly.

"No, no; every one is strange to me here. If you please, and if it would not trouble you, Sara, I had much rather dance with you."

Sara consented with a tolerably good grace; but there was a slight shadow on her face, which somewhat pained her friend.

"Is she ashamed of me, I wonder?" thought Olive. "Perhaps, because I am not beautiful. Yet, no one ever told me I was *very* disagreeable to look at. I will see."

As they danced, she watched in the tall mirror Sara's graceful, floating image, and the little pale figure that moved beside her. There *was* a contrast! Olive, who inherited all her mother's love of beauty, spiritualised by the refinement of a dawning artist-soul, felt keenly the longing regret after physical perfection. She went through the dance with less spirit, and in her heart there rung the idle echoes of some old song she knew:

"I see the courtly ladies stand,
With their dark and shining hair;
And I coldly turn aside to weep—
Oh, would that I were fair!"

The quadrille ended, she hid herself in her old corner; and Sara, whose good nature led her to perform this sacrifice to friendship, seemed to smile more pleasantly and affectionately when it was over. At least Olive thought so. She did not see her beautiful idol again for some time; and feeling little interest in any other girl, and none at all in the awkward Oldchurch "beaux," she took consolation in her own harmless fashion. This was hiding herself under the thick curtains, and looking out of the window at the moon.

Sara's voice was heard close by, talking to a young girl whom Olive knew. But Olive was too shy to join them. She greatly preferred her friend the moon.

"I laughed to see you dancing with that little Olive Rothesay, Miss Derwent. For my part, I hate dancing with girls—and as for *her*—But I suppose you wanted to show the contrast."

"Nay, that's ill-natured," answered Sara, "She is a sweet little creature, and my very particular friend."

Here Olive, blushing and happy, doubted whether she ought not to come out of the curtains. It was almost wrong to listen—only her beloved Sara often said she had no secrets from Olive.

"Yes, I know she is your friend, and Mr. Charles Geddes' great friend too; if I were you, I should be almost jealous."

"Jealous of Olive—how very comical!" and the silver laugh was a little scornful. "To think of Olive's stealing any girl's lover! She, who will probably never have one in all her life—poor thing!"

"Of course not; nobody would fall in love with her! But there is a waltz, I must run away. Will you come?"

"Presently—when I have looked in the other room for Olive?"

"Olive is here," said a timid voice. "Oh, Sara, forgive me if I have done wrong; but I can't keep anything from you. It would grieve me to think I heard what you were saying, and never told you of it."

Sara appeared confused, and with a quick impulse kissed and fondled her little friend: "You are not vexed, or pained, Olive?"

"Oh, no—that is, not much; it would be very silly if I were. But," she added, doubtfully, "I wish you would tell me one thing, Sara—not that I am proud, or vain; but still I should like to know. Why did you and Jane Ormond say just now that nobody would ever love me?"

"Don't talk so, my little pet," said Sara, looking pained and puzzled. Yet, instinctively, her eye glanced to the mirror, where their two reflections stood. So did Olive's.

"Yes, I know," she murmured. "I am little, and plain, and in figure very awkward—not graceful like you. Would that make people hate me, Sara?"

"Not hate you; but"——

"Well, go on—nay, I *will* know all!" said Olive firmly; though gradually a thought—long subdued—began to dawn painfully in her mind.

"I assure you, dear," began Sara, hesitatingly, "it does not signify to me, or to any of those who care for you; you are such a gentle little creature, we forget it all in time. But perhaps with strangers, especially with men, who think so much about beauty, this defect"——

She paused, laying her arm round Olive's shoulders—even affectionately, as if she herself were much moved. But Olive, with a cheek that whitened, and a lip that quivered more and more, looked resolutely at her own shape imaged in the glass.

"I see as I never saw before—so little I thought of myself. Yes, it is quite true—quite true."

She spoke beneath her breath, and her eyes seemed fascinated into a hard, cold gaze. Sara became almost frightened.

"Do not look so, my dear girl; I did not say that it was a positive *deformity*."

Olive faintly shuddered: "Ah, that is the word! I understand it all now."

She paused a moment, covering her face. But very soon she sat down, so quiet and pale that Sara was deceived.

"You do not mind it, then, Olive—you are not angry with me?" she said soothingly.

"Angry with you—how could I be?"

"Then you will come back with me, and we will have another dance."

"Oh, no, no!" And the cheerful good-natured voice seemed to make Olive shrink with pain. "Sara, dear Sara, let me go home!"

CHAPTER XIII

"Well, my love, was the ball as pleasant as you expected?" said Mrs. Rothesay, when Olive drew the curtains, and roused her invalid mother to the usual early breakfast, received from no hands but hers.

Olive answered quietly, "Every one said it was pleasant."

"But you," returned the mother, with an anxiety she could scarce disguise—"who talked to you?—who danced with you?"

"No one, except Sara."

"Poor child!" was the half involuntary sigh; and Mrs. Rothesay drew her daughter to her with deep tenderness.

It was a strange fate, that made the once slighted child almost the only thing in the world to which Sybilla Rothesay now clung. And yet, so rich, so full had grown the springs of maternal love, long hidden in her nature, that she would not have exchanged their sweetness to be again the petted, wilful, beautiful darling of society, as she was at Stirling. The neglected wife—the often-ailing mother—dependent on her daughter's tenderness, was happier and nearer to heaven than she had ever been in her life.

Mrs. Rothesay regarded Olive earnestly. "You look as ill as if you had been up all night; and yet you came to bed tolerably early, and I thought you slept, you lay so quiet. Was it so, darling?"

"Not quite; I was thinking," said Olive, truthfully, though her face flushed, for she would fain have kept her bitter thoughts from her mother. Just then, Mrs. Rothesay started at the sound of the hall-bell.

"Is that your father come home? He said he might, today or to-morrow."

Olive went down-stairs. It was only a letter, to say Captain Rothesay would return that day, and would bring—most rare circumstance!—some guests to visit them. Olive seemed to shrink painfully at this news.

"What, my child, are you not pleased?—It will make the house less dull for you."

"No, no—I do not wish; oh, mamma! if I could only shut myself up, and never see any one but you"—— And Olive turned very pale. At last, resolutely trying to speak without any show of trouble, she continued—"I have found out something that I never knew—at least, never thought of before—that I am different from other girls. Oh, mother! am I really deformed?"

She spoke with much agitation. Mrs. Rothesay burst into tears.

"Oh, Olive! how wretched you make me, to talk thus. Unhappy mother that I am! Why should Heaven have punished me thus?"

"Punished you, mother?"

"Nay, my child—my poor, innocent child! I did not mean that," cried Mrs. Rothesay, embracing her with a passionate revulsion of feeling.

But the word was said,—to linger for ever after on Olive's mind. It brought back the look once written on her childish memory—grown faint, but never quite erased—her father's first look. She understood it now.

Mrs. Rothesay continued weeping, and Olive had to cast aside all other feelings in the care of soothing her mother. She succeeded at last; but she learnt at the same time that on this one subject there must be silence between them for ever. It seemed, also, to her sensitive nature, as if every tear and every complaining word were a reproach to the mother that bore her. Henceforth her bitter thoughts must be wrestled with alone.

She did so wrestle with them. She walked out into her favourite meadow—now lying in the silent, frost-bound mistiness of a January day. It was where she had often been in summer with Sara, and Charles Geddes, and the little boys. Now everything seemed so wintry and lonely. What if her own future life were so—one long winter-day, wherein was neither beauty, gladness, nor love?

Olive.

"She walked out into her favourite meadow."

"I am 'deformed.' That was Sara's own word," murmured Olive to herself. "If this is felt by one who loves me, what must I appear to the world? Will not all shrink from me—and even those who pity, turn away in pain. As for loving me"——

Thinking thus, Olive's fancy began to count, almost in despair, all those whose affection she had ever known. There was Elspie, there were her parents. Yet, the love of both father and mother—how sweet soever now—had not blessed her always. She remembered the time when it was not there.

"Alas! that I should have been, even to them, a burden—a punishment!" cried the girl, in the first outburst of suffering, which became ten times keener, because concealed. Her vivid fancy even exaggerated the truth. She saw in herself a poor deformed being, shut out from all natural ties—a woman, to whom friendship would be given but in kindly pity; to whom love—that blissful dream in which she had of late indulged—would be denied for evermore. How hard seemed her doom! If it were for months only, or even years; but, to bear for a whole life this withering ban—never to be freed from it, except through death! And her lips unconsciously repeated the bitter murmur, "O God! why hast thou made me thus?"

It was scarcely uttered before her heart trembled at its impiety. And then the current of her thoughts changed. Those mysterious yearnings which had haunted her throughout childhood, until they had grown fainter under the influence of earthly ties and pleasures, returned to her now. God's immeasurable Infinite rose before her in glorious serenity. What was one brief lifetime to the ages of eternity? She felt it: she, in her weakness—her untaught childhood—her helplessness—felt that her poor deformed body enshrined a living soul. A soul that could look on Heaven, and on whom Heaven also looked—not like man, with scorn or loathing, but with a Divine tenderness that had power to lift the mortal into communion with the immortal.

Olive Rothesay seemed to have grown years older in that hour of solitary musing. She walked homewards through the silent fields, over which the early night was falling—night coming, as it were, in the midst of day, where the only light was given by the white, cold snow. To Olive this was a symbol, too—a token that the freezing sorrow which had fallen on her path might palely light her on her earthly way. Strange things for a young girl to dream of! But they whom Heaven teaches are sometimes called—Samuel-like—while to them still pertains the childish ephod and the temple-porch.

Passing on, with footsteps silent and solemn as her own heart, Olive came to the street, on the verge of the town, where was her own dwelling and Sara's. From habit she looked in at the Derwents' house. It had all the cheerful brightness given by a blazing fire, glimmering through windows not yet closed. Olive could plainly distinguish the light shining on the crimson wall; even the merry faces of the circle round the hearth. And, as if to chant the chorus of so sweet a scene, there broke out on the clear frosty air the distant carillon of Oldchurch bells—marriage-bells too—signifying that not far off was dawning another scene of love and hope; that, somewhere in the parish, was celebrated the "coming home" of a bride.

The young creature, born with a woman's longings—longings neither unholy nor impure, after the love which is the religion of a woman's heart—the sweetness of home, which is the heaven of a woman's life—felt that from both she was shut out for ever.

"Not for me—alas! not for me," she murmured; and her head drooped, and it seemed as though a cold hand were laid on her breast, saying, "Grow still, and throb no more!"

Then, lifting her eyes, she saw shining far up in the sky, beyond the mist and the frost and the gloom, one little star—the only one. With a long sigh, her soul seemed to pass upward in prayer.

"Oh, God! since Thou hast willed it so—if in this world I must walk alone, do Thou walk with me! If I must know no human love, fill my soul with Thine! If earthly joy be far from me, give me that peace of Heaven which passeth all understanding!"

And so—mournful, yet serene—Olive Rothesay reached her home.

She found her friend there. Sara looked confused at seeing her, and appeared to try, with the unwonted warmth of her greeting, to efface from Olive's mind the remembrance of what had happened the previous evening. But Olive, for the first time, shrank from these tokens of affection.

"Even Sara's love may be only compassion," she bitterly thought; but her father's nature was in the girl—his self-command—his proud reserve. Sara Derwent only thought her rather silent and cold.

There was a constraint on both—so much so that Olive heard, without testifying much pain, news which a few days before would have grieved her to the heart. This visit was a good-bye. Sara had been suddenly sent for by her grandfather, who lived in a distant county; and the summons entailed a parting of some weeks—perhaps longer.

"But I shall not forget you, Olive. I shall write to you constantly. It will be my sole amusement in the dull place I am going to. Why, nobody ever used to enter my grandfather's house except the parson, who lived some few miles off. Poor old soul! I used to set fire to his wig, and hide his spectacles. But he is dead now, I hear, and there has come in his place a young clergyman. Shall I strike up a little flirtation with *him*, eh, Olive?"

But Olive was in no jesting mood. She only shook her head.

Mrs. Rothesay looked with admiration on Sara. "What a blithe young creature you are, my dear. You win everybody's liking. I wish Olive were only half as merry as you."

Another arrow in poor Olive's heart!

"Well, we must try to make her so when I come back," said Sara, affectionately. "I shall have tales enough to tell, perhaps about that young curate. Nay, don't frown, Olive. My cousin says he is a Scotsman born, and you like Scotland. Only his father was Welsh, and he has a horrid Welsh name: Gwyrdyr, or Gwynne, or something like it. But I'll give you all information."

And then she rose—still laughing—to bid adieu; which seemed so long a farewell, when the friends had never yet been parted but for one brief day. In saying it, Olive felt how dear to her had been this girl—this first idol of her warm heart. And then there came a thought almost like terror. Though fated to live unloved, she could not keep herself from loving. And if so, how would she bear the perpetual void—the yearning, never to be fulfilled?

She fell on Sara's neck and wept. "You do care for me a little—only a little."

"A great deal—as much as ever I can, seeing I have so many people to care for," answered Sara, trying to laugh away the tears that—from sympathy, perhaps—sprang to her eyes.

"Ah, true! And everybody cares for you. No wonder," answered Olive.

"Now, little Olive, why do you put on that grave face? Are you going to lecture me about not flirting with that stupid curate, and always remembering Charles. Oh! no fear of that."

"I hope not," said Olive, quietly. She could talk no more, and they bade each other good-bye; perhaps not quite so enthusiastically as they might have done a week ago, but still with much affection. Sara had reached the door, when with a sudden impulse she came back again.

"Olive, I am a foolish, thoughtless girl; but if ever I pained you in any way, don't think of it again. Kiss me—will you—once more?"

Olive did so, clinging to her passionately. When Sara went away, she felt as though the first flower had perished in her garden—the first star had melted from her sky.

Sara gone, she went back to her old dreamy life. The romance of first friendship seemed to have been swept away like a morning cloud. From Sara there came no letters.

Olive wrote once or twice, even thrice. But a sense of wounded feeling prevented her writing again. Robert and Lyle told her their sister was quite well, and very merry. Then, over all the dream of sweet affection fell a cold silence.

In Olive's own home were arising many cares. A great change came over her father. His economical habits became those of the wildest extravagance—extravagance in which his wife and daughter were not likely to share. Little they saw of it either, save during his rare visits to his home.

Then he either spent his evenings out, or else dining, smoking, drinking, disturbed the quiet house at Oldchurch.

Many a time, till long after midnight, the mother and child sat listening to the gay tumult of voices below; clinging to each other, pale and sad. Not that Captain Rothesay was unkind, or that either had any fear for him, for he had always been a strict and temperate man. But it pained them to think that any society seemed sweeter to him than that of his wife and daughter—that any place was become dearer to him than his home.

One night, when Mrs. Rothesay appeared exhausted, either with weariness or sorrow of heart, Olive persuaded her mother to go to rest, while she herself sat up for her father.

"Nay, let some of the servants do that, not you, my child."

But Olive, innocent as she was, had accidentally seen the footman smile rudely when he spoke of "master coming home last night;" and a vague thought struck her, that such late hours were discreditable in the head of a family. Her father should not be despised in his servant's eyes.

She dismissed the household, and waited up for him alone. Twelve—one—two. The hours went by like long years. Heavily at first drooped her poor drowsy eyes, and then all weariness was dispelled by a feeling of loneliness—an impression of coming sorrow. At last, when this was gradually merging into fear, she heard the sound of the swinging gate, and her father's knock at the door—A loud, unsteady, angry knock.

"Why do you stay up for me? I don't want anybody to sit up," grumbled Captain Rothesay, without looking at her.

"But I liked to wait for you, papa."

"What, is that you, Olive?" and he stepped in with a lounging, heavy gait.

"Did you not see me before? It was I who opened the door."

"Oh, yes—but—I was thinking of something else," he said, throwing himself into the study-chair, and trying with an effort to seem just as usual. "You are—a very good girl—I'm much obliged to you. The pleasure is—I may truly say on both sides." And he energetically struck the table with his hand.

Olive thought this an odd form of speech; but her father's manner was grown so changed of late—sometimes he seemed quite in high spirits, even jocose—as he did now.

"I am glad to see you are not much tired, papa. I thought you were—you walked so wearily when you first came in."

"I tired? Nonsense, child! I have had the merriest evening in the world. I'll have another to-morrow, for I've asked them all to dine here. We'll give dinner parties to all the county."

"Papa," said Olive, timidly, "will that be quite right, after what you told me of our being now so much poorer than we were?"

"Did I? Pshaw! I don't remember. However, I am a rich man now; richer than I have ever been."

"I am so glad; because then, dear papa, you know you need not be so much away from home, or weary yourself with the speculations you told me of; but come and live quietly with us."

Her father laughed loudly. "Foolish little girl! your notion of quietness would not suit a man like me. Take my word for it, Olive, home serves as a fantastic dream till five-and-twenty, and then means nothing at all. A man's home is the world."

"Is it?"

"Ay, as I intend to show to you. By-the-by, I shall give up this stupid place, and enter into society. Your mother will like it, of course; and you, as my only child—eh, what did I say?" here he stopped hastily with a blank, frightened look—then repeated, "Yes, you, my only child, will be properly introduced to the world. Why, you will be quite an heiress, my girl," continued he, with an excited jocularity that frightened Olive. "And the world always courts such; who knows but that you may marry in spite of"——

"Oh, no—never!" interrupted Olive, turning away with bitter pain.

"Come, don't mind it," continued her father, with a reckless indifference to her feelings, quite unusual to him. "Why—my little sensible girl—you are better than any beauty in England; beauties are all fools, or worse."

And he laughed so loud, so long, that Olive was seized with a great horror, that absorbed even her own individual suffering. Was her father mad? Alas! there is a madness worse than disease, a voluntary madness, by which a man—longing at any price for excitement, or oblivion—"puts an enemy into his mouth to steal away his brains." This was the foe—the stealthy-footed demon, that had at last come to overmaster the brave and noble Angus Rothesay. As yet it ruled him not—he was no sot; but his daughter saw enough to know that the fiend was nigh upon him—that this night he was even in its grasp.

It is only the noblest kind of affection that can separate the sinner from the sin, and even while condemning, pity. Fallen as he was, Olive Rothesay looked on her father mournfully—intreatingly. She could not speak.

He seemed annoyed, and slightly confounded. "Come, simpleton, why do you stare at me?—there is nothing the matter. Go away to bed."

Olive did not move.

"Make haste—what are you waiting for? Nay, stay; 'tis a cold night—just leave out the keys of the sideboard, will you, there's a good little housekeeper," he said, coaxingly.

Olive turned away in disgust, but only for a moment. "In case you should want anything, let me stay a little longer, papa; I am not tired, and I have some work to do—suppose I go and fetch it."

She went into the inner room, slowly, quietly; and when safe out of sight, burst into tears of such shame and terror as she had never before known. Then she sat down to think. Her father thus; her mother feeble in mind or body; no one in the wide world to trust to but herself; no one to go to for comfort and counsel—none, save Heaven! She sank on her knees and prayed. As she rose, the angel in the daughter's soul was stronger than the demon in her father's.

Olive waited a little, and then walked softly into the other room. Some brandy, left on the sideboard, had attracted Captain Rothesay's sight. He had reached it stealthily, as if the act still conveyed to his dulled brain a consciousness of degradation. Once he looked round suspiciously; alas, the father dreaded his daughter's eye! Then stealthily standing with his face to the fire, he began to drink the tempting poison.

It was taken out of his hand! So noiseless was Olive's step, so gentle her movement, that he stood dumb, astonished, as though in the presence of some apparition. And, in truth, the girl looked like a spirit; for her face was very white, and her parted lips seemed as though they never had uttered, and never could utter, one living sound.

Father and daughter stood for some moments thus gazing at each other; and then Captain Rothesay threw himself into his chair, with a forced laugh.

"What's the matter, little fool? Cannot your father take care of himself? Give me the brandy again."

But she held it fast, and made no answer.

"Olive, I say—do you insult me thus?" and his voice rose in anger. "Go to bed, I command you! Will you not?"

"No!" The refusal was spoken softly—very softly—but it expressed indomitable firmness; and there was something in the girl's resolute spirit, before which that of the man quailed. With a sudden transition, which showed that the drink had already somewhat overpowered his brain, he melted into complaints.

"You are very rude to your poor father; you—almost the only comfort he has left!"

This touch even of maudlin sentiment went direct to Olive's heart. She clung to him, kissed him, begged his forgiveness, nay, even wept over him. He ceased to rage, and sat in a sullen silence for many minutes. Meanwhile Olive took away every temptation from his sight. Then she roused him gently.

"Now, papa, it is time to go to bed. Pray, come upstairs."

He—the calm, gentlemanlike, Captain Rothesay—burst into a storm of passion that would have disgraced a boor. "How dare you order me about in this manner! Cannot I do as I like, without being controlled by you—a mere chit of a girl—a very child?"

"I know I am only a child," answered Olive, meekly. "Do not be angry with me, papa; do not speak unkindly to your poor little daughter."

"My daughter! how dare you call yourself so, you white-faced, mean-looking hunchback!"——

At the word, Olive recoiled—a strong shudder ran through her frame; one long, sobbing sigh, and no more.

Her father, shocked, and a little sobered, paused in his cruel speech. For minutes they remained—he leaning back with a stupefied air—she standing before him; her face drooped, and covered with her hands.

"Olive!" he muttered, in a repentant, humbled tone.

"Yes, papa."

"I am quite ready. If you like, I'll go to bed now."

Without speaking, she lighted him up-stairs—nay, led him, for, to his bitter shame, the guidance was not un-needed. When she left him, he had the grace to whisper—

"Child, you are not vexed about anything I said?"

She looked sorrowfully into his hot fevered face, and stroked his arm. "No—no—not vexed at all! You could not help it, poor father!"

She heard her mother's feeble voice speaking to him as he entered, and saw his door close. Long she watched there, until beneath it she perceived not one glimmer of light. Then she crept away, only murmuring to herself—

"O God! teach me to endure!"

CHAPTER XIV

"What is the matter with the child to-day?" said Captain Rothesay to his wife, with whom, oh rare circumstance! he was sitting *tête-à-tête*. But this, and a few other alterations for the better had taken place in consequence of his longer stay at home than usual, during which an unseen influence had been busily at work. Poor Olive! Was it not well for her, that, to temper the first shock of her bitter destiny, there should arise, in the dreary blank of the future, duties so holy, that they stood almost in the place of joys?

"How dull the girl seems!" again observed Captain Rothesay, looking after his daughter, with a tenderness of which he afterwards appeared rather ashamed.

"Dull, is she?" said the mother; "oh, very likely poor child! She is grieving to lose her chief friend and companion, Miss Derwent. News came to her this morning that Sara is about to be married."

"Oh, indeed!" and Captain Rothesay made an attempt at departure. He hated gossiping, even of the most harmless kind. But his wife, pleased that he condescended to talk to her at all, tried to amuse him in her own easy way.

"Poor Sara! I am glad that she is going to have a home of her own— though she is young enough to marry. But I believe it was a very sudden affair; and the gentleman fell so desperately in love with her."

"More fool he!" muttered Captain Rothesay.

"Nay, he is not a fool at all; he is a very sensible, clever man, and a clergyman too; Miss Derwent said so in her brief note to Olive. But she did not mention where he lived; little indeed she told, but that his name was Gwynne"——

Captain Rothesay turned round quickly.

—"And Sara speaks of his mother being a stiff old Scotswoman. Ah, you are listening now, my dear. Let me see, I think Miss Derwent mentions her maiden name. The silly girl makes quite a boast of her lover's ancient family, on the maternal side."

"There is no silliness in that, I hope, Mrs. Rothesay?"

"Certainly not—was I not always proud of yours?" said the wife, with a meekness not newly learnt She hunted in her reticule for Sara's letter, and read.

"Ah, here is the name—Alison Balfour: do you know it?"

"I did once, when I was a boy."

"Stay! do not go away in that hasty manner. Pray, talk to me a little more, Angus; it is so dull to be confined to this sick-room. Tell me of this Alison Balfour; you know I should like to hear about your friends."

"Should you?—that is something new. If it had been always so—if you had indeed made my interests yours, Sybilla!" There was a touch of regret and old tenderness in his voice. She thought he was kind on account of her illness, and thanked him warmly. But the thanks sent him back to his usual cold self; he did not like to have his weakness noticed.

Mrs. Rothesay understood neither one state of feeling nor the other, so she said, cheerfully, "Come, now for the story of Alison Balfour."

"There is no story to tell. She was merely a young companion of my aunt Flora. I knew her for some years—in fact, until she married Mr. Gwynne. She was a noble woman."

"Really, Angus, I shall grow jealous," said Mrs. Rothesay, half in jest, half in earnest. "She must have been an old love of yours."

Her husband frowned. "Folly, Sybilla! She was a woman, and I a schoolboy!"

And yet the words galled him, for they were not far off the truth. True, Alison was old enough to have been his mother; but many a precocious lad of sixteen conceives a similar romantic passion, and Angus Rothesay had really been very much in love, as he thought, with Alison Balfour.

Even when he quitted the room, and walked out into the road, his thoughts went backward many years; picturing the old dull mansion, whose only brightness had come with her presence. He remembered how he used to walk by her side, in lonely mountain rambles—he a young boy, and she a grown woman; and how proud he was, when she stooped her tall stature to lean upon his arm. Once, she kissed him; and he lay awake all night, and many a night after, dreaming of the remembered bliss. And, as he grew a youth, what delicious sweetness in these continued dreams! what pride to think himself "in love"—and with such a woman! Folly it was—hopeless folly—for she had been long betrothed to one she loved. But that was not Owen Gwynne. Alas! Alison, like many another proud, passionate woman, had married in sudden anger, thereby wrecking her whole life! When she did so, Angus Rothesay lost his boyish dream. He had already begun to find out that it was only a dream; though his first fancy's idol never ceased to be to him a memory full of all that was noble and beautiful in womanhood.

For many years this enchanted portion of Captain Rothesay's past life had rarely crossed his mind; but when it did, it was always with a half-unconscious thought, that he himself might have been a better and a happier man, had his own beautiful Sybilla been more like Alison Balfour.

This chance news of her awakened memories connected with other scenes and characters, which had gradually melted away from Angus Rothesay's life, or been enveloped in the mist of selfishness and worldliness which had gathered over it and over him. He thought of the old uncle, Sir Andrew Rothesay, whose pride he had been; of the sweet aunt Flora, whose pale beauty had bent over his cradle with a love almost like a mother's, save that it was so very very sad. One had died estranged; the other—he would not let many weeks pass before he sought out Miss Flora Rothesay: that he was determined on! And to do so, the best plan would be first to go and see Alison—Mrs. Gwynne.

Captain Rothesay always kept his intentions to himself, and transacted his matters alone. Therefore, without the aid of wife or daughter, he soon discovered in what region lay Mr. Gwynne's curacy, and determined to hasten his customary journey to London, that he might visit the place on his way.

The night before his departure came. It was really a melancholy evening; for he had stayed at home so long, and been most of the time what his wife called "so good," that she quite regretted his going. The more so, as he was about to travel by the awful railway—then newly established—which, in the opinion of poor Mrs. Rothesay, with her delicate nerves and easily-roused terrors, entailed on him the certainty of being killed. She pleaded so much and so anxiously—even to the last—that when, in order to start at daybreak, he bade "good-bye" to her and Olive overnight, Captain Rothesay was softened even to tenderness.

"Do you really care so much about me, Sybilla?" said he, half mournfully.

She did not spring to his arms, like the young wife at Stirling, but she kissed his hand affectionately, and called him "Angus!"

"Olive!" said the father, when having embraced his wife, he now turned to his daughter, "Olive, my child! take care of your mother! I shall be at home soon, and we shall be very happy again—all three!"

As they ascended the staircase, they saw him watching them from below. Olive so content, even though her father was going away. She kissed her hand felt to him with a blithe gesture, and then saw him go in and close the door. When the house sank into quietness, a curious feeling oppressed Captain Rothesay. It seemed to take rise in his wife's infectious fears.

"Women are always silly," he argued to himself. "Why should I dread any danger? The railway is safe as a coach—and yet, that affair of poor Huskisson! Pooh! what a fool I am!"

But even while he mocked it, the vague presentiment appeared to take form in his mind; and sitting, the only person awake in the slumbering house, where no sound broke the stillness, except the falling of a few cinders, and the occasional noise of a mouse behind the wainscot, somewhat of the superstitions of his northern youth came over him. His countenance became grave, and he sank into deep thought.

It is a trite saying, that every man has that in his heart, which, if known, would make all his fellow-creatures hate him. Was it this evil spirit which now struggled in Captain Rothesay's breast, and darkened his face with storms of passion, remorse, or woe? He gave no utterance to them in words. If any secret there were, he would not trust it even to the air. But, at times, his mute lips writhed; his cheeks burned, and grew ghastly. Sometimes, too, he wore a cowed and humble look, as on the night when his daughter had stood like a pure angel to save him from the abyss on the brink of which he trod.

She had saved him, apparently. That night's shame had never occurred again. Slowly, his habits were changing, and his tastes becoming home-like. But still his lonely hours betokened some secret hidden in his soul—a secret which, if known, might have accounted for his having plunged into uproarious excitement or drunken oblivion.

At length, as by a violent effort, Angus Rothesay sat down and began to write. He wrote for several hours—though frequently his task was interrupted by long reveries, and by fits of vehement emotion. When he had finished, he carefully sealed up what he had written, and placed it in a secret drawer of his desk. Then he threw himself on a sofa, to sleep, during the brief time that intervened before daybreak.

In the grey of the morning, when he stood despatching a hasty breakfast, he was startled by a light touch on his arm.

"Little Olive!—why, I thought you were fast asleep."

"I could not sleep when papa was going away; so I rose and dressed. You will not be angry?"

"Angry?—no!" He stooped down and kissed her, more affectionately even than was his wont But he was hasty and fidgety, as most men are when starting on a journey. They were both too busy for more words until the few minutes during which he sat down to wait for the carriage. Then he took his daughter on his knee—an act of fatherly tenderness rather rare with him.

"I wish you were not going, or that I were going with you, papa," Olive whispered, nestling to him, in a sweet, childish way, though she was almost a woman now. "How tired you look! You have not been in bed all night."

"No; I had writing to do." As he spoke his countenance darkened. "Olive," he said, looking at her with sorrowful, questioning eyes.

"Well, dear papa."

"Nothing—nothing. Is the carriage ready?"

"Not yet. You will have time just for one little thing—'twill take only a minute," said Olive, persuasively.

"What is it, little one?"

"Mamma is asleep—she was tired and ill; but if you would run upstairs, and kiss her once again before you go, it would make her so much happier—I know it would."

"Poor Sybilla!" he muttered, remorsefully, and quitted the room slowly—not meeting his daughter's eyes; but when he came back, he took her in his arms, very tenderly.

"Olive, my child in whom I trust, always remember I did love you— you and your mother."

These were the last words she heard him utter, ere he went away.

CHAPTER XV

Captain Rothesay had intended to make the business-excursion wait on that of pleasure—if pleasure the visit could be called, which was entered on from duty, and would doubtless awaken many painful associations; but he changed his mind, and it was not until his return from London, that he stayed on the way, and sought out the village of Harbury.

Verbal landscape-painting is rarely interesting to the general reader; and as Captain Rothesay was certainly not devoted to the picturesque, it seems idle to follow him during his ten-mile ride from the nearest railway station to the place which he discovered was that of Mrs. Gwynne's abode, and where her son was "perpetual curate."

Her son! It seemed very strange to imagine Alison a mother; and yet, while he thought, Angus Rothesay almost laughed at himself for his folly. His boyish fancy had perforce faded at seventeen, and he was now—pshaw!—he was somewhere above forty. As for Mrs. Gwynne, sixty would probably be nearer her age. Yet, not having seen her since she married, he never could think of her but as Alison Balfour.

As before observed, Captain Rothesay was by no means keenly susceptible to beauty of scenery; otherwise, he would often have been attracted from his meditations by that through which he passed. Lovely woodlands, just bursting into the delicate green of spring; deep, still streams, flowing through meadows studded with cattle; forest-roads shadowed with stately trees, and so little frequented, that the green turf spread from hedge to hedge, and the primroses and bluebells sprung up almost in the pathway. All these composed a picture of rural loveliness which is peculiar to England, and chiefly to that part of England where Harbury is situated. Captain Rothesay scarcely noticed it, until, pausing to consider his track, he saw in the distance a church upon a hill. Beautiful and peaceful it looked—its ancient tower rising out against the sky, and the evening sun shining on its windows and gilded vane.

"That must surely be my landmark," thought Captain Rothesay; and he made an inquiry to that effect of a man passing by.

"Ay, ay, measter," was the answer, in rather unintelligible Doric; "thot bees Harbury Church, as sure as moy name's John Dent; and thot red house—conna ye see't?—thot's our parson's."

Prompted by curiosity, Rothesay observed, "Oh, Mr. Gwynne's. He is quite a young man, I believe? Do you like him, you good folks hereabout?"

"Some on us dun, and some on us dunna. He's not much of parson though; he wunna send yer to sleep wi' his long preachings. But oi say the mon's a good mon: he'll coom and see yer when you're bad, an' talk t' ye by th' hour; though he dunna talk oot o' th' Bible. But oi'm a lad o' t' forest, and 'll be a keeper some toime. That's better nor book-larning."

Captain Rothesay had no will to listen to more personal revelations from honest John Dent; so he said, quickly, "Perhaps so, my good fellow." Then added, "Mr. Gwynne has a mother living with him, I believe. What sort of person is she?"

"Her's a good-enough lady, oi reckon: only a bit too proud. Many's the blanket her's gen to poor folk; and my owd mother sees her every week—but her's never shook hands wi' her yet. Eh, measter, won ye go?"

This last remark was bellowed after Captain Rothesay, whose horse had commenced a sudden canter, which ceased not until its owner dismounted at the parsonage-gate.

This gate formed the boundary of the garden, and a most lovely spot it was. It extended to the churchyard, with which it communicated by a little wicket-door. You passed through beautiful parterres and alleys, formed of fragrant shrubs, to the spot

Where grew the turf in many a mouldering heap.

It seemed as though the path of death were indeed through flowers. Garden and churchyard covered the hill's summit; and from both might be discerned a view such as is rarely seen in level England. It was a panorama, extending some twenty or thirty miles across the country, where, through woodlands and meadow-lands, flowed the silver windings of a small river. Here and there was an old ruined castle—a manor-house rising among its ancestral trees—or the faint, misty smoke-cloud, that indicated some hamlet or small town. Save these, the landscape swept on unbroken, until it ended at the horizon in the high range of the D—shire hills.

Even to Captain Rothesay, this scene seemed strangely beautiful. He contemplated it for some time, his hand still on the unopened gate; and then he became aware that a lady, whose gardening dress and gardening implements showed she was occupied in her favourite evening employment, was looking at him with some curiosity.

The traces of life's downward path are easier to recognise than those of its ascent. Though the mature womanhood of Alison Balfour had glided into age, Rothesay had no difficulty in discovering that he was in the presence of his former friend. Not so with her. He advanced, addressed her by name, and even took her hand, before she had the slightest idea that her guest was Angus Rothesay.

"Have you, then, so entirely forgotten me—forgotten the days in our native Perthshire, when I was a bit laddie, and you, our guest, were Miss Alison Balfour?"

There came a trembling over her features—ay, aged woman as she was! But at her years, all the past, whether of joy or grief, becomes faint; else, how would age be borne? She extended both her hands, with a warm friendliness.

"Welcome, Angus Rothesay! No wonder I did not know you. These thirty years—is it not thus much?—have changed you from a boy into a middle-aged man, and made of me an old woman."

She really was an elderly lady now. It seemed almost ridiculous to think of her as his youth's idol. Neither was she beautiful—how could he ever have imagined her so? Her irregular features—unnoticed when the white and red tints of youth adorned them—were now, in age, positively plain. Her strong-built frame had, in losing elasticity, lost much of grace, though dignity remained. Looking on Mrs. Gwynne for the first time, she appeared a large, rather plain woman. Looking again, it would be to observe the noble candour that dwelt in the eyes, and the sweetness—at times even playfulness—that hovered round the mouth. Regarding her for the third time, you would see a woman whom you felt sure you must perforce respect, and might, in time, love very much, if she would let you. Of that gracious permission you would long have considerable doubt; but once granted, you would never unlove her to the end of your days. As for her loving *you*, you would not be quite clear that it did not spring from the generous benevolence of her nature, rather than from any individual warmth toward yourself; and such was the reserve of her character, that, were her affection, ever so deep, she might possibly never let you know it until the day of your death.

Yet she was capable of attachments, strong as her own nature. All her feelings, passions, energies, were on a grand scale: in her were no petty feminine follies—no weak, narrow illiberalities of judgment. She had the soul of a man and the heart of a woman.

"You were gardening, I see?" said Captain Rothesay, making the first ordinary remark that came to his mind to break the awkward pause.

"Yes; I do so every fine evening. Harold is very fond of flowers. That reminds me I must call him to you at once, as it is Wednesday,—service-night, and he will be engaged in his duties soon."

"Pray, let us enter the house; I should much like to see your son," said Angus Rothesay. He gave her his arm; and they walked together, through the green alleys of holly, to the front-door. Then Mrs. Gwynne stopped, put her hand over her eyes for a moment, removed it, and looked earnestly at her guest.

"Angus Rothesay! how strange this seems!—like a dream—a dream of thirty years. Well, let us go in."

Mechanically, and yet in a subdued, absent manner, she laid her bonnet and shawl on the hall-table, and took off her gardening gloves, thereby discovering hands, which, though large, were white and well formed, and in their round, taper delicacy, exhibited no sign of age. Captain Rothesay, without pausing to think, took the right hand.

"Ah! you wear still the ring I used to play with when a boy. I thought"—— and recollecting himself, he stopped, ashamed of his discourtesy in alluding to what must have been a painful past.

But she said, quietly, sadly, "You have a good memory. Yes, I wear it again now. It was left to me, ten years since, on the death of Archibald Maclean."

Strange that she could thus speak that name! But over how many a buried grief does the grass grow green in thirty years!

In the hall they encountered a young man.

"Harold," said Mrs. Gwynne, "give welcome to an old—a very old friend of mine—Captain Angus Rothesay. Angus, this is my son—my only son, Harold."

And she looked upon him as a mother, widowed for twenty years, looks upon an only son; yet the pride was tempered with dignity, the affection was veiled under reserve. She, who doubtless would have sustained his life with her own heart's blood, had probably never since his boyhood suffered him to know a mother's passionate tenderness, or to behold a mother's tear.

Perhaps that was the reason that Harold's whole manner was the reflection of her own. Not that he was like her in person; for nature had to him been far more bountiful. But there was a certain rigidness and harshness in his mien, and a slightly repellant atmosphere around him. Probably not one of the young lambs of his flock had ever dreamed of climbing the knee of the Reverend Harold Gwynne. Though he wore the clerical garb, he did not look at all apostle-like; he was neither a St. Paul nor a St. John. Yet a grand, noble head it was. It might have been sketched for that of a young philosopher—a Galileo or a Priestley, with the heavy, strongly-marked brows. The eyes—hackneyed as the description is, no one can paint a man without mentioning his eyes: those of Harold Gwynne were not unlike his mother's, in their open, steadfast look; yet they were not soft, like hers, but of steel-grey, diamond-clear. He carried his head very erect; and these eyes of his seemed as though unable to rest on the ground; they were always turned upwards, with a gaze—not reverent or dreamy—but eager, inquiring, and piercing as truth itself.

Such was the young man with whom Captain Rothesay shook hands, congratulating his old friend on having such a son.

"You are more fortunate than I," he said; "my marriage has only bestowed on me a daughter."

"Daughters are a great comfort sometimes," answered Mrs. Gwynne; "though, for my part, I never wished for one."

The quick, reproachful glance of Harold sought his mother's face; and shortly afterwards he re-entered his study.

"My son thinks I meant to include a daughter-in-law," was Mrs. Gwynne's remark, while the concealed playfulness about her mouth appeared. "He is soon to bring me one."

"I know it—and know her too; by this means I found you out. I should scarcely have imagined Sara Derwent the girl for you to choose."

"*He* chooses, not I. A mother, whose dutiful son has been her sole stay through life, has no right to interfere with what he deems his happiness," said Alison, gravely. And, at that moment, the young curate reappeared, ready for the duties to which he was summoned by the sharp sound of the "church-going bell."

"I will stay at home with Captain Rothesay," observed Mrs. Gwynne. Her guest made a courteous disclaimer, which ended in something about "religious duties."

"Hospitality is a duty too—at least we thought so in the north," she answered. "And old friendship is ever somewhat of a religion with me. Therefore I will stay, Harold."

"You are right, mother," said Harold. But he would not that his mother had seen the smile which curled his lip as he passed along the hall and through the garden towards the churchyard. There it faded into a look, dark and yet mournful; which, as it turned from the dust beneath his feet to the stars overhead, and then back again to the graves, seemed to ask despairingly, at once of heaven and earth, for the solution of some inward mystery.

While Harold preached, his mother and Captain Rothesay sat in the parsonage and talked of their olden days, now faint as a dream. The rising wind, which, sweeping over the wide champaign, came to moan in the hillside trees, seemed to sing the dirge of that long-past life. Yet the heart of both, even of Angus Rothesay, throbbed to its memory, as a Scottish heart ever does to that of home and the mountain-land.

Among other long unspoken names came that of Miss Flora Rothesay. "She is an old woman now—a few years older than I; Harold visits her not infrequently; and she and I correspond now and then, but we have not met for many years."

"Yet you have not forgotten her?"

"Do I ever forget?" said Alison, as she turned her face towards him. And looking thereon, he felt that such a woman never could.

Their conversation, passing down the stream of time, touched on all that was memorable in the life of both. She mentioned her husband—but merely the two events, not long distant each from each, of their marriage and his death.

"Your son is not like yourself—does he resemble Mr. Gwynne?" observed Rothesay.

"In person, yes, a little; in mind—no! a thousand times no!" Then, recollecting herself, she added, "It was not likely. Mr. Gwynne has been dead so many years that my son"—it was always *my* son—"has no remembrance of his father."

Alas! that there should be some whose memories are gladly suffered to perish with the falling of the earth above them.

A thought like this passed through the mind of Angus Rothesay. "I fancy," said he, "that I once met Mr. Gwynne; he was"—-

"My husband." Mrs. Gwynne's tone suppressed all further remark—even all recollection of the contemptible image that was intruding on her guest's mind—an image of a young, roistering, fox-hunting fool. Rothesay looked on the widow, and the remembrance passed away, or became sacred as memory itself. And then the conversation glided as a mother's heart would fain direct it—to her only son.

"He was a strange creature ever, was my Harold. In his childhood he always teased me with his 'why and because;' he would come to the root of everything, and would not believe anything that he could not quite understand. Gradually I began to glory in this peculiarity, for I saw it argued a mind far above the common order. Angus, you are a father; you may be happy in your child, but you never can understand the pride of a mother in an only son."

While she talked, her countenance and manner brightened, and Captain Rothesay saw again, not the serene, stern widow of Owen Gwynne, but the energetic, impassioned Alison Balfour. He told her this.

"Is it so? Strange! And yet I do but talk to you as I often did when we were young together."

He begged her to continue—his heart warmed as it had not done for many a day; and, to lead the way, he asked what chance had caused the descendant of the Balfours to become an English clergyman?

"From circumstances. When Harold was very young, and we two lived together in the poor Highland cottage where he was born, my boy made an acquaintance with an Englishman, one Lord Arundale, a great student. Harold longed to be a student too."

"A noble desire."

"I shared it too. When the thought came to me that my boy would be a great man, I nursed it, cherished it, made it my whole life's aim. We were not rich—I had not married for money"—and there was a faint show of pride in her lip—"yet, Harold must go, as he desired, to an English university. I said in my heart, 'He shall!' and he did."

Angus looked at Mrs. Gwynne, and thought that a woman's will might sometimes be as strong and daring as a man's.

Alison continued—"My son had only half finished his education when fortune made the poor poorer. But Scotland and Cambridge, thank Heaven were far distant I never told him one word—I lived—it matters little how—I cared not! Our fortune lasted, as I had calculated it would, till he had taken his degree, and left college rich in honours—and then"— —

She ceased, and the light in her countenance faded. Angus Rothesay gazed upon her as reverently as he had done upon the good angel of his boyish days.

"I said you were a noble woman, Alison Balfour."

"I was a mother, and I had a noble son."

They sat a long time silent, looking at the fire, and listening to the wind. There was a momentary interruption—a message from the young clergyman, to say that he was summoned some distance to visit a sick person.

"On such a stormy night as this!" said Angus Rothesay.

"Harold never fails in his duties," replied the mother, with a smile. Then turning abruptly to her guest—"You will let me talk, old friend, and about him. I cannot often talk *to* him, for he is so reserved—that is, so occupied with his clerical studies. But there never was a better son than my Harold."

"I am sure of it," said Captain Rothesay.

The mother continued—"Never shall I forget the triumph of his coming home from Cambridge. Yet it brought a pang, too; for then first he had to learn the whole truth. Poor Harold! it pained me to see him so shocked and overwhelmed at the sight of our lowly roof and mean fare; and to know that even these would not last us long. But I said to him—'My son, what signifies it, when you can soon bring your mother to your own home?' For he, already a deacon, had had a curacy offered him, as soon as ever he chose to take priest's orders."

"Then he had already decided on entering the Church?"

"He had chosen that career in his youth. Towards it his whole education had tended. But," she added, with a troubled look, "my old friend, I may tell you one doubt, which I never yet breathed to living soul—I think at this time there was a struggle in his mind. Perhaps his dreams of ambition rose higher than the simple destiny of a country clergyman. I hinted this to him, but he repelled me. Alas! he knew, as well as I, that there was now no other path open for him."

Mrs. Gwynne paused, and then went on, as though speaking more to herself than to her listener.

"The time came for Harold to decide. I did not wonder at his restlessness, for I knew how strong ambition must be in a man like him. God knows I would have worked, begged, starved, rather than he should be thus tried. I told him so the day before his ordination; but he entreated me to be silent, with a look such as I never saw on his face before—such as I trust in God I never may see again. I heard him all night walking about his room; and the next morning he was gone ere I rose. When he came back, he seemed quite excited with joy, embraced me, told me I should never know poverty more, for that he was in priest's orders, and we should go the next week to the curacy at Harbury."

"And he has never repented?"

"I think not. He is not without the honours he desired; for his fame in science is extending far beyond his small parish. He fulfils his duties scrupulously; and the people respect him, though he sides with no party, high-church or evangelical We abhor illiberality—my son and I."

"That is clear, otherwise I had never seen Alison Balfour quitting the kirk for the church."

"Angus Rothesay," said Mrs. Gwynne, with dignity, "I have learned, throughout a long life, the lesson that trifling outward differences matter little—the spirit of religion is its true life. This lesson I have taught my son from his cradle; and where will you find a more sincere, moral, or pious man than Harold Gwynne?"

"Where, indeed, mother?" echoed a voice, as Harold, opening the door, caught her last words. "But come, no more o' that, an thou lovest me!"

"Harold!"

CHAPTER XVI

Captain Rothesay found himself at breakfast on the sixth morning of his stay at Harbury—so swiftly had the time flown. But he felt a purer and a happier man every hour that he spent with his ancient friend.

The breakfast-room was Harold's study. It was more that of a man of science and learning than that of a clergyman. Beside Leighton and Flavel were placed Bacon and Descartes; dust lay upon John Newton's Sermons, while close by, rested in honoured, well-thumbed tatters, his great namesake, who read God's scriptures in the stars. In one corner by a large, unopened packet—marked "Religious Society's Tracts;" it served as a stand for a large telescope, whose clumsiness betrayed the ingenuity of home manufacture. The theological contents of the library was a vast mass of polemical literature, orthodox and heterodox, including all faiths, all variations of sect. Mahomet and Swedenborg, Calvin and the Talmud, lay side by side; and on the farthest shelf was the great original of all creeds— the Book of books.

On this morning, as on most others, Harold Gwynne did not appear until after prayers were over. His mother read them, as indeed she always did morning and evening. A stranger might have said, that her doing so was the last lingering token of her sway as "head of the household."

Harold entered, his countenance bearing the pallid restless look of one who lies half-dreaming in bed, long after he is awake and ought to have risen. His mother saw it.

"You are not right, Harold. I had far rather that you rose at six and studied till nine, as formerly, than that you should dream away the morning hours, and come down looking as you do now. Forgive me, but it is not good for you, my son."

She often called him *my son* with a beautiful simplicity, that reminded one of the holy Hebrew mothers—of Rebekah or of Hannah.

Harold looked for a moment disconcerted—not angry. "Do not mind me, mother; I shall go back to study in good time. Let me do as I judge best."

"Certainly," was all the mother's reply. She reproved—she never "scolded." Turning the conversation, she directed hers to Captain Rothesay, while Harold ate his breakfast in silence—a habit not unusual with him. Immediately afterwards he rose, and prepared to depart for the day.

"I need not apologise to Captain Rothesay," he said in his own straightforward manner, which was only saved from the imputation of bluntness by a certain manly dignity—and contrasted strongly with the reserved and courtly grace of his guest. "My pursuits can scarcely interest you, while I know, and *you* know, what pleasure my mother takes in your society."

"You will not stay away all this day too, Harold. Surely that is a little too much to be required, even by Miss Derwent," spoke the quick impulse of the mother's unconscious jealousy. But she repressed it at once—even before the sudden flush of anger awakened by her words had faded from Harold's brow. "Go, my son—your mother never interferes either with your duties or your pleasures."

Harold took her hand—though with scarce less formality than he did that of Captain Rothesay; and in a few minutes they saw him gallop down the hill and across the open country, with a speed beseeming well the age of five-and-twenty, and the season of a first love.

Mrs. Gwynne looked after him with an intensity of feeling that in any other woman would have found vent in a tear—certainly a sigh.

"You are thinking of your son and his marriage," said Angus.

"That is not strange. It is a life-crisis with all men—and it has come so suddenly—I scarcely know my Harold of two months since in my Harold now."

"To work such results, it must be an ardent love."

"Say, rather, a vehement passion—love does not spring up and flower, like my hyacinths there, in six weeks. But I do not complain. Reason, if not feeling, tells me that a mother cannot be all in all to a young man. Harold needs a wife—let him take one! They will be married soon; and if all Sara's qualities equal her beauty, this wild passion will soon mature into affection. He may be happy—I trust so!"

"But does the girl love him?"—"Of course," spoke the quick-rising maternal pride. But she almost smiled at it herself, and added—"Really, you must excuse these speeches of mine. I talk to you as I never do to any one else; but it is all for the sake of olden times. This has been a happy week to me. You must pay us another visit soon."

"I will And you must take a journey to my home, and learn to know my wife and Olive," said Rothesay. The influence of Alison Gwynne was unconsciously strengthening him; and though, from some inexplicable feeling, he had spoken but little of his wife and child, there were growing up in his mind many schemes, the chief of which were connected with Olive. But he now thought less of her appearing in the world as Captain Rothesay's heiress, than of her being placed within the shadow of Alison Gwynne, and so reflecting back upon her father's age that benign influence which had been the blessing of his youth.

He went on to tell Mrs. Gwynne more of his affairs and of his plans than he had communicated to any one for many a long year. In the midst of their conversation came the visitation—always so important in remote country districts—the every-other-day's post.

"For you—not me. I have few correspondents. So I will go to my duties, while you attend to yours," said Mrs. Gwynne, and departed.

When she came in again, Captain Rothesay was pacing the room uneasily.

"No ill news, I hope?"

"No, my kind friend—not exactly ill news, though vexatious enough. But why should I trouble you with them!"

"Nothing ever troubles me that can be of use to my friends. I ask no unwelcome confidence. If it is any relief to you to speak I will gladly hear. It is sometimes good for a man to have a woman to talk to."

"It is—it is!" And his heart opening itself more and more, he told her his cause of annoyance. A most important mercantile venture would be lost to him for want of what he called "a few paltry hundreds," to be forthcoming on the morrow.

"If it had been a fortnight—just till my next ship is due; or even one week, to give me time to make some arrangement! But where is the use of complaining! It is too late."

"Not quite," said Alison Gwynne, looking up after a few moments of deep thought; and, with a clearness which would have gained for her the repute of "a thorough woman of business," she questioned Captain Rothesay, until she drew from him a possible way of obviating his difficulty.

"If, as you say, I were in London now, where my banker or some business friend would take up a bill for me; but that is impossible!"

"Nay—why say that you have friends only in London?" replied Alison, with a gentle smile. "That is rather too unjust, Angus Rothesay. Our Highland clanship is not so clean forgotten, I hope. Come, old friend, it will be hard if I cannot do something for you. And Harold, who loves Flora Rothesay almost as much as he loves me, would gladly aid her kinsman."

"How—how! Nay, but I will never consent," cried Angus, with a resoluteness through which his first eager sense of relief was clearly discernible. Truly, there was coming upon him, with this mania of speculation, the same desperation which causes the gambler to clutch money from the starving hands of those who even yet are passionately dear.

"You *shall* consent, friend," answered Mrs. Gwynne, composedly. "Why should you not? It is a mere form—an obligation of a week, at most. You will accept that for the sake of Alison Balfour."

He clasped her hand with as much emotion as was in his nature to show.

She continued—"Well, we will talk of this again when Harold comes in to dinner. But, positively, I see him returning. There he is, dashing up the hill. I hope nothing is the matter."

Yet she did not quit the room to meet him, but sat apparently quiet, though her hands were slightly trembling, until her son came in. In answer to her question, he said—

"No, no; nothing amiss. Only Mr. Fludyer would have me go to the Hall to see his new horses; and there I found"——

"Sara!" interrupted the mother. "Well, perhaps she thought it would be a pleasant change from the dulness of Waterton during your absence; so never mind."

He did mind. He restlessly paced the room, angry with his mother, himself—with the whole world. Mrs. Gwynne might well notice how this sudden passion had changed his nature. A moralist, looking on the knotted brow, would have smiled to see—not for the first time—a wise man making of himself a slave, nay, a very fool, for the enchantments of a beautiful woman.

His mother took his arm and walked with him up and down the room, without talking to him at all. But her firm step and firm clasp seemed to soothe—almost force him into composure. She had over him at once a mother's influence and a father's control.

Meanwhile, Captain Rothesay busied, or seemed to busy himself, with his numerous letters, and very wisely kept nearly out of sight.

As soon as her son appeared a little recovered from his vexation, Mrs. Gwynne said,

"Now, Harold, if you are quite willing, I want to talk to you for a few minutes. Shall it be now or this evening?"

"This evening I shall ride over to Waterton."

"What! not one evening to spare for your mother, or"— —she corrected herself, "for your beloved books?"

He moved restlessly.

"Nay, I have had enough of study; I must have interest, amusement, excitement. I think I have drunk all the world's pleasures dry, except this one. Mother, don't keep it from me; I know no rest except I am beside Sara."

He rarely spoke to her so freely, and, despite her pain, the mother was touched.

"Go, then, go to Sara; and the matter I wished to speak upon we will discuss now."

He sat down and listened, though often only with his outward ears, to her plan, by which Captain Rothesay might be saved from his difficulty.

"It is a merely nominal thing; I would do it myself, but a man's name would be more useful than a woman's. Yours will. My son Harold will at once perform such a trifling act of kindness for his mother's friend."

"Of course—of course. Come, mother, tell me what to do; you understand business affairs much better than your son!" said Harold, as he rose to seek his guest.

Captain Rothesay scrupled a while longer; but at length the dazzling vision of coming wealth absorbed both pride and reluctance. It would be so hard to miss the chance of thousands, by objecting to a mere form. "Besides, Harold Gwynne shall share my success," he thought; and he formed many schemes for changing the comparative poverty of the parsonage into comfort and luxury. It was only when the pen was in the young man's hand, ready to sign the paper, that the faintest misgiving crossed Rothesay's mind.

"Stay, it is but for a few days—yet life sometimes ends in an hour. What if I should die, at once, before I can requite you? Mr. Gwynne, you shall not do it."

"He *shall*—I mean, he will," answered the mother.

"But not until I have secured him in some way."

"Nay, Angus; we 'auld acquaintance' should not thus bargain away our friendship," said Mrs. Gwynne, with wounded pride—Highland pride. "And besides, there is no time to lose. Here is the acceptance ready—so, Harold, sign!"

Harold did sign. The instant after, glad to escape, he quitted the room.

Angus Rothesay sank on a chair with a heart-deep sigh of relief. It was done now. He eyed with thankfulness the paper which had secured him the golden prize.

"It is but a trifle—a sum not worth naming," he muttered to himself; and so, indeed, it seemed to one who had "turned over" thousands like mere heaps of dust. He never thought that it was an amount equal to Harold's yearly income for which the young man had thus become bound.

Yet he omitted not again and again to thank Mrs. Gwynne, and with excited eagerness to point to all the prospects now before him.

"And besides, you cannot think from what you have saved me—the annoyance—the shame of breaking my word. Oh, my friend, you know not in what a whirling, restless world of commerce I live! To fail in anything, or to be thought to fail, would positively ruin me and drive me mad."

"Angus—old companion!" answered Mrs. Gwynne, regarding him earnestly, "you must not blame me if I speak plainly. In one week I have seen far into your heart—farther than you think. Be advised by me; change this life for one more calm. Home and its blessings never come too late."

"You are right," said Angus. "I sometimes think that all is not well with me. I am growing old, and business racks my head sadly sometimes. Feel it now!"

He carried to his brow her hand—the hand which had led him when a boy, which in his fantastic dream of youth he had many a time kissed; even now, when the pulses were grown leaden with age, it felt cool, calm, like the touch of some pitying and protecting angel.

Alison Gwynne said gently, "My friend, you say truly all is not well with you. Let us put aside all business, and walk in the garden. Come!"

Captain Rothesay lingered at Harbury yet one day more. But he could not stay longer, for this important business-venture made him restless. Besides, Harold's wedding was near at hand: in less than a week the mother would be sole regent of her son's home no more. No wonder that this made her grave and anxious—so that even her old friend's presence was a slight restraint Yet she bade him adieu with her own cordial sincerity. He began to pour out thanks for all kindness—especially the one kindness of all, adding—

"But I will say no more. You shall see or hear from me in a few days at farthest."

"Not until after the wedding—I can think of nothing till after the wedding," answered Mrs. Gwynne. "Now, farewell, friend! but not for another thirty years, I trust!"

"No, no!" cried Angus, warmly. He looked at her as she sat by the light of her own hearth—life's trials conquered—life's duties fulfilled—and she appeared not less divine a creature than the Alison Balfour who had trod the mountains full of joy, and hope, and energy. Holy and beautiful she had seemed to him in her youth; and though every relic of that passionate idealisation he once called love, was gone, still holy and beautiful she seemed to him in her age.

Angus Rothesay rode away from Harbury parsonage, feeling that there he had gained a new interest to make life and life's duties more sacred. He thought with tenderness of his home—of his wife, and of his "little Olive;" and then, travelling by a rather circuitous route, his thoughts rested on Harold Gwynne.

"The kind-hearted, generous fellow! I will take care he is requited double. And to-morrow, before even I reach Oldchurch, I will go to my lawyer's and make all safe on his account."

"To-morrow!" He remembered not the warning, "Boast not thyself of to-morrow."

CHAPTER XVII

Olive sat mournfully contemplating Sara Derwent's last letter—the last she knew it would be. It was written, not with the frank simplicity of their girlish confidence, but with the formal dignity of one who the next day would become a bride. It spoke of no regret, no remorse for her violated troth; it mentioned her former promise in a cold, business-like manner, without inferring any changed love, but merely stating her friends' opinion on the "evil of long engagements, and that she would be much better married at once to Mr. Gwynne, than waiting some ten years for Charles Geddes."

But to Olive this change seemed a positive sin. She shuddered to think of Sara's wicked faithlessness; she wept with pity, remembering poor Charles. The sense of wrong, as well as of misery, had entered her world at once; her idols were crumbling into dust. Life grew painful, and a morbid bitterness was settling on her mind.

She read the account that Sara had somewhat boastfully written, of her prospects, her pretty home, and of her lover's devotion to her. "This clever man—this noble man (as people call him, and most of all his mother)—I could wind him round my little finger. What think you, Olive? Is not that something to be married for? You ask if I am happy. Yes, certainly, happier than you can imagine."

"That is true, indeed," murmured Olive; and there came upon her a bitter sense of the inequalities of life. It seemed that Heaven to some gave all things; to others, nothing! But she hushed the complainings, for they seemed impious. Upon her was the influence of the faith she had been taught by Elspie, which though in the old Scotswoman it became all the mystic horrors of Calvinism, yet in Olive's gentler and higher nature, had worked out blessing instead of harm. For it was a faith that taught the peace of resting child-like beneath the shadow of that Omnipotent Will, which holds every tangled thread of fate within one mighty Hand, which rules all things, and rules them continually for good.

While thinking thus, Olive was sitting in her "bower." It was a garden-seat, placed under the thorn-tree, and shut out from sight of the house by an espalier of apple-trees. Not very romantic, certainly, but a most pleasant spot, with the sound of the "shallow river" gliding by, and of many a bird that "sang madrigals" in the meadows opposite. And Olive herself, as she sat with her hands crossed on her knee, her bending head and pensive eyes out-gazing, added no little to the scene. Many a beauty might have coveted the meek yet heavenly look which threw sweetness over the pale features of the deformed girl.

Olive, sitting with her eyes cast down, was some time before she became conscious that she was watched—long and earnestly, but by an innocent watcher—her "little knight" as he had dubbed himself, Lyle Derwent. His face looked out from the ivy-leaves at the top of the wall. Soon he had leaped down, and was kneeling at her feet, just like a young lover in a romance. Smiling, she told him so; for in truth she made a great pet of the child, whose delicate beauty pleased her artist-eye, while his gentleness won her affection.

"Well, and I will be your lover, Miss Olive," said he, stoutly; "for I love you very much indeed. I should so like to kiss you—may I?"

She stooped down; moved almost to tears.

"Why are you always so sad? why do you never laugh, like Sara or the other young ladies we know?"

"Because I am not like Sara, or like any other girl. Ah! Lyle, all is very different with me. But, my little knight, this can scarcely be understood by one so young as you."

"Though I am a little boy, I know thus much, that I love you, and think you more beautiful than anybody else in the world."

And speaking rather loudly and energetically, he was answered by a burst of derisive laughter from behind the wall.

Olive crimsoned; it was one more of those passing wounds which her sensitive nature now continually received. Was even a child's love for her deemed so unnatural, and that it should be mocked at thus cruelly? Lyle, with a quickness beyond his years, seemed to have divined her thoughts, and his gentle temper was roused into passion.

"I will kill Bob, I will! Never mind him, sweet, dear, beautiful Miss Rothesay; I love you, and I hate him."

"Hush! Lyle, hush! that is wrong." And then she was silent. The little boy stood by her side, his face still burning with indignation.

Soon Olive's trouble subsided. She whispered to herself, "It must be always thus—I will try to bear it," and then she became composed. She bade her little friend adieu, telling him she was going back into the house.

"But you will forgive all, you will not think of anything that would grieve you?" said Lyle, hesitatingly.

Olive promised, with a patient smile.

"And to prove this, will you kiss your little knight once again?"

Her soft drooping hair swept his cheek; her lips touched his. Lyle Derwent never forgot this kiss of Olive Rothesay's.

The young girl entered the house. Within it was the quiet of a Sunday afternoon. Her mother had gone to a distant church, and there was none left "to keep house," save one of the maids and the old grey cat, that dosed on the window-sill in the sunshine. The cat was a great pet of Olive's; and the moment it saw its young mistress, it was purring round her feet, following her from room to room, never resting until she took it up in her arms. The love even of a dumb animal touched her then. She sat down on her own little low chair, spread on her lap the smooth white apron which Miss Pussy loved—and so she leaned back, soothed by the monotonous song of her purring favourite, and thinking that there was at least one living creature who loved her, and whom she could make perfectly happy.

She sat at the open window, seeing only the high, green privet hedge that enclosed the front garden, the little wicket-gate, and the blue sky beyond. How still everything was! By degrees the footsteps of a few late church-goers vanished along the road; the bells ceased—first the quick, sharp clang of the new church, and then the musical peal that rang out from the grey Norman tower. There never were such bells as those of Oldchurch! But they melted away in silence; and then the dreamy quietness of the hour stole over Olive's sense.

She thought of many things—things which might have been sad, but for the slumberous peace that took away all pain. It was just the hour when she once used to sit on the floor, leaning against Elspie's knees, generally reading aloud in the Book which alone the nurse permitted on Sundays. Now and then—once in particular she remembered—old Elspie fell asleep; and then Olive turned to her favourite study, the Book of Revelations. Childlike she terrified herself over the mysterious prophecies of the latter days, until at last she forgot the gloom and horror, in reading of the "beautiful city, New Jerusalem."

She seemed to see it—its twelve gates, angel-guarded, its crystal river, its many-fruited tree—the Tree of Life. Her young but glowing fancy created out of these marvels a visible material paradise. She knew not that Heaven is only the continual presence of the Eternal. Yet she was happy, and in her dreams she never pictured the land beyond the grave but there came back to her, as though the nearest foreshadowing of it, the visions of that Sunday afternoon.

She sat a long time thinking of them, and of herself—how much older she felt since then, and how many troubles she had passed through. Troubles! Poor child!—how little knew she those of the world! But even her own small burthen seemed lightened now. She leaned her head against the window, listening to the bees humming in the garden—bees, daring Sunday workers, and even they seemed to toil with a kind of Sabbatic solemnity. And then, turning her face upwards, Olive watched many a fair white butterfly, that, having flitted awhile among the flowers, spread its wings and rose far into the air, like a pure soul weary of earth, and floating heavenward. How she wished that she could do likewise; and leaving earth behind—its flowers as well as weeds, its sunshine as its storm—soar into another and a higher existence!

Not yet, Olive—not yet! None receive the guerdon, save those who have won the goal!

A pause in the girl's reverie—caused by a light sound that broke the perfect quietness around. She listened; it was the rumbling of carriage wheels along the road—a rare circumstance; for the people of Oldchurch, if not individually devout, lived in a devout atmosphere, which made pleasure-drives on the day of rest not "respectable."

A momentary hope struck Olive that it might be her father returning home. But he was a strict man; he never travelled on Sundays. Nevertheless, Olive listened mechanically to the wheels: they dashed rapidly on—came near—stopped. Yes, it must be her father.

She flew to the hall door to welcome him. There stood, not her father, but a little hard-featured old man, Mr. Wyld, the family lawyer. Olive drew back, sorely disappointed; for if in her gentle heart lingered one positive aversion, it was felt towards this man—partly on his own account, partly because his appearance seemed always the forewarning of evil in the little household. He never came but at his departure Captain Rothesay wore a frowning brow, and indulged in a hasty temper for days and days. No marvel was there in Olive's dislike; yet she regretted having shown it.

"Mr. Wyld, I thought it was my father. I am sorry that he is not at home to receive you."

"Nay,—I did not come to see Captain Rothesay," answered the lawyer, betraying some confusion and hesitation beneath his usual smooth manner. "The fact is, my dear young lady, I bring a letter for your mother."

"From papa?" cried Olive, eagerly.

"No, not exactly; that is—. But can I see Mrs. Rothesay?"

"She is at church. She will be at home in half-an-hour, probably. Will you wait?"

He shook his head.

"Nay, there is nothing wrong?"

"Don't alarm yourself, my dear."

Olive shrank from the touch of his hand, as he led her into the parlour.

"Your papa is at my house. But I think, Miss Rothesay, as your mother is not at home, you had better read the letter yourself."

She took it. Slowly, silently, she read it through, twice; for the words seemed to dazzle and blaze before her eyes. Then she looked up helplessly. "I—I cannot understand."

"I thought the doctor wrote plainly enough, and broke the matter cautiously, too," muttered Mr. Wyld; adding aloud, "Upon my honour, my dear, I assure you your father is alive."

"Alive! Oh, my poor father!" And then she sank down slowly where she stood, as if pressed by some heavy, invisible hand. Mr. Wyld thought she had fainted; but it was not so. In another moment she stood before him, nerved by this great woe to a firmness which was awful in its rigid composure.

"I can listen now. Tell me everything!"

He told her in a few words how Captain Rothesay had come to his house the night before; and, while waiting his return, had taken up the newspaper. "Suddenly, my clerk said, he let it fall with a cry, and was immediately seized with the fit from which he has not yet recovered. There is hope, the doctor thinks; but, in case of the worst, you must come to him at once."

"Yes, yes, at once!" She rose and walked to the door, guiding herself by the wall.

"Nay, Miss Rothesay, what are you doing? You forget we cannot go without your mother."

"My mother! O, Heaven! it will kill my mother!"

And the thought brought tears, the first that had burst from her. It was well.

She recovered to consciousness and strength. In this great crisis there came to her the wisdom and forethought that lay dormant in her nature.

She became a woman—one of those of whom the world contains few—at once gentle and strong, meek and fearless, patient to endure, heroic to act.

She sat down for a moment and considered. "Fourteen miles it is to B——. If we start in an hour we shall reach there by sunset." Then she summoned the maid, and said, speaking steadily, that she might by no sign betray what might in turn be betrayed to her mother—

"You must go and meet mamma as she comes from church; or, if not, go into the church to her. Tell her there is a message come from papa, and ask her to hasten home. Make haste yourself. I will keep house the while."

The woman left the room, murmuring a little, but never thinking to disobey her young mistress, so sudden, so constraining, was the dignity which had come upon the girl. Even Mr. Wyld felt it, and his manner changed from condolence to respect.

"What can I do, Miss Rothesay? You turn from me. No wonder, when I have had the misfortune to be the bearer of such evil tidings."

"Hush!" she said. Mechanically she set wine before him. He drank talking between the draughts, of his deep sorrow, and earnest hope that no serious evil would befall his good friend, Captain Rothesay.

Olive could endure no more. She fled away, shut herself up in her own room, and fell on her knees! but no words came, save the bitter cry, "O God, have pity on us!" And there was no time, not even to pray, except within her heart.

She pressed her hands on her brow, and once more thought what she had to do. At that moment, through the quietness of the house, she heard the clock striking four. Never had time's passing seemed so awful. The day was fleeting on whose every moment perhaps hung a life.

Something she must do, or her senses would have failed. She thought of little things that might be needed when they reached her father; went into Mrs. Rothesay's room, and put up some clothes and necessaries, in case they stayed more than one day at B——; a large, warm shawl, too, for her mother might have to sit up all night. In these trifling arrangements what a horrible reality there was? And yet she scarcely felt it—she was half-stunned still.

It was past four—and Mrs. Rothesay had not come. Every minute seemed an eternity. Olive walked to the window and looked out. There was the same cheerful sunshine—the bees humming, and the butterflies flitting about, in the sweet stillness of the Sabbath afternoon, as she had watched them an hour ago. One little hour, to have brought into her world such utter misery!

She thought of it all, dwelling vividly on every accompaniment of woe—even as she remembered to have done when she first learned that Elspie would die. She pictured her mother's coming home; and almost fancied she could see her now, walking across the fields. But no; it was some one in a white dress, strolling by the hedgerow's side; and Mrs. Rothesay that day wore blue—her favourite pale blue muslin in which she looked so lovely. She had gone out, laughing at her daughter for saying this. What if Olive should never see her in that pretty dress again!

All these fancies, and more, clung to the girl's mind with a horrible pertinacity. And then, through the silence, she heard the Oldchurch bells awaking again, in the dull minute-peal which told that service-time was ended, and the afternoon funerals were taking place. Olive, shuddering, closed her ears against the sound, and then, gazing out once more, she saw her mother stand at the gate. Mrs. Rothesay looked up at the window and smiled.

Olive had never thought of that worst pang of all—how she should break the news to her mother—her timid, delicate mother, whose feeble frame quivered beneath the lightest breath of suffering. Scarcely knowing what she did, she flew down stairs.

"Not there, mamma, not there!" she cried, as Mrs. Rothesay was about to enter the parlour. Olive drew her into another room, and made her sit down.

"What is all this, my dear!—why do you look so strange! Is not your papa come home? Let us go to him."

"We will, we will! But mamma!"—One moment she looked speechlessly in Mrs. Rothesay's face, and then fell on her neck, crying, "I can't, I can't keep it from you any longer. Oh, mother, mother! there is great trouble come upon us; we must be patient; we must bear it together. God will help us."

"Olive!" The shrill terror of Mrs. Rothesay's voice rung through the room.

"Hush! we must be quiet, very quiet. Papa is dangerously ill at B——, and we must start at once. I have arranged all. Come, mamma, dearest!"

But her mother had fainted.

There was no time to lose. Olive snatched some restoratives, and then made ready to depart. Mrs. Rothesay, still insensible, was lifted into the carriage. She lay there, for some time, quite motionless, supported in her daughter's arms—to which never had she owed support before. As Olive looked down upon her, strange, new feelings came into the girl's heart. Filial tenderness seemed transmuted into a devotion passing the love of child to mother, and mingled therewith was a sense of protection, of watchful guardianship.

She thought, "What if my father should die, and we two should be left alone in the world! Then she will have none to look to save me, and I will be to her in the stead of all. Once, I think, she loved me very little; but, oh! mother, dearly we love one another now."

When Mrs. Rothesay's senses returned, she lifted her head, with a bewildered air. "Where are we going? What has happened? I can't think clearly of anything."

"Dearest mamma, do not try—I will think for us both. Be content; you are quite safe with your own daughter."

"My daughter—ah! I remember, I fainted, as I did long years ago, when they told me something about my daughter. Are you she—that little child whom I cast from my arms? and now I am lying in yours!" she cried, her mind seeming to wander, as if distraught by this sudden shock.

"Hush, mamma! don't talk; rest quiet here."

Mrs. Rothesay looked wistfully in her daughter's face, and there seemed to cross her mind some remembered sense of what had befallen. She clung helplessly to those sustaining arms—"Take care of me, Olive!—I do not deserve it, but take care of me!"

"I will, until death!" was Olive's inward vow.

And so, travelling fast, but in solemn silence, they came to B——. Alas! it was already too late! By Angus Rothesay's bed they stood—the widow and the fatherless!

CHAPTER XVIII

The tomb had scarcely closed over Captain Rothesay, when it was discovered that his affairs were in a state of irretrievable confusion. For months he must have lived with ruin staring him in the face.

His sudden death was then no mystery. The newspaper had startled him with tidings—partly false, as afterwards appeared—of a heavy disaster by sea, and the failure of his latest speculation at home. There seemed lifted against him at once the hand of Heaven and of man. His proud nature could not withstand the shock; shame smote him, and he died.

"Tell me only one thing!" cried Olive to Mr..Wyld, with whom, after the funeral, she was holding conference—she only—for her mother was incapable of acting, and this girl of sixteen was the sole ruler of the household now. "Tell me only that my father died unblemished in honour—that there are none to share misfortune with us, and to curse the memory of the ruined merchant."

"I know of none," answered Mr. Wyld. "True, there are still remaining many private debts, but they may be easily paid." And he cast a meaning glance round the luxuriously furnished room.

"I understand. It shall be done," said Olive. Misery had made her very wise—very quick to comprehend. Without shrinking she talked over every matter connected with that saddest thing—a deceased bankrupt's sale.

The lawyer was a hard man, and Olive's prejudice against him was not unfounded. Still the most stony heart has often a little softness buried deep at its core. Mr. Wyld looked with curiosity, even with kindness, on the young creature who sat opposite to him, in the dim lamp-light of the silent room, once Captain Rothesay's study. Her cheek, ever delicate, was now of a dull white; her pale gold hair fell neglected over her black dress; her hand supported her care-marked brow, as she pored over dusty papers, pausing at times to speak, in a quiet, sensible, subdued manner, of things fit only for old heads and worn hearts. Mr. Wyld thought of his own merry daughters, whom he had left at home, and felt a vague thankfulness that they were not as Olive Rothesay. Tenderness was not in his nature; but in all his intercourse with her, he could not help treating with a sort of reverence the dead merchant's forlorn child.

When they had finished their conversation, he said, "There is one matter—painful, too—upon which I ought to speak to you. I should have done so before, but I did not know it myself until yesterday."

"Know what? Is there more trouble coming?" answered Olive, sighing bitterly. "But tell me all."

"*All,* is very little. You know, my dear Miss Rothesay, that your father was speechless from the moment of his seizure. But my wife, who never quitted him—ah! I assure you she was a devoted nurse to him, was Mrs. Wyld."

"I thank her deeply, as she knows."

"My wife has just told me, that a few minutes before his death your poor father's consciousness returned; that he seemed struggling in vain to speak; at last she placed a pencil in his hand, and he wrote—one word only, in the act of writing which he died. Forgive me, my dear young lady for thus agitating you, but"——

"The paper—give me the paper!"

Mr. Wyld pulled out his pocket-book, and produced a torn and blotted scrap, whereon was written, in characters scarcely legible, the name "Harold."

"Do you know any one who bears that name, Miss Rothesay?"

"No. Yes—one," added she, suddenly remembering that the name of Sara's husband was Harold Gwynne. But between him and her father she knew of no single tie. It must be a mere chance coincidence.

"What is to be done?" cried Olive. "Shall I tell my mother?"

"If I might advise, I would say decisively, No! Better leave the matter in my hands. Harold!—'tis a boy's name," he added, meditatively. "If it were a girl's now—I executed a little commission for Captain Rothesay once."

"What did you say?" asked Olive, looking up at him with her innocent eyes. He could not meet them; his own fell confused.

"What did I say, Miss Rothesay? Oh, nothing—nothing at all; only that if I had a commission—to—to hunt out this secret."

"I thank you, Mr. Wyld; but a daughter would not willingly employ any third person to 'hunt out' her father's secret. His papers will doubtless inform me of everything; therefore we will speak no more on this subject."

"As you will" He gathered up his blue bag and its voluminous contents, and made his adieux.

But Olive had scarcely sat down again, and with her head leaning on her father's desk, had given vent to a sigh of relief, in that she was freed from Mr. Wyld's presence, when the old lawyer again appeared.

"Miss Rothesay, I merely wished to say, if ever you find out—any secret—or need any advice about that paper, or anything else, I'm the man to give it, and with pleasure in this case. Good evening!"

Olive thanked him coldly, somewhat proudly, for what she thought a piece of unnecessary impertinence. However, it quickly passed from her gentle mind; and then, as the best way to soothe all her troubles, she quitted the study, and sought her mother.

Of Mrs. Rothesay's affliction we have as yet said little. Many and various are earth's griefs; but there must be an awful individuality in the stroke which severs the closest human tie, that between two whom marriage had made "one flesh." And though in this case coldness had loosened the sacred tie, still no power could utterly divide it, while life endured. Angus Rothesay's widow remembered that she had once been the loved and loving bride of his youth. As such, she mourned him; nor was her grief without that keenest sting, the memory of unatoned wrong. From the dim shores of the past, arose ghosts that nothing could ever lay, because death's river ran eternally between.

Sybilla Rothesay was one of those women whom no force of circumstances can ever teach self-dependence or command. She had looked entirely to her husband for guidance and control, and now for both she looked to her child. From the moment of Captain Rothesay's death, Olive seemed to rule in his stead—or rather, the parent and child seemed to change places. Olive watched, guided, and guarded the passive, yielding, sorrow-stricken woman, as with a mother's care; while Mrs. Rothesay trusted implicitly in all things to her daughter's stronger mind, and was never troubled by thinking or acting for herself in any one thing.

This may seem a new picture of the maternal and filial bond, but it is frequently true. If we look around on those daughters who have best fulfilled the holy duty, without which no life is or can be blest, are they not women firm, steadfast—able to will and to act? Could not many of them say, "I am a mother unto my mother. I, the strongest now, take her in her feeble age, like a child, to my bosom—shield her, cherish her, and am to her all in all."

And so, in heart, resolved Olive Rothesay. She had made that vow when her mother lay insensible in her arms; she kept it faithfully; until eternity, closing between them, sealed it with that best of earth's blessings—the blessing that falls on a duteous daughter, whose mother is with God.

When Captain Rothesay's affairs were settled, the sole wreck of his wealth that remained to his widow and child was the small settlement from Mrs. Rothesay's fortune, on which she had lived at Stirling. So they were not left in actual poverty.

Still, Olive and her mother were poor—poor enough to make them desire to leave prying, gossiping Oldchurch, and settle in the solitude of some great town. "There," Olive said to herself, "I shall surely find means to work for her—that she may have not merely necessaries, but comforts."

And many a night—during the few weeks that elapsed before their home was broken up—she lay awake by her sleeping mother's side, planning all sorts of schemes; arranging everything, so that Mrs. Rothesay might not be annoyed with arguings or consultations. When all was matured, she had only to say, "Dearest mother, should we not be very happy living together in London?" And scarcely had Mrs. Rothesay assented, than she found everything arranged itself, as under an invisible fairy hand—so that she had but to ask, "My child, when shall we go?"

The time of departure at last arrived. It was the night but one before the sale. Olive persuaded her mother to go to rest early; for she herself had a trying duty to perform—the examining of her father's private papers. As she sat in his study—in solitude and gloom—the young girl might have been forgiven many a pang of grief, even a shudder of superstitious fear. But Heaven had given her a hero-soul, not the less heroic because it was a woman's.

Her father's business-papers she had already examined; these were only his private memoranda. But they were few,—Captain Rothesay's thoughts never found vent in words; there were no data of any kind to mark the history of a life, which was almost as unknown to his wife and daughter as to any stranger. Of letters, she found very few; he was not a man who loved correspondence. Only among these few she was touched deeply to see some, dated years back, at Stirling. Olive opened one of them. The delicate hand was that of her mother when she was young. Olive only glanced at the top of the page, where still smiled, from the worn, yellow paper, the words, "My dearest, dearest Angus;" and then, too right-minded to penetrate further, folded it up again. Yet, she felt glad; she thought it would comfort her mother to know how carefully he had kept these letters. Soon after she found a memento of herself—a little curl, wrapped in silver-paper, and marked with his own hand, "Olive's hair." Her father had loved her then—ay, and more deeply than she knew.

The chief thing which troubled Olive was the sight of the paper on which her father's dying hand had scrawled "Harold." No date of any kind had been found to explain the mystery. She determined to think of the matter no more, but to put the paper by in a secret drawer.

In doing so, she found a small packet, carefully tied and sealed. She was about to open it, when the superscription caught her eyes. Thereon she read her father's written desire that it should after his death be burnt unopened.

His faithful daughter, without pausing to think, threw the packet on the fire; even turning aside, lest the flames, while destroying, should reveal anything of the secret. Only once, forgetting herself, the crackling fire made her start and turn, and she caught a momentary glimpse of some curious foreign ornament; while near it, twisted in the flame into almost life-like motion, was what seemed a long lock of black hair. But she could be certain of nothing; she hated herself for even that involuntary glance. It seemed an insult to the dead.

Still more did these remorseful feelings awake, when, her task being almost done, she found one letter addressed thus:

"For my daughter, Olive. Not to be opened till her mother is dead, and she is alone in the world."

Alone in the world! His fatherly tenderness had looked forward, then, even to that bitter time—far off, she prayed God!—when she would be alone—a woman no longer young, without parents, husband, or child, or smiling home. She doubted not that her father had written this letter to counsel and comfort her at such a season of desolation, years after he was in the dust.

His daughter blessed him for it; and her tender tears fell upon words which he had written, as she saw by the date outside, on that night—the last he ever spent at home. She never thought of breaking his injunction, or of opening the letter before the time; and after considering deeply, she decided that it was too sacred even for the ear of her mother, to whom it would only give pain. Therefore she placed it in the private drawer of her father's desk—now her own—to wait until time should bring about the revealing of this solemn secret between her and the dead.

Then she went to bed, wearied and worn; and creeping close to her slumbering mother, thanked God that there was one warm living bosom to which she could cling, and which would never cast her out.

O mother! O daughter! who, when time has blended into an almost sisterly bond the difference of years, grow together, united, as it were, in one heart and one soul by that perfect love which is beyond even "honour" and "obedience," because including both—how happy are ye! How blessed she, who, looking on her daughter—woman grown—can say, "Child, thou art bone of my bone, and flesh of my flesh, as when I brought thee into the world!" And thrice blessed is she who can answer, "Mother, I am all thine own—I desire no love but thine—I bring to thee my every joy; and my every grief finds rest on thy bosom."

Let those who have this happiness rejoice! Let those who only have its memory pray always that God would make that memory live until the eternal meeting, at the resurrection of the just!

CHAPTER XIX

In one of the western environs of London is a region which, lying between two great omnibus outlets, is yet as retired and old-fashioned as though it had been miles and miles distant from the metropolis. Fields there are few or none, certainly; but there are quiet, green lanes (where in springtime you may pluck many a fragrant hawthorn branch), and market-gardens, and grand old trees; while on summer mornings you may continually hear a loud chorus of birds—especially larks—though these latter "blithe spirits" seem to live perpetually in the air, and one marvels how they ever contrive to make their nests in the potato-grounds below. Perhaps they do so in emulation of their human neighbours—authors, actors, artists, who in this place "most do congregate," many of them, poor souls! singing their daily songs of life out in the world, as the larks in the air; none knowing what a mean, lowly, sometimes even desolate home, is the nest whence such music springs.

Well, in this region, there is a lane * (a crooked, unpaved, winding, quaint, dear old lane!); and in that lane there is a house; and in that house there are two especially odd rooms, where dwelt Olive Rothesay and her mother.

* *Was. It is no more, now.*

Chance had led them hither; but they both—Olive especially—thanked chance, every day of their lives, for having brought them to such a delicious old place. It was the queerest of all queer abodes, was Woodford Cottage. The entrance-door and the stable-door stood side by side; and the cellar-staircase led out of the drawing-room. The direct way from the kitchen to the dining-room was through a suite of sleeping apartments; and the staircase, apparently cut out of the wall, had a beautiful little break-neck corner, which seemed made to prevent any one who once ascended from ever descending alive. Certainly the contriver of Woodford Cottage must have had some slight twist of the brain, which caused the building to partake of the same pleasant convolution.

Yet, save this slight peculiarity, it was a charming house to live in. It stood in a garden, whose high walls shut out all view, save of the trees belonging to an old dilapidated, uninhabited lodge, where an illustrious statesman had once dwelt, and which was now creeping to decay and oblivion, like the great man's own memory. The trees waved, and the birds sang therein for the especial benefit of Woodford Cottage and of Olive Rothesay. She, who so dearly loved a garden, perfectly exulted in this. Most delightful was its desolate untrimmed luxuriance—where the peaches grew almost wild upon the wall, and one gigantic mulberry-tree looked beautiful all the year through. Moreover, climbing over the picturesque, bay-windowed house, was such a clematis! Its blossoms glistened like a snow-shower throughout the day; and, in the night-time, its perfume was a very breath of Eden. Altogether the house was a grand old house—just suited for a dreamer, a poet, or an artist. An artist did really inhabit it, which had been no small attraction to draw Olive thither. But of him more anon.

At present let us look at the mother and daughter, as they sit in the one parlour to which all the glories of Meri-vale Hall and Oldchurch had dwindled. But they did not murmur at that, for they were together; and now that the first bitterness of their loss had passed away, they began to feel cheerful—even happy.

Olive was flitting in and out of the window which opened into the garden, and bringing thence her apron full of flowers to dispose about the large, somewhat gloomy, and scantily-furnished room. Mrs. Rothesay was sitting in the sunshine, engaged in some delicate needlework. In the midst of it she stopped, and her hands fell with a heavy sigh.

"It is of no use, Olive."

"What is of no use, mamma?"

"I cannot see to thread my needle. I really must be growing old."

"Nonsense, darling."—Olive often said "darling" quite in a protecting way—"Why, you are not forty yet. Don't talk about growing old, my own beautiful mamma—for you are beautiful; I heard Mr. Vanbrugh saying so to his sister the other day; and of course he, an artist, must know," added Olive, with a sweet flattery, as she took her mother's hands, and looked at her with admiration.

And truly it was not uncalled for. Over the delicate beauty of Sybilla Rothesay had crept a spiritual charm, that increased with life's decline—for her life *was* declining—even so soon. Not that her health was broken, or that she looked withered and aged; but still there was a gradual change, as of the tree which from its richest green melts into hues that, though still lovely, indicate the time, distant but certain, of autumn days, and of leaves softly falling earthwards. So, doubtless, her life's leaf would fall.

Mrs. Rothesay smiled; sweeter than any of the flatteries of her youth, now fell her daughter's tender praise. "You are a silly little girl; but never mind! Only I wish my eyes did not trouble me so much. Olive, suppose I should come to be a blind old woman, for you to take care of?"

Olive snatched away the work, and closed the strained aching eyes with two sweet kisses. It was a subject she could not bear to talk upon; perhaps because it rested often on Mrs. Rothesay's mind: and she herself had an instinctive apprehension that there was, after all, some truth in these fears concerning her mother's sight. She began quickly to talk of other matters.

"Hark, mamma, there is Mr. Vanbrugh walking in his painting-room overhead. He always does so when he is dissatisfied about his picture; and I am sure he need not be, for oh! how beautiful it is! Miss Meliora took me in yesterday to see it, when he was out."

"She seems to make quite a pet of you, my child."

"Her kitten ran away last week, which accounts for it, mamma. But indeed I ought not to laugh at her, for one must have something to love, and she has nothing but her dumb pets."

"And her brother."

"Oh, yes. I wonder if anybody else ever loved him, or if he ever loved anybody," said Olive, musingly. "But, mamma, if he is not handsome himself he admires beauty in others. What do you think?—he is longing to paint *somebody's* face, and put it in this picture; and I promised to ask. Oh, darling, do sit to him! It would not be much trouble, and I should be so proud to see my beautiful mamma in the Academy-exhibition next year."

Mrs. Rothesay shook her head.

"Nay—here he comes to ask you himself," cried Olive, as a tall, a very tall shadow darkened the window, and its corporeality entered the room.

He was a most extraordinary-looking man,—Mr. Van-brugh. Olive had, indeed, reason to call him "not handsome," for you probably would not see an uglier man twice in a lifetime. Gigantic and ungainly in height, and coarse in feature, he certainly was the very antipodes of his own exquisite creations. And for that reason he created them. In his troubled youth, tortured with the sense of that blessing which was denied him, he had said, "Providence has created me hideous: I will outdo Providence; I with my hand will continually create beauty." And so he did—ay, and where he created, he loved. He took his art for his mistress, and, like the Rhodian sculptor, he clasped it to his soul night and day, until it grew warm and life-like, and became to him in the stead of every human tie. Thus Michael Vanbrugh had lived, for fifty years, a life solitary even to moroseness; emulating the great Florentine master, whose Christian name it was his glory to bear.

He painted grand pictures, which nobody bought, but which he and his faithful little sister Meliora thought the greater for that. The world did not understand him, nor did he understand the world; so he shut himself out from it altogether, until his small and rapidly-decreasing income caused him to admit into his house as lodgers the widow and daughter.

He might not have done so, had not Miss Meliora hinted how lovely the former was, and how useful she might be as a model when they grew sociable together.

He came to make his request now, and he made it with the greatest unconcern. In his opinion everything in life tended toward one great end—Art He looked on all beauty as only made to be painted. Accordingly, he stepped up to his inmate, with the following succinct address:

"Madam, I want a Grecian head. Yours just suits me; will you oblige me by sitting?" And then adding, as a soothing and flattering encouragement: "It is for my great work—my 'Alcestis!'—one of a series of six pictures, which I hope to finish one day."

He tossed back his long iron-grey hair, and scanned intently the gentle-looking lady whom he had hitherto noticed only with the usual civilities of an acquaintanceship consequent on some months' residence in the same house.

"Excellent! madam. Your features are the very thing—they are perfect."

"Really, Mr. Vanbrugh, you are very flattering," began the widow, faintly colouring, and appealing to Olive, who looked delighted; for she regarded the old artist with as much reverence as if he had been Michael Angelo himself.

He interrupted them both. "Ay, that will just do;" and he drew in the air some magic lines over Mrs. Rothesay's head. "Good brow—Greek mouth, If, madam, you would favour me with taking off your cap. Thank you, Miss Olive. *You* understand me, I see. That will do—the white drapery over the hair—ah, divine! My 'Alcestis' to the life! Madam—Mrs. Rothesay, your head is glorious; it shall go down to posterity in my picture."

And he walked up and down the room, rubbing his hands with a delighted pride, which, in its perfect simplicity, could never be confounded with paltry vanity or self-esteem. "*My* work, *my* picture," in which he so gloried, was utterly different from, "I, the man who executed it" He worshipped—not himself at all; and scarcely so much his real painted work, as the ideal which ever flitted before him, and which it was the one great misery of his life never to have sufficiently attained.

"When shall I sit?" timidly inquired Mrs. Rothesay, still too much of a woman not to be pleased by a painter's praise.

"At once, madam, at once, while the mood is on me. Miss Rothesay, you will lead the way; you are not unacquainted with the arcana of my studio." As, indeed, she was not, having before stood some three hours in the painful attitude of a "Cassandra raving," while he painted from her outstretched and very beautiful hands.

Happy she was the very moment her foot crossed the threshold of a painter's studio, for Olive's love of Art had grown with her growth, and strengthened with her strength. Moreover, the artistic atmosphere in which she now lived had increased this passion tenfold.

"Truly, Miss Rothesay, you seem to know all about it," said Michael Vanbrugh, when, in great pride and delight, she was helping him to arrange her mother's pose, and at last became herself absorbed in admiration of "Alcestis." "You might have been an artist's daughter or sister."

"I wish I had been."

"My daughter is somewhat of an artist herself, Mr. Vanbrugh," observed Mrs. Rothesay, with maternal pride; which Olive, deeply blushing, soon quelled by an entreating motion of silence.

But the painter went on painting; he saw nothing, thought of nothing, save his "Alcestis." He was indeed an enthusiast. Olive watched how, beneath the coarse, ill-formed hand, grew images of perfect beauty; how, within the body, almost repulsive in its ugliness, dwelt a brain which could produce the grandest ideal loveliness; and there dawned in the girl's spirit a stronger conviction than ever of the majesty of the human soul.

It was a comforting thought to one like her, who, as she deemed, had been deprived of so many of life's outward sweetnesses. Between herself and Michael Vanbrugh there was a curious sympathy. To both Nature seemed to have said, "Renounce the body, in exchange for the soul."

The sitting had lasted some hours, during which it took all poor Mrs. Rothesay's gentle patience to humour Olive's enthusiasm, by maintaining the very arduous position of an artist's model. "Alcestis" was getting thoroughly weary of her duties, when they were interrupted by an advent rather rare at Woodford Cottage, that of the daily post Vanbrugh grumblingly betook himself to the substitute of a lay figure and drapery, while Mrs. Rothesay read her letter, or rather looked at it, and gave it to Olive to read: glad, as usual, to escape from the trouble of correspondence.

Olive examined the superscription, as one sometimes does, uselessly enough, when breaking the seal would explain everything. It was a singularly bold, upright hand, distinct as print, free from all caligraphic flourishes, indicating, as most writing does indicate in some degree, the character of the writer. Slightly eccentric it might be, quick, restless, in its turned-up Gs and Ys, but still it was a good hand, an honest hand. Olive thought so, and liked it. Wondering who the writer could be, she opened it, and read thus:

> "Madam—From respect to your recent affliction I have kept silence for some months—a silence which, you will allow, was more than could have been expected from me. Perhaps I should not break it now, save for the claim of a wife and mother, who are suffering, and must suffer, from the results of an act which sprung from my own folly and another's cruel—— But no; I will not apply harsh words towards one who is now no more.
>
> "Are you aware, madam, that your late husband, not two days before his death, when in all human probability he must have known himself to be a ruined man, accepted from me assistance in a matter of business, which the enclosed correspondence between my solicitor and yours will explain? This act of mine, done for the sake of an ancient friendship subsisting between my mother and Captain Rothesay, has rendered me liable for a debt so heavy, that in paying it my income is impoverished, and must continue to be so for years.
>
> "Your husband gave me no security: I desired none. Therefore I have no legal claim for requital for this great and bitter sacrifice, which makes me daily curse my own folly in having trusted living man. But I ask of you, madam, who, secured from the effects of Captain Rothesay's insolvency, have, I understand, been left in comfort, if not affluence—I ask, is it right, in honour and in honesty, that I, a clergyman with a small stipend, should suffer the penalty of a deed wherein, with all charity to the dead, I cannot but think I was grievously injured?
>
> "Awaiting your answer, I remain, madam, your very obedient,
> "Harold Gwynne."

"Harold Gwynne!" Olive, repeating the name to herself, let the letter fall on the ground. Well was it that she stood hidden from sight by the "great picture," so that her mother could not know the pang which came over her.

The mystery, then, was solved. Now she knew why in his last agony her dying father had written the name of "Harold"—her poor father, who was here accused, by implication at least, of a wilful act of dishonesty! She regarded the letter with a sense of abhorrence—so coldly cruel it seemed to her, whose tenderness for a father's memory naturally a little belied her judgment. And the heartless charge was brought by the husband of Sara Derwent! There was bitterness in every association connected with the name of Harold Gwynne.

"Well, dear, the letter!" said Mrs. Rothesay, as they passed from the studio to their own apartment.

"It brings news that will grieve you. But never mind, mamma, darling: we will bear all our troubles together." And as briefly and as tenderly as she could she explained the letter—together with the fact hitherto unknown to Mrs. Rothesay, that her husband in his last moments had evidently wished to acknowledge the debt.

Well Olive knew the effect this would produce on her mother's mind. Tears, angry exclamations, and bitter repinings; but the daughter soothed them all.

"Now, dear mamma," she whispered, when Mrs. Rothesay was a little composed, "we must answer the letter at once. What shall we say!"

"Nothing! That cruel man deserves no reply at all."

"Mamma!" cried Olive, somewhat reproachfully. "Whatever he may be, we are evidently his debtors. Even Mr. Wyld admits this, you see. We must not forget justice and honour—my poor fathers honour."

"No—no! You are right, my child. Let us do anything, if it is for the sake of his dear memory," sobbed the widow, whose love death had sanctified, and endowed with an added tenderness. "But, Olive, you must write—I cannot!"

Olive assented. She had long taken upon herself all similar duties. At once she sat down to pen this formidable letter. It took her some time; for there was a constant struggle between the necessary formality of a business letter, and the impulse of wounded feeling, natural to her dead father's child. The finished epistle was a curious mingling of both.

"Shall I read it aloud, mamma? and then the subject will be taken from your mind," said Olive, as she came and stood by her mother's chair.

Mrs. Rothesay assented.

"Well, then, here it begins—'Reverend Sir' (I ought to address him thus, you know, because he is a clergyman, though he does seem so harsh, and so unlike what a Christian pastor ought to be)."

"He does, indeed, my child—but, go on." And Olive read:

> "'Reverend Sir—I address you by my mother's desire, to say that she was quite unaware of your claim upon my late dear father. She can only reply to it, by requesting your patience for a little time, until she is able to liquidate the debt—not out of the wealth you attribute to her, but out of her present restricted means. And I, my father's only child, wishing to preserve his memory from the imputations you have cast upon it, must tell you, that his last moments were spent in endeavouring to write your name. We never understood why, until now. Oh, sir! was it right or kind of you so harshly to judge the dead? My father intended to pay you. If you have suffered, it was through his misfortune—not his crime. Have a little patience with us, and your claim shall be wholly discharged.
>
> "'Olive Rothesay.'"

"You have said nothing of Sara. I wonder if she knows this!" said the mother, as Olive folded up her letter.

"Hush, mamma! Let me forget everything that was once. Perhaps, too, she is not to blame. I knew Charles Geddes; Sara might not like to speak of me to her husband?"

Yet, with a look of bitter pain, Olive wrote the address of her letter— "Harbury Parsonage"—Sara's home! She lingered, too, over the name of Sara's husband.

"Harold Gwynne! Oh, mamma! how different names look! I cannot bear the sight of this! I hate it."

Years after, Olive remembered these words.

CHAPTER XX

If the old painter of Woodford Cottage was an ascetic and a misanthrope never was the "milk of human kindness" so redundant in any human heart as in that of his excellent little sister, Miss Meliora Vanbrugh. From the day of her birth, when her indigent father's anticipation of a bequeathed fortune had caused her rather eccentric Christian name, Miss Meliora began a chase after the wayward sprite Prosperity. She had hunted it during her whole lifetime, and never caught anything but its departing shadow. She had never grown rich, though she was always hoping to do so. She had never married, for no one had ever asked her. Whether she had loved—but that was another question. She had probably quite forgotten the days of her youth; at all events, she never talked about them now.

But though to herself her name had been a mockery, to others it was not so. Wherever she went, she always brought "better things"—at least in anticipation. She was the most hopeful little body in the world, and carried with her a score of consolatory proverbs, about "long lanes" that had most fortunate "turnings," and "cloudy mornings" that were sure to change into "very fine days." She had always in her heart a garden full of small budding blessings; and though they never burst into flowers, she kept on ever expecting they would do so, and was therefore quite satisfied. Poor Miss Meliora! if her hopes never blossomed, she also never had the grief of watching them die.

Her whole life had been pervaded by one grand desire—to see her brother president of the Royal Academy. When she was a school-girl and he a student, she had secretly sketched his likeness—the only one extant of his ugly, yet soul-lighted face—and had prefixed thereto his name, with the magic letters, "P. B. A." She felt sure the prophecy would be fulfilled one day, and then she would show him the portrait, and let her humble, sisterly love go down to posterity on the hem of his robe of fame.

Meliora told all this to her favourite, Olive Rothesay, one day when they were busying themselves in gardening—an occupation wherein their tastes agreed, and which contributed no little to the affection and confidence that was gradually springing up between them.

"It is a great thing to be an artist," said Olive, musingly.

"Nothing like it in the whole world, my dear. Think of all the stories of little peasant-boys who have thus risen to be the companions of kings, whereby the kings were the parties most honoured. Remember the stories of Francis I. and Titian, of Henry VII. and Hans Holbein, of Vandyck and Charles I.!"

"You seem quite learned in Art, Miss Vanbrugh. I wish you would impart to me a little of your knowledge."

"To be sure I will, my dear," said the proud, delighted little woman. "You see, when I was a girl, I 'read up' on Art, that I might be able to talk to Michael. Somehow, he never did care to talk with me; but perhaps he may yet.".

Olive's mind seemed wandering from the conversation, and from her employment, too; for the mignonette-bed she was weeding lost quite as many flowers as weeds. At last she said—

"Miss Meliora, do people ever grow *rich* as artists?"

"Michael has not done so," answered her friend (at which Olive began to blush for what seemed a thoughtless question). "But Michael has peculiar notions. However, I feel sure he will be a rich man yet—like Sir Joshua Reynolds, and Sir Thomas Lawrence, and many more."

Olive began to muse again. Then she said timidly, "I wonder why, with all your love for Art, you yourself did not become an artist?"

"Bless you, my dear, I should never think of such a thing. I have no genius at all for anything—Michael always said so. I an artist!—a poor little woman like me!"

"Yet some women have been painters."

"Oh, yes, plenty. There was Angelica Kauffman, and Properzia Rossi, and Elizabetta Sirani. In our day, there is Mrs. A—— and Miss B——, and the two C——s. And if you read about the old Italian masters, you will find that many of them had wives, or daughters, or sisters, who helped them a great deal. I wish I had been such an one! Depend upon it, my dear girl," said Meliora, waxing quite oracular in her enthusiasm, "there is no profession in the world that brings fame, and riches, and happiness, like that of an artist."

Olive only half believed in the innocent optimism of her companion. Still Miss Vanbrugh's words impressed themselves strongly on her mind, wherein was now a chaos of anxious thought. From the day when Mr. Gwynne's letter came, she had positively writhed under the burden of this heavy debt, which it would take years to discharge, unless a great deduction were made from their slender income. And how could she propose that—

how bear to see her delicate and often-ailing mother deprived of the small luxuries which had become necessary comforts? To their letter no answer had come—the creditor was then a patient one; but this thought the more stimulated Olive to defray the debt. Night and day it weighed her down; plan after plan she formed, chiefly in secret, for the mention of this painful circumstance was more than her mother could bear. Among other schemes, the thought of entering on that last resource of helpless womanhood, the dreary life of a daily governess; but her desultory education, she well knew, unfitted her for the duty; and no sooner did she venture to propose the plan, than Mrs. Rothesay's lamentations and entreaties rendered it impracticable.

But Miss Vanbrugh's conversation now awakened a new scheme, by which in time she might be able to redeem her father's memory, and to save her mother from any sacrifice entailed by this debt. And so—though this confession may somewhat lessen the romance of her character—it was from no yearning after fame, no genius-led ambition, but from the mere desire of earning money, that Olive Rothesay first conceived the thought of becoming an artist.

Very faint it was at first—so faint that she did not even breathe it to her mother. But it stimulated her to labour incessantly at her drawing; silently to try and gain information from Miss Meliora; to haunt the painter's studio, until she had become familiar with many of its mysteries. She had crept into Vanbrugh's good graces, and he made her useful in a thousand ways.

But labouring secretly and without encouragement, Olive found her progress in drawing—she did not venture to call these humble efforts *Art*—very slow indeed. One day, when Mrs. Rothesay was gone out, Meliora came in to have a chat with her young favourite, and found poor Olive sitting by herself, quietly crying. There was lying beside her an unfinished sketch, which she hastily hid, before Miss Vanbrugh could notice what had been her occupation.

"My dear, what is the matter with you—no serious trouble, I hope?" cried the painter's little sister, who always melted into anxious compassion at the sight of anybody's tears. But Olive's only flowed the faster—she being in truth extremely miserable. For this day her mother had sorrowfully alluded to Mr. Gwynne's claim, and had begun to propose many little personal sacrifices on her own part, which grieved her affectionate daughter to the heart.

Meliora made vain efforts at comforting, and then, as a last resource, she went and fetched two little kittens and laid them on Olive's lap by way of consolation; for her own delight and solace was in her household menagerie, from which she was ever evolving great future blessings. She had always either a cat so beautiful, that when sent to Edwin Landseer, it would certainly produce a revolution in the subjects of his animal-pictures—or else a terrier so bewitching, that she intended to present it to her then girlish, dog-loving Majesty, thereby causing a shower of prosperity to fall upon the household of Vanbrugh.

Olive dried her tears, and stroked the kittens—her propensity for such pets was not her lightest merit in Meliora's eyes. Then she suffered herself to be tenderly soothed into acknowledging that she was very unhappy.

"I'll not ask you why, my dear, because Michael used to tell me I had far too much of feminine curiosity. I only meant, could I comfort you in any way?"

There was something so unobtrusive in her sympathy, that Olive felt inclined to open her heart to the gentle Meliora. "I can't tell you all," said she, "I think it would be not quite right;" and, trembling and hesitating, as if even the confession indicated something of shame, she whispered her longing for that great comfort, money of her own earning.

"You, my dear, you want money!" cried Miss Meliora, who had always looked upon her new inmate, Mrs. Rothesay, as a sort of domestic gold-mine. But she had the delicacy not to press Olive further.

"I do. I can't tell you why, but it is for a good—a holy purpose—Oh, Miss Vanbrugh, if you could but show me any way of earning money for myself! Think for me—you, who know so much more of the world than I."

—Which truth did not at all disprove the fact, that innocent little Meliora was a very child in worldly wisdom. She proved it by her next sentence, delivered oracularly after some minutes of hard cogitation. "My dear, there is but one way to gain wealth and prosperity. If you had but a taste for Art!"

Olive looked up eagerly. "Ah, that is what I have been brooding over this long time; until I was ashamed of myself and my own presumption."

"Your presumption!"

"Yes; because I have sometimes thought my drawings were not so very, very bad; and I love Art so dearly, I would give anything in the world to be an artist!"

"You draw! You long to be an artist!" It was the only thing wanted to make Olive quite perfect in Meliora's eyes. She jumped up, and embraced her young favourite with the greatest enthusiasm. "I knew this was in you. All good people must have a love for Art. And you shall have your desire, for my brother shall teach you. I must go and tell him directly."

But Olive resisted, for her poor little heart began to quake. What if her long-loved girlish dreams should be quenched at once—if Mr. Vanbrugh's stern dictum should be that she had no talent, and never could become an artist at all!

"Well, then, don't be frightened, my dear girl. Let me see your sketches. I do know a little about such things, though Michael thinks I don't," said Miss Meliora.

And Olive, her cheeks tingling with that sensitive emotion which makes many a young artist, or poet, shrink in real agony, when the crude first-fruits of his genius are brought to light—Olive stood by, while the painter's kind little sister turned over a portfolio filled with a most heterogeneous mass of productions.

Their very oddity showed the spirit of Art that dictated them. There were no pretty, well-finished, young-ladyish sketches of tumble-down cottages, and trees whose species no botanist could ever define;—or smooth chalk heads, with very tiny mouths, and very crooked noses. Olive's productions were all as rough as rough could be; few even attaining to the dignity of drawing-paper. They were done on backs of letters, or any sort of scraps: and comprised numberless pen-and-ink portraits of the one beautiful face, dearest to the daughter's heart—rude studies, in charcoal, of natural objects—outlines, from memory, of pictures she had seen, among which Meliora's eye proudly discerned several of Mr. Vanbrugh's; while, scattered here and there, were original pencil designs, ludicrously voluminous, illustrating nearly every poet, living or dead.

Michael Vanbrugh's sister was not likely to be quite ignorant of Art. Indeed, she had quietly gathered up a tolerable critical knowledge of it. She went through the portfolio, making remarks here and there. At last she closed it; but with a look so beamingly encouraging, that Olive trembled for very joy.

"Let us go to Michael, let us go to Michael," was all the happy little woman said. So they went.

Unluckily, Michael was not himself; he had been "pestered with a popinjay," in the "shape of a would-be connoisseur, and he was trying to smooth his ruffled feathers, and compose himself again to solitude and "Alcestis." His "well, what d'ye want?" was a sort of suppressed bellow, softening down a little at sight of Olive.

"Brother," cried Miss Meliora, trying to gather up her crumbling enthusiasm into one courageous point—"Michael, I have found out a new genius! Look here, and say if Olive Rothesay will not make an artist!"

"Pshaw—a woman make an artist! Ridiculous!" was the answer. "Ha! don't come near my picture. The paint's wet Get away."

And he stood, flourishing his mahl-stick and palette—looking very like a gigantic warrior guarding the shrine of Art with shield and spear.

His poor little sister, quite confounded, tried to pick up the drawings which had fallen on the floor, but he thundered out—"Let them alone!" and then politely desired Meliora to quit the room.

"Very well, brother—perhaps it will be better for you to look at the sketches another time. Come, my dear."

"Stay, I want Miss Rothesay; no one else knows how to put on that purple chlamys properly, and I must work at drapery to-day. I am lit for nothing else, thanks to that puppy who is just gone; confound him! I beg your pardon, Miss Rothesay," muttered the old painter, in a slight tone of concession, which encouraged Meliora to another gentle attack.

"Then, brother, since your day is spoiled, don't you think if you were to look"— —

"I'll look at nothing; get away with you, and leave Miss Rothesay here—the only one of you womenkind who is fit to enter an artist's studio."

Here Meliora slyly looked at Olive with an encouraging smile, and then, by no means despairing of her kind-hearted mission, she vanished.

Olive, humbled and disconsolate, prepared for her voluntary duty as Vanbrugh's lay-figure. If she had not so reverenced his genius, she certainly would not have altogether liked the man. But her hero-worship was so intense, and her womanly patience so all-forgiving, that she bore his occasional strange humours almost as meekly as Meliora herself. To-day, for the hundredth time she watched the painter's brow smooth, and his voice soften, as upon him grew the influence of his beautiful creation. "Alcestis," calmly smiling from the canvas, shed balm into his vexed soul.

But beneath the purple chlamys poor little Olive still trembled and grieved. Not until her hope was thus crushed, did she know how near her heart it had been. She thought of Michael Vanbrugh's scornful rebuke, and bitter shame possessed her. She stood—patient model!—her fingers stiffening over the rich drapery, her eyes wearily fixed on the one corner of the room, in the direction of which she was obliged to turn her head. The monotonous attitude contributed to plunge her mind into that dull despair which produces immobility—Michael Vanbrugh had never had so steady a model.

As Olive was placed, he could not see her face unless he moved. When he did so, he quite startled her out of a reverie by exclaiming—

"Exquisite! Stay just as you are. Don't change your expression. That's the very face I want for the Mother of Alcestis. A little older I must make it—but the look of passive misery, the depressed eyelids and mouth. Ah, beautiful—beautiful! Do, pray, let me have that expression again, just for three minutes!" cried the eager painter.

He accomplished his end; for Olive's features, from long habit, had had good practice in that line;—and she would willingly have fixed them into all Le Bran's Passions, if necessary for artistic purposes. Delighted at his success, Mr. Vanbrugh suddenly thought of his model, not *as* a model, but as a human being. He wondered what had produced the look which, now faithfully transferred to the canvas, completed "a bit" that had troubled him for weeks. He then thought of the drawings, and of his roughness concerning them. Usually he hated amateurs and their productions, but perhaps these might not be so bad. He would not condescend to lift them, but fidgeting with his mahl-stick, he stirred them about once or twice—accidentally as it seemed—until he had a very good notion of what they were. Then, after half-an-hour's silent painting, he thus addressed Olive.

"Miss Rothesay, what put it into your head that you wanted to be an artist?"

Olive answered nothing. She was ashamed to speak of her girlish aspirations, such as they had been; and she could not tell the other motive—the secret about Mr. Gwynne. Besides, Vanbrugh would have scorned the bare idea of her entering on the great career of Art for money! So she was silent.

He did not seem to mind it at all, but went on talking, as he sometimes did, in a sort of declamatory monologue.

"I am not such a fool as to say that genius is of either sex; but it is an acknowledged fact that no woman ever was a great painter, poet, or musician. Genius, the mighty one, scorns to exist in weak female nature; and even if it did, custom and education would certainly stunt its growth. Look here, child,"—and, to Olive's astonishment, he snatched up one of her drawings, and began lecturing thereupon—"here you have made a design of some originality. I hate your young lady copyists of landscapes and flowers, and Jullien's paltry heads. Come, let us see this epigraph, 'Laon's Vision of Cythna,'

Upon the mountain's dizzy brink she stood.

Good! Bold enough, too!"

And the painter settled himself into a long, silent examination of the sketch. Then he said —

"Well, this is tolerable; a woman standing on a rock, a man a little distance below looking at her—both drawn with decent correctness, only overlaid with drapery to hide ignorance of anatomy. A very respectable design. But, when one compares it with the poem!" And, in his deep, sonorous voice, he repeated the stanzas from the "Revolt of Islam."

> *She stood alone.*
>
> *Above, the heavens were spread; below, the flood Was murmuring in its caves; the wind had blown Her hair apart, through which her eyes and forehead shone. A cloud was hanging o'er the western mountains; Before its blue and moveless depths were flying Grey mists, poured forth from the unresting fountains Of darkness in the north—the day was dying. Sudden the sun shone forth; its beams were lying Like boiling gold on Ocean, strange to see; And on the shattered vapours which defying The power of light in vain, tossed restlessly*
>
> *In the red heaven, like wrecks in a tempestuous sea.*
>
> *It was a stream of living beams, whose bank*
>
> *On either side by the cloud's cleft was made;*
>
> *And where its chasms that flood of glory drank,*
>
> *Its waves gushed forth like fire, and, as if swayed*
>
> *By some mute tempest, rolled on her. The shade*
>
> *Of her bright image floated on the river*
>
> *Of liquid light, which then did end and fade.*
>
> *Her radiant shape upon its verge did shiver*
>
> *Aloft, her flowing hair like strings of flames did quiver.*

"There!" cried Vanbrugh, his countenance glowing with a fierce inspiration that made it grand through all its ugliness—"there! what woman could paint *that*?—or rather, what man! Alas! how feeble we are—we, the boldest followers of an Art which is divine.—Truly there was but one among us who was himself above humanity, Michael the angel!"

He gazed reverently at the majestic head of Buonarotti, which loomed out from the shadowy corner of the studio.

Olive experienced—as she often did when brought into contact with this man's enthusiasm—a delight almost like terror; for it made her shudder and tremble as though within her own poor frame was that Pythian effluence, felt, not understood—the spirit of Genius.

Vanbrugh came back, and continued his painting, talking all the while.

"I said that it was impossible for a woman to become an artist—I mean a *great* artist. Have you ever thought what that term implies? Not only a painter, but a poet; a man of learning, of reading, of observation. A gentleman—we artists have been the friends of kings. A man of stainless virtue, or how can he reach the pure ideal? A man of iron will, indomitable daring, and passions strong, yet kept always leashed in his hand. Last and greatest, a man who, feeling within him the divine spirit, with his whole soul worships God!"

Vanbrugh lifted off his velvet cap and reverently bared his head; then he continued:

"This is what an artist should *be*, by nature. I have not spoken of what he has to make himself. Years of study incessant lie before him; no life of a carpet-knight, no easy play-work of scraping colours on canvas. Why, these hands of mine have wielded not only the pencil but the scalpel; these eyes have rested on scenes of horror, misery—crime, I glory in it; for it was all for Art. At times I have almost felt like Parrhasius of old, who exulted in his captive's dying throes, since upon them his hand of genius would confer immortality. But I beg your pardon—you are but a woman—a mere girl," added Vanbrugh, seeing Olive shudder. Yet he had not been unmindful of the ardent enthusiasm which had dilated her whole frame while listening. It touched him like the memory of his own youth. Some likeness, too, there seemed between himself and this young creature to whom nature had been so niggardly. She might also be one of those who, shut out from human ties, are the more free to work the glorious work of genius.

After a few minutes of thought, Michael again burst forth.

"They who embrace Art must embrace her with heart and soul, as their one only bride. And she will be a loving bride to them—she will stand in the place of all other joy. Is it not triumph for him to whom fate has denied personal beauty, that his hand—his flesh and blood hand—has power ta create it? What cares he for worldly splendour, when in dreams he can summon up a fairy-land so gorgeous that in limning it even his own rainbow-dyed pencil fails? What need has he for home, to whom the wide world is full of treasures of study—for which life itself is too short? And what to him are earthly and domestic ties? For friendship, he exchanges the world's worship, which *may* be his in life, *must* be, after death. For love"— —

Here the old artist paused a moment, and there was something heavenly in the melody of his voice as he continued—

"For love—frail human love—the poison-flower of youth, which only lasts an hour, he has his own divine ideal It flits continually before him, sometimes all but clasped; it inspires his manhood with purity, and pours celestial passion into his age. His heart, though dead to all human ties, is not cold, but burning. For he worships the ideal of beauty, he loves the ideal of love."

Olive listened, her mind reeling before these impetuous words.—One moment she looked at Vanbrugh where he stood, his age transfigured into youth, his ugliness into majesty, by the radiance of the immortal fire that dwelt within him. Then she dropped almost at his feet crying.

"I, too, am one of these outcasts; give me then this inner life which atones for all! Friend, counsel me—master, teach me! Woman as I am, I will dare all things—endure all things. Let me be an artist."

CHAPTER XXI

Olive Rothesay's desire,

Like all strongest hopes,
By its own energy fulfilled itself.

She became an artist—not in a week, a month, a year—Art exacts of its votaries no less service than a lifetime. But in her girl's soul the right chord had been touched, which began to vibrate unto noble music—the true seed had been sown, which day by day grew into a goodly plant.

Vanbrugh had said truly, that genius is of no sex; and he had said likewise truly, that no woman can be an artist—that is, a great artist. The hierarchies of the soul's dominion belong only to man, and it is right they should. He it was whom God created first, let him take the preeminence. But among those stars of lesser glory, which are given to lighten the nations, among sweet-voiced poets, earnest prose writers, who, by the lofty truth that lies hid beneath legend and parable, purify the world, graceful painters and beautiful musicians, each brightening their generation—among these, let woman shine!

But her sphere is, and ever must be, bounded; because, however fine her genius may be, it always dwells in a woman's breast. Nature, which gave to man the dominion of the intellect, gave to her that of the heart and affections. These bind her with everlasting links from which she cannot free herself,—nay, she would not if she could. Herein man has the advantage. He, strong in his might of intellect, can make it his all in all, his life's sole aim and reward. A Brutus, for that ambition which is misnamed patriotism, can trample on all human ties. A Michael Angelo can stand alone with his work, and so go sternly down unto a desolate old age. But there scarcely ever lived the woman who would not rather sit meekly by her own hearth, with her husband at her side, and her children at her knee, than be the crowned Corinne of the Capitol.

Thus woman, seeking to strive with man, is made feebler by the very spirit of love which in her own sphere is her chiefest strength. But sometimes chance or circumstance or wrong, sealing up her woman's nature, converts her into a self-dependent human soul. Instead of life's sweetnesses, she has before her life's greatnesses. The struggle passed, her genius may lift itself upward, expand, and grow; though never to the stature of man's. Then, even while she walks with scarce-healed feet over the world's rough pathway, heaven's glory may rest upon her upturned brow, and she may become a light unto her generation.

Such a destiny lay open before Olive Rothesay.

She welcomed it as one who has girded himself with steadfast but mournful patience unto a long and weary journey, welcomes the faint ray that promises to guide him through the desolation. No more she uttered, as was her custom in melancholy moods, the bitter complaint, "Why was I born?" but she said to herself, "I will live so as to leave the world better when I die. Then I shall not have lived in vain."

It was long before Michael Vanbrugh could thoroughly reconcile himself to the idea of a girl's becoming a painter. But by degrees he learned to view his young pupil *as* a pupil, and never thought of her sex at all. Under his guidance, Olive passed from the mere prettiness of most woman-painters to the grandeur of true Art. Strengthened by her almost masculine power of mind, she learned to comprehend and to reverence the mighty masters whom Vanbrugh loved. He led her to those heights and depths which are rarely opened to a woman's ken. And she, following, applied herself to the most abstruse of Art-studies. Still, as he had said, there were bounds that she could not pass; but as far as in her lay, she sought to lift herself above her sex's weakness and want of perseverance; and by labour from which most women would have shrunk, to make herself worthy of being ranked among those painters who are "not for an age, but for all time."

That personal deformity which she thought excluded her from a woman's natural destiny, gave her freedom in her own. Brought into contact with the world, she scarcely felt like a young and timid girl, but as a being— isolated, yet strong in her isolation; who mingles, and must mingle among men, not as a woman, but as one who, like themselves, pursues her own calling, has her own aim; and can therefore step aside for no vain fear, nor sink beneath any foolish shame. And wherever she went, her own perfect innocence wrapped her round as with a shield.

Still, little quiet Olive could do many things with an independence that would have been impossible to a girl lively and beautiful Oftentimes Mrs. Rothesay trembled and murmured at days of solitary study in the British Museum, and in various picture-galleries; long lonely walks, sometimes in winter-time extending far into the dusk of evening. But Olive always answered, with a pensive smile,

"Nay, mother; I am quite safe everywhere. Remember, I am not like other girls. Who would notice *me*?"

But she always accompanied any painful allusion of this kind by saying how happy she was in being so free, and how fortunate it seemed that there could be nothing to hinder her from following her heart's desire. She was growing as great an optimist as Miss Meliora herself, who—cheerful little soul—was in the seventh heaven of delight whenever she heard her brother acknowledge Olive's progress.

"And don't you see, my dear Miss Rothesay," she said sometimes, "that everything always turns out for the best; and that if you had not been so unhappy, and I had not come in and found you crying, you might have gone on pining in secret, instead of growing up to be an artist."

Olive assented, and confessed it was rather strange that out of her chiefest trouble should have arisen her chiefest joy.

"It almost seems," said she to her mother, laughing, "as if that hard-hearted Mr. Harold Gwynne had held the threads of my destiny, and helped to make me an artist."

"Don't let us talk about Mr. Gwynne; it is a disagreeable subject, my child," was Mrs. Rothesay's answer.

Olive did not talk about him, but she thought the more. And—though had he known it, the pelf-despising Mr. Vanbrugh would never have forgiven such a desecration of Art—it was not her lightest spur in the attainment of excellence, to feel that as soon as her pictures were good enough to sell, she might earn money enough to discharge the claim of this harsh creditor, whose very name sent a pang to her heart.

Day by day, as her mind strengthened and her genius developed, Olive's existence seemed to brighten. Her domestic life was full of many dear ties, the chief of which was that devotion, less a sentiment than a passion, which she felt for her mother. Her intellectual fife grew more intense; while she felt the stay and solace of having a fixed pursuit to occupy her whole future. Also, it was good for her to live with the enthusiastic painter and his meek contented little sister; for she learnt thereby, that life might pass not merely in endurance, but in peace, without either of those blessings which in her early romance she deemed the chief of all—beauty and love. There was a greatness and happiness beyond them both.

The lesson was impressed more deeply by a little incident that chanced about this time.

Miss Vanbrugh sometimes took Olive with her on those little errands of charity which were not unfrequent with the gentle Meliora.

"I wish you would come with me to-day," she said once, "because, to tell the truth, I hardly like to go alone."

"Indeed!" said Olive, smiling, for the little old maid was as brave as a lion among these gloomiest of all gloomy lanes, familiar to her even in dark nights, and this was a sunny spring morning.

"I am not going to see an ordinary poor person, but that Quadroon woman—Mrs. Manners, who is one of my brother's models sometimes—you know her?"

"Scarcely; but I have seen her pass through the hall. Oh, she was a grand, beautiful woman, like an Eastern queen. You remember it was she from whom Mr. Vanbrugh painted the 'Cleopatra.' What an eye she had, and what a glorious mouth!" cried Olive, waxing enthusiastic.

"Poor thing! Her beauty is sadly wasting now," said Meliora. "She seems to be slowly dying, and I shouldn't wonder if it were of sheer starvation; those models earn so little. Yesterday she fainted as she stood—Michael is so thoughtless. He had to call me to give her some wine, and then we sent the maid home with her. She lives in a poor place, Hannah says, but quite decent and respectable. I shall surely go and see the poor creature; but she looks such a desperate sort of woman, her eyes glare quite ferociously sometimes. She might be angry—so I had rather not be alone, if you will come, Miss Rothesay?"

Olive consented at once; there was in her a certain romance which, putting all sympathy aside, quite gloried in such an adventure.

They walked for a mile or two until they reached a miserable street by the river-side; but Miss Meliora had forgotten the number. They must have returned, their quest unsatisfied, had not Olive seen a little girl leaning out of an upper window,—her ragged elbows on the sill, her elf-like black eyes watching the boats up and down the Thames.

"I know that child," Olive said; "it is the poor woman's. She left it in the hall one day at Woodford Cottage, and I noticed it from its black eyes and fair hair. I remember, too—for I asked—its singular and very pretty name, *Christal*."

Talking thus, they mounted the rickety staircase, and inquired for Mrs. Manners. The door of the room was flung open from without, with a noise that would have broken any torpor less deep than that into which its wretched occupant had fallen.

"*Ma mie* is asleep; don't wake her or she'll scold," said Christal jumping down from the window, and interposing between Miss Vanbrugh and the woman who was called Mrs. Manners.

She was indeed a very beautiful woman, though her beauty was on a grand scale. She had flung herself, half-dressed, upon what seemed a heap of straw, with a blanket thrown over. As she lay there, sleeping heavily, her arm tossed above her head, the large but perfect proportions of her form reminded Olive of the reclining figure in the group of the "Three Fates."

But there was in the prematurely old and wasted face something that told of a wrecked life. Olive, prone to romance-weaving, wondered whether nature had in a mere freak invested an ordinary low-born woman with the form of the ancient queens of the world, or whether within that grand body lay ruined an equally grand soul.

Miss Meliora did not think about anything of the sort; but merely that her brother's dinner-hour was drawing near, and that if poor Mrs. Manners did not wake, they must go back without speaking to her.

But she did wake soon—and the paroxysm of anger which seized her on discovering that she had intruding guests, caused Olive to retire almost to the staircase. But brave little Miss Vanbrugh did not so easily give up her charitable purpose.

"Indeed, my good woman, I only meant to offer you sympathy, or any help you might need in your illness."

The woman refused both. "I tell you we want for nothing."

"*Ma mie*, I am so hungry!" said little Christal, in a tone between complaint and effrontery. "I will have something to eat."

"You should not speak so rudely to your mother, little girl," interposed Miss Meliora.

"My mother! No, indeed; she is only *ma mie*. My mother was a rich lady, and my father a noble gentleman."

"Hear her, Heaven! oh, hear her!" groaned the woman on the floor.

"But I love *ma mie* very much—that's when she's kind to me," said Christal; "and as for my own father and mother, who cares for them, for, as *ma mie* says, they were drowned together in the deep sea, years ago."

"Ay, ay," was the muttered answer, as Mrs. Manners clutched the child—a little, thin-limbed, cunning-eyed girl, of eight or ten years old—

and pressed her to her breast, with a strain more like the gripe of a lioness than a tender woman's clasp.

Then she fell back exhausted, and took no more notice of anybody. Meliora forgot Mr. Vanbrugh's dinner, and all things else, in making a few charitable arrangements, which resulted in a comfortable tea for little Christal and *"ma mie."*

Sleep had again overpowered the sick woman, who appeared to be slowly dying of that anomalous disease called decline, in which the mind is the chief agent of the body's decay. Meanwhile, Miss Vanbrugh talked in an undertone to little Christal, who, her hunger satisfied, stood, finger in mouth, watching the two ladies with her fierce black eyes—the very image of a half-tamed gipsy. Indeed, Miss Meliora seemed rather uneasy, and desirous to learn more of her companions, for she questioned the child closely.

"And is the person you call *ma mie* any relation to you?"

"The neighbours say she is my aunt, from the likeness. I don't know."

"And her name is Mrs. Manners—a widow, no doubt; for I remember she was in very respectable mourning when she first came to Woodford Cottage."

"Poor young creature!" she continued, sitting down beside the object of her compassion, who was, or seemed, asleep. "How hard to loose her husband so soon! and I dare say she has gone through great poverty—sold one thing after another to keep her alive. Why, I declare," added the simple and unworldly Meliora, who could make a story to fit anything, "poor soul! she has even been forced to part with her wedding-ring."

"I never had one—I scorned it!" cried the woman, leaping up with a violence that quite confounded the painter's sister. "Do you come to insult me, you smooth-tongued English lady? Ah, you shrink away. What do you know about me?"

"I don't know anything about you, indeed," said Meliora, creeping to the door; while Olive, who could not understand the cause of half she witnessed, stood simply looking on in wonder—almost in admiration,—for there was a strange beauty, like that of a Pythoness, in the woman's attitude and mien.

"You know nothing of me? Then you shall know. I come from a country where are thousands of young girls, whose mixed blood is too pure for slavery, too tainted for freedom. Lovely, accomplished, brought up delicately, they yet have no higher future than to be the white man's passing toy—cherished, wearied of, and spurned."

She paused, and Miss Vanbrugh, astonished at this sudden outburst, in language so vehement, and so above her apparent rank, had not a word to say. The woman continued:

"I but fulfilled my destiny. How could such as I hope to bear an honest man's honest name? So, when my fate came upon me, I cast all shame to the winds, and lived out my life. I followed my lover across the seas; I clung to him, faithful in my degradation; and when his child slept on my bosom, I looked at it, and was almost happy. Now what think you of me, virtuous English ladies?" cried the outcast, as she tossed back her cloud of dark crisped hair, and fixed her eyes sternly, yet mockingly, upon her visitors.

Poor Miss Vanbrugh was conscious of but one thing, that this scene was most unfit for a young girl; and that if she once could get Olive away, all future visits to the miserable woman should be paid by herself alone.

"I will see you another day, Mrs. Manners, but we cannot really stay now. Come, my dear Miss Rothesay."

And she and her charge quitted the room. Apparently, their precipitate departure still further irritated the poor creature they had come to succour; for as they descended the stairs, they heard her repeatedly shriek out Olive's surname, in tones so wild, that whether it was meant for rage or entreaty they could not tell.

Olive wanted to return.

"No, my dear, she would only insult you. Besides, I will *go* myself tomorrow. Poor wretch! she is plainly near her end. We must be merciful to the dying."

Olive walked home thoughtfully, not speaking much. When they passed out of the squalid, noisy streets, into the quiet lane that led to Woodford Cottage, she had never felt so keenly the blessing of a pure and peaceful home. She mounted to the pretty bedchamber which she and her mother occupied, and stood at the open window, drinking in the fresh odour of the bursting leaves. Scarcely a breath stirred the soft spring evening—the sky was like one calm blue lake, and therein floated, close to the western verge, "the new moon's silver boat."

She remembered how it had been one of her childish superstitions always "to wish at the new moon." How often, her desire seeming perversely to lift itself towards things unattainable, had she framed one sole wish that she might be beautiful and beloved!

Beautiful and beloved! She thought of the poor creature whose fierce words yet rang in her ear. Beautiful and beloved! *She* had been both, and what was she now?

And Olive rejoiced that her own childish longings had passed into the better wisdom of subdued and patient womanhood. Had she now a wish, it was for that pure heart and lowly mind which are more precious than beauty; for that serene peace of virtue, which is more to be desired than love.

Now her fate seemed plain before her—within her home she saw the vista of a life of filial devotion blest in

"*A constant stream of love that knew no fall.*"

As she looked forth into the world without, there rose the hope of her Art, under shadow of which the lonely woman might go down to the grave not unhonoured in her day. Remembering all this, Olive murmured no longer at her destiny. She thanked God, for she felt that she was not unhappy.

CHAPTER XXII

Perhaps, ere following Olive's fortunes, it may be as well to set the reader's mind at rest concerning the incident narrated in the preceding chapter. It turned out the olden tale of passion, misery, and death. No more could be made of it, even by the imaginative Miss Meliora.

A few words will comprise all that she discovered. Returning faithfully next day, the kind little woman found that the object of her charity needed it no more. In the night, suddenly, it was thought, the spirit had departed. There was no friend to arrange anything; so Miss Vanbrugh undertook it all. Her own unobtrusive benevolence prevented a pauper funeral. But in examining the few relics of the deceased, she was surprised to find papers which clearly explained the fact, that some years before there had been placed in a London bank, to the credit of Celia Manners, a sum sufficient to produce a moderate annuity. The woman had rejected it, and starved.

But she had not died without leaving a written injunction, that it should be claimed by the child Christal, since it was "her right." This was accomplished, to the great satisfaction of Miss Vanbrugh and of the honest banker, who knew that the man—what sort of man he had quite forgotten—who deposited the money, had enjoined that it should be paid whenever claimed by Celia or by Christal Manners.

Christal Manners was then the child's name. Miss Vanbrugh might have thought that this discovery implied the heritage of shame, but for the little girl's obstinate persistence in the tale respecting her unknown father and mother, who were "a noble gentleman and grand lady," and had both been drowned at sea. The circumstance was by no means improbable, and it had evidently been strongly impressed on Christal by the woman she called *ma mie*. Whatever relationship there was between them, it could not be the maternal one. Miss Vanbrugh could not believe in the possibility of a mother thus voluntarily renouncing her own child.

Miss Meliora put Christal to board with an old servant of hers for a few weeks. But there came such reports of the child's daring and unruly temper, that, quaking under her responsibility, she decided to send her *protégée* away to school The only place she could think of was an old-fashioned *pension* in Paris, where, during her brother's studies there, her own slender education had been acquired. Thither the little stranger was despatched, by means of a succession of contrivances which almost drove the simple Meliora crazy. For—lest her little adventure of benevolence should come to Michael's ears—she dared to take no one into her confidence, not even the Rothesays. Madame Blandin, the mistress of the *pension*, was furnished with no explanations; indeed there were none to give. The orphan appeared there under the character she so steadily sustained, as Miss Christal Manners, the child of illustrious parents lost at sea; and so she vanished altogether from the atmosphere of Woodford Cottage.

Olive Rothesay was now straining every nerve towards the completion of her first exhibited picture—a momentous crisis in every young artist's life. It was March: always a pleasant month in this mild, sheltered, neighbourhood, where she had made her home. There, of all the regions about London, the leaves come earliest, the larks soonest begin to sing, and the first soft spring breezes blow. But nothing could allure Olive from that corner of their large drawing-room which she had made her studio, and where she sat painting from early morning until daylight was spent. The artist herself formed no unpleasing picture—at least so her fond mother often thought—as Olive stood before her easel, the light from the half-closed-up window slanting downwards on her long curls, of that rare pale gold, the delight of the ancient painters, and now the especial admiration of Michael Vanbrugh To please her master, Olive, though now a woman grown, wore her hair still in childish fashion, falling in most artistic confusion over her neck and shoulders. It seemed that nature had bestowed on her this great beauty, in order to veil that defect which, though made far less apparent by her maturer growth, and a certain art in dress, could never be removed. Still there was an inexpressible charm in her purely-outlined features to which the complexion always accompanying pale-gold hair imparted such a delicate, spiritual colouring. Oftentimes her mother sat and looked at her, thinking she beheld the very likeness of the angel in her dream.

March was nearly passed. Olive's anxiety that the picture should be finished, and worthily finished, amounted almost to torture. At last, when there was but one week left—a week whose every hour of daylight must be spent in work, the hope and fear were at once terminated by her mother's sudden illness. Passing it was, and not dangerous; but to Olive's picture it brought a fatal interruption.

The tender mother more than once begged her to neglect everything but the picture. But Olive refused. Yet it cost her somewhat—ay, more than Mrs. Rothesay could understand, to give up a year's hopes. She felt this the more when came the Monday and Tuesday for sending in pictures to the Academy.

Heavily these days passed, for there was not now the attendance on the invalid to occupy Olive's mind. She was called hither and thither all over the house; since on these two days, for the only time in the year, there was at Woodford Cottage a *levée* of artists, patrons, and connoisseurs. Miss Rothesay was needed everywhere; first in the painting-room, to assist in arranging its various treasures, her taste and tact assisting Mr. Vanbrugh's artistic skill. For the thousandth time she helped to move the easel that sustained the small purchaseable picture with which Michael this year condescended to favour the Academy; and admired, to the painter's heart's content, the beloved and long-to-be-unsold "Alcestis," which extended in solitary grandeur over one whole side of the studio. Then she flitted to Miss Vanbrugh's room, to help her to dress for this important occasion. Never was there such a proud, happy little woman as Meliora Vanbrugh on the first Monday and Tuesday in April, when at least a dozen carriages usually rolled down the muddy lane, and the great surly dog, kennelled under the mulberry-tree, was never silent "from morn till dewy eve." All, thought the delighted Meliora, was an ovation to her brother. Each year she fully expected that these visiting patrons would buy up every work of Art in the studio, to say nothing of those adorning the hall—the cartoons and frescoes of Michael's long-past youth. And each year, when the carriages rolled away, and the visitants admiration remained nothing *but* admiration, she consoled herself with the thought that Michael Vanbrugh was "a man before his age," but that his time for appreciation would surely come. So she hoped on till the next April. Happy Meliora!

"Yes, you do seem happy, Miss Vanbrugh," said Olive, when she had coaxed the stiff grizzled hair under a neat cap of her own skilful manufacturing; and the painter's little sister was about to mount guard in the bay-window of the parlour, from whence she could see the guests walk down the garden, and be also ready to mark the expression of their faces as they came out of the studio.

"Happy! to be sure I am! Everybody must confess that this last is the best picture Michael ever painted"—(his sister had made the same observation every April for twenty years). "But, my dear Miss Rothesay, how wrong I am to talk so cheerfully to you, when *your* picture is not finished. Never mind, love. You have been a good, attentive daughter, and it will end all for the best."

Olive smiled faintly, and said she knew it would.

"Perhaps," continued Meliora, as a new and consolatory idea struck her, "perhaps even if you had sent in the picture, it might have been returned, or put in the octagon room, or among the miniatures, where nobody could see it; and that would have been much worse, would it not?"

"I suppose so; and, indeed, I will be quite patient and content."

Patient she was, but not content. It was scarcely possible. Nevertheless she quitted Miss Vanbrugh with smiles; and when she again sought her mother's chamber, it was with smiles too—or, at least, with that soft sweetness which was in Olive like a smile. When she had left Mrs. Rothesay to take her afternoon's sleep, she thought what she was to do to pass away the hours that, in spite of herself, dragged very wearily. This day was so different to what she had hoped. No eager delighted "last touches" to her beloved picture; no exhibiting it in its best light, in all the glory of the frame. It lay neglected below—she could not bear to look at it. The day was clear and bright—just the sort of day for painting; but Olive felt that the very sight of the poor picture would be more than she could bear. She did not go near it, but put on her bonnet and walked out.

"Courage! hope!" sang the larks to her, high up above the green lanes; but her heart was too sad to hear them. A year, a whole year, lost!—a whole year to wait for the next hope! And a year seems so long when one has scarcely counted twenty. Afterwards, how fast it flies!

"Perhaps," she said, her thoughts taking their colour from the general weariness of her spirits, "perhaps Miss Vanbrugh was right, and I might have had the picture returned. It cannot be very good, or it would not have taken such long and constant labour. Genius, they say, never toils—all comes by inspiration. It may be that I have no genius; well, then, where is the use of my labouring to excel!—indeed, where is the use of my living at all?"

"Alas! how little is known of the struggles of young, half-formed genius! struggles not only with the world, but with itself; a hopeless, miserable bearing-down; a sense of utter unworthiness and self-contempt. At times, when the inner life, the soul's lamp, burns dimly, there rises the piteous moan, 'Fool, fool! why strivest thou in vain? Thou hast deceived thyself: thou art no better than any brainless ass that plods through life.' And then the world grows so dull, and one's life seems so worthless, that one would fain blot it out at once."

Olive walked beneath this bitter cloud. She said to herself that if her picture had been a work of genius, it would have been finished long ere the time; and that if she were destined to be an artist, there would not have come this cross. No! all fates were against her. She must be patient and submit, but she felt as if she should never have courage to paint again. And now, when her work had become the chief aim and joy of her life, how hard this seemed!

She came home, drearily enough; for the sunny day had changed to rain, and she was thoroughly wet. But even this was, as Meliora would have expressed it, "for the best," since it made her feel the sweetness of having a tender mother to take off her dripping garments, and smooth her hair, and make her sit down before the bright fire. And then Olive laid her head in her mother's lap, and thought how wrong—nay, wicked—she had been. She was thinking thus, even with a few quiet tears, when Miss Meliora burst, like a stream of sunshine, into the room.

"Good news—good news!"

"What? Mr. Vanbrugh has sold his picture, as you hoped to Mr.— —."

"No, not yet!" and the least possible shadow troubled the sister's face: "but perhaps he will. And, meanwhile, what think you? Something has happened quite as good; at least for somebody else. Guess!"

"Indeed, I cannot!"

"He has sold *yours!*"

Olive's face flushed, grew white, and then she welcomed this first success, as many another young aspirant to fame has done, by bursting into tears. So did the easily-touched Mrs. Rothesay, and so did the kind Miss Meliora, from pure sympathy. Never was good fortune hailed in a more lachrymose fashion.

But soon Miss Vanbrugh, resuming her smiles, explained how she had placed Olive's nearly-finished picture in her brother's studio, where all the visitors had admired it; and one, a good friend to Art, and to young, struggling artists, had bought it.

"My brother managed all, even to the payment. The full price you will have when you have completed the picture. And, meanwhile, look here!"

She had filled one hand with golden guineas, and now poured a Danäe-stream into Olive's lap. Then, laughing and skipping about like a child, she vanished—the beneficent little fairy!—as swiftly as Cinderella's godmother.

Olive sat mute, her eyes fixed on the "bits of shining gold," which seemed to look different to all other pieces of gold that she had ever seen. She touched them, as if half-fearing they would melt away, or, like elfin money, change into withered leaves. Then, brightly smiling, she took them up, one by one and told them into her mother's lap.

"Take them, darling—my first earnings; and kiss me: kiss your happy little girl!"

How sweet was that moment—worth whole years of after-fame! Olive Rothesay might live to bathe in the sunshine of renown, to hear behind her the murmur of a world's praise, but she never could know again the bliss of laying at her mother's feet the first-fruits of her genius, and winning, as its first and best reward, her mother's proud and happy kiss.

"You will be quite rich now, my child."

"*We* will be," said Olive, softly.

"And to think that such a great connoisseur as Mr.——— should choose my Olive's picture. Ah! she will be a celebrated woman some time: I always thought she would."

"*I will!*" said the firm voice in Olive's heart, as, roused to enthusiasm by this sweet first success, she felt stirring within her the spirit whose pulses she could not mistake—woman, nay, girl as she was. Thinking on her future, the future that, with Heaven's blessing, she would nobly work out, her eye dilated and her breast heaved. And then on that wildly-heaving bosom strayed a soft, warm hand: a tender voice whispered, "My child!"

And Olive, flinging her arms round her mother's neck, hid her face there, and was a simple, trembling child once more.

It was a very happy evening for them both, almost the happiest in their lives. The mother formed a score of plans of expending this newly-won wealth, always to the winner's benefit solely; but Olive began to look grave, and at last said, timidly:

"Mamma, indeed I want for nothing; and for this money, let us spend it in a way that will make us both most content. O mother! I can know no rest until we have paid Mr. Gwynne."

The mother sighed.

"Well, love, as you will. It is yours, you know; only, a little it pains me that my child's precious earnings should go to pay that cruel debt."

"But not that they should go to redeem my father's honour?" said Olive, still gently. She had her will.

When her picture was finished, and its price received, Olive, with a joyful heart, enclosed the sum to their long-silent creditor.

"His name does not look quite so fearful now," she said, smiling, when she was addressing the letter. "I can positively write it without trembling, and perhaps I may not have to write it many times. If I grow very rich, mamma, we shall soon pay off this debt, and then we shall never hear any more of Harold Gwynne. Oh! how happy that would be!"

The letter went, and an answer arrived in due form, not to Mrs., but to Miss Rothesay:

> "Madam,—I thank you for your letter, and have pleasure in cancelling a portion of my claim. I would fain cancel the whole of it, but I must not sacrifice my own household to that of strangers.
>
> "Allow me to express my deep respect for a child so honourably jealous over a father's memory, and to subscribe myself,
>
> "Your very obedient,
>
> "Harold Gwynne."

"He is not so stony-hearted after all, mamma," said Olive, smiling. "Shall I put this letter with the other; we had better keep them both?"

"Certainly, my dear."

"Look, the envelope is edged and sealed with black."

"Is it? Oh, perhaps he has lost his mother. I think I once heard your poor papa say he knew her once. She must be now an old woman; still her loss has probably been a grief to her son."

"Most likely," said Olive, hastily. She never could bear to hear of any one's mother dying; it made her feel compassionately even towards Mr. Gwynne; and then she quickly changed the subject.

The two letters were put by in her desk; and thus, for a season at least, the Harbury correspondence closed.

CHAPTER XXIII

Seven summers more the grand old mulberry-tree at Woodford Cottage has borne leaf, flower, and fruit; the old dog that used to lie snarling under its branches, lies there still, but snarls no more. Between him and the upper air are two feet of earth, together with an elegant canine tombstone, on which Miss Rothesay, by the entreaty of the disconsolate Meliora, has modelled in clay a very good likeness of the departed.

Snap is the only individual who has passed away at Woodford Cottage; in all things else there has been an increase, not a decrease. The peaches and nectarines cover two walls instead of one, and the clematis has mounted in white virgin beauty even to the roof. Altogether, the garden is changed for the better. Trim it is not, and never would be—thanks to Olive, who, a true lover of the picturesque, hated trim gardens,—but its luxuriance is that of flowers, not weeds; and luxuriant it is, so that every day you might pull for a friend that pleasantest of all pleasant gifts, a nosegay; yea, and afterwards find, that, like charity, the more you gave the richer was your store.

Enter from the garden into the drawing-room, and you will perceive a change, too. Its dreariness has been softened by many a graceful adjunct of comfort and luxury. Half of it, by means of a crimson screen, is transformed into a painting-room. Olive would have it so; for several reasons, the chief of which was, that whether the young paintress was working or not, Mrs. Rothesay might never be out of the sound of her daughter's voice. For, alas! this same sweet love-toned voice was all the mother now knew of Olive!

Gradually there had come over Mrs. Rothesay the misfortune which she feared. She was now blind. Relating this, it may seem though we were about to picture a scene of grief and desolation: but not so. A misfortune that steals on year by year, slowly, inevitably, often comes with so light a footstep that we scarcely hear it. In this manner had come Mrs. Rothesay's blindness. Her sight faded so gradually, that its deprivation caused no despondency; and the more helpless she grew, the closer she was clasped by those supporting arms of filial love, which softened all pain, supplied all need, and were to her instead of strength, youth, eyesight!

One only bitterness did she know—that she could not see Olive's pictures. Not that she understood Art at all; but everything that Olive did *must* be beautiful. She missed nought else, not even her daughter's face, for she saw it continually in her heart Perhaps in the grey shadow of a form, which she said her eyes could still trace in the dim haze, she pictured the likeness of an Olive ten times fairer than the real one: an Olive whose cheek never grew pale with toil, whose brow was never crossed by that cloud of heart-weariness which all who labour in an intellectual pursuit must know at times. If so, the mother was saved from many of the pangs which visit those who see their beloved ones staggering under a burden which they themselves have no power either to bear or to take away.

And so, in spite of this affliction, the mother and daughter were happy, even quite cheerful sometimes. For cheerfulness, originally foreign to Olive's nature, had sprung up there—one of those heart-flowers which Love, passing by, sows according as they are needed, until they bloom as though indigenous to the soil. To hear Miss Rothesay laugh, as she was laughing just now, you would have thought she was the merriest creature in the world, and had been so all her life. Moreover, from this blithe laugh, as well as from her happy face, you might have taken her for a young maiden of nineteen, instead of a woman of six-and-twenty, which she really was. But with some, after youth's first sufferings are passed, life's dial seems to run backward.

"My child, how very merry you are, you and Miss Vanbrugh!" said Mrs. Rothesay, from her corner.

"Well, mamma, and how can we help it,—talking of my 'Charity,' and the lady who bought it. Would you believe, darling, she told Miss Vanbrugh that she did so because the background was like a view in their park, and the two little children resembled the two young Masters Fludyer—fortunate likeness for me!"

"Ay," said Miss Meliora, "only my brother would say you were very wrong to sell your picture to such stupid people, who know nothing about Art."

"Perhaps I was; but," she added whisperingly, "you know I have not sold my Academy picture yet, and mamma *must* go into the country this autumn."

"Mrs. Fludyer is a very nice chatty woman," observed the mother; "and she talked of her beautiful country-seat at Farnwood Hall. I think it would do me good to go there, Olive."

"Well, you know she asked you, dear mamma."

"Yes; but only for courtesy. She would scarcely be troubled with a guest so helpless as I," said Mrs. Rothesay, half sighing.

In a moment Olive was by her side, talking away, at first softly, and then luring her on to smiles with a merry tale,—how Mr. Fludyer, when the picture came home, wanted to have the three elder Fludyers painted in a row behind "Charity," that thus the allegorical picture might make a complete family group. "He also sent to know if I couldn't paint his horse 'Beauty,' and one or two greyhounds also, in the same picture. What a comical idea of Art this country squire must have!"

"My dear, every one is not so clever as you," said the mother. "I like Mrs. Fludyer very much, because, whenever she came to Woodford Cottage about the picture, she used to talk to me so kindly."

"And she has asked after you in all her letters since she went home. So she must be a good creature: and I, too, will like her very much indeed, because she likes my sweet mamma."

The determination was soon called into exercise; for the next half-hour, to the surprise of all parties, Mrs. Fludyer appeared.

She assigned no reason for her visit, except that being again in town, she had chosen to drive down to Woodford Cottage. She talked for half-an-hour in her mild, limpid way; and then, when the arrival of one of Olive's models broke the quiet leisure of the painting-room, she rose.

"Nay, Miss Rothesay, do not quit your easel; Miss Van-brugh will accompany me through the garden, and besides, I wish to speak to her about her clematis. We cannot make them grow in S—shire; the Hall is perhaps too cold and bleak."

"Ah, how I love a clear bracing air!" said Mrs. Rothesay, with the restlessness peculiar to all invalids—and she had been a greater invalid than usual this summer.

"Then you must come down, as I said—you and Miss Rothesay—to S—shire; our part of the country is very beautiful. I should be most happy to see you at Farnwood."

She urged the invitation with an easy grace, even cordiality, which charmed Mrs. Rothesay, to whom it brought back the faint reflex of her olden life—the life at Merivale Hall.

"I should like to go, Olive," she said, appealingly. "I feel dull, and want a change."

"You shall have a change, darling," was the soothing but evasive answer. For Olive had a tincture of the old Rothesay pride, and had formed a somewhat disagreeable idea of the position the struggling artist and her blind mother would fill as charity-guests at Farnwood Hall. So, after a little conversation with Mrs. Fludyer, she contrived that the first plan should melt into one more feasible. There was a pretty cottage, the squire's lady said, on the Farnwood estate; Miss Fludyer's daily governess had lived there; it was all fitted up. What if Miss Rothesay would bring her mother there for the summer months? It would be pleasant for all parties.

And so, very quickly, the thing was decided—decided as suddenly and unexpectedly as things are, when it seems as though not human will, but destiny held the balance.

Mrs. Fludyer seemed really pleased and interested; she talked to Miss Meliora less about her clematis than about her two inmates—a subject equally grateful to the painter's sister.

"There is something quite charming about Miss Rothesay—the air and manner of one who has always moved in good society. Do you know who she was? I should apologise for the question, but that a friend of mine, looking at her picture, was struck by the name, and desired me to inquire."

Meliora explained that she believed Olive's family was Scottish, and that her father was a Captain Angus Rothesay.

"Captain Angus Rothesay! I think that was the name mentioned by my friend."

"Shall I call Olive? Perhaps she knows your friend," observed Meliora.

"Oh no! Mrs.—that is, the lady I allude to, said they were entire strangers, and it was needless to mention her name. Do not trouble Miss Rothesay with my idle inquiry. Many thanks for the clematis; and good morning, my dear Miss Vanbrugh."

She ascended her carriage with the easy, smiling grace of one born to fortune, marrying fortune, and dwelling hand-in-hand with fortune all her life. Miss Meliora gazed in intense admiration after her departing wheels, and forthwith retired to plan out of the few words she had let fall a glorious future for her dear Miss Rothesay. There was certainly some unknown wealthy relative who would probably appear next week, and carry off Olive and her mother to affluence—in a carriage as grand as Mrs. Fludyer's.

She would have rushed at once to communicate the news to her friends, had it not been that she was stopped in the garden-walk by the apparition of her brother escorting two gentlemen from his studio—a rare courtesy with him. Meliora accounted for it when, from behind a sheltering espalier, she heard him address one of them as "my lord."

But when she told this to Olive, the young paintress was of a different opinion. She had heard the name of Lord Arundale, and recognised it as that of a nobleman on whom his love of Art and science shed more honour than his title. That was why Mr. Vanbrugh showed him respect, she knew.

"Certainly, certainly!" said Meliora, a little ashamed. "But to think that such a clever man, and a nobleman, should be so ordinary in appearance. Why, he was not half so remarkable-looking as the gentleman who accompanied him."

"What was *he* like?" said Olive smiling.

"You would have admired him greatly. His was just the sort of head you painted for your 'Aristides the Just'—your favourite style of beauty—dark, cold, proud, with such piercing, eagle eyes; they went right through me!"

Olive laughed merrily.

"Do you hear, mamma, how she runs on? What a bewitching young hero!"

"A hero, perhaps, but not exactly young; and as for bewitching, that he certainly might be, but it was in the fashion of a wizard or a magician. I never felt so nervous at the sight of any one in the whole course of my life." Here there was a knock at the drawing-room door.

"Come in," said Olive; and Mr. Vanbrugh entered.

For a moment he stood on the threshold without speaking; but there was a radiance in his face, a triumphant dignity in his whole carriage, which struck Olive and his sister with surprise.

"Brother—dear Michael, you are pleased with something; you have had good news."

He passed Meliora by, and walked up to Miss Rothesay.

"My pupil, rejoice with me; I have found at length appreciation, my life's aim has won success—I have sold my 'Alcestis.'"

Miss Vanbrugh rushed towards her brother. Olive Rothesay, full of delight, would have clasped her master's hand, but there was something in his look that repelled them both. His was the triumph of a man who exulted only in and for his Art, neither asking nor heeding any human sympathies. Such a look might have been on the face of the great Florentine, when he beheld the multitude gaze half in rapture, half in awe, on his work in the Sistine Chapel; then, folding his coarse garments round him, walked through the streets of Rome to his hermit dwelling, and sat himself down under the shadow of his desolate renown.

Michael Vanbrugh continued,

"Yes, I have sold my grand picture; the dream—the joy of a lifetime. Sold it, too, to a man who is worthy to possess it. I shall see it in Lord Arundale's noble gallery; I shall know that it, at least, will remain where, after my death, it will keep from oblivion the name of Michael Vanbrugh. Glorious indeed is this my triumph—yet less mine, than the triumph of high Art. Do you not rejoice, my pupil!"

"I do, indeed, my dear and noble master."

"And, brother, brother—you will be very rich. The price you asked for the 'Alcestis' was a thousand pounds," said Meliora.

He smiled bitterly.

"You women always think of money."

"But for your sake only, dear Michael," cried his sister; and her tearful eyes spoke the truth. Poor little soul! she could but go as far as her gifts went, and they extended no farther than to the thought of what comforts would this sum procure for Michael—a richer velvet gown and cap, like one of the old Italian painters—perhaps a journey to refresh his wearied eyes among lovely scenes of nature. She explained this, looking, not angry but just a little hurt.

"A journey! yes, I will take a journey—one which I have longed for these thirty years—I will go to Rome! Once again I will lie on the floor of the Sistine, and look up worshipingly to Michael the angel." (He always called him so.)

"And how long shall you stay, brother?"

"Stay?—Until my heart grows pulseless, and my brain dull. Why should I ever come back to this cold England?"

"No: let me grow old, die, and be buried under the shadow of the eternal City."

"He will never come back again—never," said Miss Vanbrugh, looking at Olive with a vague bewilderment. "He will leave this pretty cottage, and me, and everything."

There was a dead silence, during which poor 'Meliora sat plaiting her white apron in fold after fold, as was her habit when in deep and perplexed thought. Then she went up to her brother.

"Michael, if you will take me, I should like to go too."

"What!" cried Mrs. Rothesay, "you, my dear Miss Vanbrugh, who are so thoroughly English—who always said you hated moving from place to place, and would live and die at Woodford Cottage!"

"Hush—hush! we'll not talk about that, lest he should hear," said Meliora glancing half frightened at her brother. But he stood absorbed by the window, looking out apparently on the sky, though his eyes saw nothing—nothing! "Michael, do you quite understand—may I go with you to Rome?"

"Very well—very well, sister," he answered, in the tone of a man who is indifferent to the subject, except that consent gives less trouble than refusal. Then he turned towards Olive, and asked her to go with him to his painting-room; he wanted to consult with her as to the sort of frame that would suit the "Alcestis." Indeed, his pupil had now grown associated with all his pursuits, and had penetrated further in the depths of his inward life than any one else had been ever suffered to do. Olive gradually became to him his cherished pupil—the child of his soul, to whom he would fain transmit the mantle of his fame. He had but one regret, sometimes earnestly, and comically expressed—that she was a woman—only a woman.

They went and stood before the picture, he and Olive; Meliora stealing after her brother's footsteps, noiseless but constant as his shadow. And this ever-following, faithful love clung so closely to its object that, shadow-like, what all others beheld, by him was never seen.

Michael Vanbrugh cast on his picture a look such as no living face ever had won, or ever would win, from his cold eyes. It was the gaze of a parent on his child, a lover on his mistress, an idolator on his self-created god. Then he took his palette, and began to paint, lingeringly and lovingly, on slight portions of background or drapery—less as though he thought this needed, than as if loth to give the last, the very last, touch to a work so precious. He talked all the while, seemingly to hide the emotion which he would not show.

"Lord Arundale is an honour to his rank, a *noble man* indeed. One does not often meet such, Miss Rothesay. It was a pleasure to receive him in my studio. It did me good to talk with him, and with his friend."

Here Olive looked at Meliora and smiled. "Was his friend, then, as agreeable as himself?"

"Not so brilliant in conversation, but far the higher nature of the two, or I have read the human countenance in vain. He said frankly, that he was no artist, and no connoisseur, like Lord Arundale; but I saw from his eye, that, if he did not understand, he felt my picture."

"How so?" said Olive, with growing interest.

"He looked at Alcestis,—the 'Alcestis' I have painted,—sitting on her golden throne, waiting for death to call her from her kingdom and her lord; waiting solemnly, yet without fear. 'See,' said Lord Arundale to his friend, 'how love makes this feeble woman stronger than a hero! See how fearlessly a noble wife can die!'—'A wife who loves her husband,' was the answer, given so bitterly, that I turned to look at him. Oh, that I could have painted his head at that instant! It would have made a Heraclitus—a Timon!"

"And do you know his name? Will he come here again?"

"No: for he was leaving London to-day. I wish it had not been so, for I would have asked him to sit to me. That grand, iron, rigid head of his, with the close curling hair, would be a treasure indeed!"

"But who is he, brother?" inquired Meliora.

"A man of science; well known in the world, too, Lord Arundale said. He told me his name, but I forgot it. However, you may find a card somewhere about."

Meliora ran to the mantelpiece, and brought one to her brother. "Is this it?" He nodded. She ran for the light, and read aloud—

"*The Reverend Harold Gwynne.*"

CHAPTER XXIV

The subject of Harold Gwynne served Olive-and her mother for a full half-hour's conversation during that idle twilight season which they always devoted to pleasant talk. It was a curious coincidence which thus revived in their memories a name now almost forgotten. For, the debt once paid, Mr. Gwynne and all things connected with him had passed into complete oblivion, save that Olive carefully kept his letters.

These she had the curiosity to take from their hiding-place, and examine once more—partly for her mother's amusement, partly for her own; for it was a whim of hers to judge of character by hand-writing, and she really had been quite interested in the character which both Miss Vanbrugh and her brother had drawn.

"How strange that he should have been so near us, and we not know the fact! He seems quite to haunt us—to be our evil genius—our Daimon!"

"Hush, my dear! it is wrong to talk so. Remember, too, that he is Sara's husband."

Olive did remember it. Jestingly though she spoke, there was in her a remembrance, as mournful as a thing so long ended could be, of that early friendship, whose falseness had been her loving, heart's first blight. She had never formed another. There was a unity in her nature which made it impossible to build the shrine of a second affection on the ruins of the first. She found it so, even in life's ordinary ties. What would it have been with her had she ever known the great mystery of love?

She never had known it. She had lived all these years with a heart as virgin as mountain snows. When the one sweet dream which comes to most in early maidenhood—the dream of loving and being loved—was crushed, her heart drew back within itself, and, after a time of suffering almost as deep as if for the loss of a real object instead of a mere ideal, she prepared herself for her destiny. She went out into society, and there saw men, as they are *in society*—feeble, fluttering coxcombs, hard, grovelling men of business, some few men of pleasure, or of vice; and, floating around all, the race of ordinary mankind, neither good nor bad. Out of these classes, the first she merely laughed at, the second she turned from with distaste, the third she abhorred and despised, the fourth she looked upon with a calm indifference. Some good and clever men she had met occasionally, towards whom she had felt herself drawn with a friendly inclination; but they had always been drifted from her by the ever-shifting currents of society.

And these, the exceptions, were chiefly old, or at least elderly persons; men of long-acknowledged talent, wise and respected heads of families. The "new generation," the young men out of whose community her female acquaintances were continually choosing lovers and husbands, were much disliked by Olive Rothesay. Gradually, when she saw how mean was the general standard of perfection, how ineffably beneath her own ideal—the man she could have worshiped—she grew quite happy in her own certain lot. She saw her companions wedded to men who from herself would never have won a single thought. So she put aside for ever the half-sad dream of her youth, and married herself unto her Art.

She indulged in some of her sage reflections on men and women, courtship and wedlock, in general, when she sat at her mother's feet talking of Harold Gwynne and of his wife. "It could not have been a happy marriage, mamma,—if Mr. Gwynne be really the man that Miss Vanbrugh and her brother describe." And all day there recurred to Olive's fancy the words, "*A wife who loved her husband.*" She, at least, knew too well that Sara Derwent, when she married, could not have loved hers. Wonderings as to what was Sara's present fate, occupied her mind for a long, long time. She had full opportunity for thought, as her mother, oppressed by the sultry August evening, had fallen asleep with her hand on her daughter's neck, and Olive could not stir for fear of waking her.

Slowly she watched the twilight darken into a deeper shadow—that of a gathering thunderstorm. The trees beyond the garden began to sway restlessly about, and then, with a sudden flash, and distant thunder growl, down came the rain in torrents. Mrs. Rothesay started and woke; like most timid women, she had a great dread of thunder, and it took all Olive's powers of soothing to quiet her nervous alarms. These were increased by another sound that broke through the pouring rain—a violent ringing of the garden-bell, which, in Mrs. Rothesay's excited state, seemed a warning of all sorts of horrors.

"The house is on fire—the bolt has struck it Oh Olive, Olive, save me!" she cried.

"Hush, darling! You are quite safe with me." And Olive rose up, folding her arms closely round her mother, who hid her head in her daughter's bosom. They stood—Mrs. Rothesay trembling and cowering—Olive with her pale brow lifted fearlessly, as though she would face all terror, all danger, for her mother's sake. Thus they showed, in the faint glimmer of the lightning, a beautiful picture of filial love—to the eyes of a stranger, who that moment opened the door. She was a woman, whom the storm had apparently driven in for shelter.

"Is this Miss Vanbrugh's house—is there any one here?" she asked; her accent being slightly foreign.

Olive invited her to enter.

"Thank you; forgive my intrusion, but I am frightened—half drowned. The thunder is awful; will you take me in till Miss Vanbrugh returns?"

A light was quickly procured, and Olive came to divest the stranger of her dripping garments.

"Thank you, no! I can assist myself—I always do."

And she tried to unfasten her shawl—a rich heavy fabric, and of gaudy colours, when her trembling fingers failed; she knitted her brows, and muttered some sharp exclamation in French.

"You had better let me help you," said Olive, gently, as, with a firm hand, she took hold of the shivering woman, or girl, for she did not look above seventeen, drew her to a seat, and there disrobed her of her drenched shawl.

Not until then did Miss Rothesay pause to consider further about this incognita, arrived in such a singular manner. But when, recovered from her alarm the young stranger subsided into the very unromantic occupation of drying her wet frock by the kitchen fire, Olive regarded her with no small curiosity.

She stood, a picture less of girlish grace, than of such grace as French fashion dictates. Her tall, well-rounded form struggled through a painful compression into slimness; her whole attire had that peculiar *tournure* which we islanders term Frenchified. Nay, there was something in the very tie of her neck-ribbon which showed it never could have been done by English fingers. She appeared, all over, "a young lady from abroad."

We have noticed her dress first, because that was most noticeable. She herself was a fine, tall, well-modelled girl, who would have been graceful had fashion allowed her. She had one beauty—a column-like neck and well-set head, which she carried very loftily. Her features were somewhat large, not pretty, and yet not plain. She had a good mouth and chin; her eyes were very dark and silken-fringed; but her hair was fair.

This peculiarity caught Olive's eye at once; so much so, that she almost fancied she had seen the face before, she could not tell where. She puzzled about the matter, until the young guest, who seemed to make herself quite at home, had dried her garments, and voluntarily proposed that they should return to the drawing-room.

They did so, the stranger leading the way, and much to Olive's surprise, seeming to thread with perfect ease the queer labyrinths of the house.

By this time the storm was over, and they found Mrs. Rothesay sitting quietly waiting for tea. The young lady again apologised in her easy, foreign manner, and asked if she might stay with them until Miss Vanbrugh's return? Of course her hostess assented, and she talked for above an hour; chiefly of Paris, which she said she had just left; of French customs; music, and literature.

In the midst of this, Miss Vanbrugh's voice was heard in the hall. The girl started, as one does at the sound of some old tune, heard in youth, and forgotten for years; her gaiety ceased; she put her hand before her eyes; but when the door opened, she was her old self again.

No child "frayed with a sprite" could have looked more alarmed than Miss Meliora at the sudden vision of this elegant young damsel, who advanced towards her. The little old maid was quite overpowered with her stylish bend; her salute, French fashion, cheek to cheek; and her anxious inquiries after Miss Vanbrugh's health.

"I am quite well, thank you, madam. A friend of Mrs. Rothesay's I suppose?" was poor Meliora's bewildered reply.

"No, indeed; I have not till now had the pleasure of hearing Mrs. Rothesay's name. My visit was to yourself," said the stranger, evidently enjoying the *incognito* she had kept, for her black eyes sparkled with fun.

"I am happy to see you, madam," again stammered the troubled Meliora.

"I thought you would be—I came to surprise you. My dear Miss Vanbrugh, have you really forgotten me? Then allow me to re-introduce myself. My name is Christal Manners."

Miss Meliora looked as if she could have sunk into the earth! Year after year, from the sum left in the bank, she had paid the school-bill of her self-assumed charge; but that was all. After-thoughts, and a few prudish hints given by good-natured friends, had made her feel both ashamed and frightened at having taken such a doubtful *protégée*. Whenever she chanced to think of Christal's growing up, and coming back a woman, she drove the subject from her mind in absolute alarm. Now the very thing she dreaded had come upon her. Here was the desolate child returned, a stylish young woman, with no home in the world but that of her sole friend and protectress.

Poor Miss Vanbrugh was quite overwhelmed. She sank on a chair, "Dear me! I am so frightened—that is, so startled. Oh, Miss Rothesay, what shall I do?" and she looked appealingly to Olive.

But between her and Miss Rothesay glided the young stranger. The bright colour paled from Christa's face—her smile passed into a frown.

"Then you are not glad to see me—you, the sole friend I have in the world, whom I have travelled a thousand miles to meet—travelled alone and unprotected—you are not glad to see me? I will turn and go back again—I will leave the house—I will—I"——

Her rapid speech ended in a burst of tears. Poor Meliora felt like a guilty thing. "Miss Manners—Christal—my poor child! I didn't mean that! Don't cry—don't cry! I am very glad to see you—so are we all—are we not, Olive?"

Olive was almost as much puzzled as herself. She had a passing recollection of the death of Mrs. Manners, and of the child's being sent to school; but since then she had heard no more of her. She could hardly believe that the elegant creature before her was the little ragged imp of a child whom she had once seen staring idly down the river. However, she asked no questions, but helped to soothe the girl, and to restore, as far as possible, peace and composure to the household.

They all spent the evening together without any reference to the past. Only once, Christal—in relating how, as soon as ever her term of education expired, she had almost compelled her governess to let her come to England, and to Miss Vanbrugh,—said, in her proud way,

"It was not to ask a maintenance—for you know my parents left me independent; but I wanted to see you because I believed that, besides taking charge of my fortune, you had been kind to me when a child. How, or in what way, I cannot clearly remember; for I think," she added, laughing, "that I must have been a very stupid little girl: all seems so dim to me until I went to school. Can you enlighten me, Miss Vanbrugh?"

"Another time, another time, my dear," said the painter's sister, growing very much confused.

"Well! I thank you all the same, and you shall not find me ungrateful," said the young lady, kissing Miss Meliora's hand, and speaking in a tone of real feeling, which would have moved any woman. It quite overpowered Miss Van-brugh—the softest-hearted little woman in the world. She embraced her *protégée*, declaring that she would never part with her.

"But," she added, with a sudden thought, a thought of intense alarm, "what will Michael say?"

"Do not think of that to-night," interposed Olive. "Miss Manners is tired; let us get her to bed quickly, and we will see what morning brings."

The advice was followed, and Christal disappeared; not, however, without lavishing on Mrs. and Miss Rothesay a thousand gracious thanks and apologies, with an air and deportment that did infinite honour to the polite instruction of her *pension*.

Mrs. Rothesay, confused with all that had happened, did not ask many questions, but only said as she retired,

"I don't quite like her, Olive—I don't like the tone of her voice; and yet there was something that struck me in the touch of her hand—which is so different in different people."

"Hers is a very pretty hand, mamma. It is quite classic in shape—like poor papa's—which I remember so well!"

"There never was such a beautiful hand as your papa's. He said it descended in the Rothesay family. You have it, you know, my child," observed Mrs. Rothesay. She sighed, but softly; for, after all these years, the widow and the fatherless had learned to speak of their loss without pain, though with tender remembrance.

Thinking of him and of her mother, Olive thought, likewise, how much happier was her own lot than that of the orphan-girl, who, by her own confession, had never known what it was to remember the love of the dead, or to rejoice in the love of the living. And her heart was moved with the pity—nay, even tenderness, for Christal Manners.

When she had assisted her mother to bed—as she always did—Olive, in passing down stairs, moved by some feeling of interest, listened at the door of the young stranger. She was apparently walking up and down her room with a quick, hurried step. Olive knocked.

"Are you quite comfortable?—do you want anything?"

"Who's there? Oh! come in, Miss Rothesay."

Olive entered, and found, to her surprise, that the candle was extinguished.

"I thought I heard you moving about, Miss Manners."

"So I was. I felt restless and could not sleep. I am very tired with my journey, I suppose, and the room is strange to me. Come here—give me your hand."

"You are not afraid, my dear child?" said Olive, remembering that she was, indeed, little more than a child, though she looked so womanly. "You are not frightening yourself in this gloomy old house, nor thinking of ghosts and goblins?"

"No—no! I was thinking, if I must tell the truth," said the girl, with something very like a suppressed sob—"I was thinking of you and your mother, as I saw you standing when I first came in. No one ever clasped me so, or ever will! Not that I have any one to blame; my father and mother died; they could not help dying. But if they had just brought me into the world and left me, as I have heard some parents have done, then I should cry out, 'Wicked parents! if I grow up heartless, because I have no one to love me; and vile, because I have none to guide me,—my sin be upon your head!'"

She said these words with vehement passion. But Olive answered calmy, "Hush, Christal!—let me call you Christal; for I am much older than you. Lie down and rest. Be loving, and you will never want for love; be humble, and you will never want for guiding. You have good friends here, who will care for you very much, I doubt not. Be content, my poor, tired child!"

She spoke very softly; for the darkness quite obliterated the vision of that stylish damsel who had exhibited her airs and graces in the drawing-room. As she sat by Christal's bedside, Olive only felt the presence of a desolate orphan.

She said in her heart, "Please God, I will do her all the good that lies in my feeble power. Who knows but that, in some way or other, I may comfort and help this child!" So she stooped down and kissed Christal on the forehead, a tenderness that the girl passionately returned. Then Olive went and lay down by her blind mother's side, with a quiet and a happy heart.

CHAPTER XXV

In a week's time Christal Manners was fairly domiciled at Woodford Cottage. In what capacity it would be hard to say—certainly not as Miss Vanbrugh's *protégée*—for she assumed toward the little old maid a most benignant air of superiority. Mr. Vanbrugh she privately christened "the old Ogre," and kept as much out of his way as possible. This was not difficult, for the artist was too much wrapped up in himself to meddle with any domestic affairs. He seemed to be under some mystification that the lively French girl was a guest of Miss Rothesay's, and his sister ventured not to break this delusion. Christal's surname created no suspicions; the very name of his former model, Celia Manners, had long since passed from his memory.

So the young visitor made herself quite at home—amused the whole household with her vivacity, clinging especially to the Rothesay portion of the establishment. She served Olive as general assistant in her studio, model included—or, at least, as lay figure: for she was too strictly fashionable to be graceful in form, and not quite beautiful enough in face to attract an artist's notice. But she did very well; and she amused Mrs. Rothesay all the while with her gay French songs, so that Olive was glad to have her near.

The day after Christal's arrival, Miss Vanbrugh had summoned her chief state-councillor, Olive Rothesay, to talk over the matter. Then and there, Meliora unfolded all she knew and all she guessed of the girl's history. How much of this was to be communicated to Christal she wished Olive to decide: and Olive, remembering what had passed between them on the first night of her coming, advised that, unless Christal herself imperatively demanded to know, there should be maintained on the subject a kindly silence.

"Her parents are dead, of that she is persuaded," Olive urged. "Whoever they were, they have carefully provided for her. If they erred or suffered, let neither their sin nor their sorrow go down to their child."

"It shall be so," said the good Meliora. And since Christal asked no further questions—and, indeed, her lively nature seemed unable to receive any impressions save of the present—the subject was not again referred to.

But the time came when the little household must be broken up. Mr. Vanbrugh announced that in one fortnight he must leave Woodford Cottage, on his journey to Rome. He never thought of such mundane matters as letting the house, or disposing of the furniture; he left all those things to his active little sister, who was busy from morning till night—ay, often again from night till morning. When Michael commanded anything, it must be done, if within human possibility; and there never was any one to do it but Meliora. She did it, always;—how, he never asked or thought. He was so accustomed to her ministrations that he no more noticed them than he did the daylight. Had the light suddenly gone—then—Michael Vanbrugh would have known what it once had been.

Ere the prescribed time had quite expired, Miss Vanbrugh announced that all was arranged for their leaving Woodford Cottage. Her brother had nothing to do but to pack up his easels and his pictures; and this duty was quite absorbing enough to one who had no existence beyond his painting-room.

There was one insuperable difficulty, which perplexed Meliora. What was to be done with Christal Manners? She troubled herself about the matter night and day. At last she hinted something of it to the girl herself. And 'Miss Manners at once decided the question by saying, "I will not go to Rome."

She was of a strange disposition, as they had already found out. With all her volatile gaiety, when she chose to say, "I will!" she was as firm as a rock. No persuasions—no commands—could move her. In this case none were tried. Her fortunes seemed to arrange themselves; for Mrs. Fludyer, coming in one day to make the final arrangements for the Rothesays' arrival at Farnwood, took a vehement liking to the young French lady, as Miss Manners was generally considered, and requested that Mrs. Rothesay would bring her down to Farnwood, Olive demurred a little, lest the intrusion of a constant inmate might burden her mother: but the plan was at last decided upon—Christal's own entreaties having no small influence in turning the scale.

Thus, all things settled, there came the final parting of the two little families who for so many years had lived together in peace and harmony. The Rothesays were to leave one day, the Vanbrughs the next. Olive and Meliora were both very busy—too busy to have time for regrets. They did not meet until evening, when Olive saw Miss Vanbrugh quietly and sorrowfully watering her flowers, with a sort of mechanical interest— the interest of a mother, who meekly goes on arranging all things for the comfort and adornment of the child from whom she is about to separate. It made Olive sad; she went into the garden, and joined Meliora.

"Let me help you, dear Miss Vanbrugh. Why should you tire yourself thus, after all the fatigues of the day?"

Meliora looked up.—"Ah! true, true! I shall never do this any more, I know. But the poor flowers must not suffer; I'll take care of them while I can. Those dahlias, that I have watched all the year, want watering every night, and will do for a month to come. A month! Oh! Miss Rothesay, I am very foolish, I know, but it almost breaks my heart to say good-bye to my poor little garden!"

Her voice faltered, and at last her tears began to fall—not bitterly, but in a quiet, gentle way, like the dropping of evening rain. However, she soon recovered herself, and began to talk of her brother and of Rome. She was quite sure that there his genius would find due recognition, and that he would rival the old masters in honour and prosperity. She was content to go with him, she said; perhaps the warm climate would suit her better than England, now that she was growing—not exactly old, for she was much younger than Michael, and he had half a lifetime of fame before him—but still, older than she had been. The language would be a trouble; but then she was already beginning to learn it, and she had always been used to accommodate herself to everything. She was quite certain that this plan of Michael's would turn out for the good of both.

"And as for the poor old cottage, when you return to London you will come and see it sometimes, and write me word how it looks. You can send a bit of the clematis in a letter, too; and who knows, but if you get a very rich lady, you may take the whole cottage yourself some day, and live here again."

"Perhaps; if you will come back from Rome, and visit me here?" said Olive, smiling; for she was glad to encourage any cheerful hope.

"No, no, I shall never leave Michael—I shall never leave Michael!" She said these words over to herself many times, and then took up her watering-pot and went on with her task.

Her affectionate companion followed her for some time; but Miss Vanbrugh did not seem disposed to talk, so Olive returned to the house.

She felt in that unquiet, dreary state of mind which precedes a great change, when all preparations are complete, and there is nothing left to be done but to ponder on the coming parting. She could not rest anywhere, or compose herself to anything; but wandered about the house, thinking of that last day at Oldchurch, and vaguely speculating when or what the next change would be. She passed into the drawing-room, where Christal was amusing Mrs. Rothesay with her foreign ditties; and then she went to Mr. Vanbrugh's studio to have a last talk about Art with her old master.

He was busily engaged in packing up his casts and remaining pictures. He just acknowledged his pupil's presence and received her assistance, as he always did with perfect indifference. For, from mere carelessness, Vanbrugh had reduced the womankind about him to the condition of perfect slaves.

"There, that will do. Now bring me the great treasure of all—the bust of Michael the Angel."

She climbed on a chair, and lifted it down, carefully and reverentially, so as greatly to please the artist.

"Thank you, my pupil; you are very useful; I cannot tell what I should do without you."

"You will have to do without me very soon," was Olive's gentle and somewhat sorrowful answer. "This is my last evening in this dear old studio—my last talk with you, my good and kind master."

He looked surprised and annoyed. "Nonsense, child! If I am going to Rome, you are going too. I thought Meliora would arrange all that."

Olive shook her head.

"No, Mr. Vanbrugh; indeed, it is impossible."

"What, not go with me to Rome!—you my pupil, unto whom I meant to unfold all the glorious secrets of my art! Olive Rothesay, are you dreaming?" he cried, angrily.

She only answered him softly, that all her plans were settled, and that much as she should delight in seeing Rome, she could not think of leaving her mother.

"Your mother! What right have we artists to think of any ties of kindred, or to allow them for one moment to weigh in the balance with our noble calling?—I say *ours*, for I tell you now what I never told you before, that, though you are a woman, you have a man's soul. I am proud of you; I design to make for you a glorious future. Even in this scheme I mingled you—how we should go together to the City of Art, dwell together, work together, master and pupil. What great things we should execute! We should be like the brothers Caracci—like Titian with his scholar and adopted son. Would that you had not been a woman! that I could have made you my son in Art, and given you my name, and then died, bequeathing to you the mantle of my glory!"

Olive.

"His anger had vanished."

His rapid and excited language softened into something very like emotion; he threw himself into his painting-chair, and waited for Olive's answer.

It came brokenly—almost with tears.

"My dear, my noble master, to whom I owe so much, what can I say to you?"

"That you will go with me—that when my failing age needs your young hand, it shall be ready; and that so the master's waning powers may be forgotten in the scholar's rising fame."

Olive answered nothing but, "My mother, my mother—she would not quit England; I could not part from her."

"Fool!" said Vanbrugh, roughly; "does a child never leave a mother? It is a thing that happens every day; girls do it always when they marry." He stopped suddenly, and pondered; then he said, hastily, "Child, go away; you have made me angry. I would be alone—I will call you when I want you."

She disappeared, and for an hour she heard him walking up and down his studio with heavy strides. Soon after, there was a pause; Olive heard him call her name, and quickly answered the summons.

His anger had vanished; he stood calmly, leaning his arm on the mantelpiece, the lamp-light falling on the long unbroken lines of his velvet gown, and casting a softened shadow over his rugged features. There was majesty, even grace, in his attitude; and his aspect bore a certain dignified serenity, that well became him.

He motioned young pupil to sit down, and then said to her,

"Miss Rothesay, I wish to talk to you as to a sensible and noble woman (there are such I know, and such I believe you to be). I also speak as to one like myself—a true follower of our divine Art, who to that one great aim would bend all life's purposes, as I have done."

He paused a moment, and seeing that no answer came, continued,

"All these years you have been my pupil, and have become necessary to me and to my Art. To part with you is impossible; it would disorganise all my plans and hopes. There is but one way to prevent this. You are a woman; I cannot take you for my son, but I can take you for—my wife."

Utterly astounded, Olive heard. "Your wife—I—your wife!" was all she murmured.

"Yes. I ask you—not for my own sake, but for that of our noble Art. I am a man long past my youth—perhaps even a stern, rude man. I cannot give you love, but I can give you glory. Living, I can make of you such an artist as no woman ever was before; dying, I can bequeath to you the immortality of my fame. Answer me—is this nothing?"

"I cannot answer—I am bewildered."

"Then listen. You are not one of those foolish girls who would make sport of my grey hairs. I will be very tender over you, for you have been good to me. I will learn how to treat you with the mildness that women need. You shall be like a child to my old age. You will marry me, then, Olive Rothesay?"

He walked up to her, and took her hand, gravely, though not without gentleness; but she shrank away.

"I cannot, I cannot; it is impossible."

He looked at her one moment, neither in angry reproach, nor in wounded tenderness, but with a stern, cold pride. "I have been mistaken—pardon me." Then he quitted her, walked back to his position near the hearth, and resumed his former attitude.

There was silence. Afterwards Michael Vanbrugh felt his sleeve touched, and saw beside him the small, delicate figure of his pupil.

"Mr. Vanbrugh, my dear master and friend, look at me, and listen to what I have to say."

He moved his head assentingly, without turning round.

"I have lived," Olive continued, "for six-and-twenty years, and no one has ever spoken to me of marriage. I did not dream that any one ever would. But, since you have thus spoken, I can only answer as I have answered."

"And you are in the same mind still?"

"I am. Not because of your age, or of my youth; but because you have, as you say, no love to give me, nor have I love to bring to you; therefore for me to marry you would be a sin."

"As you will, as you will. I thought you a kindred genius—I find you a mere *woman*. Jest on at the old fool with his grey hairs—go and wed some young, gay"——

"Look at me?" said Olive, with a mournful meaning in her tone; "am I likely to marry?"

"I have spoken ill," said Vanbrugh, in a touched and humbled voice. "Nature has been hard to us both; we ought to deal gently with one another. Forgive me, Olive."

He offered her his hand; she took it, and pressed it to her heart. "Oh that I could be still your pupil—your daughter! My dear, dear master! I will never forget you while I live."

"Be it so!" He moved away, and sat down, leaning his head upon his hand. Who knows what thoughts might have passed through his mind—regretful, almost remorseful thoughts of that bliss which he had lost or scorned—life's crowning sweetness, woman's love.

Olive went up to him.

"I must go now. You will bid me good-bye—will you not, gently, kindly? You will not think the worse of me for what has passed this night?" And she knelt down beside him, pressing her lips to his hand.

He stooped and kissed her forehead. It was the first and last kiss that, since boyhood, Michael Vanbrugh ever gave to woman.

Then he stood up—the great artist only. In his eye was no softness, but the pride of genius—genius, the mighty, the daring, the eternally alone.

"Go, my pupil! and remember my parting words. Fame is sweeter than all pleasure, stronger than all pain. We give unto Art our life, and she gives us immortality."

As Olive went out, she saw him still standing, stern, motionless, with folded arms and majestic eyes; like a solitary rock whereon no flowers grow, but on whose summit heaven's light continually shines.

CHAPTER XXVI

"Well, darling, how do you feel in our new home?" said Olive to her mother, when, after a long and weary journey, the night came down upon them at Farnwood, the dark, gusty, autumn night, made wildly musical by the neighbourhood of dense woods.

"I feel quite content, my child: I am always content everywhere with you. And I like the wind; it helps me to imagine the sort of country we are in."

"A forest country, hilly and bleak. We drove through miles of forest-land, over roads carpeted with fallen leaves. The woods will look glorious this autumn time."

"That will be very pleasant, my child," said Mrs. Rothesay, who was so accustomed to see with Olive's eyes, and to delight in the vivid pictures painted by Olive's eloquent tongue, that she never spoke like a person who is blind. Even the outward world was to her no blank of desolation. Wherever they went, every beautiful place, or thing, or person, that Olive saw, she treasured in memory. "I must tell mamma of this," or "I must bring mamma here, and paint the view for her." And so she did, in words so rich and clear, that the blind mother often said she enjoyed such scenes infinitely more than when the whole wide earth lay open to her unregardful eyes.

"I wonder," said Olive, "what part of S——shire we are in. We really might have been fairy-guided hither; we seem only aware that our journey began in London and ended at Farnwood. I don't know anything about the neighbourhood."

"Never mind the neighbourhood, dear, since we are settled, you say, in such a pretty house. Tell me, is it like Woodford Cottage?"

"Not at all! It is quite modern and comfortable. And they have made it all ready for us, just as if we were come to a friend's house on a visit. How kind of Mrs. Fludyer!"

"Nay! I'm sure Mrs. Fludyer never knew how to arrange a house in her life. She had no hand in the matter, trust me!" observed the sharply-observant Christal.

"Well, then, it is certainly the same guiding-fairy who has done this for us, too. And I am very thankful to have such a quiet, pleasant coming-home."

"I, too, feel it like coming home," said Mrs. Rothesay, in a soft weary voice. "Olive, love, I am glad the journey is over; it has been almost too much for me. We will not go back to London yet awhile; we will stay here a long time."

"As long as ever you like, darling. And now shall I show you the house?"

"Showing" the house implied a long description of it, in Olive's blithest language, as they passed from room to room. It was a pretty, commodious dwelling, perhaps the prettiest portion of which was the chamber which Miss Rothesay appropriated as her mother's and her own.

"It is a charming sleeping-room, with its white draperies, and its old oak furniture; and the quaint pier-glass, stuck round with peacocks' feathers, country fashion. And there, mamma, are some prints, a 'Raising of Lazarus,' though not quite so grand as my beloved 'Sebastian del Piombo.' And here are views from my own beautiful Scotland—a 'Highland Loch,' and 'Edinburgh Castle;' and, oh, mamma! there is grand old 'Stirling,' the place where I was born! Our good fairy might have known the important fact; for, lo! she has adorned the mantelpiece with two great bunches of heather, in honour of me, I suppose. How pleasant!"

"Yes. But I am weary, love. I wish I were in bed, and at rest."

This was soon accomplished; and Olive sat down by her mother's side, as she often did, waiting until Mrs. Rothesay fell asleep.

She sat, looking about her mechanically, as one does when taking possession of a strange room. Curiously her eye marked every quaint angle in the furniture, which would in time become so familiar. Then she thought, as one of dreamy mood is apt to do under such circumstances, of how many times she should lay her head down on the pillow in this same room, and when, and how would be the *last time*. For to all things on earth must come a last time.

But, waking herself out of such pondering, she turned to look at her mother. The delicate placid face lay in the stillness of deep sleep—a stillness that sometimes startles one, from its resemblance to another and more solemn repose. While she looked, a pain entered the daughter's heart. To chase it thence, she stooped and softly kissed the face which to her was, and ever had been, the most beautiful in the world; and then, following the train of her former musings, came the thought that one day—it might be far distant, but still, in all human probability, it must come—she would kiss her mother's brow for the *last time*.

A moment's shiver, a faint prayer, and the thought passed. But long afterwards she remembered it, and marvelled that it should have first come to her then and there.

The morning that rose at Farnwood Dell—so the little house was called—was one of the brightest that ever shone from September skies. Olive felt cheerful as the day; and as for Christal, she was perpetually running in and out, making the wonderful discoveries of a young damsel who had never in all her life seen the real country. She longed for a ramble, and would not let Olive rest until the exploit was determined on. It was to be a long walk, the appointed goal being a beacon that could be seen for miles, a church on the top of a hill.

Olive quite longed to go thither, because it had been the first sight at Farnwood on which her eyes had rested. Looking out from her chamber-window, at the early morning, she had seen it gleaming goldenly in the sunrise. All was so new, so lovely! It had made her feel quite happy, just as though with that first sunrise at Farnwood had dawned a new era in her life. Many times during the day she looked at the hill church; she would have asked about it had there been any one to ask, so she determined that her first walk should be thither.

The graceful spire rose before them, guiding them all the way, which did not seem long to Olive, who revelled in the beauties unfolded along their lonely walk—a winding road, bounding the forest, on whose verge the hill stood. But Christal's Parisian feet soon grew wearied, and when they came to the ascent of the hill, she fairly sat down by the roadside.

"I will go into this cottage, and rest until you come back, Miss Rothesay; and you need not hurry, for I shall not be able to walk home for an hour," said the wilful young lady, as she quickly vanished, and left her companion to proceed to the church alone.

Slowly Olive wound up the hill, and through a green lane that led to the churchyard. There seemed a pretty little village close by, but she was too tired to proceed further. She entered the churchyard, intending to sit down and rest on one of the gravestones; but at the wicket-gate she paused to look around at the wide expanse of country that lay beneath the afternoon sunshine—a peaceful earth, smiling back the smile of heaven. The old grey church, with its circle of gigantic trees, shut out all signs of human habitation; and there was no sound, not even the singing of birds, to break the perfect quiet that brooded around.

Olive had scarcely ever seen so sweet a spot. Its sweetness passed into her soul, moving her even to tears. From the hill-top she looked on the wide verdant plain, then up into the sky, and wished for doves' wings to sail out into the blue. Never had she so deeply felt how beautiful was earth, and how happy it might be made. And was Olive not happy? She thought of all those whose forms had moved through her life's picture; very beautiful to her heart they were: beautiful and dearly loved: but now it seemed as though there was one great want, one glorious image that should have arisen above them all, melting them into a grand harmonious whole.

Half conscious of this want, Olive thought, "I wonder how it would have been with me had I ever penetrated that great mystery which crowns all life: had I ever known love!"

The thought brought back many of her conversations with Michael,—and his belief that the life of the heart and that of the brain—one so warm and rich—the other so solitary and cold—can rarely exist together. Towards the latter her whole destiny seemed now turning.

"It may be true; perchance all is well Let me think so. If on earth I must ever feel this void, may it be filled at last in the after-life with God!"

She pondered thus, but the meditations oppressed her. She was rather glad to have them broken by the appearance of a little girl, who entered from a wicket-gate at the other end of the churchyard, and walked, very slowly and quietly, to a grave-stone near where Miss Rothesay stood.

Olive approached, but the child, a thoughtful-looking little creature of about eight years old, did not see her until she came quite close.

"Do not let me disturb you, my dear," said she gently, as the little girl seemed shy and frightened, and about to run away. But Miss Rothesay, who loved all children, began to talk to her, and very soon succeeded in conquering the timidity of the pretty little maiden. For she was a pretty creature. Olive especially admired her eyes, which were large and dark, the sort of eyes she had always loved for the sake of Sara Derwent. Looking into them now, she seemed carried back once more to the days of her early youth, and of that long-vanished dream.

"Are you fond of coming here, my child?"

"Yes; whenever I can steal quietly away, out of sight of papa and grandmamma. They do not forbid me; else, you know, I ought not to do it; but they say it is not good for me to stay thinking here, and send me to go and play."

"And why had you rather come and sit here than play?"

"Because there is a secret, and I want to try and find it out. I dare not tell you, for you might tell papa and grandmamma, and they would be angry."

"But your mamma—you could surely tell mamma; I always tell everything to mine."

"Do you? and have you got a mamma? Then, perhaps you could help me in finding out all about mine. You must know," added the child, lifting up her eager face with an air of mystery, "when I was very little, I lived away from here—I never saw my mamma, and my nurse always told me that she had 'gone away.' A little while since, when I came home—my home is there," and she pointed to what seemed the vicarage-house, glimmering whitely through the trees—"they told me mamma was here, under this stone, but they would tell me nothing more. Now, what does it all mean?"

Olive perceived by these words, that the child was playing upon her mother's grave. Only it seemed strange that she should have been left so entirely ignorant with regard to the great mysteries of death and immortality. Miss Rothesay was puzzled what to answer.

"My child, if your mamma be here, it is her body only." And Olive paused, startled at the difficulty she found in explaining in the simplest terms the doctrine of the soul's immortality. At last she continued, "When you go to sleep do you not often dream of walking in beautiful places and seeing beautiful things, and the dreams are so happy that you would not mind whether you slept on your soft bed or on the hard ground? Well, so it is with your mamma; her body has been laid down to sleep, but her mind—her spirit, is flying far away in beautiful dreams. She never feels at all that she is lying in her grave under the ground."

"But how long will her body lie there? and will it ever wake?"

"Yes, it will surely wake, though how soon we know not, and be taken up to heaven and to God."

The child looked earnestly in Olive's face. "What is heaven, and what is God?"

Miss Rothesay's amazement was not unmingled with horror. Her own religious faith had dawned so imperceptibly—at once an instinct and a lesson—that there seemed something awful in this question of an utterly untaught mind.

"My poor child," she said, "do you not know who is God?—has no one told you?"

"No one."

"Then I will."

"Pardon me, madam," said a man's voice behind, calm, cold, but not unmusical; "but it seems to me that a father is the best teacher of his child's faith."

"Papa—it is papa." With a look of shyness almost amounting to fear, the child slid from the tombstone and ran away.

Olive stood face to face with the father.

He was a gentleman—a true *gentleman*; at the first glance any one would have given him that honourable and rarely-earned name. His age might be about thirty-five, but his face was cast in the firm rigid mould over which years pass and leave no trace. He might have looked as old as now at twenty; at fifty he would probably look little older. Handsome he was, as Olive discerned at a glance, but there was something in him that controlled her much more than mere beauty would have done. It was a grave dignity of presence, which indicated that mental sway which some men are born to hold, first over themselves, and then over their kind. Wherever he came, he seemed to say, "I rule—I am master here!"

Olive Rothesay, innocent as she was of any harm to this gentleman or to his child, felt as cowed and humbled as if she had done wrong. She wished she could have fled like the little girl—fled out of reach of his searching glance.

He waited for her to speak first, but she was silent; her colour rose to her very temples; she knew not whether she ought to apologise, or to summon her woman's dignity and meet the stranger with a demeanour like his own.

She was relieved when the sound of his voice broke the pause.

"I fear I startled you, madam; but I was not at first aware who was talking to my little girl. Afterwards, the few words of yours which I overheard induced me to pause."

"What words?"

"About sleep, and dreams, and immortality. Your way of putting the case was graceful—poetical Whether a child would apprehend it or not, is another question."

Olive was surprised at the half-sarcastic, half-earnest way in which he said this. She longed to ask what motive he could have had in bringing the child up in such total ignorance of the first principles of Christianity. The stranger seemed to divine her question, and answer it.

"No doubt you think it strange that my little daughter is so ill-informed in some theological points, and still more that I should have stopped you when you were kind enough to instruct her thereon. But, being a father—to say nothing of a clergyman"—(Olive looked at him in some surprise, and found that her interlocutor bore, in dress at least, a clerical appearance)—"I choose to judge for myself in some things; and I deem it very inexpedient that the feeble mind of a child should be led to dwell on subjects which are beyond the grasp of the profoundest philosopher."

"But not beyond the reverent faith of a Christian," Olive ventured to say.

He looked at her with his piercing eyes, and said eagerly, "You think so, you feel so?" then recovering his old manner, "Certainly—of course—that is the great beauty of a woman's religion. She pauses not to reason,—she is always ready to believe; therefore you women are a great deal happier than the philosophers."

It was doubtful, from his tone, whether he meant this in compliment or in sarcasm. But Olive replied as her own true and pious spirit prompted.

"It seems to me that while the intellect comprehends, the heart, or rather the soul, is the only fountain of belief. Without that, could a man dive into the infinite until he became as an angel in power and wisdom—could he 'by searching find out God'—still he could not believe."

"*Do you* believe in God?"

"I love Him!" She said no more; but her countenance spoke the rest; and her companion saw it He stood as silently gazing as a man who in the desert comes face to face with an angel.

Olive recollecting herself blushed deeply. "I ought to apologise for speaking so freely of these things to a stranger and a clergyman—in this place too."

"Can there be a fitter place, or one that so sanctifies, and at the same time justifies this conversation?" was the answer, as the speaker glanced round the quiet domain of the dead. Then Olive remembered where they stood—that she was talking to the husband over his lost wife's tomb. The thought touched her with sympathy for this man, whose words, though so earnest, were yet so piercing. He seemed as though it were his habit to tear away every flimsy veil, in order to behold the shining image of Truth.

They were silent for a moment, and then he resumed, with a smile,—the first that had yet lightened his face, and which now cast on it an inexpressible sweetness—

"Let me thank you for talking so kindly to my little daughter. I trust I have sufficiently explained why I interrupted your lessons."

"Still, it seems strange," said Olive. And strong interest conquering her diffidence, she asked how he, a clergyman, had possibly contrived to keep the child in such utter ignorance?

"She has not lived much with me," he answered; "my little Ailie has been brought up in complete solitude. It was best for a child, whose birth was soon followed by her mother's death."

Olive trembled lest she had opened a wound; but his words and manner had the grave composure of one who speaks of any ordinary event. Whatever grief he had felt, it evidently was healed. An awkward pause, during which Miss Rothesay tried to think in what way she could best end the conversation. It was broken at last by little Ailie, who crept timidly across the churchyard to her father.

"Please, papa, grandmamma wants to see you before she goes out. She is going to John Dent's, and to Farnwood, and"— —

"Hush, little chatterbox! this lady cannot be interested in our family revelations. Bid her 'good-afternoon' and come!"

He tried to speak playfully, but it was a rigid playfulness. Though a father, it was evident he did not understand children. Bowing to Olive with a stately acknowledgment, he walked on alone towards the little wicket-gate. She noticed that his eye never turned back, either to his dead wife's grave or to his living child. Ailie, while his shadow was upon her, had been very quiet; when he walked away, she sprang up, gave Olive one of those rough, sudden, childish embraces which are so sweet, and then bounded away after her father.

Miss Rothesay watched them both disappear, and then was seized with an eager impulse to know who were this strange father and daughter. She remembered the tombstone, the inscription of which she had not yet seen: for it was half-hidden by an overhanging cornice, and by the tall grass that grew close by. Olive had to kneel down in order to decipher it. She did so, and read:

"SARA,

Wife of the Reverend Harold Gwynne,

Died—, Aged 21."

Then, the turf she knelt on covered Sara! the kiss, yet warm on her lips, was given by Sara's child! Olive bowed her face in the grass, trembling violently. Far, far through long-divided years, her heart fled back to its olden tenderness. She saw again the thorn-tree and the garden-walk, the beautiful girlish face, with its frank and constant smile. She sat down and wept over Sara's grave.

Then she thought of little Ailie. Oh! would that she had known this sooner! that she might have closer clasped the motherless child, and have seen poor Sara's likeness shining from her daughter's eyes! With a yearning impulse Olive rose up to follow the little girl. But she remembered the father.

How strange—how passing strange, that he with whom she had been talking, towards whom she had felt such an awe, and yet a vague attraction, should have been Sara's husband, and the man whose influence had curiously threaded her own life for many years.

She felt glad that the mystery was now solved—that she had at last seen Harold Gwynne.

CHAPTER XXVII

Miss Rothesay was very silent during the walk home. She accounted for it to Christal by telling the simple truth—that in the churchyard she had found the grave of an early and dear friend. Her young companion looked serious, condoled in set fashion; and then became absorbed in the hateful labyrinths of the muddy road. Certainly, Miss Manners was never born for a simple rustic. Olive could not help remarking this.

"No; I was born for what I am," answered the girl, proudly. "My parents were aristocrats; so am I. Don't lecture me! Wrong or right, I always felt thus, and always shall. If I have neither friends nor relatives, I have at least my family and my name."

She talked thus, as she did sometimes, until they came to the garden-gate of Farnwood Dell. There stood an elegant carriage. Christars eyes brightened at the sight, and she trod with a more patrician air.

The maid—a parting bequest of Miss Meliora's, and who had long and faithfully served at Woodford Cottage—came anxiously to communicate that there were two ladies waiting. One of them she did not know; the other was Mrs. Fludyer. "The latter would have disturbed Mrs. Rothesay," Hannah added, "but the other lady said, 'No; they would wait.'" Whereat Olive's heart inclined towards "the other lady."

She went in and found, with Mrs. Fludyer, an ancient dame of large and goodly presence. Aged though she seemed, her tall figure was not bent; and dignity is to the old what grace is to the young. She stood a little aside, and did not speak, but Olive, labouring under the weight of Mrs. Mudyer's gracious inquiries, felt that the old lady's eyes were carefully reading her face. At last Mrs. Fludyer made a motion of introduction.

"No, I thank you," said the stranger, in the unmistakable northern tongue, which, falling from poor Elspie's lips, had made the music of Olive's childhood, and to which her heart yearned evermore. "Miss Rothesay, will you, for your father's sake, let me shake hands with his child? I am Mrs. Gwynne."

Thus it was that Olive received the first greeting of Harold's mother.

It startled—overpowered her; she had been so much agitated that day. She was surprised into that rare weakness, a hearty, even childish burst of tears. Mrs. Gwynne came up to her, with a softness almost motherly.

"You are pained, Miss Rothesay; you remember the past But I have now come to hope that everything may be forgotten, save that I was your father's old friend. For our Scottish friendship, like our pride, descends from generation to generation. Fortune has made us neighbours, let us then be friends. It is my earnest wish, and that of my son Harold."

"Your son!" echoed Olive; and then, half-bewildered by all these adventures, coincidences, and *éclaircissements*, she told how she had already met him, and how that meeting had shown to her her old companion's grave.

"That is strange, too. Never while she lived did Mrs. Harold Gwynne mention your name. And you loved her so! Well! 'twas like her—like her!" muttered Harold's mother; "but peace be with the dead!"

She walked up, and laid her hand on Olive's shoulder.

"My dear, I am an old woman; excuse my speaking plainly. You know nothing of me and of my son, save what is harsh and painful. Forget all this, and remember only that I loved your father when he was quite a child, and that I am prepared to love his daughter, if she so choose. You must not think I am taking a hasty fancy—we Scottish folk rarely do that. But I have learnt much about you lately—more than you guess—and have recognised in you the 'little Olive' of whom Angus Rothesay told me so much only a few days before his death."

"Did you see my dear father then?—did he talk of me?" cried Olive, eagerly, as, forgetting all the painful remembrances attached to the Gwynne family, she began to look at Harold's mother almost with affection.

But Mrs. Gwynne, who had unfolded herself in a way most unusual, now was relapsing into reserve. "We will talk of this another time, my dear. Now, I should much desire to see Mrs. Rothesay."

Olive went to fetch her. How she contrived to explain all that had transpired, she never clearly knew herself. However, she succeeded, and shortly re-appeared, with her mother leaning on her arm.

And, beholding the pale, worn, but still graceful woman, who, with her sightless eyes cast down, clung to her sole stay—her devoted child—Mrs. Gwynne seemed deeply moved. There was even a sort of deprecatory hesitation in her manner, but it soon passed.—She clasped the widow's hands, and spoke to her in a voice so sweet, so winning, that all pain vanished from Mrs. Rothesay's mind.

In a little while she was sitting calmly by Mrs. Gwynne's side, listening to her talking. It went into the blind woman's heart. Soft the voice was, and kind; and above all, there were in it the remembered, long unheard accents of the northern tongue. She felt again like young Sybilla Hyde, creeping along in the moonlight by the side of her stalwart Highland lover, listening to his whispers, and thinking that there was in the wide world no one like her own Angus Rothesay—so beautiful and so brave!

When Mrs. Gwynne quitted the Dell, she left on the hearts of both mother and daughter a pleasure which they sought not to repress. They were quite glad that the next day was Sunday, when they would go to Harbury, and hear Harold Gwynne preach. Olive told her mother all that had passed in the churchyard, and they agreed that he must be a very peculiar, though a very clever man. As for Christal, she had gone off with her friend, Mrs. Fludyer, and did not interfere in the conversation at all.

When Sunday morning came, Mrs. Rothesay's feeble strength was found unequal to a walk of two miles. Christal, apparently not sorry for the excuse, volunteered to remain with her, and Olive went to church alone. She was loth to leave her mother; but then she did so long to hear Mr. Gwynne preach! She thought, all the way, what kind of minister he would make. Not at all like any other, she was quite sure.

She entered the grey, still, village church, and knelt down to pray in a retired corner-pew. There was a great quietness over her—a repose like that of the morning before sunrise. She felt a meek happiness, a hopeful looking forth into life; and yet a touch would have awakened the fountain of tears.

She saw Mrs. Gwynne walk up the aisle alone, with her firm, stately step, and then the service began. Olive glanced one instant at the officiating minister;—it was the same stern face that she had seen by Sara's grave; nay, perhaps even more stern. Nor did she like his reading, for there was in it the same iron coldness. He repeated the touching liturgy of the English Church with the tone of a judge delivering sentence—an orator pronouncing his well-written, formal harangue. Olive had to shut her ears before she herself could heartily pray. This pained her; there was something so noble in Mr. Gwynne's face, so musical in his voice, that any shortcoming gave her a sense of disappointment. She felt troubled to think that he was the clergyman of the parish, and she must necessarily hear him every Sunday.

Harold Gwynne mounted his pulpit, and Olive listened intently. From what she had heard of him as a highly intellectual man, from the faint indications of character which she had herself noticed in their conversation, Miss Rothesay expected that he would have dived deeply into theological disquisition. She had too much penetration to look to him for the Christianity of a St. John—it was evident that such was not his nature; but she thought he would surely employ his powerful mind in wrestling with those knotty points of theology which might furnish arguments for a modern St. Paul.

But Harold Gwynne did neither. His sermon was a plain moral discourse—an essay such as Locke or Bacon might have written; save that he took care to translate it into language suitable to his hearers—the generality of whom were of the labouring class. Olive liked him for this, believing she recognised therein the strong sense of duty, the wish to do good, which overpowered all desire of intellectual display. And when she had once succeeded in ignoring the fact that his sermon was of a character more suited to the professor's chair than the pulpit, she listened with deep interest to his teaching of a lofty, but somewhat stern morality. Yet, despite his strong, clear arguments, and his evident earnestness, there was about him a repellent atmosphere, which prevented her inclining towards *the man*, even while she was constrained to respect the intellect of the preacher.

Nevertheless, when Mr. Gwynne ended his brief discourse with the usual prayer, that it might be "grafted inwardly" in his hearers' minds, it sounded very like a mockery—at least to Olive, who for the moment had almost forgotten that she was in a church. During the silent pause of the kneeling congregation, she raised her eyes and looked at the minister. He, too, knelt like the rest, with covered face, but his hands were not folded in prayer—they were clenched like those of a man writhing under some strong and secret agony; and when he lifted his head, his rigid features were more rigid than ever. The organ awoke, pealing forth Handel's "Hallelujah Chorus," and still the pastor sat motionless in his pulpit, his stern face showing white in the sunshine. The heavenly music rolled round him its angelic waves—they never touched his soul. Beneath, his simple congregation passed out, exchanging with one another demure Sunday greetings, and kindly Sunday smiles; he saw them not. He sat alone, like one who has no sympathy either with heaven or earth.

But there watched him from the hidden corner eyes he knew not of—the wondering, half-pitying eyes of Olive Rothesay. And while she gazed, there came into her heart—involuntarily, as if whispered by an unseen angel at her side—the words from the Litany—words which he himself had coldly read an hoar before:—

"That it may please Thee to lead into the way of truth all such as have erred and are deceived. We beseech Thee to hear us, O Lord!"

Scarcely conscious was she why she thus felt, or for whom she prayed; but, years after, it seemed to her that there had been a solemn import in these words.

Miss Rothesay was late in quitting the church. As she did so, she felt her arm lightly touched, and saw beside her Mrs. Gwynne.

"My dear, I am glad to meet you—we scarcely expected to have seen you at church to-day. Alone, too! then you must come with me to the Parsonage to lunch. You say nay? What! are we still so far enemies that you refuse our bread and salt?"

Olive coloured with sensitive fear lest she might have given pain. Besides, she felt a strong attraction towards Mrs. Gwynne—a sense of looking up, such as she had never before experienced towards any woman. For, it is needless to say, Olive's affection for her mother was the passionate, protecting tenderness of a nurse for a beloved charge—nay, even of a lover towards an idolised mistress; but there was nothing of reverential awe in it at all. Now Mrs. Gwynne carried with her dignity, influence, command. Olive, almost against her will, found herself passing down the green alley that led to the Parsonage. As she walked along—her slight small figure pressed close to her companion, who had taken her "under her arm,"—she felt almost like a child beside Harold's mother.

At the door sat little Ailie, amusing herself with a great dog. She looked restless and wearied, as a child does, kept in the house under the restrictions of "Sunday play." At the sight of her grandmother, the little girl seemed half-pleased, half-frightened, and tried to calm Rover's frolics within the bounds of Sabbatic propriety. This being impossible, Mrs. Gwynne's severe voice ordered both the offenders away in different directions. Then she apologised to Miss Rothesay.

"Perhaps," she continued, "you are surprised that Ailie was not with me this morning. But such is her father's will. My son Harold is peculiar in his opinions, and has a great hatred of cant, especially infantile cant."

"And does Ailie never go to church?"

"No! but I take care that she keeps Sunday properly and reverently at home. I remove her playthings and her baby-books, and teach her a few of Dr. Watt's moral hymns."

Olive sighed. She felt that this was not the way to teach the faith of Him who smiled with benign tenderness on the little child "set in the midst." And it grieved her to think what a wide gulf there was between the untaught Ailie, and that sincere, but stern piety over which had gathered the formality of advancing years.

Mrs. Gwynne and her guest had sat talking for some minutes, when Harold was seen crossing the lawn. His mother called him, and he came to the window with the quick response of one who in all his life had never heard that summons unheeded. It was a slight thing, but Olive noticed it, and the loving daughter felt more kindly towards the duteous son.

"Harold, Miss Rothesay is here."

He glanced in at the open window with a surprised half-confused air, which was not remarkable, considering the awkwardness of this second meeting, after their first rencontre. Remembering it, Olive heard his steps down the long hall with some trepidation. But entering, he walked up to her with graceful ease, took her hand, and expressed his pleasure in meeting her. He did not make the slightest allusion either to their former correspondence, or to their late conversation in the churchyard.

Olive's sudden colour paled beneath his unconcerned air; her faintly-quickened pulses sank into quietness; it seemed childish to have been so nervously sensitive in meeting Harold Gwynne. She felt thoroughly ashamed of herself, and was afraid lest her shyness might have conveyed to him and to his mother the impression, which she would not for worlds have given,—that she bore any painful or uncharitable remembrance of the past.

Soon the conversation glided naturally into ease and pleasantness. Mrs. Gwynne had the gift of talking well—a rare quality among women, whose conversation mostly consists of disjointed chatter, long-winded repetitions, or a commonplace remark, and—silence. But Alison Gwynne had none of these feminine peculiarities. To listen to her was like reading a pleasant book. Her terse, well-chosen sentences had all the grace of easy chat, and yet were so unaffected that not until you paused to think them over, did you discover that you might have "put them all down in a book;" and made an excellent book too.

Her son had not this gift; or, if he had, he left it unemployed. It was a great moment that could draw more than ordinary words from the lips of Harold Gwynne; and such moments seemed to have been rare indeed with him. Generally he appeared—as he did now to Olive Rothesay—the dignified, but rather silent master of the household—in whose most winning grace there was reserve, and whose very courtesy implied command.

He showed this when, after an hour's pleasant visit, Miss Rothesay moved to depart. Harold requested her to remain a few minutes longer.

"I have occasion to go to the Hall before evening service, and I shall be happy to accompany you on the way, if you do not object to my escort."

If Olive had been quite free, probably she would have answered that she did; for her independent habits made her greatly enjoy a long quiet walk alone, especially through a beautiful country. She almost felt that the company of her redoubtable pastor would be a restraint. But in all that Harold Gwynne did or said there lurked an inexplicable sway, to which every one seemed to bend. Almost against her will, she remained; and in a few minutes was walking beside him to the little wicket-gate.

Here they were interrupted by some one on clerical business. Mr. Gwynne desired her to proceed; he would overtake her ere she had descended the hill. Thither Olive went, half hoping that she might after all take her walk alone. But very soon she heard behind her footsteps, quick, firm, manly, less seeming to tread than to crush the ground. Such footsteps give one a feeling of being haunted—as they did to Olive. It was a relief when they came up with her, and she was once more joined by Harold Gwynne.

"You are exact in keeping your word," observed Miss Rothesay, by way of saying something.

"Yes, always; when I say *I will*, it is generally done. The road is uneven and rough, will my arm aid you, Miss Rothesay?"

She accepted it, perhaps the more readily because it was offered less as a courtesy than a support, and one not unneeded, for Olive was rather tired with her morning's exertions, and with the excitement of talking to strangers. As she walked, there came across her mind the thought—what a new thing it was for her to have a strong kindly arm to lean on! But it seemed rather pleasant than otherwise, and she felt gratefully towards Mr. Gwynne.

They conversed on the ordinary topics, natural to such a recent acquaintance—the beauty of the country around, the peculiarities of forest scenery, etc. etc. Never once did Harold's conversation assimilate to that which had so struck Olive when they stood beside poor Sara's grave. It seemed as though the former Harold Gwynne—the object of her girlhood's dislike, her father's enemy, her friend's husband—had vanished for ever, and in his stead was a man whose strong individuality of character already interested her. He was unlike all other men she had ever known. This fact, together with the slight mystery that hung over him, attracted the lingering romance of Olive's nature, and made her observe his manner and his words with a vigilant curiosity, as if to seek some new revelation of humanity in his character or his history. Therefore, every little incident of conversation in that first walk was carefully put by in her hidden nooks of memory, to amuse her mother with,—and perhaps also to speculate thereupon herself.

They reached Farnwood Dell, and Olive's conscience began to accuse her of having left her mother for so many hours. Therefore her adieux and thanks to Mr. Gwynne were somewhat abrupt. Mechanically she invited him in, and, to her surprise, he entered.

Mrs. Rothesay was sitting out of doors, in her garden chair. A beautiful picture she made, leaning back with-a mild sweetness, scarce a smile hovering on her lips. Her pale little hands were folded on her black dress; her soft braids of hair, already silver-grey, and her complexion, lovely as that of a young girl, showing delicately in contrast with her crimson garden-hood, the triumph of her daughter's skilful fingers.

Olive crossed the grass with a quick and noiseless step,—Harold following. "Mamma, darling!"

A light, bright as a sunburst, shone over Mrs. Rothesay's face—"My child! how long you have been away. Did Mrs. Gwynne"—

"Hush, darling!"—in a whisper—"I have been at the Parsonage, and Mr. Gwynne has kindly brought me home. He is here now."

Harold stood at a distance and bowed.

Olive came to him, saying, in a low tone, "Take her hand, she cannot see you, she is blind."

He started with surprise. "I did not know—my mother told me nothing."—And then, advancing to Mrs. Rothesay, he pressed her hand in both his, with such an air of reverent tenderness and gentle compassion, that it made his face grow softened—beautiful, divine!

Olive Rothesay, turning, beheld that look. It never afterwards faded from her memory.

Mrs. Rothesay arose, and said in her own sweet manner, "I am happy to meet Mr. Gwynne, and to thank him for taking care of my child." They talked for a few minutes, and then Olive persuaded her mother to return to the house.

"You will come, Mr. Gwynne?" said Mrs. Rothesay. He answered, hesitating, that the afternoon would close soon, and he must go on to Farnwood Hall. Mrs. Rothesay rose from her chair with the touching, helpless movement of one who is blind.

"Permit me," said Harold Gwynne, as, stepping quickly forward, he drew her arm through his, arranging her shawl with a care like a woman's. And so he led her into the house, with a tenderness beautiful to see.

Olive, as she followed silently after, felt her whole heart melted towards him. She never forgot Harold's first meeting with, and his kindness to, her mother.

He went away, promising to pay another visit soon.

"I am quite charmed with Mr. Gwynne," said Mrs. Rothesay. "Tell me, Olive, what he is like."

Olive described him, though not enthusiastically at all. Nevertheless, her mother answered, smiling, "He must, indeed, be a remarkable person. He is such a perfect gentleman, and his voice is so kind and pleasant;—like his mother, too, he has a little of the sweet Scottish tongue. Truly, I did not think there had been in the world such a man as Harold Gwynne."

"Nor I," answered Olive, in a soft, quiet, happy voice. She hung over her mother with a deeper tenderness—she looked out into the lovely autumn sunset with a keener sense of beauty and of joy. The sun was setting, the year was waning; but on Olive Rothesay's life had risen a new season and a new day.

CHAPTER XXVIII

"Well, I never in my life knew such a change as Farnwood has made in Miss Manners," observed old Hannah, the Woodford Cottage maid; who, though carefully kept in ignorance of any facts that could betray the secret of Christal's history, yet seemed at times to bear a secret grudge against her, as an interloper. "There she comes, riding across the country like some wild thing—she who used to be so prim and precise!"

"Poor young creature, she is like a bird just let out of a cage," said Mrs. Rothesay, kindly. "It is often so with girls brought up as she has been. Olive, I am glad you never went to school."

Olive's answer was stopped by the appearance of Christal, followed by one of the young Fludyer boys, with whom she had become a first-rate favourite. Her fearless frankness, her exuberant spirits, tempered only by her anxiety to appear always "the grand lady," made her a welcome guest at Farnwood Hall. Indeed, she was rarely at home, save when appearing, as now, on a hasty visit, which quite disturbed Mrs. Rothesay's placidity, and almost drove old Hannah crazy.

"He is not come yet, you see," Christal said, with a mysterious nod to Charley Fludyer. "I thought we should outride him—a parson never can manage a pony. But he will surely be here soon?"

"*Who* will be here soon?" asked Olive, considerably surprised. "Are you speaking of Mr. Gwynne?"

"Mr. Gwynne, no! Far better fun than that, isn't it, Charley? Shall we tell the secret or not? Or else shall we tell half of it, and let her puzzle it out till he comes?" The boy nodded assent "Well, then, there is coming to see you to-day a friend of Charley's, who only arrived at Farnwood last night, and since then has been talking of nothing else but his old idol, Miss Olive Rothesay. So I told him to meet me here, and, lo! he comes."

There was a hurried knock at the door, and immediately the little parlour was graced by the presence of an individual,—whom Olive did not recognise in the least. He seemed about twenty, slight and tall, of a complexion red and white; his features pretty, though rather girlish.

Olive bowed to him in undisguised surprise; but the moment he saw her his face became "celestial rosy red," apparently from a habit he had, in common with other bashful youths, of blushing on all occasions.

"I see you do not remember me, Miss Rothesay. Of course I could not expect it. But I have not forgotten you."

Olive, though still doubtful, instinctively offered him her hand. The tall youth took it eagerly, and as he looked down upon her, something in his expression reminded her of a face she had herself once looked down upon—her little knight of the garden at Oldchurch. In the impulse of the moment she called him again by his old name—"Lyle! Lyle Derwent!"

"Yes, it is indeed I!" cried the young man. "Oh, Miss Rothesay, you can't tell how glad I am to meet you again."

"I am glad, too." And Olive regarded him with that half-mournful curiosity with which we trace the lineaments of some long-forgotten face, belonging to that olden time, between which and now a whole lifetime seems to have intervened.

"Is that little Lyle Derwent?" cried Mrs. Rothesay, catching the name. "How very strange! Come hither, my dear boy! Alas, I cannot see you. Let me put my hand on your head."

But she could not reach it, he was grown so tall. She seemed startled to think how time had flown.

"He is quite a man now, mamma," said Olive; "you know we have not seen him for many years"——

Lyle added, blushing deeper than before—"The last time—I remember it well—was in the garden, one Sunday in spring—nine years ago."

"Nine years ago! Is it then nine years since my Angus died?" murmured the widow; and a grave silence spread itself over them all. In the midst of it Christal and Charley, seeing this meeting was not likely to produce the "fun" they expected, took the opportunity of escaping.

Then came the questions, which after so long a period one shrinks from asking, afraid of answer. Olive learnt that old Mr. Derwent had ceased to scold, and poor Bob played his mischievous pranks no more. Both lay quiet in Oldchurch churchyard. Worldly losses, too, had chanced, until the sole survivor of the family found himself very poor.

"I should not even have gone to college," said Lyle, "but for the kindness of my brother-in-law, Harold Gwynne."

Olive started. "Oh, true—I forgot all about that. Then he has been a good brother to you?" added she, with a feeling of pleasure and interest.

"He has indeed. When my father died, I had not a relative in the world, save a rich old uncle who wanted to put me in his counting-house; but Harold stood between us, and saved me from a calling I hated. And when my uncle turned me off, he took me home. Yes! I am not ashamed to say that I owe everything in the world to my brother Harold. I feel this the more, because he was not quite happy in his marriage. She did not suit him—my sister Sara."

"Indeed?" said Olive, and changed the conversation. After tea, Lyle, who appeared rather a sentimental young gentleman, proposed a moonlight walk in the garden. Miss Christal, after eyeing Olive and her cavalier with a mixture of amusement and vexation, as if she did not like to miss so excellent a chance of fun and flirtation, consoled herself with ball-playing and Charley Fludyer.

As their conversation grew more familiar, Olive was rather disappointed in Lyle. In his boyhood, she had thought him quite a little genius; but the bud had given more promise than the flower was ever likely to fulfil. Now she saw in him one of those not uncommon characters, who with sensitive feeling, and some graceful talent, yet never rise to the standard of genius. Strength, daring, and, above all, originality were wanting in his mind. With all his dreamy sentiment—his lip-library of perpetually quoted poets— and his own numberless scribblings (of which he took care to inform Miss Rothesay)—Lyle Der-went would probably remain to his life's end a mere "poetical gentleman."

Olive soon divined all this, and she began to weary a little of her companion and his vague sentimentalities, "in linked sweetness long drawn out." Besides, thoughts much deeper had haunted her at times, during the evening—thoughts of the marriage which had been "not quite happy." This fact scarcely surprised her. The more she began to know of Mr. Gwynne—and she had seen a great deal of him, considering the few weeks of their acquaintance—the more she marvelled that he had ever chosen Sara Derwent for his wife. Their union must have been like that of night and day, fierce fire and unstable water. Olive longed to fathom the mystery, and could not resist saying.

"You were talking of your sister a-while ago. I stopped you, for I saw it pained mamma. But now I should so like to hear something about my poor Sara."

"I can tell you little, for I was a boy when she died. But things I then little noticed, I put together afterwards. It must have been quite a romance,

I think. You know my sister had a former lover—Charles Geddes. Do you remember him?"

"I do—well!" and Olive sighed—perhaps over the remembrance of the dream born in that fairy time—her first girlish dream of ideal love.

"He was at sea when Sara married. On his return the news almost drove him wild. I remember his coming in the garden—our old garden, you know—where he and Sara used to walk. He seemed half mad, and I went to him, and comforted him as well as I could, though little I understood his grief. Perhaps I should now!" said Lyle, lifting his eyes with rather a doleful, sentimental air; which, alas! was all lost upon his companion.

"Poor Charles!" she murmured. "But tell me more."

"He persuaded me to take back all her letters, together with one from himself, and give them to my sister the next time I went to Harbury. I did so. Well I remember that night! Harold came in, and found his wife crying over the letters. In a fit of jealousy he took them and read them all through—together with that of Charles. He did not see me, or know the part I had in the matter, but I shall never forget *him*."

"What did he do?" asked Olive, eagerly. Strange that her question and her thoughts were not of Sara, but of Harold.

"Do? nothing! But his words—I remember them distinctly, they were so freezing, so stern. He grasped her arm, and said, 'Sara, when you said you loved me, you uttered *a lie!* When you took your marriage oath, you vowed *a lie!* Every day since, that you have smiled in my face, you have looked *a lie!* Henceforth I will never trust you—or any woman.'"

"And what followed?" cried Olive, now so strongly interested that she never paused to think if she had any right to ask these questions.

"Soon after, Sara came home to us. She did not stay long, and then returned to Harbury. Harold was never unkind to her—that I know. But, somehow, she pined away; the more so after she heard of Charles Geddes's sudden death."

"Alas! he died too."

"Yes; by an accident his own recklessness caused. But he was weary of his life, poor fellow! Well—Sara never quite recovered that shock. After little Ailie was born, she lingered a few weeks, and then died. It was almost a relief to us all."

"What! did you not love your sister?"

"Of course I did; but then she was older than I, and had never cared for me much. Now, as to Harold, I owe him everything. He has been to me less like a brother than a father; not in affection, perhaps that is scarcely in his nature, but in kindness and in counsel. There is not in the world a better man than Harold Gwynne."

Olive replied warmly. "I am sure of it, and I like you the more for acknowledging it." Then, in some confusion, she added, "Pardon me, but I had quite gone back to the old times, when you were my little pet. I really must learn to show more formality and respect to Mr. Derwent."

"Don't say *Mr. Derwent*. Pray call me Lyle, as you used to do."

"That I will, with pleasure. Only," she continued, smiling, "when I look up at you, I shall begin to feel quite an ancient dame, since I am so much older than you."

"Not at all," Lyle answered, with an eagerness somewhat deeper than the mannish pride of youths who have just crossed the Rubicon that divides them from their much-scorned '*teens*.' "I have advanced, and you seem to have stood still; there is scarcely any difference between us now." And Olive, somewhat amused, let her old favourite have his way.

They spoke on trivial subjects, until it was time to return to the house. Just as they were entering, Lyle said:

"Look! there is my brother-in-law standing at the gate. Oh, Miss Rothesay, be sure you never tell him of the things we have been talking about."

"It is not likely I shall ever have the opportunity. Mr. Gwynne seems a very reserved man."

"He is so; and of these matters he now never speaks at all."

"Hush! he is here;" and with a feeling of unwonted nervousness, as if she feared he had been aware of how much she had thought and conversed about him, Olive met Harold Gwynne.

"I am afraid I am an intruder, Miss Rothesay," said the latter, with a half-suspicious glance at the tall, dark figure which stood near her in the moonlight.

"What! did you not know me, brother Harold? How funny!" And he laughed: his laugh was something like Sara's.

It seemed to ring jarringly on Mr. Gwynne's ear. "I was not aware, Miss Rothesay, that you knew my brother-in-law."

"Oh, Miss Rothesay and I were friends almost ten years ago. She was our neighbour at Oldchurch."

"Indeed." And Olive thought she discerned in his face, which she had already begun to read, some slight pain or annoyance. Perhaps it wounded him to know any one who had known Sara. Perhaps—but conjectures were vain.

"I am glad you are come," she said to Harold. "Mamma has been wishing for you all day. Lyle, will you go and tell her who is here. Nay, Mr. Gwynne, surely you will come back with me to the house?"

He seemed half-inclined to resist, but at last yielded. So he made one of the little circle, and "assisted" well at this, the first of many social evenings, at Farnwood Dell But at times, Olive caught some of his terse, keen, and somewhat sarcastic sayings, and thought she could imagine the look and tone with which he had said the bitter words about "never trusting woman more."

He and Lyle went away together, and Christal, who had at last succeeded in apparently involving the light-hearted young collegian within the meshes of her smiles, took consolation in a little quiet drollery with Charley Fludyer; but even this resource failed when Charley spoke of returning home.

"I shall not go back with you to-night," said Christal. "I shall stay at the Dell. You may come and fetch me to-morrow, with the pony you lent me; and bring Mr. Derwent, too, to lead it. To see him so employed would be excellent fun."

"You seem to have taken a sudden passion for riding, Christal," said Olive, with a smile, when they were alone.

"Yes, it suits me. I like dashing along across the country—it is excitement; and I like, too, to have a horse obeying me—'tis so delicious to rule! To think that Madame Blandin should consider riding unfeminine, and that I should have missed that pleasure for so many years! But I am my own mistress now. By the way," she added, carelessly, "I wanted to have a few words with you, Miss Rothesay." She had rarely called her *Olive* of late.

"Nay, my dears," interposed Mrs. Rothesay, "do not begin to talk just yet—not until I am gone to bed; for I am very, very tired" And so, until Olive came downstairs again, Christal sat in dignified solitude by the parlour fire.

"Well," said Miss Rothesay, when she entered, "what have you to say to me, my dear child?"

Christal drew back a little at the familiar word and manner, as though she did not quite like it. But she only said, "Oh, it is a mere trifle; I am obliged to mention it, because I understand Miss Vanbrugh left my money matters under your care until I came of age."

"Certainly; you know it was by your consent, Christal."

"O yes, because it will save me trouble. Well, all I wanted to say was, that I wish to keep a horse."

"To keep a horse!"

"Certainly; what harm can there be in that? I long to ride about at my own will; go to the meets in the forest; even to follow the hounds. I am my own mistress, and I choose to do it," said Christal in rather a high tone.

"You cannot, indeed, my dear," answered Olive mildly. "Think of all the expenses it would entail—expenses far beyond your income."

"I myself am the best judge of that."

"Not quite. Because, Christal, you are still very young, and have little knowledge of the world. Besides, to tell you the plain truth—must I?"

"Certainly; of all things I hate deceit and concealment." Here Christal stopped, blushed a little; and half-turning aside, hid further in her bosom a little ornament which occasionally peeped out—a silver cross and beads. Then she said in a somewhat less angry tone, "You are right; tell me all your mind."

"I think, then, that though your income is sufficient to give you independence, it cannot provide you with luxuries. Also," she continued, speaking very gently, "it seems to me scarcely right, that a young girl like you, without father or brother, should go riding and hunting in the way you purpose."

"That still is my own affair—no one has a right to control me." Olive was silent. "Do you mean to say *you* have? Because you are in some sort my guardian, are you to thwart me in this manner? I will not endure it."

And there rose in her the same fierce spirit which had startled Olive on the first night of the girl's arrival at Woodford Cottage, and which, something to her surprise, had lain dormant ever since, covered over with the light-hearted trifling which formed Christal's outward character. "What am I to do?" thought Olive, much troubled. "How am I to wrestle with this girl? But I will do it—if only for Meliora's sake. Christal," she said affectionately, "we have never talked together seriously for a long time; not since the first night we met."

"I remember, you were good to me then," answered Christal, a little subdued.

"Because I was grieved for you—I pitied you." "Pitied!" and the angry demon again rose. Olive saw she must not touch that chord again.

"My dear," she said, still more kindly; "indeed I have neither the wish nor the right to rule you; I only advise." "And to advice I am ready to listen. Don't mistake me, Miss Rothesay. I liked you—I do still—very much indeed; but you don't quite understand or sympathise with me now."

"Why not, dear? Is it because I have little time to be with you, being so much occupied with my mother, and with my profession?"

"Ay, that is it," said Christal, loftily. "My dear Miss Rothesay, I am much obliged to you for all your kindness; but we do not suit one another. I have found that out since I visited at Farnwood Hall. There is a difference between a mere artist working for a livelihood, and an independent lady."

Even Christal, abrupt as her anger had made her, blushed for the rudeness of this speech. But false shame kept her from offering any atonement.

Olive's slight figure expressed unwonted dignity. In her arose something of the old Rothesay pride, but still more of pride in her Art. "There is a difference; but, to my way of thinking, it is often on the side of the artist."

Christal made no answer, and Olive continued, resuming her usual manner. "Come, we will not discuss this matter. All that need be decided now, is, whether or not I shall draw the sum you will require to buy your horse. I will, if you desire it; because, as you say, I have indeed no control over you. But, my dear Christal, I entreat you to pause and consider; at least till morning."

Olive rose, for she was unequal to further conversation. Deeply it pained her that this girl, whom she wished so to love, should evidently turn from her, not in dislike, but in a sort of contemptuous indifference. Still she made one effort more. As she was retiring, she went up, bade her good-night, and kissed her as usual.

"Do not let this conversation make any division between us, Christal."

"Oh no," said Christal, rather coldly. "Only," she added, in the passionate, yet mournful tone, which she had before used when at Woodford Cottage; "only, you must not interfere with me, Olive. Remember, I was not brought up like you. I had no one to control me, no one to teach me to control myself. It could not be helped! and it is too late now."

"It is never too late," cried Olive. But Christal's emotion had passed, and she resumed her lofty manner.

"Excuse me, but I am a little too old to be lectured; and, I have no doubt, shall be able to guide my own conduct. For the future, we will not have quite such serious conversations as this. Good-night!"

Olive went away, heavy at heart. She had long been unaccustomed to wrestle with an angry spirit. Indeed, she lived in an atmosphere so pure and full of love, that on it never gloomed one domestic storm. She almost wished that Christal had not come with them to Farnwood. But then it seemed such an awful thing for this young and headstrong creature to be adrift on the wide world. She determined that, whether Christal desired it or no, she would never lose sight of her, but try to guide her with so light a hand, that the girl might never even feel the sway.

Next morning Miss Manners abruptly communicated her determination not to have the horse, and the matter was never again referred to. But it had placed a chasm between Olive and Christal, which the one could not, the other would not pass. And as various other interests grew up in Miss Rothesay's life, her anxiety over this wayward girl a little ceased. Christal stayed almost wholly at Farnwood Hall; and in humble, happy, Farnwood Dell, Olive abode, devoted to her Art and to her mother.

CHAPTER XXIX

Weeks glided into months; and within the three-mile circle of the Hall, the Parsonage, and the Dell, was as pleasant a little society as could be found, anywhere. Frequent meetings, usually confined to themselves alone, produced the necessary intimacy of a country neighbourhood.

As it sometimes happens that persons, or families taught to love each other unknown, when well known learn to hate; so, on the contrary, it is no unfrequent circumstance for those who have lived for years in enmity, when suddenly brought together, to become closer friends than if there had been no former antipathy between them. So it was with the Rothesays and the Gwynnes.

Once after Mrs. Gwynne and her son had spent a long pleasant evening at the Dell, Olive chanced to light upon the packet of Harold's letters, which, years before, she had put by, with the sincere wish that she might never hear anything of him more.

"You would not wish so now, Olive—nor would I," said Mrs. Rothesay, when her daughter had smilingly referred to the fact. "The society of the Gwynnes has really proved a great addition to our happiness. How kind and warmhearted Mrs. Gwynne is—so earnest in her friendship for us, too!"

"Yes, indeed. Do you know, it struck me that it must have been from her report of us, that aunt Flora Rothesay sent the kind message which the Gwynnes brought to-day. I own, it made me happy! To think that my long-past romantic dream should be likely to come true, and that next year we should go to Scotland and see papa's dear old aunt."

"*You* will go, my child."

"And you too, darling. Think how much you would like it, when the summer comes. You will be quite strong then; and how pleasant it will be to know that good aunt Flora, of whom the Gwynnes talk so much. She must be a very, very old lady now, though Mrs. Gwynne says she is quite beautiful still. But she can't be so beautiful as my own mamma. O, darling, there never will be seen such a wondrous old lady as you, when you are seventy or eighty, Then, I shall be quite elderly myself. We shall seem just like two sisters—growing old together."

Olive never spoke, never dreamed of any other possibility than this.

Calmly, cheerfully, passed the winter, Miss Rothesay devoting herself, as heretofore, to the two great interests of her life; but she had other minor interests gathering up around her, which in some respects were of much service. They prevented that engrossing study, which was often more than her health could bear. Once when reading letters from Rome, from Mr. Vanbrugh and Meliora, Olive said,

"Mamma, I think on the whole I am happier here than I was at Woodford Cottage. I feel less of an artist and more of a woman."

"And, Olive, I am happy too—happy to think that my child is safe with me, and not carried off to Rome." For Olive had of course told her mother of that circumstance in her life, which might have changed its current so entirely. "My daughter, I would not have you leave me to marry any man in the world!"

"I never shall, darling!" she answered. And she felt that this was true. Her heart was absorbed in her mother.

Nevertheless, the other interests before mentioned, though quite external, filled up many little crevices in that loving heart which had room for so many affections. Among these was one which, in Olive's whole lifetime, had been an impulse, strong, but ever unfulfilled—love for a child. She took to her heart Harold's little daughter, less regarding it as his, than as poor Sara's. The more so, because, though a good and careful, he was not a very loving father. But he seemed gratified by the kindness that Miss Rothesay showed to little Ailie; and frequently suffered the child to stay with her, and be taught by her all things, save those in which it was his pleasure that his daughter should remain ignorant—the doctrines of the Church of England.

Sometimes in her visiting of the poor, Olive saw the frightful profanities of that cant knowledge which young or ignorant minds acquire, and by which the greatest mysteries of Christianity are lowered to a burlesque. Then she inclined to think that Harold Gwynne was right, and that in this temporary prohibition he acted as became a wise father and "a discreet and learned minister of God's Word." As such she ever considered him; though she sometimes thought he received and communicated that Word less through his heart than through his intellect. His moral character and doctrines were irreproachable, but it seemed to her as if the dew of Christian love had never fallen on his soul.

This feeling gave her, in spite of herself, a sort of awe for him, which she would not willingly have felt towards her pastor, and one whom she so much regarded and respected. Especially as on any other subject she ever held with him full and free communion, and he seemed gradually to unbend his somewhat hard nature, as a man will do who inclines in friendship towards a truly good woman.

Perhaps here it would be as well to observe, that, close and intimate friends as they were, the tie was such that none of their two households, no, not even the most tattling gossips of Farnwood and Harbury, ever dreamed of saying that Harold Gwynne was "in love" with Miss Rothesay. The good folks did chatter now and then, as country gossips will, about him and Christal Manners; and perhaps they would have chattered more, if the young lady had not been almost constantly at the Hall, whither Mr. Gwynne rarely went. But they left the bond between him and Olive Rothesay untouched, untroubled by their idle jests. Perhaps those who remembered the beautiful Mrs. Harold Gwynne, imagined the widower would never choose a second wife so *different* from his first; or perhaps there was cast about the daughter, so devotedly tending her blind mother, a sanctity which their unholy and foolish tongues dared not to violate.

Thus Olive went on her way, showing great tenderness to little Ailie, and, as it seemed, being gradually drawn by the child to the father. Besides, there was another sympathy between them, caused by the early associations of both, and by their common Scottish blood. For Harold had inherited from his father nothing but his name; from his mother everything besides. Born in Scotland, he was a Scotsman to the very core. His influence awakened once more every feeling that bound Olive Rothesay to the land of her birth—her father's land. All things connected therewith took, in her eyes, a new romance. She was happy, she knew not why—happy as she had been in her dreamy girlhood. It seemed as though in her life had dawned a second spring.

Perhaps there was but one thing which really troubled her; and that was the prohibition in her teaching of little Ailie. She talked the matter over with her mother; that is, she uttered aloud her own thoughts, to which Mrs. Rothesay meekly assented; saying, as usual, that Olive was quite right. And at last, after much hesitation, she made up her mind to speak openly on the subject with Mr. Gwynne.

For this arduous undertaking, at which in spite of herself she trembled a little, she chose a time when he had met her in one of her forest-walks, which she had undertaken, as she often did, to fulfil some charitable duty, usually that of the clergyman or the clergyman's family.

"How kind you are, Miss Rothesay; and to come all through the wintry forest, too! It was scarcely fit for you.".

"Then it certainly was not for Mrs. Gwynne. I was quite glad to relieve her; and it gives me real pleasure to read and talk with John Dent's sick mother. Much as she suffers, she is the happiest old woman I ever saw in my life."

"What makes her happy, think you?" said Harold continuing the conversation as if he wished it to be continued, and so falling naturally into a quiet arm-in-arm walk.

Olive answered, responding to his evident intention, and passing at once, as in their conversations they always did, to a subject of interest, "She is happy, because she has a meek and trusting faith in God; and though she knows little she loves much."

"Can one love Him whom one does not fully know?" It was one of the sharp searching questions that Mr. Gwynne sometimes put, which never failed to startle Olive, and to which she could not always reply; but she made an effort to do so now.

"Yes, when what we do know of Him commands love. Does Ailie, even Ailie, thoroughly know her father? And yet she loves him."

"That I cannot judge; but most true it is, we know as little of God as Ailie knows of her father—ay, and look up to Heaven with as blindfold ignorance as Ailie looks up to me."

"Alas! Ailie's is indeed blindfold ignorance!" said Olive, not quite understanding his half-muttered words, but thinking they offered a good opportunity for fulfilling her purpose. "Mr. Gwynne, may I speak to you about something which has long troubled me?"

"Troubled you, Miss Rothesay? Surely that is not my fault? I would not for the world do aught that would give pain to one so good as you."

He said this very kindly, pressing her arm with a brotherly gentleness, which passed into her heart; imparting to her not only a quick sense of pleasure, but likewise courage.

"Thank you, Mr. Gwynne. This does really pain me. It is the subject on which we talked the first time that ever you and I met, and of which we have never since spoken—your determination with respect to little Ailie's religious instruction."

"Ah!" A start, and a dark look. "Well, Miss Rothesay, what have you to say?"

"That I think you are not quite right—nay, quite wrong," said Olive, gathering resolution. "You are taking from your child her only strength in life—her only comfort in death. You keep from her the true faith; she will soon make to herself a false one."

"Nay, what is more false than the idle traditions taught by ranting parents to their offspring—the Bible travestied into a nursery talc—heaven transformed into a pretty pleasure-house—and hell and its horrors brought as bugbears to frighten children in the dark. Do you think I would have my child turned into a baby saint, to patter glibly over parrot prayers, exchange pet sweetmeats for missionary pennies, and so learn to keep up a debtor and creditor account with Heaven? No, Miss Rothesay, I would rather see her grow up a heathen."

Olive, awed by his language, which was bitter even to fierceness, at first made him no answer. At length, however, she ventured, not without trembling, to touch another chord.

"But—suppose that your child should be taken away, would you have her die as she lives now, utterly ignorant of all holy things?"

"Would I have her die an infant bigot—prattling blindly of subjects which in the common course of nature no child can comprehend? Would I have her chronicled in some penny tract as a 'remarkable instance of infant piety' a small 'vessel of mercy,' to whom the Gospel was miraculously revealed at three years old?"

"Do not—oh! do not speak thus," cried Olive, shrinking from him, for she saw in his face a look she had never seen before—an expression answering to the bitter, daring sarcasm of his tone.

"You think me a strange specimen of a Church of England clergyman? Well, perhaps you are right! I believe I am rather different to my brethren." He said this with sharp irony. "Nevertheless, if you inquire concerning me in the neighbourhood, I think you will find that my moral conduct has never disgraced my cloth."

"Never!" cried Olive warmly. "Mr. Gwynne, pardon me if I have overstepped the deference due to yourself and your opinions. In some things I cannot fathom them or you; but that you are a good, sincere, and pious man, I most earnestly believe."

"*Do you!*"

Olive started. The two words were simple, but she thought they had an under-meaning, as though he were mocking either himself or her, or both. But she thought this could only be fancy; when in a minute or two after, he said in his ordinary manner,

"Miss Rothesay, we have been talking earnestly, and you have unconsciously betrayed me into speaking more warmly than I ought to speak. Do not misjudge me. All men's faith is free; and in some minor points of Christianity, I perhaps hold peculiar opinions. As regards little Ailie, I thank you for your kind interest in this matter, which we will discuss again another time."

They had now reached John Dent's cottage. Olive asked if he would not enter with her.

"No, no; you are a far better apostle than your clergyman. Besides, I have business at home, and must return. Good morning, Miss Rothesay."

He lifted his hat with a courtly grace, but his eyes showed that reverence which no courts could command—the reverence of a sincere man for a noble-hearted woman. And so he walked back into the forest.

CHAPTER XXX

The dwelling which Miss Rothesay entered was one of the keeper's cottages, built within the forest. The door stood open, for the place was too lowly, even for robbers; and, besides, its inmates had nothing to lose. Still, Olive thought it was wrong to leave a poor bedridden old woman in a state of such unprotected desolation. As her step was heard crossing the threshold, there was a shrill cry from the inner room.

"John, John—the lad!—hast thee found the lad?"

"It is not your son—'tis I. Why, what has happened, my good Margery?" But the poor old creature fell back and wrung her hands, sobbing bitterly.

"The lad!—dun ye know aught o' the lad? Poor Reuben!—he wunnot come back no more! Alack! alack!"

And with some difficulty Olive learnt that Margery's grandson, the keeper's only child, had gone into the forest some days before, and had never returned. It was no rare thing for even practised woodsmen to be lost in this wild, wide forest; and at night, in the winter time there was no hope. John Dent had gone out with his fellows, less to find the living than to bring back the dead.

Filled with deep pity Olive sat down by the miserable grandmother; but the poor soul refused to be comforted.

"John'll go mad—clean mad! There beant nowheres such a good lad as our Reuben; and to be clemmed to death, and froze! O Lord, tak' pity on us, miserable sinners!"

For hours Olive sat by the old woman's bedside. The murky winter day soon closed in, and the snow began to fall; but still there was nothing heard save the wind howling in the forest. Often Margery started up, crying out that there were footsteps at the door, and then sank back in dumb despair.

At last there was a tramp of many feet on the frozen ground, the latch was lifted, and John Dent burst in.

He was a sturdy woodsman, of a race that are often seen in this forest region, almost giant-like in height and bulk. The snow lay thick on his uncovered head and naked breast, for he had stripped off all his upper garments to wrap round something that was clasped tightly in his arms.

He spoke to no one, looked at no one, but laid his burden before the hearth supported on his knees. It was the corpse of a boy blue and shrivelled, like that of one frozen to death. He tried to chafe and bend the fingers, but they were as stiff as iron; he wrung the melting snow out of the hair, and, as the locks became soft and supple under his hand, seemed to think there was yet a little life remaining.

"Why dunnot ye stir, ye fools! Get t' blanket—pull't off the ould woman. I tell 'ee the lad's alive."

No one moved, and then the frantic father began to curse and swear. He rushed into old Margery's room.

"Get up wi' thee. How darest thee lie hallooing there. Come and help t' lad!" and then he ran back to where poor Reuben's body lay extended on the hearth, surrounded by the other woodsmen, most of whom were pale with awe, some even melting into tears. John Dent dashed them all aside, and took his son again in his arms. Olive, from her corner, watched the writhings of his rugged features, but she ventured not to approach.

"Tak' heart, tak' heart, John!" said one of the men.

"He didna suffer much, I reckon," said another. "My owd mother was nigh froze to death in t' forest, and her said 'twas just like dropping to sleep. An' luck ye, the poor lad's face be as quiet as a child."

"John Dent, mon!" whispered one old keeper; "say thy prayers; thee doesna often do't, and thee'll want it now."

And then John Dent broke into such a paroxysm of despair, that one by one his comforters quitted the cottage. They, strong bold men, who feared none of the evils of life, became feeble as children before the awful face of Death.

One only remained—the old huntsman who had given the last counsel to the wretched father. This man, whom Olive knew, was beckoned by her to Margery's room to see what could be done.

"I'll fetch Mr. Gwynne to manage John, poor fellow! The devil's got un, sure enough; and it'll tak' a parson to drive't away. But ourn be a queer gentleman. When I get to Harbury, what mun I say!"

"Say that I am here—that I entreat him to come at once," cried Olive, feeling her strength sinking before this painful scene, from which in common charity she could not turn aside. She came once more to look at John Dent, who had crouched down before the hearth, with the stiff form of the poor dead boy extended on his knees, gazing at it with a sort of vacant, hopeless misery. Then she went back to the old woman, and tried to speak of comfort and of prayer.

It was not far to Harbury, but, in less time than Olive had expected, Harold Gwynne appeared.

"Miss Rothesay, you sent for me!"

"I did—I did. Oh, thank Heaven that you are come," eagerly cried Olive, clasping his two hands. He regarded her with a surprised and troubled look, and took them away.

"What do you wish me to do!"

"What a minister of God is able—nay, bound to do—to speak comfort in this house of misery."

The poor old woman echoed the same entreaty—

"Oh, Mr. Gwynne, you that be a parson, a man of God, come and help us."

Harold looked round, and saw he had to face the woe that no worldly comfort or counsel can lighten;—that he had entered into the awful presence of the Power, which, stripping man of all his earthly pomp, wisdom, and strength, leaves him poor, weak, and naked before his God.

The proud, the moral, the learned Harold Gwynne, stood dumb before the mystery of Death. It was too mighty for him. He looked on the dead boy, and on the living father; then cast his eyes down to the ground, and muttered within himself, "What should I do here?"

"Read to him—pray with him," whispered Olive. "Speak to him of God—of heaven—of immortality."

"God—heaven—immortality," echoed Harold, vacantly, but he never stirred.

"They say that this man has been a great sinner, and an unbeliever. Oh, tell him that he cannot deceive himself now. Death knells into his ear that there is a God—there is a hereafter. Mr. Gwynne, oh tell him that, at a time like this, there is no comfort, no hope, save in God and in His Word."

Olive had spoken thus in the excitement of the moment; then recovering herself, she asked pardon for a speech so bold, as if she would fain teach the clergyman his duty.

"My duty—yes, I must do my duty," muttered Harold Gwynne. And with his hard-set face—the face he wore in the pulpit—he went up to the father of the dead child, and said something about "patience," "submission to the decrees of Providence," and "all trials being sent for good, and by the will of God."

"Dun ye talk to me of God? I know nought about him, parson—ye never learned me."

Harold's rigid mouth quivered visibly, but he made no direct answer, only saying, in the same formal tone, "You go to church—at least, you used to go—you have heard there about 'God in his judgments remembering mercy.'"

"Mercy! ye mun easy say that; why did He let the poor lad die i' the snow, then?"

And Harold's lips hesitated over those holy words "The Lord gave and the Lord taketh away."

"He should ha' takken th' owd mother, then. She's none wanted; but the dear lad—the only one left out o' six—oh, Reuben, Reuben, wunna ye never speak to your poor father again?"

He looked on the corpse fixedly for some minutes, and then a new thought seemed to strike him.

"That's not my lad—my merry little lad!—I say," he cried, starting up and catching Mr. Gwynne's arm; "I say, you parson that ought to know, where's my lad gone to?"

Harold Gwynne's head sank upon his breast: he made no answer. Perhaps—ay, and looking at him, the thought smote Olive with a great fear—perhaps to that awful question there was no answer in his soul.

John Dent passed him by, and came to the side of Olive Rothesay.

"Miss, folk say you're a good woman. Dun ye know aught o' these things—canna ye tell me if I shall meet my poor lad again?"

And then Olive, casting one glance at Mr. Gwynne, who remained motionless, sat down beside the childless father, and talked to him of God—not the Infinite Unknown, into whose mysteries the mightiest philosophers may pierce and find no end—but the God mercifully revealed, "Our Father which is in heaven"—He to whom the poor, the sorrowing, and the ignorant may look, and not be afraid.

Long she spoke; simply, meekly, and earnestly. Her words fell like balm; her looks lightened the gloomy house of woe. When, at length, she left it, John Dent's eyes followed her, as though she had been a visible angel of peace.

It was quite night when she and Harold wont out of the cottage. The snow had ceased falling, but it lay on every tree of the forest like a white shroud. And high above, through the opening of the branches, was seen the blue-black frosty sky, with its innumerable stars. The keen, piercing cold, the utter stirlessness, the mysterious silence, threw a sense of death—white death—over all things. It was a night when one might faintly dream what the world would be, if the infidel's boast were true, and *there were no God.*

They walked for some time in perfect silence. Troubled thoughts were careering like storm-clouds over Olive's spirit. Wonder was there, and pity, and an indefined dread. As she leaned on Mr. Gwynne's arm, she had a presentiment that in the heart whose strong beating she could almost feel, was prisoned some great secret of woe or wrong, before which she herself would stand aghast. Yet such was the nameless attraction which drew her to this man, that the more she dreaded, the more she longed to discover his mystery, whatsoever it might be. She determined to break the silence.

"Mr. Gwynne, I trust you will not think it presumption in me to have spoken as I did, instead of you; but I saw how shocked and overpowered you were, nor wondered at your silence."

He answered in the low tone of one struggling under great excitement. "You noticed my silence, then?—that I, summoned as a clergyman to give religious consolation, had none to offer."

"Nay, you did attempt some."

"Ay, I tried to preach faith with my lips, and could not, because there was none in my heart. No, nor ever will be!"

Olive looked at him uncomprehending, but he seemed to shrink from her observation. "I am indeed truly grieved," she began to say, but he stopped her.

"Do not speak to me yet, I pray you."

She obeyed; though yearning with pity over him. Hitherto, in all their intercourse, whatever had been his kindness towards her, towards him she had continually felt a sense of restraint—even of fear. That controlling influence, which Mr. Gwynne seemed to exercise over all with whom he deigned to associate, was heavy upon Olive Rothesay. Before him she felt more subdued than she had ever done before any one; in his presence she unconsciously measured her words and guarded her looks, as if meeting the eye of a master. And he was a master—a man born to rule over the wills of his brethren, swaying them at his lightest breath, as the wind bends the grass of the field.

But now the sceptre seemed torn from his hand—he was a king no more. He walked along—his head drooped, his eyes fixed on the ground. And beholding him thus, there came to Olive, in the place of fear, a strong compassion, tender as strong, and pure as tender. Angel-like, it arose in her heart, ready to pierce his darkness with its shining eyes—to fold around him and all his misery its sheltering wings. He was a great and learned man, and she a lowly woman; in her knowledge far beneath him, in her faith—oh! how immeasurably above!

She began very carefully. "You are not well, I fear. This painful scene has been too much, even for you. Death seems more horrible to men than to feeble women."

"Death!—do you think that I fear Death?" and he clenched his hand as though he would battle with the great Destroyer. "No!—I have met him—stood and looked at him—until my eyes were blinded, and my brain reeled. But what am I saying? Don't heed me, Miss Rothesay; don't." And he began to walk on hurriedly.

"You are ill, I am sure; and there is something that rests on your mind," said Olive, in a quiet, soft tone.

"What!—have I betrayed anything? I mean, have you anything to charge me with! Have I left any duty unfulfilled; said any words unbecoming a clergyman?" asked he with a freezing haughtiness.

"Not that I am aware. Forgive me, Mr. Gwynne, if I have trespassed beyond the bounds of our friendship. For we are friends—have you not often said so?"

"Yes, and with truth. I respect you, Miss Rothesay. You are no thoughtless girl, but a woman who has, I am sure, both felt and suffered! I have suffered too; therefore it is no marvel we are friends. I am glad of it."

He seldom spoke so frankly, and never had done what he now did—of his own accord, to take and clasp her hand with a friendly air of confidence. Long after the pressure passed from Olive's fingers, its remembrance lingered in her heart. They walked on a little farther; and then he said, not without some slight agitation,

"Miss Rothesay, if you are indeed my friend, listen to one request I make;—that you will not say anything, think anything, of whatever part of my conduct this day may have seemed strange to you. I know not what fate it is that has thus placed you, a year ago a perfect stranger, in a position which forces me to speak to you thus. Still less can I tell what there is in you which draws from me much that no human being has ever drawn before. Accept this acknowledgment, and pardon me."

"Nay, what have I to pardon? Oh, Mr. Gwynne, if I might be indeed your friend—if I could but do you any good!"

"You do good to *me*?" he muttered bitterly. "Why, we are as far apart as earth from heaven, nay, as heaven from hell; that is if there be——. Madman that I am! Miss Rothesay, do not listen to me. Why do you lead me on to speak thus?"

"Indeed, I do not comprehend you. Believe me, Mr. Gwynne, I know very well the difference between us. I am an unlearned woman, and you"——

"Ay, tell me what I am—that is, what you think I am."

"A wise and good man; but yet one in whom great intellect may at times overpower that simple Faith, which is above all knowledge; that Love, which, as said the great apostle of our Church"——

"Silence!" His deep voice rose and fell, like the sound of a breaking wave. Then he stopped, turned full upon her, and said, in a fierce, keen, whisper, "Would you learn the truth? You shall! Know, then, that I believe in none of these things I teach—I am an infidel!"

Olive's arm fell from him.

"Do you shrink from me, then? Good and pious woman, do you think I am Satan standing by your side?"

"Oh, no, no!" She made an effort to restrain herself; it failed, and she burst into tears.

Harold looked at her.

"Meek and gentle soul! It would, perhaps, have been good for me had Olive Rothesay been born my sister."

"I would I had—I would I had! But, oh! this is awful to hear. You, an unbeliever—you, who all these years have been a minister at the altar—what a fearful thing!"

"You say right—it is fearful. Think now what my life is, and has been. One long lie—a lie to man and to God. For I do believe so far," he added, solemnly; "I believe in the one ruling Spirit of the universe—unknown, unapproachable. None but a madman would deny the existence of a God."

He ceased, and looked upwards with his piercing eyes—piercing, yet full of restless sorrow. Then he approached his companion.

"Shall we walk on, or do you utterly renounce me?" said he, with a touching, sad humility.

"Renounce you!"

"Ah! you would not, could you know all I have endured. To me, earth has been a hell—not the place of flames and torments of which your divines prate, but the true hell—that of the conscience and the soul. I, too, a man whose whole nature was athirst for truth. I sought it first among its professors; there I found that they who, too idle or too weak to demonstrate their creed, took it upon trust, did what their fathers did, believed what their fathers believed—were accounted orthodox and pious men; while those who, in their earnest eager youth, dared—not as yet to doubt, but meekly to ask a reason for their faith—they were at once condemned as impious. But I pain you: shall I go on, or cease?"

"Go on."

"Truth, still truth, I yearned for in another form—in domestic peace—in the love of woman.—My soul was famishing for any food; I snatched this—in my mouth it became ashes!" His voice seemed choking, but with an effort he continued. "After this time I gave up earth, and turned to interests beyond it. With straining eyes I gazed into the Infinite—and I was dazzled, blinded, whirled from darkness to light, and from light to darkness—no rest, no rest! This state lasted long, but its end came. Now I walk like a man in his sleep, feeling nothing, fearing nothing,—no, thou mighty Unknown, I do *not* fear! But then I hope nothing: I believe nothing. Those pleasant dreams of yours—God, Heaven, Immortality—are to me meaningless words. At times I utter them, and they seem to shine down like pitiless stars upon the black boiling sea in which I am drowning."

"Oh, God, have mercy!" moaned Olive Rothesay. "Give me strength that my own faith fail not, and that I may bring Thy light unto this perishing soul!" And turning to Harold, she said aloud, as calmly as she could, "Tell me—since you have told me thus far—how you came to take upon yourself the service of the Church; you who"— —

"Ay, well may you pause and shudder! Hear, then, how the devil—if there be one—can mock men's souls in the form of an angel of light. But it is a long history—it may drive me to utter things that you will shrink from."

"I *will* hear it." There was, in that soft, firm voice an influence which Harold perforce obeyed. She was stronger than he, even as light is stronger than darkness.

Mr. Gwynne began, speaking quietly, even humbly. "When I was a youth studying for the Church, doubts came upon my mind, as they will upon most young minds whose strivings after truth are hedged in by a thorny rampart of old worn-out forms. Then there came a sudden crisis in my life; I must either enter on a ministry in whose creed I only half believed, or let my mother—my noble, self-denying mother—starve. You know her, Miss Rothesay, though you know not half that she is, and ever was to me. But you do know what it is to have a beloved mother."

"Yes."

Infidel as he was, she could have clung to Harold Gwynne, and called him brother.

"Well, after a time of great inward conflict, I decided—for her sake. Though little more than a boy in years, struggling in a chaos of mingled doubt and faith, I bound myself to believe whatever the Church taught, and to lead souls to heaven in the Church's own road. These very bonds, this vow so blindly to be fulfilled, made me, in after years, an infidel."

He paused to look at her.

"I am listening, speak on," said Olive Rothesay.

"As you say truly, I am one whose natural bent of mind is less to faith than to knowledge. Above all, I am one who hates all falsehood, all hypocritical show. Perchance in the desert I might have learned to serve God. Face to face with Him I might have worshiped His revealings. But when between me and the one great Truth came a thousand petty veils of cunning forms and blindly taught precedents; when among my brethren I saw wicked men preaching virtue—men without brains enough to acquire a mere worldly profession, such as law or physic, set to expound the mighty mysteries of religion—then I said to myself, 'The whole system is a lie!' So I cast it from me, and my soul stood forth in its naked strength before the Creator of all."

"But why did you still keep up this awful mockery?"

"Because," and his voice sounded hoarse and hollow, "just then there was upon me a madness which all men have in youth—love. For that I became a liar in the face of Heaven, of men, and of my own soul."

"It was a great sin."

"I know it; and, being such, it fell down upon my head in a curse. Since then I have been what you now see me—a very honest, painstaking clergyman; doing good, preaching, certainly not doctrine, but blameless moralities, carrying a civil face to the world, and a heart—Oh God! whosoever and whatsoever Thou art, Thou knowest what blackest darkness there is *there!*"

She made no answer.

After a few minutes, Mr. Gwynne said, "You must forgive me, Miss Rothesay."

"I do. And so will He whom you do not know, but whom you will know yet! I will pray for you—I will comfort you. I wish I were indeed your sister, that I might never leave you until I brought you to faith and peace."

He smiled very faintly. "Thank you; it is something to feel there is goodness in the world. I did not believe in any except my mother's. Perhaps if she had known all this—if I could have told her—I had not been the wretched man I am."

"Hush; do not talk any more." And then she stood beside him for some minutes quite silent, until he grew calm.

They were on the verge of the forest, close to Olive's home. It was about seven in the evening, but all things lay as in the stillness of midnight. They two might have been the only beings in the living world—all else dead and buried under the white snow. And then, lifting itself out of the horizon's black nothingness, arose the great red moon, like an immortal soul.

"Look!" said Olive. He looked once, and no more. Then, with a sigh, he placed her arm in his, and walked with her to her own door.

Arrived there, he bade her adieu, adding, "I would bid God bless you; but in such words from me, you would not believe. How could you?"

He said this with a mournful emphasis, to which she could not reply.

"But," he continued in a tone of eager anxiety, "remember that I have trusted you. My secret is in your hands. You will be silent, I know; silent as death, or eternity.—That is, as both are to me!"

Olive promised; and he left her. She stood listening, until the echo of his footfall ceased along the frosty road; then, clasping her hands, she lifted once more the petition "for those who have erred and are deceived," the prayer which she had once uttered—unconscious how much and by whom it was needed. Now she said it with a yearning cry—a cry that would fain pierce heaven, and ringing above the loud choir of saints and angels, call down mercy on one perishing human soul.

CHAPTER XXXI

Never since her birth had Olive felt such a bewildering weight of pain, as when she awoke to the full sense of that terrible secret which she had learned from Harold Gwynne. This pain lasted, and would last, not alone for an hour or a day, but perpetually. It gathered round her like a mist. She seemed to walk blindfold, she knew not whither. Never to her, whose spiritual sense was ever so clear and strong, had come the possibility of such a mind as Harold's, a mind whose very eagerness for truth had led it into scepticism. His doubts must be wrestled with, not with the religion of precedent—not even with the religion of feeling—but by means of that clear demonstration of reason which forces conviction.

In the dead of night, when all was still—when the frosty moon cast an unearthly light over her chamber, Olive lay and thought of these things. Ever and anon she heard the striking of the clock, and remembered with horror that it heralded the Sabbath morning, when she must go to Har-bury Church—and hear, oh, with what feelings! the service read by one who did not believe a single word he uttered. Not until now had she so thoroughly realised the horrible sacrilege of Harold's daily life. For a minute she felt as though to keep his secret were associating herself with his sin.

But calmer thoughts enabled her to judge him more mercifully. She tried to view his case not as with her own eyes, but as it must appear to him. To one who disbelieved the Christian faith, the repetitions of its forms could seem but a mere idle mummery. He suffered, not for having outraged Heaven, but for having outraged his own conscience an agony of self-humiliation which must be to him a living death. Then again there awoke in Olive's heart a divine pity; and once more she dared to pray that this soul, in which was so much that was true and earnest, might not be cast out, but guided into the right way.

Yet, who should do it? He was, as he had said, drowning in a black abyss of despair, and there was no human hand to save him—none, save that feeble one of hers!

Feeble—but there was One who could make it strong. Suddenly she felt in her that consciousness which the weakest have at times felt, and which, however the rationalist may scoff, the Christian dare not disbelieve—that sense of not working, but being worked upon—by which truths come into one's heart, and words into one's mouth, involuntarily, as if some spirit, not our own, were at work within us. Such had been oftentimes the case with her; but never so strong as now. A voice seemed breathed into her soul—"Be not afraid."

She arose—her determination taken. "No," she thought, as standing at the window she watched the sun rise gloriously—"No, Lord! *my* Lord and *my* God!—I am not afraid."

Nevertheless, she suffered exceedingly. To bear the burden of this heavy secret; to keep it from her mother; to disguise it before Mrs. Gwynne; above all, to go to church, and have the ministry of such an one as Harold between her and heaven—this last was the most awful point of all; but she could not escape it without betraying him. And it seemed to her that the sin—if sin it were—would be forgiven; nay, her voluntary presence might even strike his conscience.

It was so. When Harold beheld her, his cheeks grew ashen pale. All through the service his reading at times faltered and his eyes were lowered. Once, too, during the epistle for the day, which chanced to be the sixth Sunday after Epiphany, the plain words of St. John seemed to attract his notice, and his voice took an accent of keen sorrow.

Yet, when Olive passed out of the church, she felt as though she had spent there years of torture—such torture as no earthly power should make her endure again. And it so chanced that she was not called upon to do so.

Within a week from that time Mrs. Rothesay sank into a state of great feebleness, not indicating positive danger, but still so nearly resembling illness that Olive could not quit her, even for an hour. This painful interest, engrossing all her thoughts, shut out from them even Harold Gwynne. She saw little of him, though she heard that he came almost daily to inquire at the door. But for a long time he rarely crossed the threshold.

"Harold is like all men—he does not understand sickness," said that most kind and constant friend, Mrs. Gwynne. "You must forgive him, both of you. I tell him often it would be an example for him, or for any clergyman in England, to see Olive here—the best and most pious daughter that ever lived. He thinks so too; for once, when I hoped that his own daughter might be like her, you should have heard the earnestness of his 'Amen!'"

This circumstance touched Olive deeply, and strengthened her the more in that work to which she had determined to devote herself. And a secret hope told her that erring souls are oftentimes reclaimed less by a Christian's preaching than by a Christian's life.

And so, though they did not meet again alone, and no words on the one awful subject passed between them, Harold began to come often to the Dell. Mrs. Rothesay's lamp of life was paling so gradually, that not even her child knew how soon it would cease to shine among those to whom its every ray was so precious and so beautiful—more beautiful as it drew nearer its close.

Yet there was no sorrow at the Dell, but great peace—a peace so holy that it seemed to rest upon all who entered there. These were not a few; never was there any one who gained so many kindly attentions as Mrs. Rothesay. Even the wild young Fludyers inquired after her every day. Christal, who was almost domiciled at the Hall, and seemed by some invisible attraction most disinclined to leave it, was yet a daily visitor—her high spirit softened to gentleness whenever she came near the invalid.

As to Lyle Derwent, he positively haunted them. His affections dropped off, he ceased his sentimentalities, and never quoted a single line of poetry. To Olive he appeared in a more pleasing light, and she treated him with her old regard; as for him, he adored the very ground she trod upon. A ministering angel could not have been more hallowed in his eyes. He often made Mrs. Rothesay and Olive smile with his raptures; and the latter said sometimes that he was certainly the same enthusiastic little boy who had been her knight in the garden by the river. She never thought of him otherwise; and though he often tried, in half-jesting indignation, to assure her that he was quite a man now, he seemed still a lad to her. There was the difference of a lifetime between his juvenile romance and her calm reality of six-and-twenty years.

She did not always feel so old though. When kneeling by her mother's side, amusing her, Olive still felt a very child; and there were times when near Harold Gwynne she grew once more a feeble, timid girl. But now that the secret bond between them was held in abeyance, their intercourse sank within its former boundary. Even his influence could not compete with that affection which had been the day-star of Olive's life. No other human tie could come between her and her mother.

Beautiful it was to see them, clinging together so closely that none of those who loved both had the courage to tell them how soon they must part. Sometimes Mrs. Gwynne would watch Olive with a look that seemed to ask, "Child, have you strength to bear?" But she herself had not the strength to tell her. Besides, it seemed as though these close cords of love were knitted so tightly around the mother, and every breath of her fading life so fondly cherished, that she could not perforce depart. Months might pass ere that frail tabernacle was quite dissolved.

As the winter glided away, Mrs. Rothesay seemed much better. One evening in March, when Harold Gwynne came laden with a whole basket of violets, he said—and truly—that she was looking as blooming as the spring itself. Olive coincided in this opinion—nay, declared, smiling, that any one would fancy her mother was only making pretence of illness, to win more kindness and consideration.

"As if you had not enough of that from every one, mamma! I never knew such a spoilt darling in all my life; and yet see, Mr. Gwynne, how meekly she bears it, and how beautiful and content she looks!"

It was true. Let us draw the picture which lived in Olive's memory evermore.

Mrs. Rothesay sat in a little low chair—her own chair, which no one else ever claimed. She did not wear an invalid's shawl, but a graceful wrapping-gown of pale colours—such as she had always loved, and which suited well her delicate, fragile beauty. Closely tied over her silvery hair—the only sign of age—was a little cap, whose soft pink gauze lay against her cheek—that cheek which even now was all unwrinkled, and tinted with a lovely faint rose colour, like a young girl's. Her eyes were cast down; she had a habit of doing this lest others might see there the painful expression of blindness; but her mouth smiled a serene, cheerful, holy smile, such as is rarely seen on human face, save when earth's dearest happiness is beginning to melt away, dimmed in the coming brightness of heaven. Her little thin hands lay crossed on her knee, one finger playing as she often did, with her wedding-ring, now worn to a mere thread of gold.

Her daughter looked at her with eyes of passionate yearning that threw into one minute's gaze the love of a whole lifetime. Harold Gwynne looked at her too, and then at Olive. He thought, "Can she, if she knows what I know—can she be resigned—nay, happy! Then, what a sublime faith hers must be!"

Olive seemed not to see him, but only her mother. She gazed and gazed, then she came and knelt before Mrs. Rothesay, and wound her arms round her.

"Darling, kiss me! or I shall fear you are growing quite an angel—an angel with wings."

There lurked a troubled tone beneath the playfulness; she rose up quickly, and began to talk to Mr. Gwynne.

They had a pleasant evening, all three together; for Mrs. Rothesay, knowing that Harold was lonely—since his mother and Ailie had gone away on a week's visit—prevailed upon him to stay. He read to them—Mrs.

Rothesay was fond of hearing him read; and to Olive the world's richest music was in his deep, pathetic voice, more especially when reading, as he did now, with great earnestness and emotion. The poem was not one of his own choosing, but of Mrs. Rothesay's. She listened eagerly while he read from Tennyson's "May Queen."

> Upon the chancel casement, and upon that grave of mine,
> In the early, early morning the summer sun will shine.
> I shall not forget you, mother; I shall hear you when you pass,
> With your feet above my head on the long and pleasant grass.
> Good night, good night! When I have said, good night for evermore,
> And you see me carried out from the threshold of the door,
> Don't let Effie come to see me till my grave is growing green:
> She'll be a better child to you than I have ever been.

Here Harold paused; for, looking at Olive, he saw her tears falling fast; but Mrs. Rothesay, generally so easily touched, was now quite unmoved. On her face was a soft calm. She said to herself, musingly,

"How terrible for one's child to die first. But I shall never know that pang. Go on, Mr. Gwynne."

He read—what words for him to read!—the concluding stanzas; and as he did so, the movement of Mrs. Rothesay's lips seemed silently to follow them.

> O sweet and strange it seems to me, that ere this day is done,
> The voice which now is speaking may be beyond the sun,
> For ever and for ever with those just souls and true,
> And what is life that we should moan? Why make we such ado?
> For ever and for ever all in a blessed home,
> And there to wait a little while till you and Effie come;
> To lie within the light of God, as I lie upon your breast,
> Where the wicked cease from troubling, and the weary are at rest.

After he concluded, they were all three very silent. What thoughts were in each heart? Then Mrs. Rothesay said,

"Now, my child, it is growing late. Read to us yourself, out of the best Book of all." And when Olive was gone to fetch it, she added, "Mr. Gwynne will pardon my not asking him to read the Bible, but a child's voice sounds so sweet in a mother's ears, especially when"—— She stopped, for Olive just then entered.

"Where shall I read, mamma?"

"Where I think we have come to—reading every night as we do—the last few chapters of the Revelations."

Olive read them—the blessed words, the delight of her childhood—telling of the heavenly kingdom, and the afterlife of the just. And *he* heard them: he who believed in neither. He sat in the shadow, covering his face with his hands, or lifting it at times with a blind, despairing look, like that of one who, staggering in darkness, sees afar a faint light, and yet cannot, dare not, believe in its reality.

When he bade Mrs. Rothesay good night, she held his hand, and said, "God bless you!" with more than her usual kindness. He drew back, as if the words stung him. Then he wrung Olive's hand, looked at her a moment, as if to say something, but said it not, and quitted the house.

The mother and daughter were alone. They clasped their arms round each other, and sat a little while listening to the wild March wind.

"It is just such a night as that on which we came to Farnwood, is it not, darling?"

"Yes, my child! And we have been very happy here; happier, I think, than I have ever been in my life. Remember that, love, always!"

She said these words with a beautiful, life-beaming smile. Then, leaning on Olive's shoulder, she lifted herself rather feebly, from her little chair, and prepared to walk upstairs.

"Tired, are you? I wish I could carry you, darling: I almost think I could."

"You carry me in your heart, evermore, Olive! You bear all my feebleness, troubles, and pain. God ever bless you, my daughter!"

When Olive came down once more to the little parlour, she thought it looked rather lonely. However, she stayed a minute or two, put her mother's little chair in the corner, and her mother's knitting basket beside it.

"It will be ready for her when she comes down again." Then she went upstairs to bed; and mother and daughter fell asleep, as ever, closely clasped in each other's arms.

CHAPTER XXXII

"My child!"

The feeble call startled Olive out of a dream, wherein she was walking through one of those lovely visionary landscapes—more glorious than any ever seen by day—with her mother and with Harold Gwynne.

"Yes, darling," she answered, in a sleepy, happy voice, thinking it a continuation of the dream.

"Olive, I feel ill—very ill! I have a dull pain here, near my heart. I cannot breathe. It is so strange—so strange!"

Quickly the daughter rose, and groped through the faint dawn for a light: she was long accustomed to all offices of tender care by night and by day. This sudden illness gave her little alarm; her mother had so many slight ailments. But, nevertheless, she roused the household, and applied all the simple remedies which she so well knew how to use.

But there must come a time when all physicians' arts fail: it was coming now. Mrs. Rothesay's illness increased, and the daylight broke upon a chamber where more than one anxious face bent over the poor blind sufferer who suffered so meekly. She did not speak much: she only held closely to Olive's dress, sorrowfully murmuring now and then, "My child—my child!" Once or twice she eagerly besought those around her to try all means for her restoration, and seemed anxiously to expect the coming of the physician. "For Olive's sake—for Olive's sake!" was all the reason she gave.

And suddenly it entered into Olive's mind that her mother felt herself about to die.

Her mother about to die! She paused a moment, and then flung the horror from her as a thing utterly impossible. So many illnesses as Mrs. Rothesay had passed through—-so many times as her daughter had clasped her close, and dared Death to come nigh one who was shielded by so much love! It could not be—there was no cause for dread. Yet Olive waited restlessly during the morning, which seemed of frightful length. She busied herself about the room, talking constantly to her mother; and by degrees, when the physician still delayed, her voice took a quick, sharp, anxious tone.

"Hush, love, hush!" was the soft reproof. "Be content, Olive; he will come in time. I shall recover, if it so please God."

"Of course—of course you will. Don't talk in that way, mamma!"—she dared not trust herself to say *darling*. She spoke even less caressingly than usual, lest her mother might think there was any dread upon her mind. But gradually, when she heard the strange patience of Mrs. Rothesay's voice, and saw the changes in the beloved face, she began to tremble. Once her wild glance darted upward in almost threatening despair. "God! Thou wilt not—Thou canst not—do this!" And when, at last, she heard the ringing of hoofs, and saw the physician's horse at the gate, she could not stay to speak with him, but fled out of the room.

She composed herself in time to meet him when he came downstairs. She was glad that he was a stranger, so that she had to be restrained, and to ask him in a calm, everyday voice, "What he thought of her mother?"

"You are Miss Rothesay, I believe," he answered, indirectly.

"I am."

"Is there no one to help you in nursing your mother—are you here quite alone?"

"Quite alone."

Dr. Witherington took her hand—kindly, too. "My dear Miss Rothesay, I would not deceive; I never do. If your mother has any relatives to send for, any business to arrange"——

"Ah—I see, I know! Do not say any more!" She closed her eyes faintly, and leaned against the wall. Had she loved her mother with a love less intense, less self-devoted, less utterly absorbing in its passion, at that moment she would have gone mad, or died.

There was one little low sigh; and then upon her great height of woe she rose—rose to a superhuman calm.

"You would tell me, then, that there is no hope?"

He looked on the ground, and said nothing.

"And how long—how long?"

"It may be six hours—it may be twelve; I fear it cannot be more than twelve." And then he began to give consolation in the only way that lay in his poor power, explaining that in a frame so shattered the spirit could not have lingered long, and might have lingered in much suffering. "It was best as it was," he said.

And Olive, knowing all, bowed her head, and answered, "Yes." She thought not of herself—she thought only of the enfeebled body about to be released from earthly pain, of the soul before whom heaven was even now opened.

"Does *she* know? Did you tell her?"

"I did. She asked me, and I thought it right."

Thus, both knew, mother and child, that a few brief hours were all that lay between their love and eternity. And knowing this, they again met.

With a step so soft that it could have reached no ear but that of a dying woman, Olive re-entered the room.

"Is that my child!"

"My mother—my own mother!" Close, and wild, and strong—wild as love and strong as death—was the clasp that followed. No words passed between them, not one, until Mrs. Rothesay said, faintly,

"My child, are you content—quite content?"

Olive answered, "I am content!" And in her uplifted eyes was a silent voice that seemed to say, "Take, O God, this treasure, which I give out of my arms unto Thine! Take and keep it for me, safe until the eternal meeting!"

Slowly the day sank, and the night came down. Very still and solemn was that chamber; but there was no sorrow there—no weeping, no struggle of life with death. After a few hours all suffering ceased, and Mrs. Rothesay lay quiet; sometimes in her daughter's arms, sometimes with Olive sitting by her side. Now and then they talked together, holding peaceful communion, like friends about to part for a long journey, in which neither wished to leave unsaid any words of love or counsel; but all was spoken calmly, hopefully, and without grief or fear.

As midnight approached, Olive's eyes grew heavy, and a strange drowsiness oppressed her. Many a watcher has doubtless felt this—the dull stupor which comes over heart and brain, sometimes even compelling sleep, though some beloved one lies dying. Hannah, who sat up with Olive, tried to persuade her to go down and take some coffee which she had prepared. Mrs. Rothesay, overhearing, entreated the same. "It will do you good. You must keep strong, my child."

"Yes, darling."

Olive went down in the little parlour, and forced herself to take food and drink. As she sat there by herself, in the still night, with the wind howling round the cottage, she tried to realise the truth that her mother was then dying—that ere another day, in this world she would be alone, quite alone, for evermore. Yet there she sat, wrapped in that awful calm.

When Olive came back, Mrs. Rothesay roused herself and asked for some wine. Her daughter gave it.

"It is very good—all things are very good—very sweet to me from Olive's hand. My only daughter—my life's comfort—I bless God for thee!"

After a while she said—passing her hand over her daughter's cheek—"Olive, little Olive, I wish I could see your face—just once, once more. It feels almost as small and soft as when you were a little babe at Stirling."

And saying this, there came a cloud over Mrs. Rothesay's face; but soon it went away, as she continued, "Child! listen to something I never told you—never could have told you, until now. Just after you were born, I dreamt a strange dream—that I lost you, and there came to me in your stead an angel, who comforted me and guided me through a long weary way, until, in parting, I knew that it was indeed my Olive. All this has come true, save that I did not *lose* you: I wickedly cast you from me. Ay, God forgive me! there was a time when I, a mother, had no love for the child I bore."

She wept a little, and held Olive with a closer strain as she proceeded. "I was punished, for in forsaking my child I lost my husband's love—at least not all, but for a time. But God pardoned me, and sent my child back to me as I saw her in my dream—an angel—to guard me through many troubled ways; to lead me safe to the eternal shore. And now, when I am going away, I say with my whole soul, God bless my Olive! the most loving and duteous daughter that ever mother had; and God will bless her evermore!"

One moment, with a passionate burst of anguish, Olive cried, "O mother, mother, stay! Do not go and leave me in this bitter world alone." It was the only moan she made. When she saw the anguish it caused to her so peacefully dying, she stilled it at once. And then God's comfort came down upon her; and that night of death was full of a peace so deep that it was most like happiness. In after years Olive thought of it as if it had been spent at the doors of heaven.

Toward morning Mrs. Rothesay said, "My child, you are tired. Lie down here beside me."

And so, with her head on the same pillow, and her arm thrown round her mother's neck, Olive lay as she had lain every night for so many years. Once or twice Mrs. Rothesay spoke again, as passing thoughts seemed to arise; but her mind was perfectly composed and clear. She mentioned several that she regarded—among the rest, Mrs. Gwynne, to whom she left "her love."

"And to Christal too, Olive. She has many faults; but, remember, she was good to me, and I was fond of her. Always take care of Christal."

"I will. And is there no one else to whom I shall give your love, mamma?"

She thought a minute, and answered, "Yes—to Mr. Gwynne." And, as if in that dying hour there came to the mother's heart both clear-sightedness and prophecy, she said, earnestly, "I am very glad I have known Harold Gwynne. I wish he had been here now, that I might have blessed him, and begged him all his life long to show kindness and tenderness to my child."

After this she spoke of earthly things no more, but her thoughts went, like heralds, far into the eternal land. Thither her daughter's followed likewise, until, like the martyr Stephen, Olive almost seemed to see the heavens opened, and the angels of God standing around the throne. Her heart was filled, not with anguish, but with an awful joy, which passed not even, when lifting her head from the pillow, she saw that over her mother's face was coming a change—the change that comes but once.

"My child, are you still there?".

"Yes, darling."

"That is well. All is well now. Little Olive, kiss me."

Olive bent down and kissed her. With that last kiss she received her mother's soul.

Then she suffered the old servant to lead her from the room. She never wept; it would have appeared sacrilege to weep. She went to the open door, and stood, looking to the east, where the sun was rising. Through the golden clouds she almost seemed to behold, ascending, the freed spirit upon whom had just dawned the everlasting morning.

An hour after, when she was all alone in the little parlour, lying on the sofa with her eyes closed, she heard entering a well-known step. It was Harold Gwynne's. He looked much agitated; at first he drew back, as though fearing to approach; then he came up, and took her hand very tenderly.

"Alas, Miss Rothesay, what can I say to you?"

She shed a few tears, less for her own sorrow than because she was touched by his kindness.

"I would have been here yesterday," continued he, "but I was away from Harbury. Yet, what help, what comfort, could you have received from me?"

Olive turned to him her face, in whose pale serenity yet lingered the light which had guided her through the valley of the shadow of death.

"God," she whispered, "has helped me. He has taken from me the desire of my eyes, and yet I have peace—perfect peace!"

Harold looked at her with astonishment.

"Tell me," he muttered, involuntarily, "whence comes this peace!"

"From God, as I feel him in my soul—as I read of Him in the revelation of his Word."

Harold was silent. His aspect of hopeless misery went to Olive's heart.

"Oh that I could give to you this peace—this faith!"

"Alas! if I knew what *reason* you have for yours."

Olive paused. An awful thing it was, with the dead lying in the chamber above, to wrestle with the unbelief of the living. But it seemed as if the spirit of her mother had passed into her spirit, giving her strength to speak with words not her own. What if, in the inscrutable purposes of Heaven, this hour of death was to be to him an hour of new birth?

So, repressing all grief and weakness, Olive said, "Let us talk a little of the things which in times like this come home to us as the only realities."

"To you, not to me! You forget the gulf between us!"

"Nay," Olive said, earnestly; "you believe, as I do, in one God—the Creator and Ruler of this world?"

Harold made solemn assent.

"Of this world," she continued, "wherein is so much of beauty, happiness, and love. And can that exist in the created which is not in the Creator! Must not, therefore, the great Spirit of the Universe be a Spirit of Love?"

"Your argument contradicts itself," was the desponding answer. "Can *you* speak thus—you, whose heart yet bleeds with recent suffering?"

"Suffering which my faith has changed into joy. Never until this hour did I look so clearly from this world into the world of souls—never did I so strongly feel within me the presence of God's spirit, a pledge for the immortality of mine."

"Immortality! Alas, that dream! And yet," he added, looking at her reverently, even with tenderness, "I could half believe that a life like yours—so full of purity and goodness—can never be destined to perish."

"And can you believe in human goodness, yet doubt Him who alone can be its origin? Can you think that He would give the yearning for the hereafter, and yet deny its fulfilment? That he would implant in us love, when there was nothing to love; and faith, when there was nothing to believe?"

Harold seemed struck. "You speak plain, reasonable words—not like the vain babblers of contradictory creeds. Yet you do profess a creed—you join in the Church's service?"

"Because, though differing from many of its doctrines, I think its forms of worship are pure—perhaps the purest extant. But I do not set up the Church between myself and God. I follow no ritual, and trust no creed, except so far as it is conformable to the instinct of faith—the inward revelation of Himself which he has implanted in my soul—and to that outward revelation, the nearest and clearest that He has ever given of Himself to men, the Divine revelation of love which I find here, in the life, death, and resurrection of Jesus Christ, my Lord."

As she spoke, her hand rested on the Bible out of which she had last read to her mother. It opened at the very place, and from it there dropped the little book-marker which Mrs. Rothesay always used, one worked by Olive in her childish days. The sight drew her down to the helplessness of human woe.

"Oh, my mother!—my mother!" She bowed her head upon her knees, and for some minutes wept bitterly. Then she rose somewhat calmer.

"I am going upstairs"—— Her voice failed.

"I know—I know," said Harold.

"She spoke of you: they were almost her last words. You will come with me, friend?"

Harold was a man who never wept—never could weep—but his face grew pale, and there came over him a great awe. His step faltered, even more than her own, as he followed Olive up-stairs.

Her hand trembled a moment on the latch of the door. "No," she said, as if to herself,—"no, it is not my mother; my mother is not here!"

Then she went in composedly, and uncovered the face of the dead; Harold standing beside her.

Olive was the first to speak. "See," she whispered, "how very placid and beautiful it looks!—like her and yet unlike. I never for a moment feel that it is *my mother.*"

Harold regarded with amazement the daughter newly orphaned, who stood serenely beholding her dead. He took Olive's hand, softly and with reverence, as if there were something sacred in her touch. *His* she scarcely seemed to feel, but continued, speaking in the same tranquil voice:

"Two hours ago we were so happy, she and I, talking together of holy things, and of the love we had borne each other. And can such love end with death? Can I believe that one moment—the fleeting of a breath—has left of *my mother* only this?"

She turned from the bed, and met Harold's eye—intense, athirst—as if his soul's life were in her words.

"You are calm—very calm," he murmured. "You stand here, and have no fear of death."

"No; for I have seen my mother die. Her last breath was on my mouth. I *felt* her spirit pass, and I knew that it was passing unto God."

"And you can rejoice?"

"Yes; since for all I lose on earth, heaven—the place of souls, which we call heaven, whatever or wherever that may be—grows nearer to me. It will seem the more my home, now I have a mother there."

Harold Gwynne fell on his knees at the bedside, crying out:

"Oh, God! that I could believe!"

CHAPTER XXXIII

It was again the season of late summer; and Time's soothing shadow had risen up between the daughter and her grief. The grave in the beautiful churchyard of Har-bury was bright with many months' growth of grass and flowers. It never looked dreary—nay, often seemed almost to smile. It was watered by no tears—it never had been. Those which Olive shed were only for her own loneliness, and at times she felt that even these were wrong. Many people, seeing how calm she was, and how, after a season, she fell into her old pursuits and her kindly duties to all around, used to say, "Who would have thought that Miss Rothesay would have forgotten her mother so easily?"

But *she did not forget*. Selfish, worldly mourners are they, who think that the memory of the beloved lost can only be kept green by tears. Olive Rothesay was not of these. To her, her mother's departure appeared no more like death, than did one Divine parting—with reverence be it spoken!—appear to those who stood and looked upward from the hill of Bethany. And thus should we think upon all happy and holy deaths—if we fully and truly believed the faith we own.

Olive did not forget her mother—she could as soon have forgotten her own soul. In all her actions, words, and thoughts, this most sacred memory abided—a continual presence, silent as sweet, and sweet as holy. When her many and most affectionate friends had beguiled her into cheerfulness, so that they fancied she had put aside her sorrow, she used to say in her heart, "See, mother, I can think of you and not grieve. I would not that it should pain you to know I suffer still!"

Yet human feelings could not utterly be suppressed; and there were many times, when at night-time she buried her face on the now lonely pillow, and stretched out her arms into the empty darkness, crying, "My mother, oh my mother!" But then strong love came between Olive and her agony, whispering, that wherever her spirit abided, the mother *could not* forget her child.

Olive looked very calm now, as she sat with Mrs. Gwynne in the bay-window of the little drawing-room at the Parsonage, engaged in some light work, with Ailie reading a lesson at her knee. It was a lesson too, taken from that lore—at once the most simple and most divine—the Gospels of the New Testament.

"I thought my son would prove himself right in all his opinions," observed Mrs. Gwynne, when the lesson was over and the child had run away. "I knew he would allow Ailie to learn everything at the right time."

Olive made no answer. Her thoughts turned to the day—now some months back—when, stung by the disobedience and falsehood that lay hid in a young mind which knew no higher law than a human parent's command, Harold had come to her for counsel She remembered his almost despairing words, "Teach the child as you will—true or false—I care not; so that she becomes like yourself, and is saved from those doubts which rack her father's soul."

Harold Gwynne was not singular in this. Scarcely ever was there an unbeliever who desired to see his own scepticism reflected in his child.

Mrs. Gwynne continued—"I don't think I can ever sufficiently thank you, my dear Miss Rothesay."

"Say *Olive*, as you generally do."

For her Christian name sounded so sweet and homelike from Harold's mother; especially now.

"*Olive*, then! My dear, how good you are to take Ailie so entirely under your care and teaching. But for that, we must have sent her to some school from home, and, I will not conceal from you, that would have been a great sacrifice, even in a worldly point of view, since our income is much diminished by my son's having been obliged to resign his duties altogether, and take a curate. But tell me, do you think Harold looks any better! What an anxious summer this has been!"

And Olive, hearing the heavy sigh of the mother, whose whole existence was bound up in her son, felt that there was something holy even in that deceit, or rather concealment, wherein she herself was now a sorely-tried sharer. "You must not be too anxious," she said; "you know that there is nothing dangerous in Mr. Gwynne's state of health, only his brain has been overworked."

"I suppose so; and perhaps it was the best plan for him to give up all clerical duties for a time. I think, too, that these frequent absences do him good."

"I hope so too."

"Besides, seeing that he is not positively disabled by illness, his parishioners might think it peculiar that he should continually remain among them, and yet abstain from preaching. But my Harold is a strange being; he always was. Sometimes I think his heart is not in his calling—that he would have been more happy as a man of science than as a clergyman. Yet of late he has ceased even that favourite pursuit; and though he spends whole days in his study, I sometimes find that he has not displaced one book, except the large Bible which I gave him when he went to college. God bless him—my dear Harold!"

Olive's inmost heart echoed the blessing, and in the same words. For of late—perhaps with more frequently hearing him called by the familiar home appellation, she had thought of him less as *Mr. Gwynne* than as *Harold*.

"I wonder what makes your blithe Christal so late," observed Mrs. Gwynne, abruptly, as if disliking to betray further emotion. "Lyle Derwent promised to bring her himself—much against his will, though," she added, smiling. "He seems quite afraid of Miss Manners; he says she teases him so!"

"But she suffers no one else to do it. If I say a word against Lyle's little peculiarities, she is quite indignant. I rather think she likes him—that is, as much as she likes any of her friends."

"There is little depth of affection in Christal's nature. She is too proud. She feels no need of love, and therefore cares not to win it. Do you know, Olive," continued Mrs. Gwynne, "if I must expose all my weaknesses, there was a time when I watched Miss Manners more closely than any one guesses. It was from a mother's jealousy over her son's happiness, for I often heard her name coupled with Harold's."

"So have I, more than once," said Olive. "But I thought at the time how idle was the rumour."

"It was idle, my dear; but I did not quite think so then."

"Indeed!" There was a little quick gesture of surprise; and Olive, ceasing her work, looked inquiringly at Mrs. Gwynne.

"Men cannot do without love, and having once been married, Harold's necessity for a good wife's sympathy and affection is the greater. I always expected that my son would marry again, and therefore I have eagerly watched every young woman whom he might meet in society, and be disposed to choose. All men, especially clergymen, are better married—at least in my opinion. Even you, yourself, as Harold's friend, his most valued friend, must acknowledge that he would be much happier with a second wife."

What was there in this frank speech that smote Olive with a secret pain? Was it the unconscious distinction drawn between her and all other women on whom Harold might look with admiring eyes, so that his mother, while calling her his *friend*, never dreamed of her being anything more?

Olive knew not whence came the pain, yet still she felt it was there. "Certainly he would," she answered, speaking in a slow, quiet tone. "Nevertheless, I should scarcely think Christal a girl whom Mr. Gwynne would be likely to select."

"Nor I. At first, deeming her something like the first Mrs. Harold, I had my doubts; but they quickly vanished. My son will never marry Christal Manners."

Olive, sitting at the window, looked up. It seemed to her as if over the room had come a lightness like the passing away of a cloud.

"Nor, at present," pursued Mrs. Gwynne, "does it appear to me likely that he will marry at all. I fear that domestic love—the strong, yet quiet tenderness of a husband to a wife, is not in his nature. Passion is, or was, in his youth; but he is not young now. In his first hasty marriage I knew that the fire would soon burn itself out—it has left nothing but ashes. Once he deceived himself, and sorely he has reaped the fruits of his folly. The result is, that he will live to old age without ever having known the blessing of true love."

"Is that so mournful, then?" said Olive, more as if thinking aloud than speaking.

Mrs. Gwynne did not hear the words, for she had started up at the sound of a horse's hoofs at the gate. "If that should be Harold! He said he would be at home this week or next. It is—it is he! How glad I am—that is, I am glad that he should be in time to see the Fludyers and Miss Manners before their journey to-morrow."

Thus, from long habit, trying to make excuses for her overflowing tenderness, she hurried out. Olive heard Mr. Gwynne's voice in the Hall, his anxious tender inquiry for his mother; even the quick, flying step of little Ailie bounding to meet "papa."

She paused: her work fell, and a mist came over her eyes. She felt then, as she had sometimes done before, though never so strongly, that it was hard to be in the world alone.

This thought haunted her awhile; until at last it was banished by the influence of one of those pleasant social evenings, such as were often spent at the Parsonage. The whole party, including Christal and Lyle, were assembled in the twilight, the two latter keeping up a sort of Benedick and Beatrice warfare. Harold and his mother seemed both very quiet—they sat close together, her hand sometimes resting caressingly on his shoulder or his knee. It was a new thing, this outward show of affection; but of late since his health had declined (and, in truth, he had often looked and been very ill), there had come a touching softness between the mother and son.

Olive Rothesay sat a little apart, a single lamp lighting her at her work; for she was not idle. Following her old master's example, she was continually making studies from life for the picture on which she was engaged. She took a pleasure in filling it with idealised heads, of which the originals had place in her own warm affections. Christal was there, with her gracefully-turned throat, and the singular charm of her black eyes and fair hair. Lyle, too, with his delicate, womanish, but yet handsome face. Nor was Mrs. Gwynne forgotten—Olive made great use of her well-outlined form, and her majestic sweep of drapery. There was one only of the group who had not been limned by Miss Rothesay.

"If I were my brother-in-law I should take it quite as an ill compliment that you had never asked him to sit," observed Lyle. "But," he added in a whisper, "I don't suppose any artist would care to paint such a hard, rugged-looking fellow as Gwynne."

Olive looked on the pretty red and white of the boyish dabbler in Art—for Lyle had lately taken a fancy that way too—and then at the countenance he maligned. She did not say a word; but Lyle hovering round, found his interference somewhat sharply put aside during the whole evening.

When assembled round the supper-table they talked of Christal's journey. It was undertaken by invitation of Mrs. Fludyer, to whom the young damsel had made herself quite indispensable. Her liveliness charmed away the idle lady's ennui, while her pride and love of aristocratic exclusiveness equally gratified the same feelings for her patroness. And from the mist that enwrapped her origin, the ingenious and perhaps self-deceived young creature had contrived to evolve such a grand fable of "ancient descent" and "noble but reduced family," that everybody regarded her in the same light as she regarded herself. And surely, as the quick-sighted Mrs. Gwynne often said, no daughter of a long illustrious line was ever prouder than Christal Manners.

She indulged the party with a brilliant account of Mrs. Fludyer's anticipations of pleasure at Brighton, whither the whole family at the Hall were bound.

"Really, we shall be quite desolate without a single soul left at Farnwood, shall we not, Olive?" observed Mrs. Gwynne.

Olive answered, "Yes,—very," without much considering of the matter. Her thoughts were with Harold, who was leaning back in his chair, absorbed in one of those fits of musing, which with him were not unfrequent, and which no one ever regarded, save herself. How deeply solemn it was to her at such times to feel that she alone held the key of his soul—that it lay open, with all its secrets, to her, and to her alone. What marvel was it if this knowledge sometimes moved her with strange sensations; most of all, while, beholding the reserved exterior which he bore in society, she remembered the times when she had seen him goaded into terrible emotion, or softened to the weakness of a child.

At Olive's mechanical affirmative, Lyle Derwent brightened up amazingly. "Miss Rothesay, I—I don't intend going away, believe me!"

Christal turned quickly round. "What are you saying, Mr. Derwent?"

He hung his head and looked foolish. "I mean that Brighton is too gay, and thoughtless, and noisy a place for me—I would rather stay at Harbury."

"You fickle, changeable, sentimental creature! I wouldn't be a man like you for the world!" And reckless Christal burst into a fit of laughter much louder than seemed warranted by the occasion. Lyle seemed much annoyed; whereupon his friend Miss Rothesay considerately interposed, and passed to some other subject which lasted until the hour of departure.. The three walked to the Dell together, Christal jesting incessantly, either with or at Lyle Derwent. Olive walked beside them rather silent than otherwise. She had been so used to walk home with Harold Gwynne, that any other companionship along the old familiar road seemed unnatural. As she passed along, from every bush, every tree, every winding of the lane, seemed to start some ghostlike memory; until there came over her a feeling almost of fear, to find how full her thoughts were of this one friend, how to pass from his presence was like passing into gloom, and the sense of his absence seemed a heavy void.

"It was not so while my mother lived," Olive murmured sorrowfully. "I never needed any friend but her. What am I doing! What is coming over me?"

She trembled, and dared not answer the question.

At the Dell they parted from Lyle. "I shall see you once again before you leave, I hope," he said to Christal.

"Oh, yes; you will not get rid of your tormentor so easily."

"Get rid of you, fair Cruelty! Would a man wish to put out the sun because it scorches him sometimes?" cried Lyle, lifted to the seventh heaven of poetic fervour by the influence of a balmy night and a glorious harvest moon. Which said luminary, shining on Christal's face, saw there,—she only, pale Lady Moon,—an expression fine and rare; quivering lips, eyes not merely bright, but flaming, as such dark eyes only can.

As Olive was entering the hall door, Miss Manners, a little in the rear, fell, crying out as with pain. She was quickly assisted into the house, where, recovering, she complained of having sprained her ankle. Olive, full of compassion, laid her on the sofa, and hurried away for some simple medicaments, leaving Christal alone.

That young lady, as soon as she heard Miss Rothesay's steps overhead, bounded to the half-open window, moving quite as easily on the injured foot as on the other. Eagerly she listened; and soon was rewarded by hearing Lyle's voice carolling pathetically down the road, the ditty,

"*Io ti voglio ben assai,*

Ma tu non pensi a me!"

"Tis my song, mine! I taught him!" said Christal, laughing to herself. "He thought to stay behind and escape me and my cruelty.' But we shall see—we shall see!"

Though in her air was a triumphant, girlish coquetry, yet something there was of a woman's passion, too. But she heard a descending step, and had only just, time to regain her invalid attitude and her doleful countenance, when Olive entered.

"This accident is most unfortunate," said Miss Rothesay, "How will you manage your journey to-morrow?"

"I shall not be able to go," said Christal in a piteous voice, though over her averted face broke a comical smile.

"Are you really so much hurt, my dear?"

"Do you doubt it?" was the sharp reply. "I am sorry to trouble you; but I really am unable to leave the Dell."

Very often did she try Olive's patience thus; but the faithful daughter always remembered those last words, "Take care of Christal."

So, excusing all, she tended the young sufferer carefully until midnight, and then went down-stairs secretly to perform a little act of self-denial, by giving up an engagement she had made for the morrow. While writing to renounce it, she felt, with a renewed sense of vague apprehension, how keen a pleasure it was she thus resigned—a whole long day in the forest with her pet Ailie, Ailie's grandmamma, and—Harold Gwynne.

CHAPTER XXXIV

Midnight was long past, and yet Olive sat at her desk; she had finished her note to Mrs. Gwynne, and was poring over a small packet of letters carefully separated from the remainder of her correspondence. If she had been asked the reason of this, perhaps she would have made answer that they were unlike the rest—solemn in character, and secret withal. She never looked at them but her expression changed; when she touched them she did it softly and tremulously, as one would touch a living sacred thing.

They were letters which at intervals during his various absences she had received from Harold Gwynne.

Often had she read them over—so often, that, many a time waking in the night, whole sentences came distinctly on her memory, vivid almost as a spoken voice. And yet scarcely a day passed that she did not read them over again. Perhaps this was from their tenor, for they were letters such as a man rarely writes to a woman, or even a friend to a friend.

Let us judge, extracting portions from them at will.

The first, dated months back, began thus: "You will perhaps marvel, my dear Miss Rothesay, that I should write to you, when for some time we have met so rarely, and then apparently like ordinary acquaintance. Yet, who should have a better right than we to call each other *friends*? And like a friend you acted, when you consented that there should be between us for a time this total silence on the subject which first bound us together by a tie which we can neither of us break if we would. Alas! sometimes I could almost curse the weakness which had given you—a woman—to hold my secret in your hands. And yet so gently, so nobly have you held it, that I could kneel and bless you. You see I can write earnestly, though I speak so coldly."

"I told you, after that day when we two were alone with death (the words are harsh, I know, but I have no smooth tongue), I told you that I desired entire silence for weeks, perhaps months. I must 'commune with my own heart and be still.' I must wrestle with this darkness alone. You assented; you forced on me no long argumentative homilies—you preached to me solely with your life, the pure beautiful life of a Christian woman. Sometimes I tried to read carefully the morality of Jesus, which I, and sceptics worse than I, must allow to be perfect of its kind, and it struck me how nearly you approached to that divine life which I had thought impossible to be realised."

"I have advanced thus far into my solemn seeking. I have learned to see the revelation—imputedly divine—clear and distinct from the mass of modern creeds with which it has been overladen. I have begun to read the book on which—as you truly say—every form of religion is founded. I try to read with my own eyes, putting aside all received interpretations, earnestly desiring to cast from my soul all long-gathered prejudices, and to bring it, naked and clear, to meet the souls of those who are said to have written by divine inspiration."

"The book is a marvellous book. The history of all ages can scarcely show its parallel. What diversity, yet what unity! The stream seems to flow through all ages, catching the lights and shadows of different periods, and of various human minds. Yet it is one and the same stream—-pure and shining as truth. Is it truth?—is it divine?"

"I will confess, candidly, that if the scheme of a worlds history with reference to its Creator, as set forth in the Bible, were true, it would be a scheme in many things worthy of a divine benevolence: such as that in which you believe. But can I imagine Infinity setting itself to work out such trivialities? What is even a world? A mere grain of dust in endless space! It cannot be. A God who could take interest in man, in such an atom as I, would be no God at all. What avails me to have risen unto more knowledge, more clearness in the sense of the divine, if it is to plunge me into such an abyss as this? Would I had never been awakened from my sleep—the dull stupor of materialism into which I was fast sinking. Then I might, in the end, have conquered even the last fear, that of 'something after death,' and have perished like a soulless clod, satisfied that there was no hereafter. Now, if there should be? I whirl and whirl; I can find no rest. I would I knew for certain that I was mad. But it is not so."

"You answer, my kind friend, like a woman—like the sort of woman I believed in in my boyhood—when I longed for a sister, such a sister as you. It is very strange, even to myself, that I should write to any one as freely as I do to you. I know that I could never speak thus. Therefore, when I return home, you must not marvel to find me just the same reserved being as ever—less to you, perhaps, than to most people, but still reserved. Yet, never believe but that I thank you for all your goodness most deeply."

"You say that, like most women, you have little power of keen philosophical argument. Perhaps not; but there is in you a spiritual sense that may even transcend knowledge. I once heard—was it not you who said so?—that the poet who 'reads God's secrets in the stars' soars nearer Him than the astronomer who calculates by figures and by line. As, even in the material universe, there are planets and systems which mock all human ken; so in the immaterial world there must be a boundary where all human reasoning fails, and we can trust to nothing but that inward inexplicable sense which we call faith. This seems to me the great argument which inclines us to receive that supernatural manifestation of the all-pervading Spirit which is termed 'revelation.' And there we go back again to the relation between the finite—humanity, and the infinite—Deity.'"

"One of my speculations you answer by an allegory—Does not the sun make instinct with life not only man, but the meanest insect, the lowest form of vegetable existence? He shines. His light at once revivifies a blade of grass and illumines a world. If thus it is with the created, may not it be also with the Creator? There is something within me that answers to this reasoning.

"If I have power to conceive the existence of God, to look up from my nothingness unto His great height, to desire nearer insight into His being, there must be in my soul something not unworthy of Him—something that, partaking His divinity, instinctively turns to the source whence it was derived. Shall I, suffering myself to be guided by this power, seek less to doubt than to believe?

"I remember my first mathematical tutor once said to me, 'If you would know anything, begin by doubting everything.' I did begin, but I have never yet found an end."

"I will take your advice, my dear friend; advice given so humbly, so womanly. Yet I think you deal with me wisely. I am a man who never could be preached or argued into belief. I must find out the truth for myself. And so, according to your counsel, I will again carefully study the Bible, and especially the life of Jesus of Nazareth, which you believe the clearest revelation which God has allowed of Himself to earth. Finding any contradictions or obscurities, I will remember, as you say, that Scripture was not, and does not pretend to be, written visibly and actually by the finger of God, but by His inspiration conveyed through many human minds, and of course always bearing to a certain extent the impress of the mind through which it passes. Therefore, while the letter is sometimes apparently contradictory, the spirit is invariably one and the same. I am to look to *that*, first? Above all, I am to look to the only earthly manifestation of Divine perfection—Jesus Christ, the Saviour of all men? *I will.*

"You see how my mind echoes your words, my friend! I am becoming, I think, more like you. All human affections are growing closer and dearer unto me. I can look at my good and pious mother without feeling, as I did at times, that she is either a self-deceiver or deceived. I do not now shrink from my little daughter, nor think with horror that she owes to me that being which may lead her one day to 'curse God and die.' Still I cannot rest at Harbury. All things there torture me. As for resuming my duties as a minister, that seems all but impossible. What an accursed hypocrite I have been! If this search after truth should end in a belief anything like that of the Church of England, I shall marvel that Heaven's lightning has not struck me dead."

... "You speak hopefully of the time when we shall hold one faith, and both give thanks unto the merciful God who has lightened my darkness. I cannot say this *yet* ; but the time may come. And if it does, what shall I owe to you, who, by your outward life, first revived my faith in humanity—by your inward life, my faith in God? You have solved to me many of those enigmas of Providence which, in my blindness, I thought impugned eternal justice. Now I see that love—human and divine—is sufficient to itself, and that he who loves God is one with God. There may be a hundred varying forms of doctrine, but this one truth is above all and the root of all.—I hold to it, and I believe it will save my soul. If ever I lift up a prayer worthy to reach the ear of God, it is that He may bless you, my friend, and comforter."

And here, reader, for a moment, we pause. Following whither our object led, we have gone far beyond the bounds usually prescribed to a book like this; After perusing the present chapter, you may turn to the title-page, and reading thereon, "Olive, a *Novel*" may exclaim, "Most incongruous—most strange!" Nay, some may even accuse us of irreverence in thus bringing into a fictitious story those subjects which are acknowledged as most vital to every human soul, but yet which most people are content, save at set times and places, tacitly to ignore. There are those who sincerely believe that in such works as this it is profanity even to name the Holy Name. Yet what is a novel, or, rather, what is it that a novel ought to be? The attempt of one earnest mind to show unto many what humanity is—ay, and more, what humanity might become; to depict what is true in essence through imaginary forms; to teach, counsel, and warn, by means of the silent transcript of human life. Human life without God! Who will dare to tell us we should paint *that*?

Authors, who feel the solemnity of their calling, cannot suppress the truth that is within them. Having put their hands to the plough, they may not turn aside, nor look either to the right or the left. They must go straight on, as the inward voice impels; and He who seeth their hearts will guide them aright.

CHAPTER XXXV

Some days passed in quiet uniformity, broken only by the visits of good-natured Lyle, who came, as he said, to amuse the invalid. Whether that were the truth or no, he was a frequent and always welcome guest at the Dell. Only he made the proviso, that in all amusements which he and Christal shared, Miss Rothesay should be in some way united. So, morning after morning, the sofa whereupon the invalid gracefully reclined was brought into the painting-room, and there, while Olive worked, she listened, sometimes almost in envy, to the gay young voices that mingled in song, or contended in the light battle of wits. How much older, graver, and sadder, she seemed than they!

Harold Gwynne did not come. This circumstance troubled Olive. Not that he was in the habit of paying long morning visits, like young Derwent; but still when he was at Harbury, it usually chanced that every few days they met somewhere. So habitual had this intercourse become, that a week's complete cessation of it seemed a positive pain.

Ever, when Olive rose in the morning, the sun-gilded spire of Harbury Church brought the thought, "I wonder will he come to-day!" And at night, when he did not come, she could not conceal from herself, that looking back on the past day, over all its duties and pleasures, there rose a pale mist. She seemed to have only half lived. Alas, alas!

Olive knew, though she hardly would acknowledge it to herself, that for many months this interest in Harold Gwynne had been the one great interest of her existence. At first it came in the form of a duty, and as such she had entered upon it. She was one of those women who seem born ever to devote themselves to some one. When her mother died, it had comforted Olive to think there was still a human being who stretched out to her entreating hands, saying, "I need thee! I need thee!" Nay, it even seemed as if the voice of the saint departed called upon her to perform this sacred task. Thereto tended her thoughts and prayers. And thus there came upon her the fate which has come upon many another woman,—while thus devoting herself she learned to love. But so gradual had been the change that she knew it not.

"Why am I restless?" she thought. "One is too exacting in friendship; one should give all and ask nothing back. Still, it is not quite kind of him to stay away thus. But a man is not like a woman. He must have so many conflicting and engrossing interests, whilst I"— — Here her thought broke and dissolved like a rock-riven wave. She dared not yet confess that she had no interest in the world save what was linked with him.

"If he comes not so often," she re-commenced her musings, "even then I ought to be quite content. I know he respects and esteems me; nay, that he has for me a warm regard. I have done him good, too; he tells me so. How fervently ought I to thank God if any feeble words of mine may so influence him, as in time to lead him from error to truth. My friend, my dear friend! I could not die, knowing or fearing that the abyss of eternity would lie between my spirit and his. Now, whatever may part us during life"— —

Here again she paused, overcome with the consciousness of great pain. If there was gloom in the silence of a week, what would a whole life's silence be? Something whispered that even in this world it would be very bitter to part with Harold Gwynne.

"You are not painting, Miss Rothesay; you are thinking," suddenly cried Lyle Derwent.

Olive started almost with a sense of shame. "Has not an artist a right to dream a little?" she said. Yet she blushed deeply. Were her thoughts wrong, that they needed to be thus glossed over? Was there stealing into her heart a secret that taught her to feign?

"What! are you, always the idlest of the idle, reproving Miss Rothesay for being idle too?" said Christal, somewhat sharply. "No wonder she is dull, and I likewise. You are getting as solemn as Mr. Gwynne himself. I almost wish he would come in your place."

"Do you? Then 'reap the misery of a granted prayer' for there is a knock It may be my worthy brother-in-law himself."

"If so, for charity's sake, give me your arm and help me into the next room. I cannot abide his gloomy face."

"O woman!—changeful—fickle—vain!" laughed the young man, as he performed the duty of supporting the not very fragile form of the fair Christal.

Olive was left alone. Why did she tremble? Why did her pulse sink, slower and slower? She asked herself this question, even in self-disdain. But there was no answer.

Harold entered.

"I am come with a message from my mother," said he; but added anxiously, "How is this, Miss Rothesay? You look as if you had been ill?"

"Oh, no! only weary with a long morning's work. But will you sit!"

He received, as usual, the quiet smile—the greeting gentle and friendly. He was deceived by them as heretofore.

"Are you better than when last I was at the Parsonage? I have seen nothing of you for a week, you know."

"Is it so long? I did not note the time." He "did not note the time." And she had told every day by hours—every hour by minutes!

"I should have come before," he continued, "but I have had so many things to occupy me. Besides, I am such poor company. I should only trouble you."

"You never trouble me."

"It is kind of you to say so. Well, let that pass. Will you now return with me and spend the day? My mother is longing to see you."

"I will come," said Olive, cheerfully. There was a little demur about Christars being left alone, but it was soon terminated by the incursion of a tribe of the young lady's "friends," whom she had made at Farnwood Hall.

Soon Olive was walking with Mr. Gwynne along the well-known road. The sunshine of the morning seemed to gather and float around her. She remembered no more the pain—the doubt—the weary waiting. She was satisfied now!

Gradually they fell into their old way of conversing. "How beautiful all seems," said Harold, as he stood still, bared his head, and drank in, with a long sighing breath, the sunshine and the soft air. "Would that I could be happy in this happy world!"

"It is God's world, and as He made it—good; but I often doubt whether He meant it to be altogether happy."

"Why so?"

"Because life is our time of education—our school-days. Our holidays, I fancy, are to come. We should be thankful," she added, smiling, "when we get our brief play-hours—our pleasant Saturday afternoons—as now. Do you not think so?"

"I cannot tell; I am in a great labyrinth, from which I must work my way out alone. Nevertheless, my friend, keep near me." Unconsciously she pressed his arm. He started, and turned his head away. The next moment he added, in a somewhat constrained voice, "I mean—let me have your friendship—your silent comforting—your prayers-Yes! thus far I believe. I can say, 'Pray God for me,' doubting not that He will hear—you, at least, if not me. Therefore, let me go on and struggle through this darkness."

"Until comes the light! It will come—I know it will!" Olive looked up at him, and their eyes met. In hers was the fulness of joy, in his a doubt—a contest. He removed them, and walked on in silence. The very arm on which Olive leaned seemed to grow rigid—like a bar of severance between them.

"I would to Heaven!" Harold suddenly exclaimed as they approached Harbury—"I would to Heaven I could get away from this place altogether. I think I shall do so. My knowledge and reputation in science is not small. I might begin a new life—a life of active exertion. In fact, I have nearly decided it all."

"Decided what? It is so sudden. I do not quite understand," said Olive, faintly.

"To leave England for ever. What do you think of the plan?"

What thought she? Nothing. There was a dull sound in her ears as of a myriad waters—the ground whereon she stood seemed reeling to and fro—yet she did not fall. One minute, and she answered.

"You know best. If good for you, it is a good plan."

He seemed relieved and yet disappointed. "I am glad you say so. I imagined, perhaps, you might have thought it wrong."

"Why wrong?"

"Women have peculiar feelings about home, and country, and friends. I shall leave all these. I would not care ever to see England more. I would put off this black gown, and with it every remembrance of the life of vile hypocrisy which I have led here. I would drown the past in new plans—new energies—new hopes. And, to do this, I must break all ties, and go alone. My poor mother! I have not dared yet to tell her. To her, the thought of parting would be like death, so dearly does she love me."

He spoke all this rapidly, never looking towards his silent companion. When he ceased, Olive feebly stretched out her hand, as if to grasp something for support, then drew it back again, and, hid under her mantle, pressed it tightly against her heart. On that heart Harold's words fell, tearing away all its disguises, laying it bare to the bitter truth. "To me," she thought—"to me, also, this parting is like death. And why? Because I, too, love him—dearer than ever mother loved son, or sister brother; ay, dearer than my own soul. Oh miserable me!"

"You are silent," said Harold. "You think I am acting cruelly towards one who loves me so well Human affections are to us secondary things.

We scarcely need them; or, when our will demands, we can crush them altogether."

"I—I have heard so," said she, slowly.

"Well, Miss Rothesay?" he asked, when they had nearly reached the Parsonage, "what are you thinking of?"

"I think that, wherever you go, you ought to take your mother with you; and little Ailie, too. With them your home will be complete."

"Yet I have friends to leave—one friend at least—*yourself.*"

"I, like others, shall miss you; but all true friends should desire, above all things, each other's welfare. I shall be satisfied if I hear at times of yours."

He made no reply, and they went in at the hall door.

There was much to be done and talked of that afternoon at the Parsonage. First, there was a long lesson to be given to little Ailie; then, at least an hour was spent in following Mrs. Gwynne round the garden, and hearing her dilate on the beauty of her hollyhocks and dahlias.

"I shall have the finest dahlias in the country next year," said the delighted old lady.

Next year! It seemed to Olive as if she were talking of the next world.

In some way or other the hours went by; how, Olive could not tell. She did not see, hear, or feel anything, save that she had to make an effort to appear in the eyes of Harold, and of Harold's mother, just as usual—the same quiet little creature—gently smiling, gently speaking—who had already begun to be called "an old maid"—whom no one in the world suspected of any human passion—least of all, the passion of *love*.

After this early dinner Harold went out. He did not return even when the misty autumn night had begun to fall. As the daylight waned and the firelight brightened, Olive felt terrified at herself. One hour of that quiet evening commune, so sweet of old, and her strength and self-control would have failed. Making some excuse about Christal, she asked Mrs. Gwynne to let her go home.

"But not alone, my dear. You will surely wait until Harold comes in?"

"No, no! It will be late, and the mist is rising. Do not fear for me; the road is quite safe; and you know I am used to walking alone," said Olive, feebly smiling.

"You are a brave little creature, my dear. Well, do as you will."

So, ere long, Olive found herself on her solitary homeward road. It lay through the churchyard. Closing the Parsonage-gate, the first thing she did was to creep across the long grass to her mother's grave.

"Oh, mother, mother! why did you go and leave me? I should never have loved any one if my mother had not died!"

And burning tears fell, and burning blushes came. With these came also the horrible sense of self-degradation which smites a woman when she knows that, unsought, she has dared to love.

"What have I done," she cried, "O earth, take me in and cover me! Hide me from myself—from my misery—my shame." Suddenly she started up. "What if he should pass and find me here! I must go. I must go home."

She fled out of the churchyard and down the road. For a little way she walked rapidly, then gradually slower and slower. A white mist arose from the meadows; it folded round her like a shroud; it seemed to creep even into her heart, and make its beatings grow still. Down the long road, where she and Harold had so often passed together, she walked alone. Alone—as once had seemed her doom through life—and must now be so unto the end.

It might be the *certainty* of this which calmed her. She had no maiden doubts or hopes; not one. The possibility of Harold's loving her, or choosing her as his wife, never entered her mind.

Since the days of her early girlhood, when she wove such a bright romance around Sara and Charles, and created for herself a beautiful ideal for future worship, Olive had ceased to dream about love at all. Feeling that its happiness was for ever denied her, she had altogether relinquished those fancies in which young maidens indulge. In their place had come the intense devotion to her Art, which, together with her passionate, love for her mother, had absorbed all the interests of her secluded life. Scarcely was she even conscious of the happiness that she lost; for she had read few of those books which foster sentiment; and in the wooings and weddings she heard of were none that aroused either her sympathy or her envy. Coldly and purely she had moved in her sphere, superior to both love's joy and love's pain.

Reaching home, Olive sought not to enter the house, where she knew there could be no solitude. She went into the little arbour—her mother's favourite spot—and there, hidden in the shadows of the mild autumn night, she sat down, to gather up her strength, and calmly to think over her mournful lot.

She said to herself, "There has come upon me that which I have heard is, soon or late, every woman's destiny. I cannot beguile myself any longer. It is not friendship I feel: it is love. My whole life is threaded by one thought—the thought of him. It comes between me and everything else on earth—almost between me and Heaven. I never wake at morning but his name rises to my heart—the first hope of the day; I never kneel down at night but in my prayer, whether in thought or speech, that name is mingled too. If I have sinned, God forgive me; He knows how lonely and desolate I was—how, when that one best love was taken away, my heart ached and yearned for some other human love. And this has come to fill it. Alas for me!

"Let me think. Will it ever pass away? There are feelings which come and go—light girlish fancies. But I am six-and-twenty years old. All this while I have lived without loving any man. And no one has ever wooed me except my master, Vanbrugh, whose feeling for me was not love at all. No, no! I am, as they call me, 'an old maid,' destined to pass through life alone and unloved.

"Perhaps, though I have long ceased to think on the subject—perhaps my first girlish misery was true, and there is in me something repulsive—something that would prevent any man's seeking me as a wife. Therefore, even if my own feelings could change, it is unlikely there will ever come any soothing after-tie to take away the memory of this utterly hopeless love.

"Hopeless I know it is. He admires beauty and grace—I have neither. Yet I will not do him the injustice to believe he would despise me for this. Even once I overheard him say, there was such sweetness in my face, that he had never noticed my being 'slightly deformed.' Therefore, did he but love me, perhaps—O fool!—dreaming fool that I am! It is impossible!

"Let me think calmly once more. He has given me all he could—kindness, friendship, brotherly regard; and I have given him love—a woman's whole and entire love, such as she can give but once, and be beggared all her life after. I to him am like any other friend—he to me is all my world. Oh, but it is a fearful difference!

"I will look my doom in the face—I will consider how I am to bear it. No hope is there for me of being loved as I love. I shall never be his wife: never be more to him than I am now; in time, perhaps even less. He will go out into the world, and leave me, as brothers leave sisters (even supposing he regards me as such). He will form new ties; perhaps he will marry; and then my love for him would be sin!"

Olive pressed her hands tightly together, and crushed her hot brow upon them, bending it even to her knees. Thus bowed, she lay until the fierce struggle passed.

"I do not think that misery will come. His mother, who knows him best, was surely right when she said he would never take a second wife. Therefore I may be his friend still. Neither he nor any one will ever know that I loved him otherwise than as a sister might love a brother. Who would dream there could be any other thought in me—a pale, unlovely thing—a woman past her youth (for I seem very old now)? It ought not to be so; many women are counted young at six-and-twenty; but it is those who have been nurtured tenderly in joyous homes. While I have been struggling with the hard world these many years. No wonder I am not as they—that I am quiet and silent, without mirth or winning grace, a creature worn out before her time, pale, joyless, *deformed*. Yes, let me teach myself that word, with all other truths that 'can quench this mad dream. Then, perhaps knowing all hope vain, I may be able to endure.

"What am I to do? Am I to try and cleanse my heart of this love, as if it were some pollution? Not so. Sorrow it is—deep, abiding sorrow; but it is not sin. If I thought it so, I would crush it out, though I crushed my life out with it. But I need not. My heart is pure—O God, Thou knowest!

"Another comfort I have. He has not deceived me, as men sometimes deceive, with wooing that seems like love, and yet is only idle, cruel sport. He has ever treated me as a friend—a sister—nothing more! Therefore, no bitterness is there in my sorrow, since he has done no wrong.

"I will not cease from loving—I would not if I could. Better this suffering than the utter void which must otherwise be in my heart eternally, seeing I have neither father, mother, brother, nor sister, and shall never know any nearer tie than the chance friendships which spring up on the world's wayside, and wither where they spring. I know there are those who would bid me cast off this love as it were a serpent from my bosom. No! Rather let it creep in there, and fold itself close and secret. What matter, even if its sweet sting be death?

"But I shall not die. How could I, while he lived, and might need any comfort that I could give? Did he not say, 'Keep near me!' Ay, I will! Though a world lay between us, my spirit shall follow him all his life long. Distance shall be nothing—years nothing! Whenever he calls, 'Friend I need thee.' I will answer, 'I am here!' If I could condense my whole life's current of joy into one drop of peace for him, I would pour it out at his feet, smile content, and die. And when I am dead—he will know how I loved him—Harold—my Harold."

Such were her thoughts—though no words passed her lips—except the last. As she rose and went towards the house, she might even have met him and not trembled—she had grown so calm.

It was already night—but the mist had quite gone—there was only the sky and its stars.

CHAPTER XXXVI

I know that I am promulgating a new theory of love; I know that in Olive Rothesay I dare to paint a woman full of all maidenly virtues, who has yet given her heart away unrequited—given it to a man who knows not of the treasure he has never sought to win. The case, I grant, is rare. I believe that a woman seldom bestows her love save in return for other love—be it silent or spoken—real or imaginary. If it is not so, either she has deceived herself, or has been deceived.

But the thing is quite possible—ay, and happens sometimes—that a woman unselfish, unexacting in all her affections, more prone to give than to receive, thinking perhaps very little of love or marriage, may be unconsciously attracted by some imagined perfection in the other sex, and be thus led on through the worship of abstract goodness until she wakes to find that she has learned to love *the man*. For what is love in its purest and divinest sense, but that innate yearning after perfection which we vainly hope to find in some other human soul; this is as likely to be felt by a woman as by a man—ay, and by one most pure from every thought of unfeminine boldness, vanity, or sin.

I know, too, that from many a sage and worthy matron my Olive has for ever earned her condemnation, because, at last discovering her mournful secret, she did not strive in horror and shame to root out this misplaced attachment. Then, after years of self-martyrdom, she might at last have pointed to her heart's trampled garden, and said, "Look what I have had strength to do!" But from such a wrecked and blasted soil what aftergrowth could ever spring?

Better, a thousand times, that a woman to whom this doom has come unwittingly, without her seeking—as inevitably and inexorably as fate—should pause, stand steadfast, and look it in the face, without fear. She cannot disguise it, or wrestle with it, or fly from it Let her meet it as she would meet death—solemnly, calmly, patiently. Let her draw nigh and look upon the bier of her life's dead hope, until the pale image grows beautiful as sleep; then cover it—bury it—if she can. Perhaps it may one day rise from the grave, wearing a likeness no longer human, but divine.

It is time that we women should begin to teach and to think thus. It is meet that we—maidens, wives, mothers, to whom the lines have fallen in more pleasant places—should turn and look on that pale sisterhood—some carrying meekly to the grave their heavy unuttered secret, some living unto old age, to bear the world's smile of pity, even of derision, over an "unfortunate attachment." Others, perhaps, furnishing a text whereupon prudent mothers may lesson romantic daughters, saying, "See that you be not like these 'foolish virgins;' give not *your* heart away in requital of fancied love; or, madder still, in worship of ideal goodness—give it for nothing but the safe barter of a speedy settlement, a comfortable income, a husband, and a ring."

Olive Rothesay, be not ashamed, nor afraid. Hide the arrow close in thy soul—lay over it thy folded hands and look upwards. Far purer art thou than many a young creature, married without love, living on in decent dignity as the mother of her husband's children, the convenient mistress of his household, and so sinking down into the grave, a pattern of all matronly virtue. Envy her not! A thousand times holier and happier than such a destiny is that silent lot of thine.

With meekness, yet with courage, Olive Rothesay prepared to live her appointed life. At first it seemed very bitter, as must needs be. Youth, while it is still youth, cannot at once and altogether be content to resign love. It will yearn for that tie which Heaven ordained to make its nature's completeness; it will shrink before the long dull vista of a solitary, aimless existence. Sometimes, wildly as she struggled against such thoughts, there would come to Olive's fancy dreams of what her life might have been. The holiness of lovers' love, of wedded love, of mother-love, would at times flit before her imagination; and her heart, still warm, still young, trembled to picture the lonely old age, the hearth blank and silent, the utter isolation from all those natural ties whose place not even the dearest bonds of adopted affection can. ever entirely fill. But, whenever these murmurings arose, Olive checked them; often with a feeling of intolerable shame.

She devoted herself more than ever to her Art, trying to make it as once before the chief interest and enjoyment of her life. It would become the same again, she hoped. Often and often in the world's history had been noted that of brave men who rose from the wreck of love, and found happiness in fame. But Olive had yet to learn that, with women, it is rarely so.

She felt more than ever the mournful change which had come over her, when it happened that great success was won by one of her later pictures—a picture unconsciously created from the inspiration of that sweet love-dream. When the news came—tidings which a year ago would have thrilled her with pleasure—Olive only smiled faintly, and a few minutes after went into her chamber, locked the door, and wept.

There was not, and there could not be, any difference made in her ordinary way of life. She still went to the Parsonage, and walked and talked with Harold, as he seemed always to expect. She listened to all his projects for the future—a future wherein she, alas! had no part Eagerly she strove to impress this fact upon her mind—to forget herself entirely, to think only of him, and what would be best for his happiness. Knowing him so well, and having over him an influence which he seemed rather to like, and which, at least, he never repelled, she was able continually to reason, to cheer him, and sympathise with him. He often thanked her for this, little knowing how every quiet word of hers was torn from a bleeding heart.

Walking home with her at nights, as usual, he never saw the white face turned upwards to the stars—the eyes wherein tears burned, but would not fall; the lips compressed in a choking agony, or opened to utter ordinary words in which his ear detected not one tremulous or discordant tone. When he sat in the house, absorbed in anxious thought, little he knew what looks were secretly fastened on his face, to learn by heart every beloved lineament, against the time when his visible likeness would be beheld no more.

Thus miserably did Olive struggle. The record of that time, its every day, its every hour, was seared on her heart as with a burning brand. Afterwards she never thought of it but with a shudder, marvelling how she had been able to endure all and live.

At last the inward suffering began to be outwardly written on her face. Some people said—Lyle Derwent first—that Miss Rothesay did not look so well as she used to do. But indeed it was no wonder, she was so engrossed in her painting, and worked far too much for her strength. Olive neither dissented nor denied: but she never complained, and still went painting on. Harold himself saw she was ill, and sometimes treated her with almost brotherly tenderness. Often he noticed her pale face, paler than ever beneath his eye, or, in wrapping her from the cold, observed how she shivered and trembled. And then Olive would go home and cry out in her misery,

"How long? how long? Oh, that this would cease, or else I die!"

She was quite alone at the Dell now, for Mrs. Fludyer had paid a flying visit home, and had taken back with her both Christal and the somewhat unwilling Lyle. Solitude, once sweet and profitable, now grew fearful unto Olive's tortured mind. And to escape it she had no resource, but that which she knew was to her like a poison-draught, and for which she yet thirsted evermore—the daily welcome at the Parsonage. But the web of circumstances, which she herself seemed to have no power to break, was at length apparently broken for her. One day she received a letter from her father's aunt, Miss Flora Rothesay, inviting—nay, entreating—her to visit Edinburgh, that the old lady might look upon the last of her race.

For a moment Olive blessed this chance of quitting the scenes now become so painful. But then, Harold might need her. In his present conflict of feeling and of purpose he had no confidant save herself. She would have braved years of suffering if her presence could have given him one hour's relief from care. But of this she must judge, so she set off at once to the Parsonage.

"Well, my dear," said Mrs. Gwynne, with a smiling and mysterious face, "of course you will go at once! It will do your health a world of good. Harold said so only this morning."

"Then he knew of the letter?"

"Why, to tell the truth, I believe he originated the plan. He saw you wanted change—he has such a regard for you, Olive."

Then *he* had done it all! He could let her part from him, easily, as friend from friend. Yet, what marvel! they were nothing more. She answered, quietly, "I will go."

She told him so when he came in. He seemed much pleased; and said, with more than his usual frankness,

"I should like you to know aunt Flora. You see, I call her *my* aunt Flora, too, for she is of some distant kin, and I have dearly loved her ever since I was a boy."

It was something to be going to one whom Harold "dearly loved." Olive felt a little comfort in her proposed journey.

"Besides, she knows you quite well already, my dear," observed Mrs. Gwynne. "She tells me Harold used often to talk about you during his visit with her this summer."

"I had a reason," said Harold, his dark cheek changing a little. "I wished her to know and love her niece, and I was sure her niece would soon learn to love *her*."

"Why, that is kind, and like yourself, my son. How thoughtfully you have been planning everything for Olive."

"Olive will not be angry with me for that?" he said, and stopped. It was the first time she had ever heard him utter her Christian name. At the sound her heart leaped wildly, but only for an instant. The next, Harold had corrected himself, and said, "*Miss Rothesay*" in a distinct, cold, and formal tone. Very soon afterwards he went away.

Mrs. Gwynne persuaded Olive to spend the day at the Parsonage. They two were alone together, for Harold did not return. But in the afternoon their quietness was broken by the sudden appearance of Lyle Derwent.

"So soon back from Brighton! Who would have thought it!" said Mrs. Gwynne, smiling.

Lyle put on his favourite sentimental air, and muttered something about "not liking gaiety, and never being happy away from Farnwood."

"Miss Rothesay is scarcely of your opinion; at all events, she is going to try the experiment by leaving us for a while."

"Miss Rothesay leaving us!"

"It is indeed true, Lyle. You see I have not been well of late, and my kind friends here are over-anxious for me; and I want to see my aunt in Scotland."

"It is to Scotland you are going?—all that long dreary way? You may stay there weeks, months! and that while what will become of me—I mean of us all at Farnwood?"

His evident regret touched Olive deeply. It was something to be missed, even by this boy: he always seemed a boy to her, partly because of olden times, partly because he was so boy-like and unsophisticated in mind and manner.

"My dear Lyle, how good of you to think of me in this manner! But indeed I will not forget you when I am away."

"You promise that?" cried Lyle, eagerly.

Olive promised; with a sorrowful thought that none asked this pledge—none needed it—save the affectionate Lyle!

He was still inconsolable, poor youth! He looked so drearily pathetic, and quoted such doleful poetry, that Mrs. Gwynne, who, in her matter-of-fact plainness, had no patience with any of Lyle's "romantic vagaries," as she called them, began to exert the dormant humour by which she always quenched his little ebullitions. Olive at last considerately came to the rescue, and proposed an evening stroll about the garden, to which Lyle gladly assented.

There he still talked of her departure, but his affections were now broken by real feeling.

"I shall miss you bitterly," he said, in a low tone; "but if your health needs change, and this journey is for your good, of course I would not think of myself at all."

—The very expressions she had herself used to Harold! This coincidence touched her, and she half reproached herself for feeling so coldly to all her kind friends, and chiefly to Lyle Derwent, who evidently regarded her with much affection. But all other affections grew pale before the one great love. Every lesser tie that would fain come in the place of that which was unattainable, smote her with only a keener pain.

Still, half remorsefully, she looked on her old favourite, and wished that she could care for him more. So thinking, her manner became gentler than usual, while that of Lyle grew more earnest and less dreamy.

"I wish you would write to me while you are away, Miss Rothesay; or, at all events, let me write to you."

"That you may; and I shall be so glad to hear all about Harbury and Farnwood." Here she paused, half-shaming to confess to herself that for this reason chiefly would she welcome the letters of poor Lyle.

"Is that all? Will you not care to hear about *me*? Oh, Miss Rothesay," cried Lyle, "I often wish I was again a little boy in the dear old garden at Oldchurch."

"Why so?"

"Because—because"—and the quick blood rose in his cheek. "No, no, I cannot tell you now; but perhaps I may, some time."

"Just as you like," answered Olive, absently. Her thoughts, wakened by the long-silent name, were travelling over many years; back to her old home, her happy girlhood. She almost wished she had died then, while she was young. But her mother!

"No, I am glad I lived to comfort *her*." she mused. "Perhaps it may be true that none ever leave earth until they are no longer needed there. So I will even patiently live on."

Unable to talk more with Lyle, Olive re-entered the Parsonage. Harold sat reading.

"Have you long come in?" she asked in a somewhat trembling voice.

He answered, "About an hour."

"I did not see you enter."

"It was not likely; you were engaged with my brother-in-law. Therefore I would not disturb you, but took my book."

He spoke in the abrupt, cold manner he sometimes used. Olive thought something had happened to annoy him. She sat down and talked with him until the cloud passed away.

Many times during the evening Lyle renewed his lamentations over Miss Rothesay's journey; but Harold never uttered one word of regret. When Olive departed, however, he offered to accompany her home.

"Nay—it is such a rainy night—perhaps"——

"Very well, since you choose it so," and he sat down again. But Olive saw she had wounded his pride, *only* his pride; she said this to her heart, to keep down its unconscious thrill. She replied, hesitatingly:

"Still, as we shall not have many more walks together, if"——

"I will come," he said, smiling.

And he came. Moreover, he contrived to keep her beside him. Lyle, poor fellow, went whistling in solitude down the other side of the road, until at the Dell he said goodnight, and vanished.

Harold had talked all the way on indifferent subjects, never once alluding to Olive's departure. He did so now, however, but carelessly, as if with an accidental thought.

"I wonder whether you will return before I leave Har-bury—that is, if I should really go. I should like to see you once again. Well, chance must decide."

Chance! when she would have controlled all accidents, provided against all hindrances, woven together all purposes, to be with him for one single day!

At once the thought broke through the happy spell which, for the time, his kindness had laid upon her. She felt that it was *only* kindness; and as such he meant it, no more! In his feelings was not the faintest echo of her own. A sense of womanly pride arose, and with it a cruel pang of womanly shame. These lasted while she bade him good-night, somewhat coldly; then both sank at once, and there remained to her nothing but helpless sorrow.

She listened for the last sound of his footsteps down the road. But she heard them not; and thought, half-sighing, how quickly he must have walked away!

A very few days intervened between Miss Rothesay's final decision and her departure. During this time, she only once saw Harold Gwynne. She thought he might have met her a little oftener, seeing they were so soon to part. But he did not; and the pain it gave warned her that all was happening for the best. Her health failing, her cheerful spirit broken, even her temper growing embittered with this mournful struggle, she saw that in some way or other it must be ended. She was thankful that all things had arranged themselves so plainly before her.

There was planned no farewell meeting at the Parsonage; but Mrs. Gwynne spent at the Dell the evening before Olive's departure. Harold would have come, his mother said, but he had some important matters to arrange; he would, however, appear some time that evening. However, it grew late, and still his welcome knock was not heard. At last one came; it was only Lyle, who called to bid Miss Rothesay good-bye. He did so dolorously enough, but Olive scarcely felt any pain.

"It is of no use waiting," said Mrs. Gwynne. "I think I will go home with Lyle—that is, if he will take my son's place for the occasion. It is not quite right of Harold; he does not usually forget his mother."

Olive instinctively hinted some excuse. She was ever prone to do so, when any shadow of blame fell on Harold.

"You are always good, my dear. But still he might have come, even for the sake of proper courtesy to you."

Courtesy!

Mrs. Gwynne entreated Olive to call at the Parsonage on her journey next morning. It would not hinder her a minute. Little Ailie was longing for one good-bye, and perhaps she might likewise see Harold. Miss Rothesay assented. It would have been hard to go away without one more look at him—one more clasp of his hand.

Yet both seemed denied her. When Olive reached the Parsonage, he was not there. He had gone out riding, little Ailie thought; no one else knew anything about him.

"It was very wrong and unkind," said Mrs. Gwynne in real annoyance.

"Oh, no, not at all," was all that Olive murmured. She took Ailie on her knee, and hid her face upon the child's curls.

"Ah, dear Miss Rothesay, you must come back soon," whispered the little girl. "We can't do without you. We have all been much happier since you came to Harbury; papa said so, last night."

"Did he?"

"Yes; when I was crying at the thought of your going away, and he came to my little bed, and comforted me, and kissed me. Oh, you don't know how sweet papa's kisses are! Now, I get so many of them. Before he rode out this morning he gave me half-a-dozen here, upon my eyes, and said I must learn all you taught me, and grow up a good woman, just like you. What! are you crying? Then I will cry too."

Olive laid her thin cheek to the rosy one of Harold's daughter; she wept, but could not speak.

"What kisses you are giving me, dear Miss Rothesay, and just where papa gives me them, too. How kind! Ah, I love you—I love you dearly."

"God bless and take care of you, my dear child—almost as dear as though you had been born my own," was Mrs. Gwynne's farewell, as she bestowed on Olive one of her rare embraces. And then the parting was over.

Closing her eyes—her heart;—striving to make her thoughts a blank, and to shut out everything save the welcome sense of blind exhaustion that was creeping over her, Olive lay back in the carriage, and was whirled from Harbury.

She had a long way to go across the forest-country until she reached the nearest railway-station. When she arrived, it was already late, and she had barely time to take her seat ere the carriages started. That moment her quick ear caught the ringing of a horse's hoofs, and as the rider leaped on the platform she saw it was Harold Gwynne. He looked round eagerly—more eagerly than she had ever seen him look before. The train was already moving, but they momently recognised each other, and Harold smiled—his own frank affectionate smile. It fell like a sunburst upon Olive Rothesay.

Her last sight of him was as he stood with folded arms, intently watching the winding northward line. Then, feeling that this had taken away half her pain, she was borne upon her solitary journey.

CHAPTER XXXVII

There is not in the world a more exquisite sight than a beautiful old age. It is almost better than a beautiful youth. Early loveliness passes away with its generation, and becomes at best only a melancholy tradition recounted by younger lips with a half-incredulous smile. But if one must live to be the last relic of a past race, one would desire in departing to leave behind the memory of a graceful old age. And since there is only one kind of beauty which so endures, it ought to be a consolation to those whom fate has denied the personal loveliness which charms at eighteen, to know that we all have it in our power to be beautiful at eighty.

Miss, or rather Mrs. Flora Rothesay—for so she was always called—appeared to Olive the most beautiful old lady she had ever beheld. It was a little after dusk on a dull wet day, when she reached her journey's end. Entering, she saw around her the dazzle of a rich warm fire-light, her cloak was removed by light hands, and she felt on both cheeks the kiss of peace and salutation.

"Is that Olive Rothesay, Angus Rothesay's only child? Welcome to Scotland—welcome, my dear lassie!"

The voice lost none of its sweetness for bearing, strongly and unmistakably, the ".accents of the mountain tongue." Though more in tone than phrase, for Mrs. Flora Rothesay spoke with all the purity of a Highland woman.

Surely the breezes that rocked Olive's cradle had sung in her memory for twenty years, for she felt like coming home the moment she set foot in her native land. She expressed this to Mrs. Flora, and then, quite overpowered, she knelt and hid her face in the old lady's lap, and her excitement melted away in a soft dew—too sweet to seem like tears.

"The poor lassie! she's just wearied out!" said Mrs. Flora, laying her hands on Olive's hair. "Jean, get her some tea. Now, my bairn, lift up your face. Ay, there it is—a Rothesay's, every line! and with the golden hair too. Ye have heard tell of the weird saying, about the Rothesays with yellow hair? No? We will not talk of it now." And the old lady suddenly looked thoughtful—even somewhat grave. When Olive rose up, she made her bring a seat opposite to her own arm-chair, and there watched her very intently.

Olive herself noticed her aunt with curious eyes. Mrs. Flora's attire was quite a picture, with the ruffled elbow-sleeves and the long, square boddice, over which a close white kerchief hid the once lovely neck and throat of her whom old Elspie had chronicled—and truly—as "the Flower of Perth." The face, Olive thought, was as she could have imagined Mary Queen of Scots grown old. But age could never obliterate the charm of the soft languishing eyes, the almost infantile sweetness of the mouth. Therein sat a spirit, ever lovely, because ever loving; smiling away all natural wrinkles—softening down all harsh lines. You regarded them no more than the faint shadows in a twilight landscape, over which the soul of peace is everywhere diffused. There was peace, too, in the very attitude—leaning back, the head a little raised, the hands crossed, each folded round the other's wrist. Olive particularly noticed these hands. On the right was a marriage-ring which had outlasted two lives, mother and daughter; on the left, at the wedding-finger, was another, a hoop of gold with a single diamond. Both seemed less ornaments than tokens—gazed on, perhaps, as the faint landmarks of a long past journey, which now, with its joys and pains alike, was all fading into shadow before the dawn of another world.

"So they called you 'Olive,' my dear," said Mrs. Flora. "A strange name! the like of it is not in our family."

"My mother gave it me from a dream she had."

Olive.

"Now, my bairn, lift up your face."

Olive.   "Now, my bairn, lift up your face."

"Ay, I mind it; Harold Gwynne told me, saying that Mrs. Rothesay had told *him*. Was she, then, so sweet and dainty a creature—your mother? Once Angus spoke to me of her—little Sybilla Hyde. She was his wife then, though we did not know it. Poor Angus, we loved him very much—better than he thought. Tears again, my dearie!"

"They do not harm me, Aunt Flora."

"And so you know my dear Alison Balfour? She was younger than I, and yet you see we have both grown auld wives together. Little Olive, ye have come to me in a birthday gift, my dear. I am eighty years old to-day—just eighty years, thank the Lord!"

The old lady reverently raised her blue eyes—true Scottish eyes—limpid and clear as the dew on Scottish heather. Cheerful they were withal, for they soon began to flit hither and thither, following the motions of Jean's "eident hand" with most housewifely care. And Jean herself, a handmaid prim and ancient, but youthful compared to her mistress, seemed to watch the latter's faintest gesture with most affectionate observance. Of all the light traits which reveal character, none is more suggestive than the sight of a mistress whom her servants love.

After tea Mrs. Mora insisted on Olive's retiring for the night. "Your room has a grand view over the Braid Hills. They call them hills here; but oh! if ye had seen the blue mountains sweeping in waves from the old house at home. Night and day I was wearying for them, for years after I came to live at Morningside. But one must e'en dree one's weird!"

She always spoke in this rambling way, wandering from the subject, after the fashion of old age. Olive could have listened long to the pleasant stream of talk, which seemed murmuring round her, wrapping her in a soft dream of peace. She laid down her tired head on the pillow, with an unwonted feeling of calmness and rest. Even the one weary pain that ever pursued her sank into momentary repose. Her last waking thought was still of Harold; but it was more like the yearning of a spirit from beyond the grave.

Just between waking and sleeping Olive was roused by music. Her door had been left ajar, and the sound she heard was the voices of the household, engaged in their evening devotion. The tune was that sweetest of all Presbyterian psalmody, "plaintive Martyrs." Olive caught some words of the hymn—it was one with which she had often, often been lulled to sleep in poor old Elspie's arms. Distinct and clear its quaint rhymes came back upon her memory now:

> *The Lord's my shepherd, I'll not want,*
> *He makes me down to lie*
> *In pastures green, He leadeth me*
> *The quiet waters by.*
>
> *Yea, though I walk in death's dark vale,*
> *Yet will I fear none ill;*
> *For Thou art with me, and Thy rod*
> *And staff me comfort still.*

Poor lonely Olive lay and listened. Then rest, deep and placid, came over her, as over one who, escaped from a stormy wrack and tempest, falls asleep amid the murmur of "quiet waters," in a pleasant land.

She awoke in the morning, as if waking in another world. The clear cold air, thrilled with sunshine, filled her room. It was the "best room," furnished with a curious mingling of the ancient and the modern. The pretty chintz couch laughed at the oaken, high-backed chair, stiff with a century of worm-eaten state. On either side the fireplace hung two ancient engravings, of Mary Stuart and "bonnie Prince Charlie," both garnished with verses, at once remarkable for devoted loyalty and eccentric rhythm. Between the two was Sir William Ross's sweet, maidenly portrait of our own Victoria. Opposite, on a shadowed wall, with one sunbeam kissing the face, was a large well-painted likeness, which Olive at once recognised. It was Mrs. Flora Rothesay, at eighteen. No wonder, Olive thought, that she was called "the Flower of Perth." But strange it was, that the fair flower had been planted in no good man's bosom; that this lovely and winning creature had lived, bloomed, withered—"an old maid." Olive, looking into the sweet eyes that followed her everywhere—as those of some portraits do—tried to read therein the foreshadowing of a life-history of eighty years. It made her dreamy and sad, so she arose and looked out upon the sunny slopes of the Braid Hills until her cheerfulness returned. Then she descended to the breakfast-table.

It was too early for the old lady to appear, but there were waiting three or four young damsels—invited, they said, to welcome Miss Rothesay, and show her the beauties of Edinburgh. They talked continually of "dear Auntie Mora," and were most anxious to "call cousins" with Olive herself, who, though she could not at all make out the relationship, was quite ready to take it upon faith. She tried very hard properly to distinguish between the three Miss M'Gillivrays, daughters of Sir Andrew Rothesay's half-sister's son, and Miss Flora Anstruther, the old lady's third cousin and name-child, and especially little twelve-years-old Maggie Oliphant, whose grandfather was Mrs. Flora's nephew on the mother's side, and first cousin ta Alison Balfour.

All these conflicting relationships wrapped Olive in an inexplicable net; but it was woven of such friendly arms that she had no wish to get free. Her heart opened to the loving welcome; and when she took her first walk on Scottish ground, it was with a sensation more akin to happiness than she had felt for many a long month.

"And so you have never before seen your aunt," said one of the M'Gillivrays;—for her life, Olive could not tell whether it was Miss Jane, Miss Janet, or Miss Marion, though she had tried for half-an-hour to learn the difference. "You like her of course—our dear old Auntie Flora?"

"Aunt to which of you?" said Olive, smiling.

"Oh, she is everybody's Auntie Flora; no one ever calls her anything else," observed little Maggie Oliphant, who, during all their walk clung tenaciously to Miss Rothesay's hand, as most children were prone to do.

"I think," said the quiet Miss Anstruther, lifting up her brown eyes, "that in all *our* lives put together, we will never do half the good that Aunt Flora has done in hers. Papa says, every one of her friends ought to be thankful that she has lived an old maid!"

"Yes, indeed, for who else would have had patience with her cross old brother Sir Andrew, until he died?" said Janet M'Gillivray.

"And who," added her sister, "would have come and been a mother to us when we lost our own, living with us, and taking care of us for seven long years?"

"I am sure," cried blithe Maggie, "my brothers and I used often to say, that if Auntie Flora had been young, and any disagreeable husband had come to steal her from us, we would have hooted him away down the street, and pelted him with stones."

Olive laughed; and afterwards said, thoughtfully, "She has then lived a happy life—has this good Aunt Flora!"

"Not always happy," answered the eldest and gravest of the M'Gillivrays. "My mother once heard that she had some great trouble in her youth. But she has outlived it, and conquered it in time. People say such things are possible: I cannot tell," added the girl, with a faint sigh.

There was no more said of Mrs. Flora, but oftentimes during the day, when some passing memory stung poor Olive, causing her to turn wearily from the mirth of her young companions, there came before her in gentle reproof the likeness of the aged woman who had lived down her one great woe—lived, not only to feel but to impart cheerfulness.

A few hours after, Olive saw her aunt sitting smiling amidst a little party which she had gathered together, playing with the children, sympathising with those of elder growth, and looked up to by old and young with an affection passing that of mere kindred. And then there came a balm of hope to the wounded spirit that had felt life's burden too heavy to be borne.

"How happy you are, and how much everyone loves you!" said Olive, when Mrs. Flora and herself were left alone, and their hearts inclined each to each with a vague sympathy.

"Yours must have been a noble woman's life."

"I have tried to make it so, as far as I could, my dear bairn; and the little good I have done has come back upon me fourfold. It is always so."

"And you have been content—nay happy!"

"Ay, I have! God quenched the fire on my own hearth, that I might learn to make that of others bright My dear, one's life never need be empty of love, even though, after seeing all near kindred drop away, one lingers to be an old maid of eighty years."

CHAPTER XXXVIII

"No letters to-day from Harbury!" observed Mrs. Mora, as, some weeks after Olive's arrival, they were taking their usual morning airing along the Queen's Drive. "My dear, are you not wearying for news from home?"

"Aunt Flora's house has grown quite home-like to me," said Olive, affectionately. It was true. She had sunk down, nestling into its peace like a tired broken-winged dove. As she sat beside the old lady, and drank in the delicious breezes that swept across from the Lothians, she was quite another creature from the pale drooping Olive Rothesay who had crept wearily up Harbury Hill. Still, the mention of the place even now took a little of the faint roses from her cheek.

"I am glad you are happy, my dear niece," answered Mrs. Flora; "yet others should not forget you."

"They do not. Christal writes now and then from Brighton, and Lyle Derwent indulges me with a long letter every week," said Olive, trying to smile. She did not mention Harold. She had hardly expected him to write; yet his silence grieved her. It felt like a mist of cold estrangement rising up between them. Yet—as sometimes she tried to think—perhaps it was best so!

"Alison Gwynne was aye the worst of all correspondents," pursued the old lady, "but Harold might write to you: I think he did so once or twice when he was living with me here, this summer."

"Yes;" said Olive, "we have always been good friends."

"I know that. It was not little that we talked about you. He told me all that happened long ago between your *father* and himself. Ah, that was a strange, strange thing!"

"We have never once spoken of it—neither I nor Mr. Gwynne."

"Harold could not. He was sair grieved, and bitterly he repented having 'robbed' you. But he was no the same man then that he is now. Ah, that gay young wife of his—fair and fause, fair and fause! It's ill for a man that loves such a woman. I would like well to see my dear Harold wed to some leal-hearted lassie. But I fear me it will never be."

Thus the old lady's talk gently wandered on. Olive listened in silence, her eyes vacantly turned towards the wide open country that sweeps down from Duddingston Loch. The yellow harvest-clad valley smiled; but beneath the same bright sky the loch lay quiet, dark, and still. The sunshine passed over it, and entered it not. Olive wistfully regarded the scene, which seemed a symbol of her own fate. She did not murmur at it, for day by day her peace was returning. She tried to respond with cheerfulness to the new affections that greeted her on every side; to fill each day with those duties, that by the alchemy of a pious nature are so often transmuted into pleasures. She was already beginning to learn the blessed and heaven-sent truth, that no life ought to be wrecked for the love of one human being, and that no sinless sorrow is altogether incurable.

The rest of the drive was rather dull, for Mrs. Flora, usually the most talkative, cheerful old lady in the world, seemed disposed to be silent and thoughtful. Not sad—sadness rarely comes to old age. All strong feelings, whether of joy or pain, belong to youth alone.

"Ye will ride with Marion M'Gillivray the day?" said Mrs. Flora, after a somewhat protracted silence. "You bairns will not want an auld wifie like me."

Olive disclaimed this, affirming, and with her whole heart, that she was never so happy as when with her good Aunt Flora.

"'Tis pleasant to hear ye say the like of that. But it must be even so—for this night I would fain bide alone at home."

The carriage stopped in Abercromby Place.

"I will see ye again the morn," the old lady observed, as her niece descended. And then, after looking up pleasantly to the window, that was filled with a whole host of juvenile M'Gillivrays vehemently nodding and smiling, Aunt Flora pulled down her veil and drove away.

"I thought you would be given up to us for to-day," said Marion, as she and Olive, now grown almost into friends, strolled out arm-in-arm along the shady walks of Morning-side.

"Indeed! Did Aunt Flora say"——

"She said nothing—she never does. But for years I have noticed this 20th of September; because, when she lived with us, on this day, after teaching us in the morning, she used to go to her own room, or take a long, lonely walk,—come back very pale and quiet, and we never saw her again that night. It was the only day in the year that she seemed wishful to keep away from us. Afterwards, when I grew a woman, I found out why this was."

"Did she tell you?"

"No; Aunt Flora never talks about herself. But from her maid and foster-sister, an old woman who died a while ago, I heard a little of the story, and guessed the rest—one easily can," added quiet Marion.

"I think I guess, too. But let me hear, that is, if I *may* hear?"

"Oh yes. 'Tis many, many years ago. Aunt Flora was quite a girl then, and lived with Sir Andrew, her elder brother. She had 'braw wooers' in plenty, according to Isbel Græme (you should have seen old Isbel, cousin Olive). However, she cared for nobody; and some said it was for the sake of a far-away cousin of her own, one of the 'gay Gordons.' But he was anything but 'gay'—delicate in health, plain to look at, and poor besides. While he lived he never said to her a word of love; but after he died,—and that was not until both were past their youth,—there came to Aunt Flora a letter and a ring. She wears it on her wedding finger to this day."

"And this 20th of September must have been the day *he* died," said Olive.

"I believe so. But she never says a word, and never did."

The two walked on silently. Olive was thinking of the long woe-wasted youth—the knowledge of love requited came too late—and then of her who after this great blow could gird up her strength and endure for nearly fifty years. Ay, so as to find in life not merely peace, but sweetness. Olive's own path looked less gloomy to the view. From the depths of her forlorn heart uprose a feeble-winged hope; it came and fluttered about her pale lips, bringing to them

The smile of one, God-satisfied; and earth-undone.

Marion turned round and saw it. "Cousin Olive, how very mild, and calm, and beautiful you look! Before you came, Aunt Flora told us she had heard you were 'like a dove.' I can understand that now. I think, if I were a man, I should fall in love with you."

"With me; surely you forget! Oh no, Marion, not with me; that would be impossible!"

Marion coloured a little, but then earnestly continued, "I don't mean any one who was young and thoughtless, but some grave, wise man, who saw your soul in your face, and learned, slowly and quietly, to love you for your goodness. Ay, in spite of—of"——(here the frank, plain-speaking Marion again hesitated a little, but continued boldly) "any little imperfection which may make you fancy yourself different to other people. If that is your sole reason for saying, as you did the other day, that"——

"Nay, Marion, you have talked quite enough of me."

"But you will forgive me! I could hate myself if I have pained you, seeing how much I love you, how much every one learns to love you."

"Is it so? Then I am very happy!" And the smile sat long upon her face.

"Can you guess whither I am taking you?" said Marion, as they paused before a large and handsome gateway. "Here is the Roman Catholic convent—beautiful St. Margaret's, the sweetest spot at Morningside. Shall we enter?"

Olive assented. Of late she had often thought of those old tales of forlorn women, who, sick of life, had hidden themselves from the world in solitudes like this. Sometimes she had almost wished she could do the same. A feeling deeper than curiosity attracted her to the convent of St. Margaret's.

It was indeed a sweet place; one that a weary heart might well long after. The whole atmosphere was filled with a soft calm—a silence like death, and yet a freshness as of new-born life. When the heavy door closed, it seemed to shut out the world; and without any sense of regret or loss, you passed, like a passing soul, into another existence.

They entered the little convent-parlour. There, on the plain, ungarnished walls, hung the two favourite pictures of Catholic worship; one, thorn-crowned, ensanguined, but still Divine; the other, the Mother lifted above all mothers in blessedness and suffering. Olive gazed long upon both. They seemed meet for the place. Looking at them, one felt as if all trivial earthly sorrows must crumble into dust before these two grand images of sublime woe.

"I think," said Miss Rothesay, "if I were a nun, and had known ever so great misery, I should grow calm by looking at these pictures."

"The nuns don't pass their time in that way I assure you," answered Marion M'Gillivray. "They spend it in making such things as these." And she pointed to a case of babyish ornaments, pin-cushions, and artificial flowers.

"How very strange," said Olive, "to think that the interests and duties of a woman's life should sink down into such trifles as these. I wonder if the nuns are happy?"

"Stay and judge, for here comes one, my chief friend here, Sister Ignatia." And Sister Ignatia—who was, despite her quaint dress, the most bright-eyed, cheerful-looking little Scotchwoman imaginable—stole in, kissed Marion on both cheeks, smiled a pleasant welcome on the stranger, and began talking in a manner so simple and hearty, that Olive's previous notions of a "nun" were cast to the winds. But, after a while, there seemed to her something painfully solemn in looking upon the sister's, where not one outward line marked the inward current which had run on for forty years—how, who could tell? All was silence now.

They went all over the convent. There was a still pureness pervading every room. Now and then a black-stoled figure crossed their way, and vanished like a ghost. Sister Ignatia chattered merrily about their work, their beautiful flowers, and their pupils of the convent school. Happy, very happy, she said they all were at St. Margaret's; but it seemed to Olive like the aimless, thoughtless happiness of a child. Still, when there came across her mind the remembrance of herself—a woman, all alone, struggling with the world, and with her own heart; looking forward to a life's toil for bread and for fame, with which she must try to quench one undying thirst—when she thus thought, she almost longed for such an existence as this quiet monotony, without pleasure and without pain.

"You must come and see our chapel, our beautiful chapel," said Sister Ignatia. "We have got pictures of our St. Margaret and all her children." And when they reached the spot—a gilded, decorated, flower-garden temple, she pointed out with great interest the various memorials of the sainted Scottish Queen.

Olive thought, though she did not then say, that noble Margaret, the mother of her people, the softener of her half-savage lord, the teacher and guide of her children, was more near the ideal of womanhood than the simple, kind-hearted, but childish worshippers, who spent their lives in the harmless baby-play of decking her shrine with flowers.

"Yet these are excellent women," said Marion M'Gillivray, when, on their departure, Olive expressed her thoughts aloud. "You cannot imagine the good they do in their restricted way. But still, if one must lead a solitary life I would rather be Aunt Flora!"

"Yes, a thousand, thousand times! There is something far higher in a woman who goes about the world, keeping her heart consecrated to Heaven, and to some human memories; not shrinking from her appointed work, but doing it meekly and diligently, hour by hour through, life's long day; waiting until at eve God lifts the burden off, saying, 'Faithful handmaid, sleep!'"

Olive spoke softly, but earnestly. Marion did not quite understand her. But she thought everything Miss Rothesay said must be true and good, and was always pleased to watch her the while, declaring that whenever she talked thus her face became "like an angels."

Miss Rothesay spent the evening very happily, though in the noisy household of the M'Gillivrays. She listened to the elder girls' music, and let the younger tribe of "wee toddling bairnies" climb on her knee and pull her curls. Finally, she began to think that some of these days there would be great pleasure in becoming an universal "Aunt Olive" to the rising generation.

She walked home, escorted valiantly by three stout boys, who guided her by a most circuitous route across Bruntsfield Links, that she might gain a moonlight view of the couchant lion of Arthur's Seat. They amused her the whole way home with tales of High-school warfare. On reaching the garden-gate she was half surprised to hear the unwonted cheerfulness of her own laugh. The sunshine she daily strove to cast around her was falling faintly back upon her own heart.

"Good-night, good-night, Allan, and Charlie, and James. We must have another merry walk soon," was her gay adieu as the boys departed, leaving her in the garden-walk, where Mrs. Flora's tall hollyhocks cast a heavy shadow up to the hall-door.

"You seem very happy, Miss Rothesay." The voice came from some one standing close by. The next instant her hand was taken in that of Harold Gwynne.

But the pressure was very cold. Olive's heart, which had leaped up within her, sank down heavily, so heavily, that her greeting was only the chilling words,

"I did not expect to see you here!"

"Possibly not; but I—I had business in Edinburgh. However, it will not, I think, detain me long." He said this sharply even bitterly.

Olive, startled by the suddenness of this meeting, could make no answer, but as they stood beneath the lamp she glanced at the face, whose every change she knew so well. She saw that something troubled him. Forgetful of all besides, her heart turned to him in sympathy and tenderness.

"There is nothing wrong, surely! Tell me, are you quite well, quite happy? You do not know how glad I am to see you, my dear friend."

And her hand alighted softly on his arm like a bird of peace. Harold pressed it and kept it there, as he often did; they were used to that kind of friendly familiarity.

"You are very good, Miss Rothesay. Yes, all is well at Harbury. Pray, be quite easy on that account But I thought, hearing how merry you were at the garden-gate, that amidst your pleasures here you scarcely remembered us at all."

His somewhat vexed tone went to Olive's heart. But she only answered, "You were not quite right there. I never forget my friends."

"No, no! I ought to have known that. Forgive me; I speak rudely, unkindly; but I have so many things to embitter me just now. Let us go in, and you shall talk my ill-humour away, as you have done many a time."

There was a repentant accent in his voice as he drew Olive's arm in his. And she—she looked, and spoke, and smiled, as she had long learned to do. In the little quiet face, the soft, subdued manner, was no trace of any passion or emotion.

"Have you seen Aunt Flora?" said Olive, as they stood together in the parlour.

"No. When I came she had already retired. I have only been here an hour. I passed that time in walking about the garden. Jean told me you would come in soon."

"I would have come sooner had I known. How weary you must be after your journey! Come, take Aunt Flora's chair here, and rest."

He did indeed seem to need rest. As he leaned back with closed eyes on the cushions she had placed, Olive stood and looked at him a moment. She thought, "Oh, that I were dead, and become an invisible spirit, that I might comfort and help him. But I shall never do it. Never in this world!"

She pressed back two burning tears, and then began to move about the room, arranging little household matters for his comfort. She had never done so before, and now the duties seemed sweet and homelike, like those of a sister, or—a wife. Once she thought thus—but she dared not think again. And Harold was watching her, too; following her—as she deemed—with the listless gaze of weariness. But soon he turned his face from her, and whatever was written thereon Olive read no more.

He was to stay that night, for Mrs. Flora's house was always his home in Edinburgh. But he seemed disinclined to talk. One or two questions Olive put about himself and his plans, but they seemed to increase his restlessness.

"I cannot tell; perhaps I shall go; perhaps not at all. We will talk the matter over to-morrow—that is, if you are still kind enough to listen."

She smiled. "Little doubt of that, I think."

"Thank you! And now I will say good-night," observed Harold, rising.

Ere he went, however, he looked down curiously into Olive's face.

"You seem quite strong and well now, Miss Rothesay. You have been happy here?"

"Happy—oh, yes! quite happy."

"I thought it would be so—I was right! Though still—But I am glad, very glad to hear it. Good-night."

He shook her hand—an easy, careless shake; not the close, lingering clasp—how different they were! Then he went quickly up-stairs to his chamber.

But hour after hour sped; the darkness changed to dawn, the dawn to light, and still Olive lay sleepless. Her heart, stirred from its serenity, again swayed miserably to and fro. Vainly she argued with herself on her folly in giving way to these emotions; counting over, even in pitiful scorn, the years that she had past her youth.

"Three more, and I shall be a woman of thirty. Yet here I lie, drowning my pillow with tears, like a love-sick girl. Oh that this trouble had visited me long ago, that I might have risen up from it like the young grass after rain! But now it falls on me like an autumn storm—it tears me, it crushes me; I shall never, never rise."

When it was broad daylight, she roused herself, bathed her brow in water, shut out the sunbeams from her hot, aching eyes, and then lay down again and slept.

Sleeping, she dreamed that she was walking with Harold Gwynne, hand-in-hand, as if they were little children. Suddenly he took her in his arms, clasping her close as a lover his betrothed; and in so doing pressed a bright steel into her heart. Yet it was such sweet death, that, waking, she would fain have wished it true.

But she lifted her head, saw the sunlight dancing on the floor, and knew that the morning was come—that she must rise once more to renew her life's bitter strife.

CHAPTER XXXIX

Olive dressed herself carefully in her delicate-coloured morning-gown. She was one of those women who take pains to appear freshest and fairest in the early hours of the day; to greet the sun as the flowers greet him—rich "in the dew of youth." Despite her weary vigil, the balmy morning brought colour to her cheek and a faint sweetness to her heart. It was a new and pleasant thing to wake beneath the same roof as Harold Gwynne; to know that his face would meet her when she descended—that she would walk and talk with him the whole day long.

Never did any woman think less of herself than Olive Rothesay. Yet as she stood twisting up her beautiful hair, she felt glad that it *was* beautiful. Once she thought of what Marion had told her about some one saying she was "like a dove." Who said it? Not Harold—that was impossible. Arranging her dress, she looked a moment, with half-mournful curiosity, at the pale, small face reflected in the mirror.

"Ah, no! There is no beauty in me. Even did he care for me, I could give him nothing but my poor heart. I can give him that still. It can do him no harm to love him—the very act of loving is blessedness to me."

So thinking, she left her chamber.

It was long before the old lady's time for rising. There was no one in the breakfast-room, but she saw Harold walking on the garden terrace. Very soon he came in with some heliotrope in his hand. He did not give it to Olive, but laid it by her plate, observing, half-carelessly,

"You were always fond of heliotropes, Miss Rothesay."

"Thank you for remembering my likings;" and Olive put the flowers in her bosom. She fancied he looked pleased; and suddenly she remembered the meaning given to the flower, "I love you!" At the thought, she began to tremble all over, though contemning her own folly the while. Even had the words been true, she and Harold were both too old for such sentimentalities.

They breakfasted alone. Harold still looked pale and weary, nor did he deny the fact that he had scarcely slept. He told her all the Harbury news, but spoke little of himself or of his plans. "They were yet uncertain," he said, "but a few more days would decide all." And then he remained silent until, a little time after, they were standing together at the window. From thence it was a pleasant view. Close beneath, a little fountain rose in slender diamond threads, and fell again with a soft trickling, like a Naiad's sigh. Bees were humming over the richest of autumn flower-gardens, which sloped down, terrace after terrace, until its boundary was hid in the little valley below. Beyond—looking in the clear September air so close that you could almost see the purple of the heather—lay the Braid Hills, a horizon-line soft as that which enclosed the Happy Valley of Prince Rasselas.

Harold stood and gazed.

"How beautiful and calm this is! It looks like a quiet nest—a *home* for a man's tired heart and brain. Tell me, friend, do you think one could ever find such in this world?"

"A home!" she repeated, somewhat confusedly, for his voice had startled her.—"You have often said that man needed none; that his life was in himself—the life of intellect and of power. It is only we women who have a longing after rest and home."

Harold made no immediate reply; but after a while he said,

"I want to have a quiet talk with you, Miss Rothesay. And I long to see once more my favourite haunt, the Hermitage of Braid. 'Tis a sweet place, and we can walk and converse there at our leisure. You will come?"

She rarely said him nay in anything, and he somehow unconsciously used a tone of command, like an elder brother;—but there was such sweetness in being ruled by him! Olive obeyed at once; and soon, for the thousandth time, she and Harold were walking out together arm-in-arm.

If ever there was a "lover's walk," it is that which winds along the burnside in the Hermitage of Braid. On either side

The braes ascend like lofty wa's,

shutting out all but the small blue rift of sky above. Even the sun seems slow to peep in, as if his brightness were not needed by those who walk in the light of their own hearts. And the little birds warble and the little burnie runs, as if neither knew there was a weary world outside, where many a heart, pure as either, grows dumb amidst its singing, and freezes slowly as it flows.

Olive walked along by Harold's side in a happy dream. He looked so cheerful, so "good"—a word she had often used, and he had smiled at—meaning those times when, beneath her influence, the bitterness melted from him. Such times there were—else she could never have learned to love him as she did. Then, as now, his eyes were wont to lighten, and his lips to smile, and there came an almost angelic beauty over his face.

"I think," he said, "that my spirit is changing within me. I feel as if I had never known life until now. In vain I say unto myself that this must be a mere fantasy of mine; I, who am marked with the 'frost of eild,' who will soon be—let me see—seven-and-thirty years old. What think you of that age?"

His eyes, bent on her, spoke more than mere curiosity; but Olive, unaware, looked up and smiled.

"Why, I am getting elderly myself; but I heed it not. One need mind nothing if one's heart does not grow old."

"Does yours?"

"I hope not. I would like to lead a life like Aunt Flora's—a quiet stream that goes on singing to the end."

"Look me in the face, Olive Rothesay," said Harold, abruptly. "Nay—pardon me, but I speak like one athirst, who would fain know if any other human thirst is ever satisfied. Tell me, do you look back on your life with content, and forward with hope? Are you happy?"

Olive's eyes sank on the ground.

"Do not question me so." she said trembling. "In life there is nothing perfect; but I have peace, great peace. And for you there might be not only peace, but happiness."

Again there fell between them one of those pauses which rarely come save between two friends or lovers, who know thoroughly—in words or in silence—each other's hearts. Then Harold, guiding the conversation as he always did, changed it suddenly.

"I am thinking of the last time I walked here—when I came to Edinburgh this summer. There was with me one whom I regarded highly, and we talked—as gravely as you and I do now, though on a far different theme."

"What was it?"

"One suited to the season and the place, and my friend's ardent youth. He was in love, poor fellow, and he asked me about his wooing. Perhaps you may think he chose an adviser ill fitted to the task?"

Harold spoke carelessly—and waiting Olive's reply, he pulled a handful of red-brown leaves from a tree that overhung the path, and began playing with them.

"You do not answer, Miss Rothesay. Come, there is scarcely a subject that we have not discussed at some time or other, save this. Let us, just for amusement, take my friend's melancholy case as a text, and argue concerning what young people call 'love.'"

"As you will."

"A cold acquiescence. You think, perhaps, the matter is either above or beneath *me*—that I can have no interest therein?" And his eyes, bright, piercing, commanding, seemed to force an answer.

It came, very quietly and coldly.

"I have heard you say that love was the brief madness of a man's life; if fulfilled, a burden—if unfulfilled or deceived, a curse."

"I said so, did I? Well, you give my opinions—what think you *of me*? Answer truly—like a friend."

She did so. She never could look in Harold's eyes and tell him what was not true.

"I think you are one of those men in whom strong intellect prevents the need of love. Youthful passion you may have felt; but true, deep, earnest love you never did know, and, as I believe, never will! Nay, forgive me if I err; I only take you on your own showing."

"Thank you, thank you! You speak honestly and frankly—that is something for a woman," muttered Harold; and then there was a long, awkward pause. How one poor heart ached the while!

At last, fearing that her silence annoyed him, Olive took courage to say, "You were going to talk to me about your plans. Do so now; that is, if you are not angry with me," she added, with a little deprecatory soothing.

It seemed to touch him. "Angry! How could you think so? I am never angry with you. But what do you desire to hear about? Whither I am going, and when? Do you, then, wish—I mean, advise me to go?"

"Yes, if it is for your good. If leaving Harbury would give you rest on that one subject of which we never speak."

"But of which I, at least, think night and day, and never without a prayer—(I can pray now)—for the good angel who brought light into my darkness," said Harold, solemnly. "That comfort is with me, whatever else may—But you wanted to hear about my going abroad?"

"Yes, tell me all. You know I like to hear."

"Well, then, I have only to decide, and I might depart immediately; to America, I think. I should engage in science and literature. Mine would be a safe, sure course; but, at the beginning, I might have a hard struggle. I do not like to take any one to share it."

"Not your mother, who loves you so?"

"No, because her love would be sorely tried. We should be strangers in a strange land; perhaps poverty would be added to our endurance; I should have to labour unceasingly, and my temper might fail. These are hard things for a woman to bear."

"You do not know what a woman's affection is!" said Olive earnestly. "How could she be desolate when she had you with her! Little would she care for being poor! And if, when sorely tried, you were bitter at times, the more need for her to soothe you. We can bear all things for those we love."

"Is it so?" Harold said, thoughtfully, his countenance changing, and his voice becoming soft as he looked upon her. "Do you think that any woman—I mean my mother, of course—would love *me* with this love?"

And once more Olive taught herself to answer calmly, "I do think so."

Again there was a silence. Harold broke it by saying, "You would smile to know how childishly my last walk here haunts me; I really must go and see that love-stricken friend of mine. But you, I suppose, take no interest in his wooing?"

"O yes! I like to hear of young people's happiness."

"But he was not quite happy. He did not know whether the woman he loved loved him. He had never asked her the question."

"Why not?"

"There were several reasons. First, because he was a proud man, and, like many others, had been deceived *once*. He would not again let a girl mock his peace. And he was right. Do you not think so?"

"Yes, if she were one who would act so cruelly. But no true woman ever mocked at true love. Rarely, *knowingly*, would she give cause for it to be cast before her in vain. If your friend be worthy, how knows he but that she may love him all the while?"

"Well, well, let that pass. He has other reasons." He paused and looked towards her, but Olive's face was drooped out of sight. He continued,— "Reasons such as men only feel. You know not what an awful thing it is to cast one's pride, one's hope—perhaps the weal or woe of one's whole life—upon a woman's light 'Yes' or 'No.' I speak," he added, abruptly, "as my friend, the youth in love, would speak."

"Yes, I know—I understand. Tell me more. That is, if I may hear."

"Oh, certainly. His other reasons were,—that he was poor; that, if betrothed, it might be years before they could marry; or, perhaps, as his health was feeble, he might die, and never call her wife at all. Therefore, though he loved her as dearly as ever man loved woman, he held it right, and good, and just, to keep silence."

"Did he imagine, even in his lightest thought, that she loved him?"

"He could not tell. Sometimes it almost seemed so."

"Then he was wrong—cruelly wrong! He thought of his own pride, not of *her*. Little he knew the long, silent agony she must bear—the doubt of being loved causing shame for loving. Little he saw of the daily struggle: the poor heart frozen sometimes into dull endurance, and then wakened into miserable throbbing life by the shining of some hope, which passes and leaves it darker and colder than before. Poor thing! Poor thing!"

And utterly forgetting herself, forgetting all but the compassion learnt from sorrow, Olive spoke with strong agitation.

Harold watched her intently. "Your words are sympathising and kind. Say on! What should he, this lover, do?"

"Let him tell her that he loves her—let him save her from the misery that wears away youth, and strength, and hope."

"What! and bind her by a promise which it may take years to fulfil?"

"If he has won her heart, she is already bound. It is mockery to talk as the world talks, of the sense of honour that leaves a woman 'free.' She is not free. She is as much bound as if she were married to him. Tell him so! Bid him take her to his heart, that, come what will, she may feel she has a place there. Let him not insult her by the doubt that she dreads poverty or long delay. If she loves him truly, she will wait years, a whole lifetime, until he claim her. If he labour, she will strengthen him; if he suffer, she will comfort him; in the world's fierce battle, her faithfulness will be to him rest, and help, and balm."

"But," said Harold, his voice hoarse and trembling, "what if they should live on thus for years, and never marry? What if he should die?"

"Die!"

"Yes. If so, far better that he should never have spoken—that his secret should go down with him to the grave."

"What, you mean that he should die, and she never know that he loved her! O Heaven! what misery could equal that!"

As Olive spoke, the tears sprang into her eyes, and, utterly subdued, she stood still and let them flow.

Harold, too, seemed strangely moved, but only for a moment. Then he said, very softly and quietly, "Miss Rothesay, you speak like one who feels every word. These are things we learn in but one school. Tell me—as a friend, who night and day prays for your happiness—are you not speaking from your own heart? You love, or you have loved?"

For a moment Olive's senses seemed to reel. But his eyes were upon her—those truthful, truth-searching eyes.

"Must I look in his face and tell him a lie?" was her half-frenzied thought. "I cannot, I cannot! And the whole truth he will never, never know."

Dropping her head, she answered, in one word—"Yes!"

"And, with a woman like you, to love once is to love for evermore?"

Again Olive bent her head, and that was all. There was a sound as of crushed leaves, and those with which Harold had been playing fell scattered on the ground. He gave no other sign of emotion or sympathy.

For many minutes they walked on slowly, the little laughing brook beside them seeming to rise like a thunder-voice upon the dead silence. Olive listened to every ripple, that fell as it were like the boom of an engulphing wave. Nothing else she heard, or felt, or thought, until Harold spoke.

His tone was soft and very kind, and he took her hand the while. "I thank you for this confidence. You must forgive me if I did wrong in asking it. Henceforth I shall ask no more. If your life be happy, as I pray God it may, you will have no need of me. If not, hold me ever to your service as a true friend and brother."

She stooped, she leaned her brow upon the two clasped hands—her own and his—and wept as if her heart were breaking.

But very soon all this ceased, and she felt a calmness like death. Upon it broke Harold's cold, clear voice—as cold and clear as ever.

"Once more, let me tell you all I owe you—friendship, counsel, patience,—for I have tried your patience much. I pray you pardon me! From you I have learned to have faith in Heaven, peace towards man, reverence for women. Your friendship has blessed me—may God bless you."

His words ceased, somewhat tremulously; and she felt, for the first time, Harold's lips touch her hand.

Quietly and mutely they walked home; quietly and mutely, nay, even coldly, they parted. The time had come and passed; and between their two hearts now rose the silence of an existence.

CHAPTER XL

Olive and Harold parted at Mrs. Flora's gate. He had business in town, he said, but would return to dinner. So he walked quickly away, and Olive went in and crept upstairs. There, she bolted her door, groped her way to the bed, and lay down. Life and strength, hope and love, seemed to have ebbed from her at once. She felt no power or desire to weep. Once or twice, she caught herself murmuring, half aloud,

"It is all over—quite over. There can be no doubt now."

And then she knew, by this utter death of hope, that it must have lived *once*—a feeble, half-unconscious life, but life it was. Despite her reason, and the settled conviction to which she had tutored herself, she must have had some faint thought that Harold loved her. Now, this dream gone, she might perhaps rise, as a soul rises from the death of the body, into a new existence. But of that she could not yet think. She only lay, motionless as a corpse, with hands folded, and eyes firmly closed. Sometimes, with a strange wandering of fancy, she seemed to see herself thus, looking down, as a spirit might do upon its own olden self, with a vague compassion. Once she even muttered, in a sort of childish way,

"Poor little Olive! Poor, crushed, broken thing!"

Thus she lay for many hours, sometimes passing into what was either a swoon or a sleep. At last she roused herself, and saw by the shadows that it was quite late in the day. There is great mournfulness in waking thus of one's own accord, and alone; hearing the various noises of the busy mid-day household, and feeling as if all would go on just the same without thought of us, even if we had died in that weary sleep.

Olive wished she had!—that is, had Heaven willed it. She could so easily have crept out of the bitter world, and no one would have missed her. Still, if it must be, she would try once more to lift her burden, and pursue her way.

There was a little comfort for her the minute she went downstairs. Entering the drawing-room, she met Mrs. Flora's brightest smile.

"My dear lassie, welcome! Have you been sleeping after your weary walk this morning?"

"This morning!" echoed poor Olive. She had half forgotten what had happened then, there had come such a death-like cloud between.

"Ye were both away at the Hermitage, Harold said. Ah! poor Harold!"

Olive stood waiting to hear some horrible tidings. All misfortunes seemed to come so naturally now; she felt as though she would scarcely have wondered had they told her Harold was dead.

"My dear Harold is gone away."

"Gone away," repeated Olive, slowly, as her cold hands fell heavily on her lap. She gave no other sign.

"Ah," continued the unconscious old lady, "something has gone ill with the lad. He came in here, troubled like, and said he must just depart at once."

"He was here, then?"

"Only for a wee while. I would have sent for ye, my dearie, but Jean said you were sleeping, and Harold said we had best not waken you, for you had seemed wearied. He could not wait longer, so he bade me bid you farewell, Lassie—lassie, stay!" But Olive had already crept out of the room.

He was gone then. That last clasp of his hand was indeed the last. O miserable parting! Not as between two who love, and loving can murmur the farewell, heart to heart, until its sweetness lingers there long after its sound has ceased; but a parting that has no voice—no hope—wherein one soul follows the other in a wild despair, crying, "Give me back my life that is gone after thee;" and from the void silence there comes no answer, until the whole earth grows blank and dark like an universal grave.

For many days after *that* day, Olive scarcely lifted her head. There came to her some friendly physical ailment, cold or fever, so that she had an excuse to comply with Mrs. Flora's affectionate orders, and take refuge in the quietness of a sick-chamber. There, such showers of love poured down upon her, that she rose refreshed and calmed. After a few weeks, her spirit came to her again like a little child's, and she was once more the quiet Olive Rothesay, rich in all social affections, and even content, save for the one never ceasing pain.

After a season of rest, she began earnestly to consider her future, especially with respect to her Art. She longed to go back to it, and drink again at its wells of peace. For dearly, dearly she loved it still. Half-smiling, she began to call her pictures her children, and to think of the time when they, a goodly race, would live, and tell no tale of their creator's woe. This

Art-life—all the life she had, and all she would leave behind—must not be sacrificed by any miserable contest with an utterly hopeless human love. Therefore she determined to quit Harbury, and at once, before she began to paint her next picture. Her first plan had been to go and live in London, but this was overruled by Mrs. Flora Rothesay.

"Bide here with me, my dear niece. Come and dwell among your ain folk, your father's kin."

And so it was at last fixed to be. But first Olive must go back to Farnwood, to wind up the affairs of her little household, and to arrange about Christal. She had lately thought a good deal of this young girl; chiefly, perhaps, because she was now so eagerly clinging to every interest that could occupy her future life. She remembered, with a little compunction, how her heart had sprung to Christal on her first coming, and how that sympathy had slowly died away, possibly from its being so lightly reciprocated. Though nominally one of the household at the Dell, Miss Manners had gradually seceded from it; so that by degrees the interest with which Olive had once regarded her melted down into the mere liking of duty. Whether this should be continued, became now a matter of question. Olive felt almost indifferent on the subject, but determined that Christal herself should decide. She never would give up the girl, not even to go and live in the dear quiet household of Aunt Flora. Having thus far made up her mind, Miss Rothesay fixed the day for her return to Farnwood—a return looked forward to with a mixture of fear and yearning. But the trial must be borne. It could not be for long.

Ever since his departure Olive had never heard the sound of Harold's name. Mrs. Flora did not talk of him at all. This, her niece thought, sprang from the natural forgetfulness of old age, which, even when least selfish, seems unconsciously to narrow its interest to the small circle of its own daily life. But perhaps the old lady was more quick-sighted than Olive dreamed; for such a true and tried heart could hardly be quite frozen, even with the apathy of eighty years.

A few days before Olive's journey Mrs. Flora called her into her own room.

"I have something to say to ye, lassie. Ye'll listen to the auld wife?"

"Aunt Flora!" said Olive, in affectionate reproach, and, sitting down at her feet, she took the withered hand, and laid it on her neck.

"My sweet wee lassie—my bonnie, bonnie birdie!" said the tender-hearted old lady, who often treated her grand-niece as if she were a child. "If I had known sooner that poor Angus had left a daughter! My dearie, come back soon."

"In a month, Auntie Flora."

"A month seems long. At eighty years one should not boast of the morrow. That is why I will tell ye now what rests on my mind."

"Well, dear aunt, let me hear it."

"'Tis anent the worldly gear that I will leave behind me. I have been aye careful of the good things Heaven lent me."

—She paused; but Olive, not quite knowing what to say, said nothing at all Mrs. Flora continued:

"God has given me great length of days—I have seen the young grow auld, and the auld perish. Some I would fain have chosen to come after me, have gone away before me; some have enough, and need no more. Of all my kith and kin there is none to whom the bit siller can do good, but my niece Olive, and Harold Gwynne. Does that grieve ye, lassie? Nay, his right is no like yours. But he comes of blood that was sib to ours. Alison Balfour was a Gordon by the mother's side."

As Mrs. Flora uttered the name, Olive felt a movement in the left hand that lay on her neck; the aged fingers were fluttering to and fro over the diamond ring. She looked up, but there was perfect serenity on the face. And, turning back, she prayed that the like peace might come to *her* in time.

"Before ye came," continued Mrs. Flora, "I thought to make Harold my heir, and that he should take the name of Gordon—for dearly I loved that name in auld lang syne. Ah, lassie! even in this world God can wipe away all tears from our eyes, so that we may look clearly forth unto the eternal land."

"Amen, amen!" murmured Olive Rothesay—ay, though while she uttered the prayer, her own tears blindingly rose. But her aunt's soft cold hand glided silently on her drooped head, pressing its throbbings into peace.

"I am wae to think," continued the old lady, "that ye are the last of the Rothesay line. The *name* must end, even should Olive marry."

"I shall never marry, Aunt Flora! I shall live as you have done—God make my life equally worthy!"

"Is it so? I thought it was different. Then, Olive, my child! may God comfort thee with his peace."

Mrs. Flora kissed her on the forehead, and asked no more. Shortly afterwards, she again began to speak about her will. She wished to be just, she said, and to leave her property where it would be most required. Her heart inclined chiefly to her niece, as being a woman, struggling alone through the world; whereas Harold, firmly settled in his curacy, would not need additional fortune.

"Oh, but he does need it; you little know how sorely!" cried Olive.

"Eh, my dear? He, a minister!"

Olive drew back, afraid lest she had betrayed too much of the secret so painfully shared between her and Harold Gwynne. She trembled and blushed beneath the old lady's keen eyes. At last she said, beseechingly,

"Aunt Flora, do not question me—I cannot, ought not, to tell you any more than this—that there may come a time when this money might save him from great misery."

"Misery aye follows sin," said Mrs. Flora, almost sternly, "Am I deceived in him, my dear Harold—poor Alison's son?"

"No, no, no! He is noble, just, and true. There is no one like him in the whole world," cried Olive; and then stopped, covered with blushes. But soon the weakness passed. "Listen to me, Aunt Flora, for this once. Harold Gwynne,"—she faltered not over the name,—"Harold Gwynne is, and will be always, my dear friend and brother. I know more of his affairs than any one else; and I know, too, that he may be in great poverty one day. For me, I have only myself to work for, and work I must, since it is the comfort of my life. As to this fortune, I need it not—how should I? I entreat you, leave all to him."

Mrs. Flora wrapped her arms round her niece without speaking—nor did she again refer to the subject.

But the night before Olive left Edinburgh, she bade her farewell with a solemn blessing—the more solemn, as it was given in words taken out of the Holy Book which she had just closed—words never used lightly by the aged Presbyterian.

"*The Lord bless thee and keep thee!*

The Lord cause His face to shine upon thee!

The Lord give thee thy heart's desire, and fulfil all thy mind."

Olive rose with an indescribable sense of hope and peace. As she left the room she looked once more at her aunt.

Mrs. Flora sat in her crimson chair, her hands laid on her knee, her face grave, but serene, and half-lifted, like one who hearkens to some unseen call A secret consciousness struck Olive that in this world she should never more hear the voice, or see the face, of one who had been truly a saint on earth.

It was indeed so.

CHAPTER XLI

Coming home!—coming home! In different ears how differently sound the words! They who in all their wanderings have still the little, well-filled, love-expectant nest whereto they may wing their way, should think sometimes of the many there are to whom the whole wide world is all alike; whose sole rest must be in themselves; who never can truly say, "I am going home," until they say it with eyes turned longingly towards a Home unseen.

Something of this mournfulness felt Olive Rothesay. It was dreary enough to reach her journey's end alone, and have to wait some hours at the small railway station; and then, tired and worn, to be driven for miles across the country through the gloomiest of all gloomy November days. Still, the dreariness passed, when she saw, shining from afar, the light from the windows of Farnwood Dell. As the chaise stopped, out came running old Hannah, the maid, with little Ailie too; while awaiting her in the parlour, were Christal and Mrs. Gwynne. *No one else!* Olive saw that in one moment, and blamed herself for having wished—what she had no right to hope—what had best not be.

Mrs. Gwynne embraced her warmly—Christal with dignified grace. The young lady looked gay and pleased, and there was a subdued light in her black eyes which almost softened them into sweetness. The quick restless manner in which she had indulged at times since she came to Farnwood seemed melting into a becoming womanliness, Altogether, Christal was improved.

"Well, now, I suppose you will be wanting to hear the news of all your friends," said Miss Manners, with smiles bubbling round her pretty mouth. "We are not all quite the same as you left us. To begin with—let me see—Mr. Harold Gwynne"——

"Of that, Miss Christal, I will beg you not to speak. It is a painful subject to me," observed Mrs. Gwynne, with a vexed air. "You need not look at me so earnestly, dear, kind Olive! All is well with me and with my son; but he has done what I think is not exactly good for him, and it somewhat troubles me. However, we will talk of this another time."

"More news do you want, Olive?" (Christal now sometimes called her so.) "Well, then, Dame Fortune is in the giving mood. She has given your favourite Mr. Lyle Derwent a fortune of £1000 a year, and a little estate to match!"

"I am so glad! for his sake, good dear Lyle!"

"*Dear* Lyle!" repeated Christal, turning round with a sparkle either of pleasure or anger in her glittering eyes; but it was quenched before it reached those of Olive. "Well, winning is one thing, deserving is another!" she continued, merrily. "I could have picked out a dozen worthy, excellent young men, who would have better merited the blessing of a rich uncle, ay, and made a better use of his money too."

"Lyle would thank you if he knew."

"That he ought, and that he does, and that he shall do, every day of his life!" cried Christal, lifting up her tall figure with a sudden haughtiness, not the less real because she laughed the while; then with one light bound she vanished from the room.

Olive, left alone with Mrs. Gwynne, would fain have taken her hands, and said as she had oft done before. "Friend, tell me all that troubles you—all that concerns you and *him*." But now a faint fear repelled her. However, Harold's mother, understanding her looks, observed,

"You are anxious, my dear. Never was there such a faithful friend to me and to my son! I wish you had been here a week ago, and then you might have helped me to persuade him not to go away."

"He is gone, then, to America?"

"America!—who mentioned America?" said Mrs. Gwynne, sharply. "Has he told you more than he told me?"

Olive, sorely repentant, tried to soothe the natural jealousy she had aroused. "You know well Mr. Gwynne would be sure to tell his plans to his mother; only I have heard him talk of liking America—of wishing to go thither."

"He has not gone then. He has started with his friend Lord Arundale, to travel all through Europe. It is a pity, I think, for one of his cloth, and it shows a wandering and restless mind. I know not what has come over my dear Harold."

"Was it a sudden journey?—is it long since he went?" said Olive, shading her eyes from the fire-light.

"Only yesterday. I told him you were coming to-day; and he desired me to say how grieved he was that he thus missed you, but it was unavoidable.

He had kept Lord Arundale waiting already, and it would not be courteous to delay another day. You will not mind?"

"Oh no! oh no!" The hand was pressed down closer over the eyes.

Mrs. Gwynne pursued. "Though I have all confidence in my son, yet I own this sudden scheme has troubled me. His health is better;—why could he not stay at Harbury?"

Olive, wishing to discover if she knew anything of her son's sad secret, observed, "It is a monotonous life that Mr. Gwynne leads here—one hardly suited for him."

"Ah, I know," said the mother, sighing. "His heart is little in his calling. I feared so, long ago. But it is not that which drives him abroad; for I told him if he still wished to resign his duties to his curate, we would give up the Parsonage, and he should take pupils. There is a charming little house in the neighbouring village that would suit us. But no; he seemed to shrink from this plan too. He said he must go entirely away from Harbury."

"And for how long?"

"I cannot tell—he did not say. I should think, not above a year—his mother may not have many more years to spend with him;" and there was a little trembling of Mrs. Gwynne's mouth; but she continued with dignity: "Do not imagine, Olive, that I mean to blame my son. He has done what he thought right. Against my wish, or my happiness, he would not have done it at all. So I did not let him see any little pain it might have given me. 'Twas best not. Now we will let the subject rest."

But, though they spoke no more, Olive speculated vainly on what had induced Harold to take this precipitate journey. She thought she had known him so thoroughly—better than any one else could. But in him lay mysteries beyond her ken. She could only still rest on that which had comforted her in all she suffered;—an entire faith in him and in his goodness.

Mrs. Gwynne sat an hour or two, and then rose to return to the Parsonage. "We must be home before it is dark, little Ailie and I. We have no one to take care of us now."

Some pain was visible as she said this. When she took her grandchild by the hand, and walked down the garden, it seemed to Olive that the old lady's step was less firm than usual. Her heart sprang to Harold's mother.

"Let me walk with you a little way, Mrs. Gwynne. I am thoroughly rested now; and as for coming back alone, I shall not mind it."

"What a little trembling arm it is for me to lean on!" said Mrs. Gwynne, smiling, when, after some faint resistance, she had taken Olive for a companion. "'Tis nothing like my Harold's, and yet I am glad to have it. I am afraid I shall often have to look to it now Harold is away. Are you willing, Olive?"

"Quite, quite willing;—nay, very glad!"

Olive went nearly all the way to Harbury. She was almost happy, walking between Harold's mother and Harold's child. But when she parted from them she felt alone, bitterly alone. Then first she began to realise the truth, that the dream of so many months was now altogether ended! It had been something, even after her sorrow began, to feel that Harold was near! that, although days might pass without her seeing him, still he *was* there—within a few miles. Any time, sitting wearily in her painting room, she might hear his knock at the door; or in any walk, however lonely and sad, there was at least the possibility of his crossing her path, and, despite her will, causing her heart to bound with joy. Now, all these things could not be again. She went homeward along the dear old Harbury road, knowing that no possible chance could make his image appear to brighten its loneliness; that where they had so often walked, taking sweet counsel together as familiar friends, she must learn to walk alone. Perhaps, neither there nor elsewhere, would she ever walk with Harold more.

In her first suffering, in her brave resolve to quit Harbury, she had not thought how she should feel when all was indeed over. She had not pictured the utter blankness of a world wherein Harold was not. The snare broken and her soul escaped, she knew not how it would beat its broken wings in the dun air, meeting nothing but the black, silent waste, ready once more to flutter helplessly down into the alluring death.

Olive walked along with feet heavy and slow. In her eyes were no tears—she had wept them all away long since. She did not look up much; but still she saw, as one sees in a dream, all that was around her—the white, glittering grass, the spectral hedges, the trees laden with a light snow, silent, motionless, stretching their bare arms up to the dull sky. No, not the sky, that seemed far, far off; between it and earth interposed a mist, so thick and cold that it blinded sight and stifled breath. She could not look up at God's dear heaven—she almost felt that through the gloom the pitying Heaven could not look at her. But after a while the mist changed a little, and then Olive drew her breath, and her thoughts began to form themselves as she went along.

"I am now alone, quite alone. I must shut my life up in myself—look to no one's help, yearn for no one's love. What I receive I will take thankfully; but I have no claim upon any one in this wide world. Many pleasant friendships I have, many tender ties, but none close enough to fill the void in my heart—none to love as I could love—as I did love for many years. Oh, mother, why did you go away? Why did I love again—lose again? Always loving only to lose."

Many times she said to herself, "I am alone—quite alone in the world;" and at last the words seemed to strike the echo of some old remembrance. But it was one so very dim, that for a long time Olive could not give it any distinct form. At last she recollected the letter which, ten years ago, she had put away in a secret drawer of her father's desk. Strange to say, she had never thought of it since. Perhaps this was because, at the time, she had instinctively shuddered at the suggestions it gave, and so determined to banish them. And then the quick, changing scenes of life had prevented her ever recurring to the subject Now, when all had come true, when on that desert land which, still distant, had seemed so fearful to the girl's eyes, the woman's feet already stood, she turned with an eager desire to the words which her father had written—*"To his daughter Olive when she was quite alone in the world."*

Reaching home, and hearing Christal warbling some Italian song, Olive went at once to her own apartment, half parlour, half studio. There was a fire lit, and candles. She fastened the door, that she might not be interrupted, and sat down before her desk.

She found some difficulty in opening the secret drawer, for the spring was rusty from long disuse, and her own fingers trembled much. When at last she held the letter in her hand, its yellow paper and faded ink struck her painfully. It seemed like suddenly coming face to face with the dead.

A solemn, anxious feeling stole over her. Ere breaking the seal, she lingered long; she tried to call up all she remembered of her father—his face—his voice—his manners. Very dim everything was! She had been such a mere child until he died, and the ten following years were so full of action, passion, and endurance, that they made the old time look pale and distant. She could hardly remember how she used to feel then, least of all how she used to feel towards her father. She had loved him, she knew, and her mother had loved him, ay, long after love became only memory. He had loved them, too, in his quiet way. Olive thought, with tender remembrance, of his kiss, on that early morning when, for the last time, he had left his home. And for her mother! Often, during Mrs. Rothesay's declining days, had she delighted to talk of the time when she was a young, happy wife, and of the dear love that Angus bore her. Something, too, she hinted of her own faults, which had once taken away that love, and something in Olive's own childish memory told her that this was true. But she repelled the thought, remembering that her father and mother were now together before God.

At length with an effort she opened the letter. She started to see its date—the last night Captain Rothesay ever spent at home—the night, which of all others, she had striven to remember clearly, because they were all three so happy together, and he had been so kind, so loving, to her mother and to her. Thinking of him on this wise, with a most tender sadness, she began to read:

"Olive Rothesay—My dear Child!—It may be many—many years—(I pray so, God knows!) before you open this letter. If so, think of me as I sit writing it now—or rather as I sat an hour ago—by your mother's side, with your arms round my neck. And, thus thinking of me, consider what a fierce struggle I must have had to write as I am going to do—to confess what I never would have confessed while I lived, or while your mother lived. I do it, because remorse is strong upon me; because I would fain that my Olive—the daughter who may comfort me, if I live—should, if I die, make atonement for her father's sins. Ay, sins. Think how I must be driven, thus to humble myself before my own child—to unfold to my pure daughter that—But I will tell the tale plainly, without any exculpation or reserve.

"I was very young when I married Sybilla Hyde. God be my witness, I loved her then, and in my inmost heart I have loved her evermore. Remember, I say this—hear it as if I were speaking from my grave—Olive, *I did love your mother*. Would to Heaven she had loved me, or shown her love, only a little more!

"Soon after our marriage I was parted from my wife for some years. You, a girl, ought not to know—and I pray may never know—the temptations of the world and of man's own nature. I knew both, and I withstood both. I came back, and clasped my wife to the most loving and faithful heart that ever beat in a husband's breast. I write this even with tears—I, who have been so cold. But in this letter—which no eye will ever see until I and your mother have lain together long years in our grave—I write as if I were speaking, not as now, but as I should speak then.

"Well, between my wife and me there came a cloud. I know not whose was the fault—perhaps mine, perhaps hers; or, it might be, both. But there the cloud was—it hung over my home, so that I could find therein no peace, no refuge. It drove me to money-getting, excitement, amusement—at last to crime!

"In the West Indies there was one who had loved me, in vain,—mark you, I said *in vain*,—but with the vehemence of her southern blood. She was a Quadroon lady—one of that miserable race, the children of planters and slaves, whose beauty is their curse, whose passion knows no law except a blind fidelity. And, God forgive me! that poor wretch was faithful unto me.

"She followed me to England without my knowledge. Little she had ever heard of marriage; she found no sacred-ness in mine. I did not love her—not with a pure heart as I loved Sybilla. But I pitied her. Sometimes I turned from my dreary home—where no eye brightened at mine, where myself and my interests were nothing—and I thought of this woman, to whom I was all the world. My daughter Olive, if ever you be a wife, and would keep your husband's love, never let these thoughts enter and pollute his mind. Give him your whole heart, and he will ask no other. Make his home sweet and pleasant to him, and he will not stray from it. Bind him round with cords of love—fast—fast. Oh, that my wife had had strength so to encircle me!

"But she had not; and so the end came! Olive, you are not my *only* child.

"I have no desire to palliate my sin. Sin, I know it was, heavy and deadly; against God's law, against my trusting wife, and against that hapless creature on whom I brought a whole lifetime of misery. Ay, not on her alone, but on that innocent being who has received from me nothing but the heritage of shame, and to whom in this world I can never make atonement. No man can! I felt this when she was born. It was a girl, too—a helpless girl. I looked on the little face, sleeping so purely, and remembered that on her brow would rest through life a perpetual stain; and that I, her father, had fixed it there. Then there awoke in me a remorse which can never die. For, alas, Olive, I have more to unfold! My remorse, like my crimes, was selfish at the root, and I wreaked it on her, who, if guilty, was less guilty than I.

"One day I came to her, restless and angry, unable to hide the worm that was continually gnawing at my heart. She saw it there, and her proud spirit rose; she poured on me a torrent of reproachful words. I answered them as one who had erred like me was sure to answer. Poor wretch! I reviled her as having been the cause of my misery. When I saw her in her fury, I contrasted her image with that of the pale, patient, trusting creature I had left that morning—my wife, my poor Sybilla—until, hating myself, I absolutely loathed *her*—the enchantress who had been my undoing. With her shrill voice yet pursuing me, I precipitately left the house. Next day mother and child had disappeared! Whither, I knew not; and I never have known, though I left no effort untried to solve a mystery which made me feel like a *murderer*.

"Nevertheless, I believe that they are still alive—these wretched two. If I did not, I should almost go mad at times.

"Olive, have pity on your father, and hearken to what I implore. Whilst I live, I shall continue this search—but I may die without having had the chance of making atonement. In that case I entreat of my daughter Olive to stand between her father and his sin. If you have no other ties—if you never marry, but live alone in the world—seek out and protect that child! Remember, she is of your own blood—*she*, at least, never wronged you. In showing mercy to her, you do so to me, your father; who, when you read this, will have been for years among the dead, though the evil that he caused may still remain unexpiated. Oh! think that this is his voice crying out from the dust, beseeching you to absolve his memory. Save me from the horrible thought, now haunting me evermore, that the being who owes me life may one day heap curses on her father's name!

"Herewith enclosed you will find instructions respecting an annuity I wish paid to—to the woman. It was placed in——'s bank by Mr. Wyld, whom, however, I deceived concerning it—I am now old enough in the school of hypocrisy. Hitherto the amount has never been claimed.

"Olive, my daughter, forgive me! Judge me not harshly. I never would have asked this of you while your mother lived—your mother, whom *I loved*, though I wronged her so grievously. In some things, perhaps, she erred towards me; but I ought to have shown her more sympathy, and have dealt gently with her tender nature, so unlike my own. May God forgive us both!—God, in whose presence we shall both be, when you, our daughter, read this record. And may He bless you evermore, prays your loving father,

"Angus Rothesay.

"Celia Manners was her name. Her child she called *Christal*."

It ceased—this voice from the ten years' silent grave of Angus Rothesay. His daughter sat motionless, her fixed eyes blindly out-gazing, her whole frame cold and rigid, frozen into a statue of stone.

CHAPTER XLII

Rivetted by an inexplicable influence, Olive had read the letter through, without once pausing or blenching;—read it as though it had been some strange romance of misery, not relating to herself at all. She felt unable to comprehend or realise it, until she came to the name—"Christal." Then the whole truth burst upon her, wrapping her round with a cold horror, and, for the time, paralysing all her faculties. When she awoke, the letter was still in her hand, and from it still there stood out clear the name, which had long been a familiar word. Therefore, all this while, destiny had been leading her to work out her father's desire. The girl who had dwelt in her household for months, whom she had tried to love, and generously sought to guide, was—*her sister*.

But what a chaos of horror was revealed by this discovery! Olive's first thought was of her mother, who had showered kindness on this child of shame; who, dying, had unconsciously charged her to "take care of Christal."

With a natural revulsion of feeling, Olive thrust the letter from her. Its touch seemed to pollute her fingers.

"Oh, my mother—my poor, wronged mother!—well for you that you never lived to see this day. You—so good, so loving, so faithfully remembering him even to the last. But I—I have lived to shrink with abhorrence from the memory of my own father."

Suddenly she stopped, aghast at thinking that she was thus speaking of the dead—the dead from whom her own life had sprung.

"I am bewildered," she murmured. "Heaven help me! I know not what I say or do." And Olive fell on her knees.

She had no words to pray with; but, in such time of agony, all her thoughts were prayers. After a while these calmed her, and made her strong to endure one more trial—different from, perhaps even more awful than, all the rest.

Much sorrow had been her life's portion; but never until this hour had Olive Rothesay stood face to face with crime. She had now to learn the crowning lesson of virtue—how to deal with vice. Not by turning away in saintly pride, but by boldly confronting it, with an eye stern in purity, yet melting in compassion; remembering ever—

How all the souls that were, were forfeit once; And He who might the vantage best have took Found out the remedy.

Angus Rothesay's daughter read over once more the record of his sin. In so doing, she was struck with the depth of that remorse which, to secure a future expiation, threw aside pride, reserve, and shame. How awful must have been the repentance which had impelled such a confession, and driven a father to humble himself in the dust before his own child! She seemed to hear, rising from the long-closed grave, that mournful, beseeching cry, "Atone my sin!" It silenced even the voice of her mother's wrongs.

This duty then remained, to fulfil which—as it would appear—Olive had been left alone on earth. The call seemed like that of fate; nay, she half-shuddered to think of the almost supernatural chance, which had arranged everything before her, and made her course so plain. But it had often happened so. Her life appeared as some lives do, all woven about with mysteries; threads of guidance, first unseen, and then distinctly traced, forcing on the mind that sweet sense of invisible ministry which soothes all suffering, and causes a childlike rest on the Omnipotence which out of all evil continually evolves good.

With this thought there dawned upon Olive a solemn sense of calm. To lay down this world's crown of joys, and to take up its cross—no longer to be ministered unto, but to minister,—this was to be her portion henceforth, and with this holy work was her lonely life to be filled.

"I will do it," she cried. "O my poor father, may God have forgiven you, as my mother would, and as I now do! It is not mine to judge your sin; enough for me is the duty to atone it. How can this be best fulfilled?"

She sat long in silence, mournfully pondering. She tried to collect every scattered link of memory respecting what she had heard of Christal's mother. For such, she now knew, was the woman who, for the time, had once strongly excited her girlish imagination. That visit and its incidents now came vividly back upon her memory. Much there was which made her naturally revolt from the thought of this unhappy creature. How could it be otherwise with her mother's child? Still, amidst all, she was touched by the love of this other most wretched mother, who—living and dying—had renounced her maternal claim; and impressed upon her daughter's mind a feigned story, rather than let the brand of illegitimate birth rest upon the poor innocent.

Suddenly she heard from the next room Christal's happy, unconscious voice, singing merrily.

"My sister!" Olive gasped. "She is my sister—my father's child."

And there came upon her, in a flood of mingled compassion and fear, all that Christal would feel when she came to know the truth! Christal—so proud of her birth—her position—whose haughty nature, inherited from both father and mother, had once struggled wrathfully against Olive's mild control. Such a blow as this would either crush her to the earth, or, rousing up the demon in her, drive her to desperation. Thinking thus, Olive forgot everything in pity for the hapless girl;—everything, save an awe-struck sense of the crime, which, as its necessary consequence, entailed such misery from generation to generation.

It seemed most strange that Christal had lived for so many years, cherishing her blind belief, nay, not even seeking to investigate it when it lay in her power. For since the day she returned from France, she had never questioned Miss Vanbrugh, nor alluded to the subject of her parentage. Such indifference seemed incredible, and could only be accounted for by Christal's light, careless nature, her haughtiness, or her utter ignorance of the world.

What was Olive to do? Was she to reveal the truth, and thus blast for ever this dawning life, so full of hope? Was her hand to place the stigma of shame on the brow of this young creature?—a girl too! There might come a time when some proud, honourable man, however loving, would scruple to take to his bosom as a wife, one—whose mother had never owned that name. But then—was Olive to fix on herself the perpetual burden of this secret—the continual dread of its betrayal—the doubt, lest one day, chance might bring it to Christal's knowledge, perhaps when the girl would no longer be shielded by a sister's protection, or comforted by a sister's love?

While she struggled in this conflict, she heard a voice at the door.

"Olive—Olive!"—the tone was more affectionate than usual. "Are you never coming? I am quite tired of being alone. Do let me into the studio!"

Olive sprang to her desk and hid the letter therein. Then, without speaking—she had no power to speak—she mechanically unlocked the door.

"Well, I am glad to get at you at last," cried Christal, merrily. "I thought you were going to spend the night here. But what is the matter? You are as white as a ghost. You can't look me in the face. Why, one would almost imagine you had been planning a murder, and I was the 'innocent, unconscious victim,' as the novels have it."

"You—a victim!" cried Olive, in great agitation. But by an almost superhuman effort she repressed it, and added, quietly, "Christal, my dear, don't mind me. It is nothing—only I feel ill—excited."

"Why, what have you been doing?"

Olive instinctively answered the truth. "I have been sitting here alone—thinking of old times—reading old letters."

"Whose? nay, but I will know," answered Christal, half playfully, half in earnest, as though there was some distrust in her mind.

"It was my father's—my poor father's."

"Is that all? Oh, then don't vex yourself about any old father dead and gone. I wouldn't! Though, to be sure, I never had the chance. Little I ever knew or cared about mine."

Olive turned away, and was silent; but Christal, who seemed, for some reason best known to herself, to be in a particularly unreserved and benignant humour, said kindly, "You poor little trembling thing, how ill you have made yourself! You can scarcely stand alone; give me your hand, and I'll help you to the sofa."

But Olive shrank as if there had been a sting in the slender fingers which lay on her arm. She looked at them, and a slight circumstance, long forgotten, rushed back upon her memory,—something she had noticed to her mother the first night that the girl came home. Tracing the beautiful hereditary mould of the Rothesay line, she now knew why Christal's hand was like her own father's.

A shiver of instinctive repugnance came over her, and then the mysterious voice of kindred blood awoke in her heart. She took and passionately clasped that hand—the hand of *her sister*.

"O Christal! let us love one another—we two, who have no other tie left to us on earth."

But Christal was rarely in a pathetic mood. She only shrugged her shoulders, and then stroked Olive's arm with a patronising air. "Come, your journey has been too much for you, and you had no business to wander off that way with Mrs. Gwynne; you shall lie down and rest a little and then go to bed."

But Olive was afraid of night and its solitude. She knew there was no slumber for her. When she was a little recovered, feeling unable to talk, she asked Christal to read aloud.

The other looked annoyed. "Pleasant! to be a mere lady's companion and reader! Miss Rothesay forgets who I am, I think," muttered she, though apparently not meaning Olive to hear her.

But Olive did hear, and shuddered at the hearing.

Miss Manners carelessly took up the newspaper, and read the first paragraph which caught her eye. It was one of those mournful episodes which are sometimes revealed at the London police-courts. A young girl—a lady swindler—had been brought up for trial there. In her defence came out the story of a life, cradled in shame, nurtured in vice, and only working out its helpless destiny—that of a rich man's deserted illegitimate child. The report added, that "The convict was led from the dock in a state of violent excitement, calling down curses on her parents, but especially on her father, who, she said, had cruelly forsaken her mother. She ended by exclaiming that it was to him she herself owed all her life of misery, and that her blood was upon his head."

"It *was* upon his head," burst forth Christal, whose sympathies, as by some fatal instinct, seemed attracted by a case like this. "If I had been that girl, I would have hunted my vile father through the world. While he lived, I would have heaped my miseries in his path, that everywhere they might torture and shame him. When he died, I would have trampled on his grave and cursed him!"

She stood up, her eyes flashing, her hands clenched in one of those paroxysms which to her came so rarely, but, when roused, were terrible to witness. Her mother's soul was in the girl. Olive saw it, and from that hour knew that, whatever it cost her, the secret of Christal's birth must be buried in her own breast for evermore.

Most faithfully Miss Rothesay kept her vow. But it entailed upon her the necessity of changing her whole plans for the future. For some inexplicable reason, Christal refused to go and live with her in Edinburgh, or, in fact, to leave Farnwood at all. Therefore Olive's despairing wish to escape from Harbury, and all its bitter associations, was entirely frustrated. It would be hard to say whether she lamented or rejoiced at this. The brave resolve had cost her much, yet she scarcely regretted that it would not be fulfilled. There was a secret sweetness in living near Harbury—in stealing, as it were, into a daughter's place beside the mother of him she still so fervently loved. But, thinking of him, she did not suffer now. For all great trials there is an unseen compensation; and this last shock, with the change it had wrought, made her past sorrows grow dim. Life became sweeter to her, for it was filled with a new and holy interest. It could be so filled, she found, even when love had come and vanished, and only duty remained.

She turned from all repining thoughts, and tried to make for herself a peaceful nest in her little home. And thither, above all, she desired to allure and to keep, with all gentle wiles of love, her sister. *Her sister!* Often, yearning for kindred ties, she longed to fall on Christal's neck, and call her by that tender name! But she knew it could never be, and her heart had been too long schooled into patience, to murmur because in every human tie this seemed to be perpetually her doom—that—save one who was gone—none upon earth had ever loved her as much as she loved them.

Harold Gwynne wrote frequently from Rome, but only to his mother. However, he always mentioned Miss Rothesay, and kindly. Once, when Mrs. Gwynne was unable to write herself, she asked Olive to take her place, and indulge Harold with a letter.

"He will be so glad, you know. I think of all his friends there is none whom my son regards more warmly than you," said the mother. And Olive could not refuse. Why, indeed, should she feel reluctance? He had never been her lover; she had no right to feel wounded, or angry at his silence. Certainly, she would write.

She did so. It was a quiet, friendly letter, making no reference to the past—expressing no regret, no pain. It was scarcely like the earnest letters which she had once written to him—that time was past. She tried to make it an epistle as from any ordinary acquaintance—easy and pleasant, full of everything likely to amuse him. She knew he would never dream how it was written—with a cold, trembling hand and throbbing heart, its smooth sentences broken by pauses of burning blinding tears.

She said little about herself or her own affairs, save to ask that, being in Rome, he would contrive to find out the Vanbrughs, of whom she had heard nothing for a long time. Writing, she paused a moment to think whether she should not apologise for giving him this trouble. But then she remembered his words—almost the last she had heard him utter—that she must always consider him "as a friend and brother."

"I will do so," she murmured. "I will not doubt him, or his true regard for me. It is all he can give; and while he gives me that, I shall endure life contentedly, even unto the end."

CHAPTER XLIII

It was mid-winter before the inhabitants of the Dell were visited by their friend, Lyle Derwent, now grown a rich and important personage. Olive rather regretted his apparent neglect, for it grieved her to suspect a change in any one whom she regarded. Christal only mocked the while, at least in outside show. Miss Rothesay did not see with what eagerness the girl listened to every sound, nor how every morning, fair and foul, she would restlessly start to walk up the Harbury road and meet the daily post.

It was during one of these absences of hers that Lyle made his appearance. Olive was sitting in her painting-room, arranging the contents of her desk. She was just musing, for the hundredth time, over her father's letter, considering whether or not she should destroy it, lest any unforeseen chance—her own death, for instance—might bring the awful secret to Christars knowledge. Lyle's entrance startled her, and she hastily thrust the letter within the desk. Consequently her manner was rather fluttered, and her greeting scarcely so cordial as she would have wished it to be. The infection apparently communicated itself to her visitor, for he sat down, looking agitated and uncomfortable.

"You are not angry with me for staying so long away, are you, Miss Rothesay?" said Lyle, when he had received her congratulations on his recent acquisitions. "You don't think this change in fortune will make any change in my heart towards you?"

Olive half smiled at his sentimental way of putting the matter, but it was the young man's peculiarity. So she frankly assured him that she had never doubted his regard towards her. At which poor Lyle fell into ecstasies of delight.

They had a long talk together about his prospects, in all of which Olive took a warm and lively interest. He told her of his new house and grounds; of his plan of life, which seemed very Arcadian and poetical indeed. But he was a simple-minded, warm-hearted youth, and Miss Rothesay listened with pleasure to all he said. It did her good to see that there was a little happiness to be found in the world.

"You have drawn the sweetest possible picture of rural felicity," she said, smiling; "I earnestly hope you may realise it, my dear Lyle—But I suppose one must not call you so any more, since you are now Mr. Derwent, of Hollywood."

"Oh, no; call me Lyle, nothing but Lyle. It sounds so sweet from your lips—it always did, even when I was a little boy."

"I am afraid I have treated you quite like a boy until now. But you must not mind it, for the sake of old times."

"Do you remember them still?" asked Lyle, a tone of deeper earnestness stealing through his affectations of sentiment. "Do you remember how I was your little knight, and used to say I loved you better than all the world?"

"I do indeed. It was an amusing rehearsal of what you will begin to enact in reality some of these days. You will make a most poetical lover."

"Do you think so? O Miss Rothesay, do you really think so?" And then his eagerness subsided into vivid blushes, which really caused Olive pain. She began to fear that, unwittingly, she had been playing on some tender string, and that there was more earnest feeling in Lyle than she had ever dreamed of. She would not for the world have jested thus, had she thought there was any real attachment in the case. So, a good deal touched and interested, she began to talk to him in her own quiet, affectionate way.

"You must not mistake me, Lyle; you must not think I am laughing at you. But I did not know that you had ever considered these things. Though there is plenty of time—as you are only just twenty-one. Tell me candidly—you know you may—do you think you were ever seriously in love?"

"It is very strange for you to ask me these questions."

"Then do not answer them. Forgive me, I only spoke from the desire I have to see you happy: you, who are so mingled with many recollections; you, poor Sara's brother, and my own little favourite in olden time." And speaking in a subdued and tender voice, Olive held out her hand to Lyle.

He snatched it eagerly. "How I love to hear you speak thus! Oh, if I could but tell you all."

"You may, indeed," said Olive, gently. "I am sure, my dear Lyle, you can trust me. Tell me the whole story."

—"The story of a dream I had, all my boyhood through, of a beautiful, noble creature, whom I reverenced, admired, and at last have dared to love," Lyle answered, in much agitation.

Olive felt quite sorry for him. "I did not expect this," she said. "You poetic dreamers have so many light fancies. My poor Lyle, is it indeed so? You, whom I should have thought would choose a new idol every month, have you all this while been seriously and heartily in love, and with one girl only? Are you quite sure it was but one?" And she half smiled.

He seemed now more confused than ever. "One cannot but speak truth to you," he murmured. "You make me tell you everything, whether I will or no. And if I did not, you might hear it from some one else, and that would make me very miserable."

"Well, what was it?"

"That though I never loved but this my beautiful lady, once,—only once, for a very little while, I assure you,—I was half disposed to like some one else whom you know."

Olive thought a minute, and then said, very seriously, "Was it Christal Manners?"

"It was. She led me into it, and then she teased me out of it. But indeed it was not love—only a mere passing fancy."

"Did you tell her of your feelings?"

"Only in some foolish verses, which she laughed at."

"You should not have done that. It is very wicked to make any pretence about love."

"O! dearest Miss Rothesay, you are not angry with me? Whatever my folly, you must know well that there is but one woman in the world whom I ever truly loved—whom I do love, most passionately! It is *yourself*."

Olive looked up in blank astonishment. She almost thought that sentiment had driven him crazy. But he went on with an earnestness that could not be mistaken, though it was mingled with some extravagance.

"All the good that is in me I learned from you when I was a little boy. I thought you an angel even then, and used to dream about you for hours. When I grew older, I made you an idol. All the poetry I ever wrote was about you—your golden hair, and your sweet eyes. You seemed to me then, and you seem now, the most beautiful creature in the whole world."

"Lyle, you are mocking me," said Olive, sadly.

"Mocking you! It is very cruel to tell me so," and he turned away with an expression of deep pain.

Olive began to wake from the bewilderment into which his words had thrown her. But she could not realise the possibility of Lyle Derwent's loving *her*, his senior by some years, many years older than he in heart; pale, worn, *deformed*. For the sense of personal defect which had haunted her throughout her life was present still. But when she looked again at Lyle, she regretted having spoken to him so harshly.

"Forgive me," she said. "All this is so strange; you cannot really mean it. It is utterly impossible that you can love me. I am old, compared with you; I have no beauty, nay, even more than that"—— here she paused, and her colour sensitively rose.

"I know what you would say," quickly added the young man. "But I think nothing of it—nothing! To me you are, as I said, like an angel. I have come here to-day to tell you so; to ask you to share my riches, and teach me to deserve them. Dearest Miss Rothesay, be not only my friend, but—my wife?"

There was no doubting him now. The strong passion within gave him dignity and manhood. Olive scarcely recognised in the earnest wooer before her, the poesy-raving, blushing, sentimental Lyle. Great pain came over her. She had never dreamed of one trial—that of being loved by another as hopelessly as she herself loved.

"You do not answer, Miss Rothesay? What does your silence mean? That I have presumed too much! You think me a boy; a foolish, romantic boy; but I can love you, for all that, with my whole heart and soul."

"Oh, Lyle, why talk to me in this way? You do not know how deeply it grieves me."

"It grieves you—you do not love me, then? Well," he added, sighing, "I could hardly expect it at once; but you will grant me time, you will let me try to prove myself worthy of you—you will give me hope?"

Olive shook her head mournfully. "Lyle, dear Lyle, forget all this. It is a mere dream; it will pass, I know it will. You will choose some young girl who is suited for you, and to whom you will make a good and happy husband."

Lyle turned very pale. "That means to say that you think me unworthy to be yours."

"No—no—I did not say you were unworthy; you are dear to me, you always were, though not in *that* way. It goes to my very heart to inflict even a momentary pain; but I cannot, cannot marry you!"

Much agitated, Olive hid her face. Lyle moved away to the other end of the room. Perhaps, with manhood's love was also dawning manhood's pride.

"There must be some reason for this," he said at last. "If I am dear to you, though ever so little, a stronger love for me might come in time. Will it be so?"

"No, never!"

"Are you quite sure?"

"Quite sure."

"Perhaps I am too late," he continued, bitterly. "You may already love some one else. Tell me, I have a right to know."

She blushed crimson, and then arose, not without dignity. "I think, Lyle, you go too far; we will cease this conversation."

"Forgive me, forgive me!" cried Lyle, melted at once, and humbled too. "I will ask no more—I do not wish to hear. It is misery enough for me to know that you can never be mine, that I must not love you any more!"

"But you may regard me tenderly still. You may learn to feel for me as a sister—an elder sister. That is the fittest relation between us. You yourself will think so, in time." And Olive truly believed what she said. Perhaps she judged him rightly: that this passion was indeed only a boyish romance, such as most men have in their youth, which fades painlessly in the realities of after years. But now, at least, it was most deep and sincere.

As Miss Rothesay spoke, once more as in his childish days Lyle threw himself at her feet, taking both her hands, and looking up in her face with the wildest adoration.

"I must—must worship you still; I always shall! You are so good—so pure; I look up to you as to some saint. I was mad to think of you in any other way. But you will not forget me; you will guide and counsel me always. Only, if you should be taken away from me—if you should marry"——

"I shall never marry," said Olive, uttering the words she had uttered many a time, but never more solemnly than now.

Lyle regarded her for a long and breathless space, and then laying his head on her knees, he wept like a child.

That moment, at the suddenly-opened door there stood Christal Manners! Like a vision, she came—and passed. Lyle never saw her at all. But Olive did; and when the young man had departed, amidst all her own agitation, there flashed before her, as it were an omen of some woe to come—that livid face, lit with its eyes of fire.

Not long had Olive to ponder, for the door once more opened, and Christal came in. Her hair had all fallen down, her eyes had the same intense glare, her bonnet and shawl were still hanging on her arm. She flung them aside, and stood in the doorway.

"Miss Rothesay, I wish to speak with you; and that no one may interrupt us, I will do this." She bolted and locked the door, and then clenched her fingers over the key, as if it had been a living thing for her to crush.

Olive sat utterly confounded. For in her sister she saw two likenesses; one, of the woman who had once shrieked after her the name of "Rothesay,"—the other, that of her own father in his rare moments of passion, as she had seen him the night he had called her by that opprobrious word which had planted the sense of personal humiliation in her heart for life.

Christal walked up to her. "Now tell me—for I *will* know—what has passed between you and—him who just now went hence."

"Lyle Derwent?"

"Yes. Repeat every word—every word!"

"Why so? You are not acting kindly towards me," said Olive, trying to resume her wonted dignity, but still speaking in a placable, quiet tone. "My dear Christal, you are younger than I, and have scarcely a right to question me thus."

"Right! When it comes to that, where is yours? How dare you suffer Lyle Derwent to kneel at your feet? How dare you, I say!"

"Christal—Christal! Hush!"

"I will not! I will speak. I wish every word were a dagger to stab you—wicked, wicked woman! who have come between me and my lover—for he is my lover, and I love him."

"You love him?"

"You stole him from me—you bewitched him with your vile flatteries. How else could he have turned from *me* to *you*?"

And lifting her graceful, majestic height, she looked contemptuously on poor shrinking Olive—ay, as her father—the father of both—had done before. Olive remembered the time well. For a moment a sense of cruel wrong pressed down her compassion, but it rose again. Who was most injured, most unhappy—she, or the young creature who stood before her, shaken by the storm of rage.

She stretched out her hands entreatingly.—"Christal, do listen. Indeed, indeed, I am innocent. I shall never marry that poor boy—never! I have just told him so."

"He has asked you, then?"—and the girl almost gnashed her teeth—"Then he has deceived me. No, I will not believe that. It is you who are deceiving me now. If he loved you, you were sure to love him."

"What am I to do—how am I to convince you? How hard this is!"

"Hard! What, then, must it be to me? You did not think this passion was in me, did you? You judged me by that meek cold-blooded heart of yours. But mine is all burning—burning! Woe be to those who kindled the fire."

She began to walk to and fro, sweeping past Olive with angry strides. She looked, from head to foot, her mother's child. Hate and love, melting and mingling together, flashed from her black, southern eyes. But in the close mouth there was an iron will, inherited with her northern blood. Suddenly she stopped, and confronted Olive.

"You consider me a mere girl. But I learned to be a woman early. I had need."

"Poor child!—poor child!"

"How dare you pity me? You think I am dying for love, do you? But no! It is pride—only pride! Why did I not always scorn that pitiful boy? I did once, and he knows it. And afterwards, because there was no one else to care for, and I was lonely, and wanted a home—haughty, and wanted a position—I have humbled myself thus."

"Then, Christal, if you never did really love him"——

"Who told you that? Not I!" she cried, her broken and contradictory speech revealing the chaos of her mind.

"I say, I did love him—more than you, with your cold prudence, could ever dream of! What could such an one as you know about love? Yet you have taken him from me.

"I tell you, no! Never till this day did he breathe one word of love to me. I can show you his letters."

"Letters! He wrote to you, then, and I never knew it. Oh! how I hate you! I could kill you where you stand!"

She went to the open desk, and began searching there with trembling hands.

"What—what are you going to do?" cried Olive, with sudden terror.

"To take his letters, and read them. I do it in your presence, for I am no dishonourable thief. But I will know everything. You are in my power—you need not stir or shriek."

But Olive did shriek, for she saw that Christal's hand already touched the one fatal letter. A hope there was that she might pass it by, unconscious that it contained her doom! But no! her eye had been attracted by her own name, mentioned in the postscript.

"More wicked devices against me!" cried the girl, passionately. "But I will find out this plot too," and she began to unfold the paper.

"The letter—give me that letter. Oh, Christal! for the happiness of your whole life, I charge you—I implore you not to read it!" cried Olive, springing forward, and catching her arm. But Christal thrust her back with violence. "'Tis something you wish to hide from me; but I defy you! I *will* read!"

Nevertheless, in the confusion of her mind, she could not at once find the passage where she had seen her own name. She began, and read the letter all through, though without a change of countenance until she reached the end. Then the change was so awful, none could be like it, save that left by death on the human face. Her arms fell paralysed, and she staggered dizzily against the wall.

Trembling, Olive crept up and touched her; Christal recoiled, and stamped on the ground, crying:

"It is all a lie, a hideous lie! *You* have forged it—to shame me in the eyes of my lover."

"Not so," said Olive, most tenderly; "no one in the wide world knows this, but we two. No one ever shall know it! Oh, would that you had listened to me, then I should still have kept the secret, even from you! My sister—my poor sister!"

"*Sister!* And you are his child, his lawful child, while I—— But you shall not live to taunt me. I will kill you, that you may go to your father, and mine, and tell him that I cursed him in his grave!"

As she spoke, she wreathed her arms round Olive's slight frame, but the deadly embrace was such as never sister gave. With the marvellous strength of fury, she lifted her from the floor, and dashed her down again. In falling, Olive's forehead struck against the marble chimney-piece, and she lay stunned and insensible on the hearth.

Christal looked at her sister for a moment,—without pity or remorse, but in motionless horror. Then she unlocked the door and fled.

CHAPTER XLIV

When Olive returned to consciousness she was lying on her own bed, the same whereon her mother had died. Olive almost thought that she herself had died too, so still lay the shadows of the white curtains, cast by the one faint night-lamp that was hidden on the floor. She breathed heavily in a kind of sigh, and then she was aware of some watcher close beside, who said, softly, "Are you sleeping, my dear Olive?"

In her confused fancy, the voice seemed to her like Harold's. She imagined that she was dead, and that he was sitting beside her bier—sorrowfully—perhaps even in tenderness, as he might look on her *then*. So strong was the delusion, that she feebly uttered his name.

"It is Harold's mother, my dear. Were you dreaming about my son?"

Olive was far too ill to have any feeling of self-betrayal or shame; nor was there any consecutive memory in her exhausted mind. She only stretched out her hands to Harold's mother with a sense of refuge and peace.

"Take care of me! Oh, take care of me!" she murmured; and as she felt herself drawn lovingly to that warm breast—the breast where Harold had once lain—she could there have slept herself into painless death, wherein the only consciousness was this one thought of him.

But, after an hour or two, the life within her grew stronger, and she began to consider what had happened. A horrible doubt came, of something she had to hide.

"Tell me, do tell me, Mrs. Gwynne, have I said anything in my sleep? Don't mind it, whatever it be. I am ill, you know."

"Yes, you have been ill for some days. I have been nursing you."

"And what has happened in this house, the while? Oh, where is Christal,—poor Christal?"

There was a frown on Mrs. Gwynne's countenance—a frown so stern that it brought back to Olive's memory all that had befallen. Earnestly regarding her, she said, "Something has happened—something awful. How much of it do you know?"

"Everything! But, Olive, we must not talk."

"*I* must not be left to think, or I should lose my senses again. Therefore, let me hear all that you have found out, I entreat you!"

Mrs. Gwynne saw she had best comply, for there was still a piteous bewilderment in Olive's look. "Lie still," she said, "and I will tell you. I came to this house when that miserable girl was rushing from it. I brought her back—I controlled her, as I have ere now controlled passions as wild as hers, though she is almost a demon."

"Hush, hush!" murmured Olive.

"She told me everything. But all is safe, for I have possession of the letter; and I have nursed you myself, alone."

"Oh, how good, how wise, how faithful you have been!"

"I would have done all and more for your sake, Olive, and for the sake of your unhappy father. But, oh! that ever I should hear this of Angus Rothesay. Alas! it is a sinful, sinful world. Never knew I one truly good man, save my son Harold."

The mention of this name fell on Olive's wandering thoughts like balm, turning her mind from the horror she had passed through. Besides, from her state of exhaustion, everything was growing dim and indistinct to her mind.

"You shall tell me more another time," she said; and then, sinking back on her pillow, still holding fast the hand of Harold's mother, she lay and slept till morning.

When, in the daylight, she recovered a little more, Mrs. Gwynne told her all that had happened. From the moment that Christal saw her sister carried upstairs, dead, as it were, her passion ceased. But she exhibited neither contrition nor alarm. She went and locked herself up in her chamber, from whence she had never stirred. She let no one enter except Mrs. Gwynne, who seemed to have over her that strong rule which was instinctive in such a woman. She it was who brought Christal her meals, and compelled her to take them; or else, in her sullen misery, the girl would, as she threatened, have starved herself to death. And though many a stormy contest arose between the two, when Mrs. Gwynne, stern in her justice, began to reprove and condemn, still she ever conquered so far as to leave Christal silent, if not subdued.

Subdued she was not. Night after night, when Olive was recovering, they heard her pacing up and down her chamber, sometimes even until dawn. A little her spirit had been crushed, Mrs. Gwynne thought, when there was hanging over her what might become the guilt of murder; but as soon as Olive's danger passed, it again rose. No commands, no persuasions, could induce Christal to visit her sister, though the latter entreated it daily, longing for the meeting and reconciliation.

But in illness there is great peace sometimes, especially after a long mental struggle. In the dreamy quiet of her sick-room, all things belonging to the world without, all cares, all sufferings, grew dim to Olive. Ay, even her love. It became sanctified, as though it had been an affection beyond the grave. She lay for hours together, thinking of Harold; of all that had passed between them—of his goodness, his tender friendship; of hers to him, more faithful than he would ever know.

It was very sweet, too, to be nursed so tenderly by Harold's mother—to feel that there was growing between them a bond like that of parent and child. Often Mrs. Gwynne even said so, wishing that in her old age she could have a daughter like Olive; and now and then, when Olive did not see, she stole a penetrating glance, as if to observe how her words were received.

One day when Olive was just able to sit up, and looked, in her white drapery and close cap, so like her lost mother,—Mrs. Gwynne entered with letters. Olive grew pale. To her fancy every letter that came to Harbury could only be from Rome.

"Good tidings, my dear; tidings from Harold. But you are trembling."

"Everything sudden startles me now. I am very weak, I fear," murmured Olive. "But you look so pleased!—All is well with him?"

"All is quite well. He has written me a long letter, and here is one for you!"

"For me!" The poor pale face lighted up, and the hand was eagerly stretched out. But when she held the letter, she could not open it for trembling. In her feebleness, all power of self-control vanished. She looked wistfully at Harold's writing, and burst into tears.

Mrs. Gwynne regarded Olive for a moment, as *his* mother naturally would, jealous over her own claim, yet not blaming the one whose only blame was "loving where *she* did." But she said nothing, or in any way betrayed the secret she had learnt. Perhaps, after all, she was proud that her son should be so truly loved, and by such a woman.

Leaning over Olive, she soothed her with great tenderness. "You are indeed too weak to hear anything of the world without. I ought to have taken better care of you, my dear child. Nay, never mind because you gave way a little," she said seeing the burning blushes that rose one after the other in Olive's face. "It was quite natural. The most trifling thing must agitate one who has been so very, very ill. Come, will you read your letter, or shall I put it by till you are stronger?"

"No, no, I should like to read it. He is very good to write to me,—very good indeed. I felt his kindness the more from being ill; that is why it made me weep," said Olive, faintly.

"Certainly, my dear; but I will leave you now, for I have not yet read mine. I am sure Harold would be pleased to know how glad *we both* are to hear from him," said Mrs. Gwynne, with a light but kindly emphasis. And then Olive was left alone.

Oh that Harold had seen her as she sat! Oh that *he* had heard her broken words of thankful joy, when she read of his welfare! Then he might at last have felt what blessedness it was to be so loved; to reign like a throned king in a pure woman's heart, where no man had ever reigned before, and none ever would, until that heart was dust.

Harold wrote much as he had always done, perhaps a little more reservedly, and with a greater degree of measured kindliness. He took care to answer every portion of Olive's letter, but wrote little about himself, or his own feelings. He had not been able to find out the Vanbrughs, he said, though he would try every possible means of so doing before he left Rome for Paris. Miss Rothesay must always use his services in everything, when needed, he said, nor forget how much he was "her sincere and faithful friend."

"He is that, and will be always! I am content, quite content;" and she gazed down, calmly smiling at the letter on her knee.

This news from Rome seemed to have given her new life. Hour by hour she grew rapidly better, and the peace in her own heart made it the more to yearn over her unhappy sister, who, if sinning, had been sinned against, and who, if she erred much, must bitterly suffer too.

"Tell Christal I long to see her," she said. "To-morrow I shall be quite strong, I think, and then I will go to her room myself, and never quit her until we are reconciled."

But Christal declared no power should induce her to meet Olive more.

"Alas! what are we to do?" cried Olive, sorrowfully; and the whole night, during which she was disturbed by the restless sounds in Christars room, she lay awake, planning numberless compassionate devices to soothe and win over this obdurate heart. Something told her they would not be in vain; love rarely is! When it was almost morning, she peacefully fell asleep.

It was late when she awoke, and then the house, usually so quiet, seemed all astir. Hasty feet were passing in all directions, and Mrs. Gwynne's voice, sharpened and agitated, was heard in the next room. Very soon she stood by Olive's bed, and told her troubled tale.

Christal had fled! Ere any one had risen, whilst the whole household must have been asleep, she had effected her escape. It was evidently done with the greatest ingenuity and forethought. Her door was still bolted, and she had apparently descended from the window, which was very low, and made accessible by an espalier. But the flight, thus secretly accomplished, had doubtless been long arranged and provided for, since all her money and ornaments, together with most of her attire, had likewise disappeared. In whatever way the scheme had been planned and executed, the fact was plain that it had thoroughly succeeded. Christal was gone; whither, there was at first not a single clue to tell.

But when afterwards her room was searched, they found a letter addressed to Miss Rothesay. It ran thus:

"I would have killed myself days since, but that I know in so doing, I should release you from a burden and a pang which I wish to last your life, as it must mine. Also, had I died, I might have gone to hell, and there met him whom I hate,—my wicked, wicked father. Therefore I would not die.

"But I will not stay to be tyrannised over, or insulted by hypocritical pity. I will neither eat your bread, nor live upon the cowardly charity of—— the man who is dead. I intend to work for my own maintenance; most likely, to offer myself as a teacher in the school where I was brought up. I tell you this plainly; though I tell you, at the same time, that if you dare to seek me there, or drag me thence.—— But no! you will be glad to be freed from me forever.

"One thing only I regret; that, in justice to my own mother, I must no longer think tenderly of *yours*. For yourself all is ended between us. Pardon I neither ask nor grant; I only say, Farewell.

"Christal Manners."

The letter was afterwards apparently re-opened, and a hasty postscript added:

"Tell Lyle Derwent that I have gone for ever; or, still better, that I am dead. But if you dare to tell him anything more, I will hunt you through the world, but I will be revenged."

Mrs. Gwynne read this letter aloud. It awoke in the stern, upright, God-fearing Scotswoman, less of pity, than a solemn sense of retributive justice, which she could scarcely repress, even though it involved the condemnation of him whose memory was mingled with the memories of her youth.

But Olive, more gentle, tried to wash away her dead father's guilt with tears; and for her living sister she offered unto Heaven that beseeching never offered in vain, a pure heart's humble prayers.

CHAPTER XLV

Many a consultation was held between Mrs. Gwynne and Olive, as to what must be done concerning that hapless child: for little more than a child she was in years, though her miserable destiny had nurtured in her so much of woman's suffering, and more than woman's sin. Yet still, when Olive read the reference to Mrs. Rothesay, she thought there might yet be a lingering angel sitting in poor Christal's heart.

"Oh that some one could seek her out and save her, some one who would rule and yet soothe her; who, coming from us, should not be mingled with us in her fancy, so that no good influence might be lost."

"I have thought of this," answered Mrs. Gwynne. "But, Olive, it is a solemn secret—your father's, too. You ought never to reveal it, except to one bound to you by closest ties. If you married, your husband would have a right to know it, or you might tell your brother."

"I do not quite understand," said Olive, yet she changed colour a little.

Mrs. Gwynne kindly dropped her eyes, and avoided looking at her companion, as she said, "You, my dear, are my adopted daughter; therefore, my son should be to you as a brother. Will you trust Harold?"

"Trust him? There is nothing with which I could not trust him," said Olive, earnestly. She had long found out that praise of Harold was as sweet to his mother's heart as to her own.

"Then trust him in this. I think he has almost a right—or one day he may have."

Mrs. Gwynne's latter words sank indistinctly, and scarcely reached Olive. Perhaps it was well; such light falling on her darkness might have blinded her.

Ere long the decision was made. Mrs. Gwynne wrote to her son and told him all. He was in Paris then, as she knew. So she charged him to seek out the school where Christal was. Sustained by his position as a clergyman, his grave dignity, and his mature years, he might well and ably exercise an unseen guardianship over the girl. His mother earnestly desired him to do this, from his natural benevolence, and for *Olive's sake*.

"I said that, my dear," observed Mrs. Gwynne, "because I know his strong regard for you, and his anxiety for your happiness."

These words, thrilling in her ear, made broken and trembling the few lines which Olive wrote to Harold, saying how entirely she trusted him, and how she implored him to save her sister.

"I am ready to do all you wish," wrote Harold in reply. "O my dear friend, to whom I owe so much, most happy should I be if in any way I could do good to you and yours!"

From that time his letters came frequently and regularly. Passages from them will best show how his work of mercy sped.

"Paris, Jan.—I have had no difficulty in gaining admittance to the *pension*, for I chanced to go in Lord Arundale's carriage, and Madame Blandin would receive any one who came under the shadow of an English *milord*. Christal is there, in the situation she planned. I found out speedily,—as she, poor girl, will find,—how different is the position of a poor teacher from that of a rich pupil. I could not speak with her at all. Madame Blandin said she refused to see any English friends: and, besides, she could not be spared from the schoolroom. I must try some other plan... Do not speak again of this matter being 'burdensome' to me. How could it be so, when it is for you and your sister? Believe me, though the duty is somewhat new, it is most grateful to me for your sake, my dear friend."

... "I have seen Christal. It was at mass. She goes there with some Catholic pupils, I suppose. I watched her closely, but secretly. Poor girl! a life's anguish is written in her face. How changed since I last saw it! Even knowing all, I could not choose but pity her. When she was bending before a crucifix, I saw how her whole frame trembled with sobs. It seemed not like devotion—it must be heart-broken misery. I came closer, to meet her when she rose. The moment she saw me her whole face blazed. But for the sanctity of the place, I think she could not have controlled herself. I never before saw at once such anger, such defiance, and yet such bitter shame. She turned away, took her little pupils by the hand, and walked out of the chapel. I dared not follow her; but many times since then I have watched her from the same spot, taking care that she should not see me. Who would think that haggard woman, sharp in manner, careless in dress—you see how closely I observe her—was the blithe Christal of old! But I sometimes fancied, even from her sporting, that there was the tigress-nature in that girl. Poor thing! And she had the power of passionately loving, too. Ah! we should all be slow to judge. We never can look into the depths of one another's hearts."

... "Christal saw me to-day. Her eye was almost demoniacal in its threatening. Perhaps the pity she must have read in mine only kindled hers with wrath the more. I do not think she will come to the chapel again."

... "My dear Miss Rothesay, I do not like playing this underhand game—it almost makes me despise myself. Yet it is with a good intent; and I would do anything from my friendship for you.

"I have heard much about your sister to-day from a girl who is a *pensionnaire* at Madame Blandin's. But fear not, I did the questioning skillfully, nor betrayed anything. My friend, you know me well as you say; but even you know not how wisely I can acquire one secret and hold fast another. An honourable school of hypocrisy I learnt in, truly! But to my subject. Little Clotilde does not love her instructress. Poor Christal seems to be at war with the whole household. The pupil and the poor teacher must be very different in Madame Blandin's eyes. No wonder the girl is embittered—no marvel are those storms of passion, in which, according to Clotilde, she indulges, 'just as if she were a great English *miladi*, when she is nobody at all, as I told her once,' said the triumphant little French girl.

"'And what did she answer?' asked I.

"'She went into a great fury, and shook me till I trembled all over; then she threw herself on her own bed, at one end of the dormitory, and all that night, whenever I woke, I heard her crying and moaning. I would have been sorry for her, except that she was *only* the teacher—a poor penniless *Anglaise*.'

"This, my friend, is the lesson that Christal must soon have to learn. It will wring her heart, and either break it or soften it. But trust me, I will watch over her continually. Ill fitted I may be, for the duty is more that of 'a woman'—such a woman as yourself. But you have put something of your own nature into mine. I will silently guard Christal as if I had been her own brother,—and yours."

... "The crisis must be coming, from what the little girl tells me. Miss Manners and Madame Blandin have been at open war for days. Clotilde is in great glee since the English teacher is going away. Poor forlorn Christal! whither can she go? I must try and save her, before it is too late."

... "I sit down at midnight to inform you of all that has happened this day, that you may at once answer and tell me what further I am to do. I went once more to visit Madame Blandin, who poured out upon me a whole stream of reproaches against Christal."

—"'She was *un petit diable* always; and now, though she has been my own pupil for years, I would rather turn her out to starve than keep her in my house for another day.'

"'But,' said I, 'you might at least find her some other situation.'

"'I offered, if she would only tell me who she is, and what are her connections. I cannot recommend as a governess a girl without friends—a *nobody*.'

"'Yet you took her as a pupil.'

"'Oh, Monsieur, that was a different matter; and then I was so liberally paid. Now, if you should be a relative'——

"'I am not, as I told you,' said I, indignant at the woman's meanness. 'But I will see this poor girl, nevertheless, if she will permit me.'

"'Her permission is no matter. No one cares for Miss Manners's whims now,' was the careless reply, as Madame ushered me into the deserted schoolroom, and then quickly vanished. She evidently dreaded a meeting with her refractory teacher. Well she might, for there sat Christal—but I will tell you all minutely. You see how I try to note down every trifle, knowing your anxiety.

"Christal was sitting at the window, gazing at the high, blank, convent-like walls. Dull, helpless misery was in every line of her face and attitude. But the moment she saw me she rose up, her eyes darting fire.

"'Have you come to insult me, Mr. Gwynne? Did I not send you word I would see no one? What do you mean by haunting me in this way?'

"I spoke to her very quietly, and begged her to remember I was a friend, and had parted from her as such only three months before.

"'But you know what has happened since? Attempt not to deceive me—you do! I read it in your eyes long ago, at the chapel. You are come to pity the poor nameless wretch—the—Ah! you know the horrible word. Well, do I look like that? Can you read in my face my mother's shame?'

"She was half beside herself, I saw. It was an awful thing to hear her, a young girl, talk thus to me, ay, and without one natural blush. I said to her, gently, 'that I knew the unhappy truth; but, as regarded herself, it could make no difference of feeling in any right-judging mind, nor would with those who had loved her, and who now anxiously wished to hear from me of her welfare.'

"'You mean your mother, who hates me as I hate her; and Olive Rothesay, whom I tried to murder!' (Friend, you did not tell me that.)

"I drew back the hand I had offered. Forgive me, Olive!—let me this once call you so!—forgive me that I felt a momentary abhorrence for the miserable creature who might have taken your precious life away. Yet you would not tell the fact—even to me! Remembering this, I turned again to your sister, who cannot be altogether evil since she is dear to you. I said, and solemnly I know, for I was greatly moved,

"'Christal, from your own lips have I first heard of this. Your sister's were sealed, as they would have been on that other secret. Are you not softened by all this goodness?'

"'No! She thinks to crush me down with it, does she? But she shall not do so. If I grow wicked, ay, worse than you ever dream of, I shall be glad. It will punish her for the wrong her father did, and so I shall be revenged upon his child. Remember, it is all because of him! As to his daughter, I could have loved her once, until she came between me and '——

"'I know all that,' said I, heedlessly enough; but I was not thinking of Christal just then. She rose up in a fury, and demanded what *right* I had to know? I answered her as, after a struggle with myself, I thought best—*how*, I will tell you one day; but I must hasten on now. She was calmed a little, I saw; but her passion rose again when I mentioned Lyle.

"'Speak of that no more,' she cried. 'It is all passed and gone. There is no feeling in my heart but hatred and burning shame. Oh that I had never been born!'

"I pitied her from my soul, as she crouched down, not weeping, but groaning out her misery. Strange that she should have let me see it; but she was so humbled now; and perceiving that I trusted her, perhaps she was the more won to trust me—I had considered this when I spoke to her as I did. My dear friend Olive, I myself am learning what I fain would teach this poor girl—that there is sometimes great evil done by that selfishness which we call a just pride.

"While we were talking, I very earnestly, and she listening much subdued, there entered Madame Blandin. At sight of her the evil spirit awoke again in unhappy Christal. She did not speak, but I saw the flaming of her eyes—the haughtiness of her gesture. It was not tempered by the woman's half-insulting manner.

"'I am come to make one last offer to Mademoiselle—who will do well to accept it, always with the advice of her English friend, or—whatever he may be,' she added, smirking.

"'I have already told you, Madame, that I am a clergyman, and that this young lady is my mother's friend,' said I, striving hard to restrain my anger, by thinking of one for whom I ought and would endure all things.

"'Then Monsieur can easily explain the mystery about Mademoiselle Christal; and she can accept the situation. For her talents I myself will answer. It is merely requisite that she should be of Protestant principles and of good parentage. Now, of course, the latter is no difficulty with a young lady who was once so enthusiastic about her high family.'

"Christal looked as if she could have sprung at her tormentor, and torn her limb from limb. Then, turning deadly white, she gasped out, 'Take me away; let me hide my head anywhere.'

"Madame Blandin began to make bitter guesses at the truth. I feared lest she would drive the girl mad, or goad her on to the perpetration of some horrible crime. I dared not leave her in the house another hour. A thought struck me. 'Come, Christal!' I said, 'I will take you home with me.'

"'Home with you! What then would they say of me—the cruel, malicious world? I am beginning to be very wise in crime, you see!' and she laughed frightfully. 'But it matters not what is done by my mother's child. I will go.'

"'You shall,' I said, gravely, 'to the care of my friend, Lady Arundale. It will be enough for her to hear that you come from Harbury, and are known to me.'

"Christal resisted no more. I brought her to share the kindness of good Lady Arundale, who needed no other guarantee than that it was a kindness asked by me. Olive (may I begin to call you so? Acting as your brother, I feel to have almost a right)—Olive, be at rest. To-night, ere I sat down to write, I heard that your sister was quietly sleeping beneath this hospitable roof. It will shelter her safely until some other plan can be formed. I also feel at peace, since I have given peace to you. Peace, too, I see in both our futures, when this trouble is overpast. God grant it!—He to whom, as I stand at this window, and look up at the stars shining down into the midnight river, I cry, 'Thou art *my* God!'"

—"I have an awful tale to tell—one that I should fear to inform you, save that I can say, 'Thank God with me that the misery has passed—that He has overruled it into good.' So, reading this, do not tremble—do not let it startle you—feeble, as my mother tells me, you still are. '*Poor little Olive.*' She calls you so."

"Last night, after I closed my letter, I went out to take my usual quiet ramble before going to rest. I went to the Pont Neuilly, near which Lord Arundale resides. I walked slowly, for I was thinking deeply—of what it matters not now. On the whole, my thoughts were happy—so happy that I did not see how close to me was standing Misery—misery in the shape of a poor wretch, a woman! When I did see her, it was with that pang, half shame, half pity, which must smite an honest man, to think how vile and cruel are some among his brethren. I went away to the other wall of the bridge—I could not bear that the unhappy creature should think I watched her crouching there. I was just departing without again looking round, when my eye was unconsciously caught by the glitter of white garments in the moonlight.

"She was climbing the parapet to leap into the arms of Death!

"I know not how that awful moment passed—what I said—or did, for there was no time for words. But I saved her. I held her fast, though she struggled with miraculous strength. Once she had nearly perilled both our lives, for we stood on the very edge of the bridge. But I saved her.—Olive, cry with me, 'Thank God, thank God!'

"At last, half-fainting, she sank on the ground, and I saw her face. It was Christal's face! If I had not been kept wandering here, filled with these blessed thoughts (which, please Heaven! I will tell you one day), your sister might have perished! Say again with me—thank God! His mercy is about us continually.

"I cannot clearly tell what I did in that first instant of horror. I only remember that Christal, recognising me, cried out in piteous reproach, 'You should have let me die! you should have let me die!' But she is saved—Olive, be sure that she is saved. Her right spirit will come into her again. It is coming even now, for she is with kind Lady Arundale, a woman almost like yourself. To her, when I carried Christal home, I was obliged to reveal something of the truth, though not much. How the miserable girl contrived to escape, we cannot tell; but it will not happen again. Do not be unhappy about your sister; take care of your own health. Think how precious you are to my mother and to—all your friends. This letter is abrupt, for my thoughts are still bewildered, but I will write again soon. Only let me hear that you are well, and that in this matter you trust to me."

... "I have not seen Christal for many days until yesterday. She has had a severe illness; during which Lady Arundale has been almost like a mother to her. We thought it best that she should see no one else; but yesterday she sent for me, and I went. She was lying on a sofa, her high spirit utterly broken. She faintly smiled when I came in, but her mouth had a patient sunken look, such as I have seen you wear when you were ill last year. She reminded me of you much—I could almost have wept over her. Do you not think I am strangely changed? I do sometimes—but no more of this now.

"Christal made no allusion to the past. She said, 'She desired to speak to me about her future—to consult me about a plan she had.' It was one at which I did not marvel She wished to hide herself from the world altogether in some life which in its eternal quiet might be most like death.

"I said to her, 'I will see what can be done, but it is not easy. There are no convents or monasteries open to us Protestants.'

"Christal looked for a moment like her own scornful self. '*Us* *Protestants?*' she echoed; and then she said, humbly, 'One more confession can be nothing to me now. I have deceived you all;—I am, and I have ever been—a Roman Catholic.'

"She thought, perhaps, I should have blamed her for this long course of religious falsehood. I blame *her!* (Olive, for God's sake do not let my mother read all I write to you. She shall know everything soon, but not now.)

"'But you will not thwart me,' Christal said; 'though you are an English clergyman, you will find me some resting-place, some convent where I can hide, and no one ever hear of me any more.'

"I found that to oppose her was useless: little religion she ever seemed to have had, so that no devoteeism urged her to this scheme: she only wanted rest. You will agree with me that it is best she should have her will, for the time at least?"

... "I have just received your letter. Yes! yours is a wise and kindly plan; I will write at once to Aunt Flora about it. Poor Christal! perhaps she may find peace as a novice at St. Margaret's. Some little fear I had in communicating the scheme to her; for she still shudders at the very mention of her father's name, and she might refuse to go to her father's land. But she is so helpless in body and mind, that in everything she has at last implicitly trusted to my guidance."

"I suppose you, too, have heard from Edinburgh? Dear Aunt Flora! who, despite her growing feebleness, is continually seeking to do good. I, like you, judged it better not to tell her the whole story; but only that Christal was an orphan who had suffered much. At St. Margaret's she will see no one but the good nuns, until, as your aunt proposes, you yourself go to Edinburgh. You may be your sister's saving angel still."

"Christal is gone. Lady Arundale herself will take her safe to St. Margaret's, where your aunt has arranged all Olive, we must not fail both to go to Edinburgh soon. Something tells me this will be the last good deed done on earth by our noble aunt Flora. For what you say in your last letter, thank you! But why do you talk of gratitude? All I ever did was not half worthy of you. You ask of myself, and my plans? I have thought little of either lately, but I shall now. Tell my mother that all her letters came safe, and welcome—especially *the first* she wrote."

"Lord Arundale stays abroad until the year's close. For me, in the early spring, when I have finished my duties with him, I shall come home. *Home!* Thank God!"

CHAPTER XLVI

Night and day there rung in Olive's heart the last words of Harold's letter, "I shall come home!" Simple they were; but they seemed so strangely joyful—so full of hope. She could not tell why, but thinking of him now, her whole world seemed to change. He was coming back! With him came spring and sunshine, youth and hope!

It was yet early in the year. The little crocuses peeped out—the violets purpled the banks. Now and then came soft west winds, sighing sweetness over the earth. Not a breeze passed her by—not a flower sprang in her sight—not one sunny day dawned to ripen the growing year, but Olive's heart leaped within her; for she said, "He will come with the spring—he will come with the spring!"

How and with what mind he would come—whether he would tell her he loved her, or ask her to be his wife—she counted none of these things. Her love was too unselfish, too utterly bound up in him. She only thought that she would see his face, clasp his hand, and walk with him—the same as in the dear old time. Not quite, perhaps, for she was conscious that in the bond between them had come a change, a growth. How, she knew not, but it had come. Sometimes she sat thinking—would he tell her all those things which he had promised, and what could they be? And, above all, would he call her, as in his letters, *Olive*? Written, it looked most beautiful in her sight; but when spoken, it must be a music of which the world could hold no parallel.

A little she strove to temper her happiness, for she was no love-sick girl, but a woman, who, giving her heart—how wholly none but herself could tell—had given it in the fear of God, and in all simplicity. Having known the sorrow of love, she was not ashamed to rejoice in love's joy. But she did so meekly and half-tremblingly, scarcely believing that it was such, lest it should overpower her. She set herself to all her duties, and above all, worked sedulously at a picture which she had begun.

"It must be finished before Harold comes home," said Harold's mother. "I told him of it in my letters, you know."

"Indeed. I do not remember that. And yet for this long while you have let me see all your letters, I think."

"All—except one I wrote when you were ill. But never mind it, my dear, I can tell you what I said—or, perhaps Harold will," answered Mrs. Gwynne, her face brightening in its own peculiar smile of heartfelt benevolence and lurking humour. And then the brief conversation ceased.

For a while longer these two loving hearts waited anxiously for Harold's coming. At last he came.

It was in the sweetest month, the opening gate of the summer year—April Mrs. Gwynne and Olive, only they two, had spent the day together at Harbury; for little Ailie, a child too restless to be ruled by quiet age, was now sent away to school. Mrs. Gwynne sat in her armchair, knitting. Olive stood at the window, thinking how beautiful the garden looked, just freshened with an April shower; and how the same passing rain-cloud, melting in the west, had burst into a most gorgeous sunset Her happiness even took a light tone of girlish romance. Looking at the thorn-tree, now covered with pale green leaves, she thought with a pleasant fancy, that when it was white with blossoms Harold, would be here. And her full heart, hardly conscious why, ran over with a trembling joy.

Nevertheless, amidst all her own hope, she remembered tenderly her poor sister far away. And also Lyle, whom since that day he parted from her she had never seen. Thinking, "How sweet it is to feel happy!" she thought likewise—as those who have suffered ever must—"Heaven make all the world happy too!"

It was just after this silent aspiration, which of all others must bring an answering blessing down, that the long-desired one came home. His mother heard him first.

"Hark—there's some one in the hall. Listen, Olive! It is his voice—I know it is! He is come home—my son!—my dear son, Harold." And with eager, trembling steps, she hurried out.

Olive stayed behind. She had no right to go and meet him, as his mother did. And after one wild throb, her heart sank, so faintly that she could hardly stand.

His voice—his long silent voice! Hearing it, the old feeling came over her. She shuddered, even with a sort of fear. "Heaven save me from myself! Heaven keep my heart at peace! Perhaps he will not suffer himself to love me, or does not wish me to love him. I have thought so sometimes. Yes! I am quite calm—quite ready to meet him now." And she felt herself growing all white and cold as she stood.

The door opened, and Harold came in alone. Not one step could she advance to meet him, not one word of welcome fell from her lips,—nor from his, which were pale as her own. But as he clasped her hands and held them fast, she felt him gazing down upon her—now, for the first time, beginning to read her heart. Something in that fond—ay, it was a fond look—was drawing her closer to him—something that told her she was dearer than any friend. It might have happened so—that moment might have proved the crowning moment of life, which blends two hearts of man and woman into one love, making their being complete, as God meant it should be.

But at the same instant Mrs. Gwynne came in. Their hands fell from one another; Harold quitted Olive's side, and began talking to his mother.

Olive stood by herself in the window. She felt as if her whole destiny was changing—melting from cloud to glory—like the sunset she had watched an hour before. Whatever was the mystery that had kept him silent, she believed that in the secret depth of his heart Harold loved her. Once she had thought, that were this knowledge true, the joy would overpower her reason. Now, it came with such a solemnity, that all agitation ceased. Her hands were folded on her heart, her eyes looked heavenwards. Her prayer was,—"O God, if this happiness should be, make me worthy of it—worthy of him!—If not, keep us both safe until the eternal meeting!"

Then, all emotion having passed away, she went back quietly to Harold and his mother.

They were sitting together on the sofa, Harold holding his mother's hand in one of his. When Olive approached, he stretched out the other, saying, "Come to us, little Olive,—come! Shall she, mother?"

"Yes," was Mrs. Gwynne's low answer. But Olive heard it. It was the lonely heart's first welcome home.

For an hour afterwards she sat by Harold's side in the gathering darkness, feeling her hand safe clasped in his. Never was there any clasp like Harold's—so firm, yet soft—so gentle, yet so close and warm. It filled her with a sense of rest and protection—she, long tossed about in the weary world. Once or twice she moved her hand, but only to lay it again in his, and feel his welcoming fingers close over it, as if to say, "Mine—mine—always mine!"

So they sat and talked together—she, and Harold, and Harold's mother—talked as if they were one loving household, whose every interest was united. Though, nevertheless, not one word was spoken that might break the seal upon any of their hearts.

"How happy it is to come home!" said Harold. "How blessed to feel that one has a home! I thought so more strongly than ever I had done before, one day, at Home, when I was with Olive's old friend, Michael Vanbrugh."

"Oh, tell me of the Vanbrughs," cried Olive eagerly. "Then you did see them at last, though you never said anything about it in your letters?"

"No; for it was a long story, and both our thoughts were too full. Shall I tell it now? Yet it is sad, it will pain you, Olive." And he pressed her hand closer while he spoke.

She answered, "Still, tell me all." And she felt that, so listening, the heaviest worldly sorrow would have fallen light.

"I was long before I could discover Mr. Vanbrugh, and still longer before I found out-his abode. Day after day I met him, and talked with him at the Sistine, but he never spoke of his home, or asked me thither. He had good reason."

"Were they so poor then? I feared this," said Olive compassionately.

"Yes, it was the story of a shattered hope. As I think, Vanbrugh was a man to whom Fortune could never come. He must have hunted her from him all his life, with his pride, his waywardness, his fitful morose ambition. I soon read his character—for I had read another very like it, once. But that is changed now, thank God," said Harold, softly. "Well, so it was: the painter dreamed his dream, the little sister stayed at home and starved."

"Starved! oh, no! you cannot mean that!"

"It would have been so, save for Lord Arundale's benevolence, when we found them out at last. They lived in a miserable house, which had but one decent room—the studio. 'Michael's room must always be comfortable,' said Miss Meliora—I knew her at once, Olive, after all you had told me of her. The poor little woman! she almost wept to hear the sound of my English voice, and to talk with me about you. She said, 'she was very lonely among strangers, but she would get used to it in time. She was not well too, but it would never do to give way—it might trouble Michael She would get better in the spring.'"

"Poor Meliora! But you were very kind to her—you went to see her often?—I knew you would."

"There was no time," Harold answered, sadly. "The day after this we sought out Michael Vanbrugh, in his old haunt, the Sistine Chapel. He was somewhat discomposed, because his sister had not risen in time to set his palette, and get all things ready in his painting-room at home. I went thither, and found her—dying."

Harold paused—but Olive was too much moved to speak. He went on—

"So sudden was the call that she would not believe it herself. She kept saying continually, that she must contrive to rise before Michael came back at night. Even when she knew she was dying, she seemed to think only of him; but always in her simple, humble way. I remember how she talked, brokenly, of some draperies she had to make for his model that day—asking me to get some one else to do it, or the picture would be delayed. Once she wept, saying, 'who would take care of Michael when she was gone?' She would not have him sent for—he never liked to be disturbed when he was at the Sistine. Towards evening she seemed to lie eagerly listening, but he did not come home. At last she bade me give her love to Michael: she wished he had come, if only to kiss her before she died—he had not kissed her for thirty years. Once more, just when she seemed passing into a death-like sleep, she half-roused herself, to beg some one would take care that Michael's tea was all ready for him against he came home. After this she never spoke again."

"Poor Meliora! poor simple, loving soul!" And Olive melted into quiet tears. After a while she inquired in what way this blow had fallen upon Michael Vanbrugh.

"Strangely, indeed," said Harold. "It was I who told him first of his sister's death. He received the news quite coldly—as a thing impossible to realise! He even sat down to the table, as if he expected her to come in and pour out his tea; but afterwards, leaving the meal untouched, he went and shut himself up in his painting-room, without speaking a word. And then I quitted the house."

"But you saw him again?"

"No; for I left Rome immediately. However, I had a friend who watched over him and constantly sent me news. So I learnt that after his sister's death a great change came over him. His one household stay gone, he seemed to sink down helpless as a child. He would wander about the house, as though he missed something—he knew not what; his painting was neglected, he became slovenly in his dress, restless in his look. No one could say he grieved for his sister, but he missed her—as one misses the habit of a lifetime. So he gradually changed, and grew speedily to be a worn-out, miserable old man. A week since I heard that his last picture had been bought by the Cardinal F——, and that Michael Vanbrugh slept eternally beneath the blue sky of Rome."

"He had his wish—he had his wish!" said Olive, gently. "And his faithful little sister had hers; for nothing ever parted them. Women are content thus to give up their lives to some one beloved. The happiness is far beyond the pain."

"You told me so once before," answered Harold, in a low tone. "Do you remember? It was at the Hermitage of Braid."

He stopped, thinking she would have replied; but she was silent. Her silence seemed to grow over him like a cloud. When the lights came in, he looked the same proud, impassive Harold Gwynne, as in the old time. Already his clasp had melted from Olive's hand. Before she could guess the reason why, she found him speaking, and she answering coldly, indifferently. All the sweetness of that sweet hour had with it passed away.

This sudden change so pained her, that very soon she began to talk of returning home. Harold rose to accompany her, but he did so with the formal speech of necessary courtesy—"Allow me the pleasure, Miss Rothesay." It stung her to the heart.

"Indeed, you need not, when you are already tired. It is still early. I had much rather go home alone."

Harold sat down again at once.

She prepared to depart. She shook hands with his mother, and then with himself, saying in a voice that, lest it should tremble, she made very low, quiet, and cold, how glad she was that he had come home safe. However, before she reached the garden gate, Harold followed her.

"Excuse me, but my mother is not easy for you to set off thus; and we may as well return to our old custom of walking home together—just once more."

What could he mean? Olive would have asked him, but she dared not. Even yet there was a veil between their hearts. Would it ever be drawn aside?

There were few words spoken on the way to Farnwood, and those few were of ordinary things. Once Olive talked of Michael Vanbrugh and his misfortunes.

"You call him unfortunate; how know you that?" said Harold, quickly. "He needed no human affection, and so, on its loss, suffered no pain; he had no desire save for fame; his pride was never humbled to find himself dependent on mere love. The old painter was a great and a happy man."

"Great he was, but not happy. I think I had rather be the poor little sister who spent her life for him."

"Ay, in a foolish affection which was all in vain."

"Affection is never in vain. I have thought sometimes that as to give is better than to receive, they who love are happier than they who are loved."

Harold was silent. He remained so until they stood at Miss Rothesay's door. Then bidding her good-bye, he took her two hands, saying, as if inquiringly, "Olive?"

"Yes," she answered, trembling a little—but not much—for her dream of happiness was fading slowly away, and she was sinking back into her old patient, hopeless self. That olden self alone spoke as she added, "Is there anything you would say to me?"

"No, no—nothing—only good night." And he hastily walked away.

An hour after, Olive closed her heavy eyes, that burned with long weeping, and lay down to sleep, thinking there was no blessing like the oblivion of night, after every weary day! She lay down, little knowing what mystery of fate that quiet night was bearing in its bosom.

From her first sleep she started in the vague terror of one who has been suddenly awakened. There was a great noise—knocking—crashing—a sound of mingled voices—and, above all, her name called. Anywhere, waking or sleeping, she would have known *that* voice, for it was Harold Gwynne's. At first, she thought she must still be dreaming some horrible dream; but consciousness came quick, as it often does at such a time. Before the next outcry was raised she had guessed its meaning. Upon her had come that most awful waking—the waking in a house on fire.

There are some women who in moments of danger gain an almost miraculous composure and presence of mind. Olive was one of these. Calmly she answered Harold's half-frenzied call to her from without her door.

"I am awake and safe; the fire is not in my room. Tell me, what must I do?"

"Dress quickly—there is time. Think of all you can save, and come," she heard Harold reply. His passionate cry of "Olive!" had ceased; he was now as self-possessed as she.

Her room was light as day, with the reflection of the flames that were consuming the other end of the long straggling house. She dressed herself, her hands never trembling—her thoughts quick, vivid, and painfully minute. There came into her mind everything she would lose—her household mementos—the unfinished picture—her well-beloved books. She saw herself penniless—homeless—escaping only with life. But that life she owed to Harold Gwynne. How everything had chanced she never paused to consider. There was a sweetness, even a wild gladness, in the thought of peril from which Harold had come to save her.

She heard his voice eager with anxiety. "Miss Rothesay! hasten. The fire is gaining on us fast!" And added to his was the cry of her faithful old servant, Hannah, whom he had rescued too. He seemed to stand firm amidst the confusion and terror, ruling every one with the very sound of his voice—that knew no fear, except when it trembled with Olive's name.

"Quick—quick! I cannot rest till I have you safe. Olive! for God's sake, come! Bring with you anything you value, only come!"

She had but two chief treasures, always kept near her—her mother's portrait, and Harold's letters; the letters she hid in her bosom, the picture she carried in her arms. Thus laden, she quitted the burning house.

It was an awful scene. The utter loneliness of the place precluded any hope of battling with the fire; but, the night being still and windless, it advanced slowly. Sometimes, mockingly, it almost seemed to die away, and then rose up again in a hurricane of flame.

OLIVE AND HAROLD.

Olive and Harold stood on the lawn, she clinging to his hand like a child. "Is there no hope of saving it—my pretty cottage—my dear home, where my mother died!"

"Since you are safe, let the house burn—I care not," muttered Harold. He seemed strangely jealous even of her thoughts—her tears. "Be content," he said—"you see, much has been done." He pointed to the lawn strewn with furniture. "All is there—your picture—your mother's little chair—everything I thought you cared for I have saved."

"And my life, too. Oh! it is so sweet to owe you all!"

He quitted her for a moment to speak to some of the men whom he had brought with him from Harbury, then he came back, and stood beside Olive on the lawn—she watching the doomed house—he only watching her.

"The night is cold—you shiver. I am glad I thought to bring this." He took off his plaid and wrapped her in it, holding his arm round her the while. But she scarcely felt it then. Through the yawning, blazing windows, she saw the fire within, lighting up in its laughing destruction the little parlour where her mother used to sit, twining round the white-curtained bed whereon her mother's last breath had been sighed away peacefully in her arms. She stood speechless, gazing upon this piteous household ruin, wherein were engulfed so many memories. But very soon there came the crash of the sinking roof, and then a cloud of dense smoke and flame arose, sweeping over where she and Harold stood, falling in showers of sparks around their feet.

Instinctively, Olive clung to Harold, hiding her blinded eyes upon his arm. She felt him press her to him, for an instant only, but with the strong true impulse, taught by one only feeling.

"You must not stay here," he said. "Come with me home!"

"Home!" and she looked wistfully at the ruins of her own. 2 D

"Yes—to my home—my mother's. You know for the present it must indeed be yours. Come!"

He gave her his arm to lean on. She tried to walk, but, quite overpowered, staggered, fainted, and fell. When she awoke, she felt herself borne like a child in Harold's arms. No power had she to move or speak—all was a dizzy dream. Through it, she faintly heard him whisper as though to himself; "I have saved her—I hold her fast—little Olive—little Olive!"

When they reached the Parsonage door, he stood still a moment, passionately looking down upon her face. One minute he strained her closer to his heart, and then placed her in his mother's arms.

"She is safe—oh thank God!" cried Mrs. Gwynne. "And you, too, my dear son—my brave Harold!" And she turned to him as he stood, leaning breathless against the wall.

He tried to speak, but in vain. There was one gasp; the blood poured in a torrent from his mouth, and he fell down at his mother's feet.

CHAPTER XLVII

"He has given his life in saving mine. Oh, would that I had died for thee—my Harold—my Harold!"

This was evermore Olive's cry during the days of awful suspense, when they knew not but that every hour might be Harold's last. He had broken a bloodvessel in the lungs; through some violent mental emotion, the physician said. Nothing else could have produced such results in his usually strong and manly frame.

"And it was for me—for me!" moaned Olive. "Yet I doubted him—I almost called him cruel. Oh, that I should never have known his heart until now!"

Every feeling of womanly shame vanished before the threatening shadow of death. Night and day, Olive hovered about the door of Harold's room, listening for any sound. But there was always silence. No one passed in and out except his mother,—his mother, on whom Olive hardly dared to look, lest—innocent though she was—she might read reproach in Mrs. Gwynne's sorrowful eye. Once, she even ventured to hint this.

"I angry, because it was in saving you that this happened to my son? No, Olive, no! Whatever God sends, we will bear together."

Mrs. Gwynne said this kindly, but her heart seemed frozen to every thought except one. She rarely quitted Harold's chamber, and scarcely noticed any person—not even Olive.

One night, or rather early morning, during the time of great crisis, she came out, and saw Olive standing in the passage, with a face whereon was written such utter woe, that before it even the mother's sorrow paled. It seemed to move Mrs. Gwynne deeply.

"My dear, how long have you been here?"

"All night."

"Poor child—poor child!"

"It is all I can do for him and you. If I could only"——

"I guess what you would say. No, no! He must be perfectly quiet; he must not see or hear *you*." And the mother turned away, as though she had said too much. But what to Olive was it now to know that Harold loved her? She would have resigned all the blessing of his love to bring to him health and life. So crushed, so hopeless was her look, that Harold's mother pitied her. Thinking a moment, she said:

"He is fast asleep now. If it would comfort you, poor child, to look at him for one moment—but it must be only one"——

Olive bowed her head—she was past speaking—and followed Mrs. Gwynne. With a step as silent and solemn as though she were going to look on death, she went and looked on the beloved of her heart.

Harold lay; his face perfectly blanched, his dark hair falling heavily on the pillow, as if never to be stirred by life or motion more. They stood by his bed—the mother that bore him, and the woman who loved him dearer than her own soul. These two—the strongest of all earthly loves—so blended in one object, constrained them each to each. They turned from gazing on Harold, and sank into one another's arms.

For a few more days continued this agonised wrestling with death, during which they who would have given their life for Harold's could only look on and pray. During this time there came news to Olive from the world without—news that otherwise would have moved her, but which was now coldly received, as of no moment at all. Lyle Derwent had suddenly married; his heart, like many another, being "won in the rebound." And Mrs. Flora Rothesay had passed away; dying, in the night, peacefully, and without pain, for they found her in the attitude of sleep.

But even for her Olive had no tears. She only shuddered over the letter, because it spoke of death. All the world seemed full of death. She walked in its shadow night and day. Her only thought and prayer was, "Give me his life—only his life, O God!"

And Harold's life was given her. But the hope came very faintly at first, or it might have been too much to bear. Day by day it grew stronger, until all present danger was gone. But there were many chances to be guarded against; and so, as soon as this change for the better arrived, Olive came to look at him in his sleep no more. His mother was very cautious over his every look and word, so that Olive could not even learn whether he had ever given any sign that he thought of her. And now that his health was returning, her womanly reserve came back; she no longer lingered at his door; even her joy was restrained and mingled with a trembling doubt.

At length, Harold was allowed to be moved to his mother's dressing-room. Very eager and joyful Mrs. Gwynne was, ransacking the house for pillows to make him lie easy on the sofa; and plaids to wrap him in;—full of that glad, even childish excitement with which we delight to hail the recovery of one beloved, who has been nearly lost. The pleasure extended itself over the whole household, to whom their master was very dear. Olive only sat in her own room, listening to every footstep.

Mrs. Gwynne came to her at last "It is all done, my dear, and he is not so weak as we feared. But he is very much exhausted still. We must take great care even now."

"Certainly," answered Olive. She knew what the anxious mother meant, and dared not utter the longing at her heart.

"I hardly know what to do," said Mrs. Gwynne, restlessly. "He has been asking to see you."

"To see me! And—may I!"——

"I told him not to-day, and I was right. Child, look at your own face now! Until you can calm yourself, you shall not see my Harold." Without offering any opposition, Olive sat down. Mrs. Gwynne was melted. "Nay," she said, "you shall do as you will, little patient one! I left him asleep now; you shall stay by him until he wakes. Come."

She took her to the door, but quitted her there, perhaps remembering the days when she too was young.

Olive entered noiselessly, and took her place by Harold's side. He was sleeping; though it was not the death-like sleep in which she had beheld him, that mournful night; but a quiet, healthful slumber. His whole face seemed softened and spiritualised, as is often the case with strong men, whom a long illness has brought low. With childlike helplessness there seems to come a childlike peace. Olive knew now why Mrs. Gwynne had said, a few days since, that Harold looked as he had done when he was a little boy—his mother's only boy.

For a few minutes Olive sat silently watching. She felt how utterly she loved him—how, had he died, the whole world would have faded from her like a blank dream. And even now, should she have to part from him in any way——

"I cannot—I cannot It would be more than I could bear." And from the depth of her heart rose a heavy sigh.

Harold seemed to hear it. He moved a little, and said, faintly. "Who is there?"

"It is I."

"Olive—little Olive." His white cheek flushed, and he held out his hand.

She, remembering his mother's caution, only whispered, "I am so glad—so glad!"

"It is a long time since I saw you," he said brokenly. "Stand so that I can look at you, Olive!" She obeyed. He looked long and wistfully at her face. "You have been weeping, I see. Wherefore?"

"Because I am so happy to think you are better."

"Is that true? Do you think so much of me?" And a pale but most joyful smile broke over his face; though, leaving it, the features trembled with emotion. Olive was alarmed.

"You must not talk now—not one word. Remember how very ill you have been. I will sit by you here. Oh, what can I ever do or say in gratitude for all you have done for me?"

"Gratitude!" Harold echoed the word, as if with pain, and then lay still, looking up at her no more. Gradually there came a change over his countenance, as if some bitter thought were slowly softening into calmness. "Olive," he said, "you speak of gratitude, then what must be mine to you? In those long hours when I lay conscious, but silent, knowing that there might be but a breath between me and eternity, how should I have felt had I not learnt from you that holy faith which conquers death?"

"Thank God! thank God! But you are weak, and must not speak."

"I must, for I am stronger now; I draw strength from your very presence—you, who have been my life's good angel. Let me tell you so while I can."

"While you can!"

"Yes; for I sometimes think that, though I am thus far better, I shall never be quite myself again; but slowly, perhaps without suffering, pass away from this world."

"Oh, no!—oh, no!" And Olive clasped his hand tighter, looking up with a terrified air. "You cannot—shall not die! I—I could not bear it" And then her face was dyed with a crimson blush—soon washed away by a torrent of tears.

Harold turned feebly round, and laid his right hand on her head. "Little Olive! To think that you should weep thus, and I should be so calm!" He waited awhile, until her emotion had ceased. Then he said, "Lift up your face; let me look at you. Nay, tremble not, for I am going to speak very solemnly;—of things that I might never have uttered, save for such an hour as this. You will listen, my own dear friend, my sister, as you said you would be?"

"Yes—yes, always!"

"Ah! Olive, you thought not that you were more to me than any friend—any sister—that I loved you—not calmly, brotherly—but with all the strength and passion of my heart, as a man loves the woman he would choose out of all the world to be his wife."

These words trembled on lips white as though they had been the lips of death. Olive heard; but she only pressed his hand without speaking.

Harold went on. "I tell you this, because now, when I feel so changed that all earthly things grow dim, I am not too proud to say I love you. Once I was. You stole into my heart before I was aware. Oh! how I wrestled against this love—I, who had been once deceived, so that I believed in no woman's truth. At last, I resolved to trust in yours, but I would try to be quite sure of it first You remember how I talked to you, and how you answered, in the Hermitage of Braid? Then I knew you loved, but I thought you loved not me."

"How could you think so? Oh! Harold—Harold!"

As she uttered his name, tremulously as a woman breathes for the first time the beloved name in the beloved ear, Harold started. But still he answered calmly,

"Whether that thought was true or not, would not change what I am about to say now. All my pride is gone—I only desire that you should know how deeply I loved you: and that, living or dying, I shall love you evermore."

Olive tried to answer—tried to tell him the story of her one great love—so hopeless, yet so faithful—so passionate, yet so dumb. But she could utter nothing save the murmur—"Harold! Harold!" And therein he learnt all.

Looking upon her, there came into his face an expression of unutterable joy. He made an effort to raise himself, but in vain. "Come," he murmured, "come near me, Olive—my little Olive that loves me!—is it not so?"

"Ever—from the first, you only—none but you!"

"Kiss me, then, my own faithful one," he said faintly.

Olive leaned over him, and kissed him on the eyes and mouth. He tried to fold his arms round her, but failed.

"I have no strength at all," he said, sorrowfully. "I cannot take her to my heart—my darling—my wife! So worn-out am I—so weak."

"But I am strong," Olive answered. She put her arm under his head, and made him lean on her shoulder. He looked up smiling.

"Oh, this is sweet, very sweet! I could sleep—I could almost die—thus"——

"No, God will not let you die, my Harold," whispered Olive; and then neither spoke again.

Overpowered by an emotion which was too much for his feeble strength, Harold lay quiet By degrees, when the room darkened—for it was evening—his breathing grew deeper, and he fell asleep, his head still resting on Olive's shoulder.

She looked down upon him—his wasted face—his thin hand, that, even in slumber, still clung helplessly to hers. What a tide of emotion swept through her heart! It seemed that therein was gathered up for him every tenderness that woman's soul could know. She loved him at once with the love of mother, sister, friend, and wife—loved him as those only can who have no other kindred tie—nothing in the whole wide world to love beside. She laid her cheek against his hair—but softly, lest she should waken him.

"I thought to have led a whole long lonely life for thy sake, Harold! And I would have led it, without murmuring, either against Heaven or thee, knowing my own un-worthiness. But since it is not to be so, I will give thee instead a whole life of faithful love—a wife's love—such as never was wife's before."

And then, over long years, her fancy went back, discerning how all things had worked together to this end. She saw how patience had ripened into hope, and suffering into joy. Not one step of the whole weary way had been trodden in vain—not one thorn had pierced her feet, that had not while entering there distilled a saving balm.

Travelling over many scenes, her memory beheld Harold, as in those early days when her influence and her prayers had changed his heart, and led him from darkness to light. Again, as in the first bitterness of her love for him; when continually he tortured her, never dreaming of the wounds he gave. And once more, as in the time, when knowing her fate, she had calmly prepared to meet it, and tried to make herself a true friend unto him—he so unresponsive, cold, and stern. Remembering him thus, she looked at him as he lay, turning for rest and comfort to her—only her. Once more she kissed his forehead as he slept, and then her lips uttered the words with which Mrs. Flora had blessed her.

"O God, I thank Thee, for Thou hast given me my heart's desire!"

Soon after, Mrs. Gwynne entered the room. But no blush came to Olive's cheek—too solemn was her joy.

"Hush!" she whispered; "do not wake him. He loves me—I know it now. You will not be angry?—I have loved him always."

"I knew it, Olive."

Harold's mother stood a long time in silence. Heaven only knows what struggle there might have been in her heart—so bound up as it was in him—her only child. Ere it ended—he awoke.

"Mother!—is not that my mother?"

"Yes!" Mrs. Gwynne answered. She went up and kissed them both, first her son, and afterwards Olive. Then, without speaking, she quitted the room, leaving them alone together.

CHAPTER XLVIII

It was a Sunday afternoon, not bright, but dull. All the long day the low clouds had been dropping freshness down;—the soft May-rain, which falls warm and silent, as if the spring were weeping itself away for very gladness. Through the open window came the faint odour which the earth gives forth during rain—an odour of bursting leaves and dew-covered flowers. On the lawn you could almost "have seen the grass grow." And though the sky was dull and grey, still the whole air was so full of summer, so rich in the promise of what the next day would be, that you did not marvel to hear the birds singing as merrily as if it had been sunshine. There was one thrush to which Olive had stood listening for half-an-hour. He sat sheltered in the heart of the great syringa bush. Though the rain kept dropping continually from its flowers, he poured out a song so long and merry, that he even disturbed his friends in the parlour—the happy silent three—mother, son, and the son's betrothed.

Mrs. Gwynne, who sat in the far corner, put down her book—the best Book, for Sunday and all other days—the only one she ever read now. Harold, still feeble, lying back in his armchair by the window, listened to the happy bird.

"Do you like to hear it, or shall I close the window?" said Olive, coming towards him.

"Nay, it does me good; everything does me good now," he answered, smiling. And then he lay a long time, quietly looking on the garden and the misty view beyond. Olive sat, looking alone at him; watching him in that deep peace, that satisfied content with which our eyes drink in every lineament beloved, when, all sorrow past, the fulness of love has come. No need had she to seek his, as though asking restlessly, "Do you love me?" In her own love's completeness she desired no demonstration of his. To her it was perfect joy only to sit near him and to look at his face; the face which, whether seen or remembered, shone distinct from every other face in the wide world; and had done so from the first moment when it met her sight. Very calm and beautiful it was now; so beautiful, that even his mother turned round and looked at him for a moment with dimmed eyes.

"You are sure you feel quite well to-day? I mean as well as usual. You are not sitting up too long, or wearying yourself too much?"

"Oh, no, mother! I think I could even exert myself more; but there is such sweetness in this dreamy life. I am so happy! It will be almost a pain to go back to the troublesome world again."

"Do not say so, my son. Indeed, we must have you quite well soon—the sooner the better—and then you will return to all your old duties. When I sat in church this morning, I was counting how many Sundays it would possibly be before I heard my son Harold's voice there again."

Harold moved restlessly.

"What say you, Olive, my dear?" continued Mrs. Gwynne. "Will it not be a pleasure to hear him in his own pulpit again? How soon, think you, will he be able to preach?"

"I cannot tell," answered Olive, in a low voice; and she looked anxiously at her betrothed. For well she knew his heart, and well she guessed that though that heart was pure and open in the sight of God and in *her* sight, it might not be so in that of every man. And although his faith was now the Christian faith—even, in many points, that of the Church—still Olive doubted whether he would ever be a Church of England minister again. No wonder that she watched his face in anxious love, and then looked from him to his mother, who, all unconscious, continued to speak.

"In truth, all your parishioners will be glad to have you back. Even Mrs. Fludyer was saying so yesterday; and noticing that it was a whole year since you had preached in your own church. A long absence! Of course, it could not be helped; still it was rather a pity. Please God, it shall not happen again—shall it, Harold?"

"Mother—mother!" His hands were crushed together, and with a look of pain. Olive stole to his side.

"Perhaps we are talking too much. Shall we go away, Harold, and leave you to sleep?"

"Hush, Olive! hush!" he whispered. "I have thought of this before. I knew I must tell it to her—all the truth."

"But not now—not now. Wait till you are stronger; wait a week—a day."

"No, not an hour. It is right!"

"What are you talking to my son about?" said Mrs. Gwynne, with a quick jealousy, which even yet was not altogether stilled.

Neither of the betrothed spoke.

"You are not hiding anything from me, Harold; from me, your mother!"

"My mother—my noble, self-denying, mother!" murmured Harold, as if thinking aloud. "Surely, if I sinned for her, God will forgive me!"

"Sinned for me! What are you talking of, Harold? Is there anything in your mind—anything I do not know?" And her eyes—still tender, yet with a half-formed suspicion—were fixed searchingly on her son. And when, as if to shield him even from his mother, Olive leaned over him, Mrs. Gwynne's voice grew stern with reproof.

"Stand aside, Olive. Let me see his face. Not even you have a right to interpose between me and my son."

Olive moved a little aside. Very meek was she—as one had need to be whom Mrs. Gwynne would call daughter and Harold wife. Yet by her meekness she had oftentimes controlled them both. She did so now.

"Olive—darling," whispered Harold, his eyes full of love; "my mother says right Let her come and sit by me a little. Nay, stay near, though. I must have you in my sight—it will strengthen me."

She pressed his hand, and went away to the other end of the room.

Then Harold said, tenderly, "Mother, I want to tell you something."

"It is no misfortune—no sin? O, my son, I am too old to bear either!" she answered, as she sat down, trembling a little.

"My own mother—my mother that I love, dearer now than ever in my life before—listen to me, and then judge me. Twelve or fourteen years ago, there was a son—an only son—who had a noble mother. She had sacrificed everything for him—the time came when he had to sacrifice something for her. It was a point of conscience; light, perhaps, *then*—but still it caused him a struggle. He must conquer it, and he did so. He stifled all scruples, pressed down all doubts, and became a minister of a Church in whose faith he did not quite believe."

"Go on," said Mrs. Gwynne, hurriedly. "I had a fear once—a bitter fear. But no matter! Go on!"

"Well, he did this sin, for sin it was, though done for his mother's sake. He had better have supported her by the labour of his hands, than have darkened his soul by a lie. But he did not think of that then. All the fault was his—not his mother's; mind—I say *not his mother's*."

She looked at him, and then looked away again.

"He could blame no one but himself—he never did—though his first faint doubts grew, until they prisoned him like a black mist, through which he could see neither earth nor heaven. Men's natures are different; his was not meant for that of a quiet village priest. Circumstances, associations, habits of mind—all were against him. And so his scepticism and his misery increased, until in despair of heaven, he plunged into the oblivion of an earthly passion. He went mad for a woman's beauty,—for her beauty only!"

Harold pressed his hand upon his brow, as if old memories stung him still. His betrothed saw it, but she felt no pain. She knew that her own love had shone down into his heart's dark depths, removing every stain, binding up every wound. By that love's great might she had saved him, won him, and would have power to keep him evermore.

"Mother," Harold pursued, "I must pass on quickly to the end. This man's one error seemed to cause all fate to rise against him that he might become an infidel to God and to man. At last he had faith in no living soul except his mother. This alone saved him from being the vilest wretch that ever crawled, as he was already the most miserable."

A faint groan—only one—broke from the depth of the mother's heart, but she never spoke.

"There was no escape—his pride shut out that. So, year after year, he fulfilled his calling, and lived his life, honestly, morally—towards man, at least; but towards Heaven it was one long, awful lie. For he—a minister in God's temple—was in his heart an infidel."

Harold stopped. In his strong excitement he had forgotten his mother. She, letting go his hand, glided to her knees; there she knelt for a long time, her lips moving silently. At last she rose, her grand figure lifted to its utmost height, her face very stern, her voice without one tone of tremulous age, or mother's anguish.

"And this hypocrite in man's sight—this blasphemer in the face of God—is my son Harold?"

"Was, but is not—never will be more. Oh, mother, have mercy! for Heaven has had mercy too.—I am no sceptic now. I believe, ay, fervently and humbly believe."

Mrs. Gwynne uttered a great cry, and fell on his neck. Never since the time when he was a child in her arms had he received such a passionate clasp—an embrace mingled with weeping that shook the whole frame of the aged mother. For a moment she lifted her head, murmured a thanksgiving for the son who "was dead, and alive again—was lost and found," and then she clung to him once more.

"Olive kept aloof, until, seeing what a ghastly paleness was coming over the face of her betrothed, she came and stood beside him, saying,

"Do not talk more, you are too weak. Let me tell the rest."

"You there, Olive? Go! Leave my son to me; you have no part here."

But Harold held his betrothed fast. "Nay, mother. Take her and bless her, for it was she who saved your son."

And then, in a few broken words, he told the rest of the tale; told it so that not even his mother could be wounded by the thought of a secret known to Olive and concealed from her—of an influence that over her son was more powerful than her own. Afterwards, when Olive's arms were round her neck, and Olive's voice was heard imploring pardon for both, her whole heart melted within her. Solemnly she blessed her son's betrothed, and called her "daughter."

"Now, my Harold!" she said, when, all trace of emotion having passed from either, she sat quietly by her son's side. "Now I understand all. Olive is right; with your love of action, and a spirit that would perhaps find a limitation in the best forms of belief, you never can be again a minister of the English Church. We must not think of it any more."

"But, mother, how shall we live? That is what tortures me! Whither shall we turn if we go from Harbury? Alone, I could bear anything, but you"——

"No matter for me! My Harold," she added, a little moved, "if you had trusted me, and told me your sufferings at any time all these years,—I would have given up everything here, and lived, as I once did, when you were a youth at college. It was not hard then, nor would it have been now. O my son, you did not half know your mother!"

He looked at her, and slowly, slowly there rose in his eyes—those clear, proud, manly eyes!—two great crystal tears. He was not ashamed of them; he let them gather and fall. And Olive loved him dearer, ay, ten thousand times, even though these tears—the first and last she ever beheld him shed—were given not to her, but to his mother.

Mrs. Gwynne resumed.

"Let us think what we must do; for we have no time to lose. As soon as you are quite strong, you must give up the curacy, and we will leave Harbury."

"Leave Harbury! your dear old home, from which you have often said you could never part! Oh, mother, mother!"

"It is nothing—do not think of it, my son! Afterwards, what must you do?"

"I cannot tell. Olive, think for me!" said Harold, looking helplessly towards her.

Olive advised—timidly at first, but growing firmer as she proceeded—that he should carry out his old plan of going to America. They talked over the project for a long time, until it grew matured. Ere the afternoon closed, it was finally decided on—at least, so far as Harold's yet doubtful health permitted.

"But I shall grow strong now, I know. Mother—Olive! my heart is lightened of the load of years!"

And truly it seemed so. Nay, when tea-time came he even rose and walked across the room with something of his old firm step, as if the returning health were strong within him.

After tea, Harbury bells broke out in their evening chime. Mrs. Gwynne rose; Olive asked if she were thinking of going to church!

"Yes—to thank God!"

"Go with her, Olive," said Harold, as he watched his mother from the room. Olive followed, but Mrs. Gwynne said she would rather go to church alone, and Harold must not be left. Olive stayed with her a few minutes, rendering all those little services which youth can so sweetly pay to age. And sweet too was the reward when Harold's mother kissed her, and once more called her "daughter." So, full of content, she went down-stairs to her betrothed.

Harold was again sitting in his favourite arm-chair by the window. The rain had lately ceased, and just at the horizon there had come to the heavy grey sky a golden fringe—a line of watery light, so dazzling that the eye could scarcely bear it. It filled the whole room, and fell like a glory on Harold's head. Olive stood still to look at him. Coming closer, she saw that he was not asleep, though his eyes were cast down in painful thought. Something in his expression reminded her of that which he had worn on the night when he first came to Edinburgh, and she had leaned over him, longing to comfort him—as she had now a right to do. She did so! He felt the kiss on his brow, and smiled.

"Little Olive—good little Olive, she always comes when I most need her," he said, fondly.

"Little Olive is very happy in so doing. And now tell me what you were thinking of, that you pressed your lips together, and knotted your forehead—the broad beautiful forehead that I love? It was not good of you, my Harold."

"Do not jest, Olive; I cannot. If I go abroad, I must go alone. What will become of my mother and Ailie?"

"They shall stay and comfort me. Nay, you will not forbid it. How could I go on with my painting, living all alone?"

"Ay, there is another sting," he answered. "Not one word say you;—but I feel it. How many years you may have still to work on alone!"

"Do you think I fear that? Nay—I do not give my heart like some women I have known—from dread of living to be an old maid, or to gain a house, a name, and a husband;—I gave it for love, pure love! If I were to wait for years—if I were never your wife at all, but died only your betrothed, still I should die satisfied. Oh, Harold, you know not how sweet it is to love you, and be loved by you—to share all your cares, and rejoice in all your joys! Indeed—indeed I am content."

"You might, my gentle one, but not I. Little you think how strong is man's pride—how stronger still is man's love. We will not look to such a future—I could not bear it. If I go, you shall go with me, my wife! Poor or not, what care I, so you are mine?"

He spoke hurriedly, like the proud Harold of old—ay, the pride mingled with a stronger passion still. But Olive smiled both down.

"Harold," she said, parting his hair with her cool soft hands, "do not be angry with me! You know I love you dearly. Sometimes I think I must have loved you before you loved me, long. Yet I am not ashamed of this."

"Ah!" he muttered, "how often ignorantly I must have made you suffer, how often, blindly straggling with my own pride, have I tortured you. But still—still I loved you. Forgive me, dear!"

"Nay, there is nothing to forgive. The joy has blotted out all the pain."

"It shall do so when you are once mine. That must be soon, Olive—soon."

She answered firmly, though a little blushing the while: "It should be to-morrow; if for your good. But it would not be. You must not be troubled with worldly cares. To see you so would break my heart. No—you must be free to work, and gain fame and success. My love shall never fetter you down to anxious poverty. I regard your glory even dearer than yourself, you see!"

Gradually she led him to consent to her entreaty that they should both work together for their dearest ones; and that in the home which she with her slender means could win, there should ever be a resting-place for Mrs. Gwynne and for little Ailie.

Then they put aside all anxious talk, and sat in the twilight, with clasped hands, speaking softly and brokenly; or else never speaking at all; only feeling that they were together—they two, who were all in all to each other, while the whole world of life went whirling outside, never touching that sweet centre of complete repose. At last, Olive's full heart ran over.

"Oh, Harold!" she cried, "this happiness is almost more than I can bear. To think that you should love me thus—me poor little Olive! Sometimes I feel—as I once bitterly felt—how unworthy I am of you."

"Darling! why?"

"Because I have no beauty; and, besides—I cannot speak it, but you know—you know!"

She hid her face burning with blushes. The words and act revealed how deeply in her heart lay the sting which had at times tortured her her whole life through—shame for that personal imperfection with which Nature had marked her from her birth, and which, forgotten in an hour by those who learned to love her, still seemed to herself a perpetual humiliation. The pang came, but only for the last time, ere it quitted her heart for ever.

For, dispelling all doubts, healing all wounds, fell the words of her betrothed husband—tender, though grave: "Olive, if you love me, and believe that I love you, never grieve me by such thoughts again. To me you are all beautiful—in heart and mind, in form and soul."

Then, as if silently to count up her beauties, he kissed her little hands, her soft smiling mouth, her long gold curls. And Olive hid her face in his breast, murmuring,

"I am content, since I am fair in your sight, my Harold—my only love!"

CHAPTER XLIX

Late autumn, that season so beautiful in Scotland, was shining into the house at Morningside. She, its mistress, who had there lived from middle life to far-extended years, and then passed from the weakness of age to the renewed youth of immortality, was seen no more within its walls. But her spirit seemed to abide there still; in the flowers which at early spring she had planted, for other hands to gather; in the fountain she had placed, which sang its song of murmuring freshness to soothe many an ear and heart, when *she*, walking by the streams of living waters, needed those of earth no more.

Mrs. Flora Rothesay was dead; but she had lived one of those holy lives whose influence remains for generations. So, though now her name had gradually ceased from familiar lips, and from her house and garden walks, her image faded slowly in the thoughts of those who best loved her; still she lived, even on earth, in the good deeds she had left behind—in the happiness she had created wherever her own sore-wounded footsteps trod.

In the dwelling from which she had departed there seemed little change. Everything looked as it had done more than a year before, when Olive had come thither, and found rest and peace. There were fewer flowers in the autumnal garden, and the Hermitage woods beyond were all brown and gold; but there was the same clear line of the Braid Hills, their purple slopes lying in the early morning sun. No one looked at them, though, for the breakfast-room was empty. But very soon there stole into it, with the soft footstep of old, with the same quiet smile,—Olive Rothesay.

No, reader! Neither you nor any one else will ever see Olive *Rothesay* more. She wears on her finger a golden ring, she bears a new name—the well-beloved name.—She is Harold Gwynne's wife now.

To their fortunes Heaven allowed, as Heaven sometimes does, the sweetness of a brave resolve, the joy of finding that it is not needed. Scarcely had Olive and her betrothed prepared to meet their future and go on, faithfully loving, though perhaps unwedded for years, when a change came. They learned that Mrs. Flora Rothesay, by a will made a little before her death, had devised her whole fortune to Harold, on condition that he should take the name of his ancestors on the mother's side, and be henceforth Harold Gordon Gwynne. She made no reservations, save that she wished her house and personal property at Morningside to go to her grand-niece Olive, adding in the will the following sentence:

"I leave her this and *no more,* that she may understand how deeply I reverenced her true woman's nature, and how dearly I loved herself."

And Olive did understand all; but she hid the knowledge in her rejoicing heart, both then and always. It was the only secret she ever kept from her husband.

She had been married some weeks only; yet she felt as if the old life had been years gone by, so faint and dreamlike did it seem. Hers was a very quiet marriage—a quiet honeymoon; fit crowning of a love which had been so solemn, almost sad, from its beginning to its end. Its *end?*—say, rather, its new dawn;—its fulfilment in a deeper, holier bond than is ever dreamed of by girlish sentiment or boyish passion—the still, sacred love of marriage. And, however your modern infidels may doubt, and your free-thinking heart-desecrators scoff, *that* is the true love—the tie which God created from the beginning, making man and woman to be one flesh, and pronouncing it "good."

It is good! None can question it who sees the look of peace and full contentment—a look whose like one never beholds in the wide world save then, as it sits smiling on the face of a bride who has married for true love. Very rare it is, indeed—rare as such marriages ever are; but one sees it sometimes;—we saw it, reader, a while since, on a young wife's face, and it made us think of little Olive in her happy home at Morningside.

She stood by the window for a minute or two, her artist-soul drinking in all that was beautiful in the scene; then she went about her little household duties, already grown so sweet. She took care that Mrs. Gwynne's easy-chair was placed in its proper angle by the fire, and that Harold had beside his plate the great ugly scientific book which he always liked to read at breakfast. Indeed, it was a saying of Marion M'Gillivray's—from whose bonnie face the cloud had altogether passed, leaving only a thoughtful gravity meet for a girl who would shortly leave her maiden home for one far dearer—Marion often said that Mr. Gwynne was trying to make his wife as learned as himself, and that his influence was robbing their Scottish Academy of no one knew how many grand pictures. Perhaps it might be—it was a natural and a womanly thing that in her husband's fame Olive should almost forget her own.

When she had seen all things ready, Olive went away upstairs, and stood by a child's bed—little Ailie's. Not the least sweet of all her new ties was it, that Harold's daughter was now her own. And tender, like a mother's, was the kiss with which she wakened the child. There was in her hand a book—a birthday gift; for Ailie was nine years old that day.

"Oh, how good you are to me, my sweet, dear, new mamma!" cried the happy little one, clinging round Olive's neck. "What a pretty, pretty book! And you have written in it my name—'Ailie.' But," she added, after a shy pause, "I wish, if you do not mind, that you would put there my whole long name, which I am just learning to write."

"That I will, my pet. Come, tell me what shall I say—word for word, 'Alison'"———

"Yes, that is it—my beautiful long name—which I like so much, though no one ever calls me by it—*Alison Sara Gwynne.*"

"Sara! did they call you Sara?" said Olive, letting her pen fall. She took the little girl in her arms, and looked long and wistfully into the large oriental eyes—so like those which death had long sealed. And her tears rose, remembering the days of her youth. How strange—how very strange, had been her whole life's current, even until now! She thought of her who was no more—whose place she filled, whose slighted happiness was to herself the summit of all joy. But Heaven had so willed it, and to that end had made all things tend. It was best for all. One moment her heart melted, thinking of the garden at Oldchurch, the thorn-tree at the river-side, and afterwards of the long-closed grave at Harbury, over which the grass waved in forgotten silence. Then, pressing Ailie to her bosom, she resolved that while her own life lasted she would be a faithful and most loving mother unto poor Sara's child.

A *Mother!*—The word brought back—as it often did when Harold's daughter called her by that name—another memory, never forgotten, though sealed among the holy records of the past. Even on her marriage-day the thought had come—"O thou, to whom in life I gave all love, all duty,—now needed by thee no more, both pass unto *him.* If souls can behold and rejoice in the happiness of those beloved on earth, mother, look down from heaven and bless my husband!"

Nor did it wrong the dead, if this marriage-bond involved another, which awakened in Olive feelings that seemed almost a renewal of the love once buried in Mrs. Rothesay's grave. And Harold's wife inly vowed, that while she lived, his mother should never want the devotion and affection of a daughter.

In the past fading memories of Olive's former life was one more, which now grew into a duty, over whose fulfilment, even amidst her bridal happiness, she pondered continually; and talked thereof to her husband, to whom it was scarcely less absorbing.

Since they came home to Morningside, they had constantly sought at St. Margaret's for news of Christal Manners.

Many times Olive had written to her, but no answer came. The silence of the convent walls seemed to fold itself over all revelations of the tortured spirit which had found refuge there. However, Christal had taken no vows. Mrs. Flora and Harold had both been rigid on that point, and the good nuns reverenced their order too much to admit any one who might have sought it from the impulse of despair, rather than from any pious "vocation."

Olive's heart yearned over her sister. On this day she resolved to make one more effort to break the silence between them. So, in the afternoon, she went to the convent quite alone, walking through the pleasant lanes where she had formerly walked with Marion M'Gillivray. Strange contrast between the present and the past! When she stood in the little convent parlour, and remembered how she had stood there with a bursting heart, that longed for any rest—any oblivion, to deaden its cruel pain,—Olive trembled with her happiness now. And she felt how solemn is the portion of those whose cup God has thus crowned, in order that they may pour it out before Him continually, in offerings of thanksgiving and of fruitful deeds.

Sister Ignatia entered—the same bright-eyed, benevolent, simple soul. "Ah, you are come again this week, too, my dear Mrs. Harold Gwynne—(I can hardly remember your new name even yet)—but I fear your coming is vain; though, day after day, I beseech your sister to see you."

"She will not, then?" said Olive, sighing.

"No. Yet she says she has no bitterness against you. How could she? However, I ask no questions, for the past is all forgotten here. And I love the poor young creature. Oh, if you knew her fasts, her vigils, and her prayers! God and the Holy Mother pity her, poor broken-hearted thing!" said the compassionate nun.

"Speak to her once more. Do not tell her I am here: only speak of me to her," said Olive. And she waited anxiously until Sister Ignatia came back.

"She says she is glad you are happy, and married to that good friend of hers, to whom she owes so much; but that she is dead to the world, and wishes to hear of no one any more. Still, when I told her you lived at Morningside, she began to tremble. I think—I hope, if she were to see you suddenly, before she had time to reflect—only not now—you look so agitated yourself."

"No, no; I can always be calm at will—I have long learned that. Your plan is kind: let it be to-day. It may end in good, please God. Where is my dear sister?"

"She is sitting in the dormitory of the convent-school. She stays a great deal with our little girls, and takes much care of them, especially of some orphans that we have."

Olive sighed. Well she read unhappy Christal's reason. But it showed some softening of the stony heart. Almost hopeful she followed Sister Ignatia to the dormitory.

It was a long, narrow room, lined with tiny white beds. Over its pure neatness good fairies might have continually presided. Through it swept the fresh air coming from the open window which overlooked the garden. And there, darkening it with her tall black shadow, stood the only present occupant of the room, Christal Manners.

She wore a garb half-secular, half-religious. Her black serge dress betrayed no attention to fashion, scarcely even to neatness; her beautiful hair was all put back under a white linen veil, and her whole appearance showed that last bitter change in a woman's nature, when she ceases to have a woman's instinctive personal pride. Olive saw not her face, except the cheek's outline, worn to the straightness of age. Nor did Christal observe Olive until she had approached quite close.

Then she gave a wild start, the old angry flush mounted to her temples, and sank.

"Why did you come here?" she said hoarsely; "I sent you word I wished to see no one—that I was utterly dead to the world."

"But not to me—oh, not to me, my sister!"

"Sister!" she repeated, with flashing eyes, and then crossed herself humbly, muttering, "The evil spirit must not rise again. Help me, Blessed Mother—good saints, help me!"

She told her rosary over once, twice, and then turned to Olive, subdued.

"Now say what you have to say to me. I told you I had no anger in my heart—I even asked your forgiveness. I only desire to be left alone—to spend the rest of my bitter life in penance and prayer."

"But I cannot leave you, my sister."

"I wish you would not call me so, nor take my hand, nor look at me as you do now—as you did the first night I saw you, and again on that awful,

awful day!" And Christal sank back on one of the little beds—the thornless pillow where some happy child slept—and there sobbed bitterly.

More than once she motioned Olive away, but Olive would not go. "Do not send me away! If you knew how I suffer daily from the thought of you!"

"You suffer! happy as they tell me you are—you, with your home and your husband!"

"Ah, Christal, even my husband grieves—my husband, who would do anything in the whole world for your peace. You have forgotten Harold."

A softness came over Christal's face. "No, I have not forgotten him. Day and night I pray for him who saved more than my life—my soul. For that deed may God bless him!—and God pardon me."

She said this, shuddering, too, as at some awful memory. After a while, she spoke to Olive in a gentler tone, for the first time lifting her eyes to her sister's face.

"You seem well in health, and you have a peaceful look. I am glad of it—I am glad you are happy, and married to Harold Gwynne. He told me of his love for you."

"But he could not tell you all. If I am happy, I have suffered too. We must all suffer, some time; but suffering ends in time."

"Not with me—not with me. But I desire not to talk of myself."

"Shall I talk then about your friend Harold—your *brother*? He told me to say he would ever be so to you," said Olive, striving to awaken Christal's sympathies. And she partly succeeded; for her sister listened quietly, and with some show of interest, while she spoke of Harold and of their dear home.

"It is so near you, too; we can hear the convent bells when we walk in our pretty garden. You must come and see it, Christal."

"No, no; I have rest here; I will never go beyond these walls. As soon as I am twenty-one I shall become a nun, and then I, with all my sorrows, will be buried out of sight for evermore."

So said she; and Olive did not contradict her at the time. But she thought that if there was any strength in faithful affection and earnest prayers, the peace of a useful life, spent, not in barren solitude, but in the fruitful garden of God's world, should be Christal's portion yet.

One only doubt troubled her. After considering for a long time she ventured to say:

"I have told you now nearly all that has happened among us this year. You have spoken of all your friends, save one." She hesitated, and at last uttered the name of Lyle.

"Hush!" said Christal. But her cheek's paleness changed not; her heavy eye neither kindled nor drooped. "Hush! I do not wish to hear that name. It has passed out of my world for ever—blotted out by the horrors that followed."

"Then you have forgotten"——

"Forgotten all. It was but a dream of my old vain life—it troubles me no more."

"Thank God!" murmured Olive, though in her heart she marvelled to think how many false reflections there were of the one true love—the only love that can endure—such as had been hers.

She bade an affectionate farewell to her sister, who went with her to the outer court of the convent. Christal did not ask her to come again, but she kissed her when they parted, and once looked back ere she again passed into the quiet silent home which she had chosen as her spirit's grave.

Olive walked on quickly, for the afternoon was closing.

Very soon she heard overtaking her a footstep, whose sound quickened her pulse even now. "How good and thoughtful of him, my dear Harold—my husband!"

My husband! Never did she say or think the words but her heart swelled with inexpressible emotion, remembering the old time, the long silent struggle, the wasting pain. Yet she would have borne it all a thousand times—ay, even had the end come never in her life on earth,—rather than not have known the sweetness of loving—the glory of loving one like him.

Harold met her with a smile. "I have been waiting long—I could not let my little Olive walk home alone."

She, who had walked through the world alone for so many weary years! But she would never do so any more. She clung to her husband's arm, clasping over it both her little hands in a sweet caressing way: and so they went on together.

Olive told him all the good news she had to tell, and he rejoiced with her for Christal's sake. He agreed that there was hope and comfort for their sister still; for he could not believe there was in the whole world a heart so hard and cold, that it could not be melted by Olive's gentle influence, and warmed by the shining of Olive's spirit of love.

They were going home, when she saw that her husband looked tired and dull—he had been poring over his books all day. For though now independent of the world, as regarded fortune, he could not relinquish his scientific pursuits; but was every day adding to his acquirements, and to the fame which had been his when only a poor clergyman at Harbury. So, without saying anything, Olive led him down the winding road that leads from Edinburgh towards the Braid Hills, laughing and talking with him the while, "to send the cobwebs out of his brain," as she often told him. Though at the time she never let him see how skilfully she did this, lest his man's dignity should revolt at being so lovingly beguiled. For he was still as ever the very quintessence of pride. Well for him his wife had not that quality—yet perhaps she loved him all the better for possessing it.

At the gate of the Hermitage Harold paused. Neither of them had seen the place since they last stood there. At the remembrance he seemed greatly moved.

His wife looked lovingly up to him. "Harold, are you content? You would not send me from you?—you would not wish to live your whole life without me now?"

"No—no!" he cried, pressing her hand close to his heart. The mute gesture said enough—Olive desired no more.

They walked on a long way, even climbing to the summit of the Braid Hills. The night was coming on fast,—the stormy night of early winter—for the wind had risen, and swept howling over the heathery ridge.

"But I have my plaid here, and you will not mind the cold, my lassie—Scottish born," said Harold to his wife. And in his own cheek, now brown with health, rose the fresh mountain-blood, while the bold mountain-spirit shone in his fearless eyes. No marvel that Olive looked with pride at her husband, and thought that not in the whole world was there such another man!

"I glory in the wind," cried Harold, tossing back his head, and shaking his wavy hair, something lion-like. "It makes me strong and bold. I love to meet it, to wrestle with it; to feel myself in spirit and in frame, stern to resist, daring to achieve, as a man should feel!"

And on her part, Olive with her clinging sweetness, her upward gaze, was a type of true woman.

"I think," Harold continued, "that there is a full rich life before me yet. I will go forth and rejoice therein; and if misfortune come, I will meet it—thus!"

He planted his foot firmly on the ground, lifted his proud head, and looked out fearlessly with his majestic eyes.

"And I," said Olive, "thus."

She stole her two little cold hands under his plaid, laid her head upon them, close to his heart, and, smiling, nestled there.

And the loud fierce wind swept by, but it harmed not them, thus warm and safe in love. So they stood, true man and woman, husband and wife, ready to go through the world without fear, trusting in each other, and looking up to Heaven to guide their way.